Rock Chick Reckoning

Published by Kristen Ashley
Discover other titles by Kristen Ashley at:
www.kristenashley.net

ISBN: 0-6157-8160-8
ISBN-13: 9780615781600

Rock Chick Reckoning

Kristen Ashley

Dedication

This book is dedicated to Rick Chew and Jim Gonzalez
I love you. I miss you.
I wish you were still right next door.
Yahtzee!

Acknowledgement

A shout out to my Sir Will, William Womack, my uncle, my friend and the premier Rock Guru. Stella's set lists would be nowhere near as cool if Will didn't feed the burn in my soul for kickass music. Love you, Will.

Author's Note

I would guess my readers understand, considering you're reading a series entitled *Rock Chick*, that music means a great deal to me. Frequently in my writing I will use music to explain feelings, define characters or add emotion to the narrative. And if I had a wish, I would wish to be able to make music one way or another but, alas, I do not play an instrument (though have tried to learn) and my singing leaves something to be desired.

So it was a thrill for Stella Gunn to inhabit my headspace and, through Stella, to be able to play a guitar, sing super sexy, entrance a crowd, give a one woman private concert to a hot guy and write set lists.

Stella chose her music with great care. Therefore, if you haven't before or have only done it in passing, I encourage you to experience fully the music Stella chose to explain her emotions by looking up the lyrics and listening to the songs mentioned in this book. Indeed, if you can, listening to the songs while reading the scenes may enhance the experience (it does for me). Most specifically Pearl Jam's "Black", Billy Joel's "And So It Goes", Journey's "Open Arms" and Blink-182's "All the Small Things". They're all fantastic songs but the lyrics expose Stella's soul. Unfortunately, without permission from the artists, I cannot include the lyrics in the narrative and being a self-published author without a great deal of resources, I'm not in a place where I could request that permission (alas).

Further, if you wish to know how Stella sounded singing in my head, find the Cowboy Junkies' version of "I'm So Lonesome I Could Cry" and Sarah McLachlan's version of "Blackbird" from the *I Am Sam* soundtrack.

Or don't and experience her just how she is in your head.

Enjoy listening *and* reading.

And always remember to *rock on!*

Chapter 1

No One Got in the Way of Me and My Band

Stella

The phone rang.

My eyes opened and I looked at the clock.

Three thirty-seven.

In the morning.

I reached for the phone. "Hello?"

I sounded awake and alert. This was because it wasn't unusual for me to be up at an ungodly hour in the morning. Not only did I have loads of practice taking frantic phone calls in the hours before dawn, but also I was lead singer and guitarist of a rock band. Most of the time, I was just stumbling through the door after a gig at an ungodly hour in the morning.

"Stella?" It was Buzz, my bass player. He sounded messed up. On the phone at an ungodly hour in the morning he always sounded messed up.

"Hey Buzz, what's up?" I asked.

His answer could be anything. He needed me to bail him out of jail. He needed me to give him a ride home because he was somewhere, drunk out of his skull and thankfully responsible enough to call someone. Unthankfully, that someone was always me. He was stuck on a billboard on 8th promoting Earth, Wind and Fire's upcoming concert with no way to get down (don't ask).

But I was guessing it had to do with Lindsey.

"It's Linnie," Buzz said.

I was right.

"Buzz, I don't—"

"She's in bed, she ain't movin'. Something's weird. It just ain't right. I'm scared to even touch her. Stella Bella, fuck..." he whispered. "I think she overdosed."

I shot upright in my huge, super king-sized bed and my Saint Bernard, Juno, who was lying full out (thus explaining my need for a huge, super king-sized bed), sat up too and gave a woof.

"Have you called 911?" I asked Buzz.

"No, I called you."

Yep, that's about right.

Of course he'd call me. I was Stella Michelle Gunn, lead singer and lead guitarist of the Blue Moon Gypsies. I posted bond (mostly for Pong, my drummer, but for all of them on occasion). I soothed drunken angry men (again, predominately Pong, but they all were good at getting drunk *and* angry). I counseled relationships on the brink of collapse (this was not my strong suit; for your information, the parties concerned always broke up). I listened when the world just *did not* understand (and the world didn't understand much according to Leo, who played rhythm guitar and regularly got stoned and reflective). I extricated not-so-horny-anymore saxophonists named Hugo from mini-orgies with gonzo groupies gone bad.

And apparently I was an emergency paramedic.

"Call 911," I ordered

"But—"

"*Now!*" I snapped.

I hung up and swung out of bed. Juno woofed again and lumbered out of bed behind me.

My first thought was Mace.

In these situations (and there were a lot of them, although not always involving overdosed junkies who used to be sweet girls that were now addicted to smack) my first thought was always Kai "Mace" Mason, the tallest, hottest, coolest, most amazing guy I'd ever met. Mace with the jade green eyes. Mace with the thick, dark hair. Mace with the fantastic bod. Mace with the strong, masculine, long-fingered hands that could run so light across your skin you could almost hear them whisper.

Mace would know what to do. Mace would take care of Buzz and Lindsey, at the same time shielding me and Juno.

"Sleep," Mace's ultra-deep voice would say in my ear after hanging up the phone, which he *always* answered, and kissing my shoulder or my neck or the spot behind my ear, his lips making me tremble. "I'll take care of it."

Then he'd go and take care of it and I would sleep.

But Mace was gone. He'd broken up with me a year before.

Now it was just me. As always.

My second thought was to shove thoughts of Mace aside.

My third thought was to find my jeans.

I yanked off my nightgown and tugged on a pair of old Levi's and my bra. I grabbed a capped-sleeved white blouse with red stitching at the top and dangling tassels that you would expect a girl named Heidi to wear while yodeling in the mountains of Germany.

Just for your information, I loved that effing top.

Also, for your information, I had no idea how to yodel and didn't want to know how.

I sat on the bed and pulled on my brown cowboy boots, dusty not from riding the range but from standing on dirty stages in dark bars.

Then I grabbed my keys, shoved my cell phone in my back pocket and snatched Juno's leash off a hook by the door.

"Let's go, Juno," I called, slapping my hand against my thigh.

Juno thumped over to me, not with great excitement, wagging tail and lolling tongue, ready for adventure. Instead Juno was resigned to her fate, which consisted of yet another interruption to her beauty sleep, of which she needed a lot.

"Buzz thinks Linnie's overdosed. Probably just passed out," I told Juno as we headed out of my room and into the hall. "We'll be back home soon."

⌲

I drove my old, beat-up, dirty, fading red Ford van by Buzz's place but no one was home. That meant they were at Lindsey's.

By the time I got there so had the ambulance and the police. Lights flashing, the front yard of Lindsey's broken down house held not just straggling tufts of grass, weeds and patches of dirt, but also uniformed police officers and pajama'ed neighbors.

Worse, parked on the street was a shiny black Ford Explorer.

I knew what that meant.

One of the Nightingale Boys was there.

"What the eff?" I whispered, a chill sliding over my skin for several reasons. I parked in front of the squad car that was parked in front of the Explorer.

The Nightingale Boys were famous in certain circles of Denver—the circles occupied by cops, felons and others in need of their unique services. They were on the Nightingale Private Investigations Team, all of them highly qualified, intensely skilled, morally dubious, but totally super cool.

Mace was one of them.

I clipped the leash on Juno and swung out my door, Juno following me on a huge, big dog sigh.

Please don't let Mace be here, please don't let Mace be here, my brain chanted.

Then I switched topics.

Please let Linnie be okay, please let Linnie be okay.

I rounded the back of my van. The door to Lindsey's house opened and Luke Stark, Hot Guy and Nightingale Man, walked out. Black super short hair, killer, trimmed mustache that ran down the sides of his mouth, mouth-watering handsome and body designed by the gods.

I knew Luke. I'd met him when I dated Mace. I knew him now because he was living with my friend, Ava Barlow.

His eyes scanned the yard and stalled on me.

Okay, cool. No worries. All was well. I could deal with Luke. Luke was good. Luke was great.

I smiled at Luke.

The door opened again and Mace walked out.

Fuck! My brain shouted and my smile vanished.

My eyes did a sweep of all that was Mace.

I wanted to find fault in him, I really did. I wanted him to be growing a paunch. I wanted him to be developing a bald spot. I wanted him to look like he was wasting away, pining for me. Something, anything but what he was. Tall at six foot four, flat, tight abs, square jaw and, last but not least, arresting green eyes and great skin that showed the Hawaiian ancestry that he got from his Mom's side.

He didn't scan the yard. His eyes came direct to me like he sensed me there.

When his eyes caught my eyes I worked hard to keep my face blank.

Mace didn't appear to have to work hard at all. His expression didn't change. Not in the slightest.

I felt it like I always felt it when I remembered him, when I remembered us or when, on the odd occasion, I'd see him. That sharp kick in the gut and the sharper desire to flee.

I held my ground. I was ashamed to admit holding my ground took a lot, even after a year.

Luke hesitated.

Mace approached.

Bad luck. I would have preferred Luke to approach.

Effing hell, but my luck sucked.

Juno went wild. Finally happy with our ungodly hour adventure, Juno was straining at the leash, wanting more than anything, even hard food covered in melted bacon grease, to get at Mace. Juno loved Mace. She took Mace's defection almost harder than me. She'd pouted and waited at the door for him for months after he broke it off. She hadn't seen him in ages.

I held on tight to the lead, but struggled to keep my big dog still.

"Juno, sit," Mace commanded, five feet away.

Juno sat, as always, obeying Mace without hesitation, but she wasn't happy about it. Her tail swept the dirt, her tongue lolled, her life brightened.

Mace got close and Juno butted his hand with her wet nose, neck stretched to the max, but keeping her doggie-heiny to the ground.

I watched as Mace's long fingers slid through the fur on top of Juno's head and the gut kick feeling came back. Jealous of my own damn dog.

How far had I sunk?

I straightened my spine and tipped my head back to look at him.

"Go home, Stella," Mace said when my eyes caught his.

Not "hey", not "how are you?", not "you look good", not "I made the worst mistake in my life breaking up with you. Please forgive me and marry me and live with me until we both die at the same exact time, holding hands when we're one hundred and seven."

To hide my disappointment at his non-greeting, my eyes went to the door of the house then they scanned the area. Luke had moved to talk to Willie Moses, another friend of mine and a police sergeant for the Denver Police Department. The ambulance was still there, but I saw no paramedics.

Something was not right.

I looked back at Mace.

"Is Linnie okay?" I asked.

"Go home."

Yep, something was not right.

"Is Linnie okay?" I repeated.

"Stella, nothin' you can do here. Go home."

Oh hell. Something was *definitely* not right.

"Buzz called me. Said Linnie overdosed. Did she overdose? Is Buzz in there?" I asked.

"I'll talk to Buzz. He'll call you in the morning," Mace responded unhelpfully.

I felt fear begin to tear at my insides and I started to move around him, pulling Juno with me.

"I need to see Buzz," I declared.

His fingers wrapped around my upper arm in a way that couldn't be ignored. I stopped on a lurch. Juno stopped with me and I stared at his hand for two beats, then up at him.

"Take your hand off me, Mace," I demanded, my voice soft and low, my meaning clear.

He gave up the right to touch me a year ago. He gave up the right to tell me to go home. He even gave up the right to pet my damn dog. Maybe that last was pushing it, but I felt like pushing it at that moment.

He didn't move his hand. In fact his fingers tightened. It didn't hurt but it certainly made his meaning clear, too.

"Either you go to the van or I carry you there. Your choice, Stella."

He meant it.

This pissed me off.

I didn't get pissed-off very often. I didn't have the time. My life was music and my life was the band. When we weren't playing, we were loading or unloading our gear. When we weren't loading or unloading, we were rehearsing. When we weren't rehearsing, I was finding us gigs. When I wasn't finding us gigs, I was practicing guitar. When I wasn't practicing guitar, I was getting my bandmates out of trouble. When I wasn't getting my bandmates out of trouble, I was hanging out with Juno and cooking fabulous gourmet meals-for-one, because Juno was a big dog with not a lot of energy, thus she didn't do much so I had to find some way to amuse myself, and Juno liked the scraps. When I wasn't hanging out with Juno and cooking, I was shooting the shit with my girlfriends on the phone or meeting them somewhere.

The rest of the time, of which there wasn't much, I was sleeping.

As you could see, I didn't have time to be pissed-off.

But really, who the hell did he think he was? He couldn't break my heart one day and then get in the way of me and a member of my band the next.

Nunh-unh.

No way.

No one got in the way of me and my band.

I leaned into him.

"Tell me what's going on," I demanded on a quiet hiss.

"Buzz'll call in the morning." He kept attempting to blow me off.

"What the fuck is going on?" I demanded on a not-at-all quiet shout.

I felt, rather than saw, the eyes that turned to us.

"Stella, lower your voice," Mace ordered.

That pissed me off more.

"I'm goin' in there," I told him.

"You aren't goin' in there," he told me, and his hand stayed where it was.

Effing hell.

I changed tactics. "Why are you doing this?"

This caught him off-guard, I saw it. His usually blank-but-broody look disappeared and I saw his eyes flash in the dim illumination of Lindsey's porch light.

"I'm protecting you," he answered, his voice low. The words seemed torn from him as if he didn't want to say them.

There was the gut kick feeling again and more fear started tearing through my insides.

"It isn't your job to protect me anymore, Mace," I reminded him and watched the flash in his eyes again.

Erm, excuse me? What in the heck was that all about?

"You're right. It's not," he replied and dropped my arm.

Big time gut kick.

Sheesh. He gave up easily.

Oh well, so be it.

I started to move away.

"Lindsey's dead. Executed," Mace said to my back.

I stopped moving and turned to stare, unable to process what he just said.

"What?" I whispered.

7

Mace got close again. "She was executed. Somewhere else, brought back here," Mace answered.

"But…" I started then stopped then started again, "but, Buzz said he thought she overdosed. How could—?"

"Bullet to the forehead. No blood because she was moved from wherever they whacked her. She was put in bed, covers pulled up, fuck knows why. Her face, except for the bullet hole in her forehead, looks normal, but the back of her head is gone."

I turned my eyes away from Mace, bile sliding up the back of my throat at the vision he created. I swallowed it down.

I saw Luke standing across the yard still talking to Willie, but my mind was elsewhere.

It was on Lindsey, the sweet girl who came to one of our gigs two years ago and fell in love with Buzz on sight. She was plump and pretty and she loved rock 'n' roll. And because she was plump and pretty and sweet-as-hell, we all loved her.

How she got caught up with heroin and that life no one knew, not even Buzz. Everyone tried to pull her out of it—the entire band, mostly Buzz and me and, for a short time, Mace. But she slid down into that world no matter how hard we tried to stop her. Buzz didn't give up, nor did I, but I was losing patience. She was hanging with bad dudes, doing stuff that was not good, all to get her fix. She'd started to bring these bad dudes to gigs. That was where I drew the line.

Now she was dead.

"Linnie," I whispered.

Juno felt my mood and pushed my hand with her nose. I absentmindedly stroked her head as I heard Luke's phone ring and watched, unfocused and not knowing what to feel (sad, definitely; angry, heck yeah), as Luke pulled his phone out of his black cargo pants.

"Kitten." I heard as if from far away, so far away it was like a dream.

It was Mace's voice calling me "Kitten", his nickname for me, a nickname I earned because he said I "purred" when I was content. Normally this purring happened post-orgasm, but there were other times too. I was content a lot when I'd been with Mace.

It was something I hadn't heard in a year. It was one of the seven hundred and twenty-five thousand things I missed most about Mace.

A touch, whisper-soft, slid across the small of my back and I shivered.

"Linnie," I whispered again.

Then I watched in distracted fascination as whatever Luke heard over the phone changed his entire body. I was fascinated because I could swear Luke looked scared.

Men like Luke didn't get scared.

I shook my head and jerked out of my daze.

"I have to get to Buzz," I announced.

"Stella."

I took off, walking swiftly across the yard.

As I marched, I heard Luke shout, "*Mace!*" and Mace's name came from Luke's lips like a bark, sharp and ferocious.

I didn't let that register. My mind was centered on Buzz.

Then gunshots rang out.

Yes.

Gunshots.

There were shouts of surprise, rapid movement, and I saw the dirt around me explode as the bullets pounded into it around my cowboy boots, one after the other after the other.

For a second I stood frozen, not comprehending this drastic turn of events. Then I felt a stinging burn in my hip and cried out, but for some reason my hands went to my head, and unfortunately belatedly, I started to run for my effing life.

I ran two steps before I was picked up at the waist, shifted, thrown over Mace's shoulder, and he ran in a half crouch as the bullets whizzed around us.

He stopped, wrenched open the backdoor to the Explorer and tossed me in. He made a quick whistling noise through his teeth and Juno jumped up with me, jarring me. Pain sliced through my hip and I cried out again.

Mace slammed the door almost before Juno's hind-end cleared it. He got in the passenger seat; Luke was already in at the driver's side. My dog and I barely settled before we rocketed from the curb.

I hadn't even noticed Luke starting the truck. It was like he hit the ignition through a mind meld, one with the vehicle. None of that normal turn the key and go business for Super Cool Luke.

Mace hit a button on the dash and the cab was filled with ringing.

Juno woofed just to be part of the action. Not wanting to do much of anything, just not wanting anyone to forget she was around. This was her way.

I put my hand to my hip. I felt something wet there and pulled my hand away.

The wet on my hand was dark. Blood.

I'd been shot. Effing hell, I'd been *shot*.

With a bullet. An honest-to-goodness bullet.

Jesus!

"Um, Mace—" I started, trying not to sound panicky.

"This is Jack." A voice filled the cab.

"One second," Mace said to me in an undertone.

"Ava just called in, said someone opened fire on her, Daisy, Ally, Indy, Tod and Stevie. They were outside a gay club on Broadway. I lost contact with her in the middle of the call," Luke informed Jack, who I also knew from my days as Mace's girlfriend. He was another Nightingale Man, built strong, tough, solid and scary.

I gasped at this news. Ava and the girls had been shot at? What was going on?

"Copy that. I'm on it," Jack's voice replied.

"Someone just shot at Stella at the scene," Mace added.

They weren't shooting at me, were they? My brain asked.

Since I didn't actually utter the words, no one answered.

"Fuck," Jack snapped.

"Call Lee and check Roxie, Jules and Jet," Luke ordered.

"Copy," Jack said.

"Out," Luke clipped, and hit a button on the console while Jack repeated the same word. "I don't fuckin' like this," Luke finished on a mutter.

You could sense his fear, clear and edgy, filling the cab. He wasn't even hiding it. His woman had been shot at, and not only did he not like it, he was terrified that she was in danger. Mingled with the out-and-out panic I felt at the general situation, not to mention the fact I was bleeding from a gunshot wound, was a sense of beauty that Super Cool Luke cared about Ava enough to let his tough guy image take that kind of direct hit.

Mace was silent, but he leaned forward and pulled his cell out of his back pocket.

"Um, Mace——" I started again, thinking now the time was ripe to share the fact I was bleeding.

"Two seconds," Mace replied.

Apparently the time wasn't ripe.

I looked around the backseat for something to press against my wound. I was probably bleeding all over the seat. I saw a blanket on the floor opposite me, leaned over and grabbed it. I lifted a butt cheek, shoved it under, sat on it and pressed its edge to my hip. Why I cared about bloodstains on the seat of the Explorer, don't ask me, but it was something to worry about that didn't involve me and my friends getting shot at, at four o'clock early on a Wednesday morning. So I went with it.

Mace hit some buttons on his cell, but the phone rang in the cab before he connected.

Luke hit a button on the console.

"Stark," he answered.

"Luke, get to Jules. Now. She called in. Drive-by, AK-47. They shot out Nick and Jules's windows," Jack told us.

"Goddamn it!" Luke clipped.

"Sid," Mace replied what I thought was nonsensically.

"Call Vance. Call Lee. We need a rendezvous point," Luke demanded to Jack. "Call Louie and find out what the fuck is goin' on with Ava."

"Copy. Out," Jack said.

Disconnect.

Luke took a turn without slowing so I went flying, and so did Juno. My big dog and I became a tangle of furry limbs and not-furry-limbs. Once we were on the straight and narrow and my ass cheek was back on the blanket again, I thought it best to buckle in.

Mace was looking around the seat at me. His eyes watched me click the buckle, then without a word he turned back to the front.

"Hang tight, Juno," I whispered after I buckled in and I reached across myself with the hand that wasn't bloody and stroked Juno's head.

Juno woofed a calm woof.

Good to know my dog was cool in a crisis, though it would have been better if I'd never needed that knowledge.

Mace was on the phone. "Ike," he said. "Yeah. Call Matt and Bobby. Sid's made a move. We need confirmation on Ava and the girls. Ava reported to Luke they were under fire and he lost contact. Louie's with them. They were outside that gay club on Broadway." Pause. "Yeah, out."

He flipped his phone shut as Luke took another turn without slowing and we all leaned with it.

"Um, Mace——" I began yet again.

"There." Mace ignored me and pointed at a cherry-condition, red, circa 1980-something Camaro illuminated by the streetlights and headed our way.

Luke hit the brakes, executed a swift, tight, three-point turn in the middle of the road (scaring the effing beejeezus out of me, by the way) and raced up behind the Camaro. Once there, he flashed his lights.

Leaning to my side and looking between the seats, I saw the driver's hand wave. The Camaro slowed and Luke shot round it. I looked behind us and the Camaro followed as I heard the bleeping sound of the phone being dialed on the dash. I turned back around to the front, one ring and connect.

"I'm okay," a woman's voice said.

"Nick?" Mace asked.

"He's okay too."

"Have you contacted Vance?" Mace went on.

"Yeah, he's heading back from Albuquerque now," the woman said, and I knew this was Jules, a more recent friend of mine. I'd met her a few months ago when she'd come with some of my friends to a gig. She was married to one of the Nightingale Men, Vance Crowe. In fact, they were just back from their honeymoon.

For your information, it was just my bad luck that after one of the Nightingale Men broke up with me, one of my closest friends hooked up with *the* Nightingale Man, Lee Nightingale. Her name was India "Indy" Savage. I'd known her for years. Now she and her best friend Ally (a Nightingale herself, Lee's sister), both close friends of mine, were mixed up with the Nightingale posse.

This meant for almost a year I hadn't had a lot to do with my friends. They knew about me and Mace because they guessed, but they also didn't know because I didn't share details, not during our five month relationship and not after it ended. It was too precious to share, not even with Ally, whose brother was my now-ex-boyfriend's employer, and it had never gotten to the point where it wasn't. When it was over I just got busy. But then again, they were all busy, too. As the months passed, Indy and Ally added Rock Chicks to the club and all of them were claimed by Nightingale Men along the way.

As I said, it was bad luck. What I didn't say was it was super shitty bad luck.

Also, for your information, I was the Queen of Super Shitty Bad Luck, and getting shot was only the most recent example of that fact.

"Follow us," Luke told Jules.

"Gotcha," Jules replied.

Disconnect.

The dash phone started ringing immediately and Luke pressed a button.

Without a greeting, Jack informed the cab, "Ava's fine."

I expelled a breath I didn't know I was holding. Luke's fear disappeared.

"Louie returned fire, got the girls and boys in Daisy's limo. Everyone's safe, no one was hit. They're headed to The Castle. Lee says that's the rendez-vous."

"Copy that. The others?" Luke asked.

"Soon to be in transit but not good. Both Eddie and Hank got callouts. Both houses were hit by drive-bys after they were gone. AK-47s again. Roxie and Jet were sleeping. They're okay. Lee's just been in to get a vehicle. He's picking them up and heading toward The Castle."

To keep you up to date, Eddie was Lee's best friend, Jet was his fiancée. Hank was Lee's brother, Roxie was living with him.

See how this all came around and went around? Sucks for me because I lost Mace. Though the girls were happy as clams, getting married, having babies (Jules was pregnant), living the good life of being a Hot Guy's Woman. The life I tasted and loved but lost and would never have again.

"Fuckin' Sid," Luke clipped, breaking into my thoughts.

"Fuckin' Sid," Jack agreed.

"Ike's mobilizing Matt and Bobby," Mace put in. "He was looking for Ava. Now he needs an alternate assignment."

"Copy that. I'll call him," Jack responded.

"Out," Luke said and hit a button.

Silence.

"War," Mace declared.

"Fuck yeah," Luke replied.

I didn't know what they meant, but I didn't like the sound of it.

Effing hell.

Chapter 2

Hunky Dory

Stella

When they referred to "The Castle", they meant an actual castle. I didn't know Denver *had* a castle, but there it was, right in front of us.

We'd driven to the ritzy part of Englewood, down a winding lane in a heavily wooded area, and all lit up with a shitload of lights that would make even your average environmentalist shudder was a stone castle, complete with turrets and a moat.

During the drive I decided that it was evident that I was not going to die of my wound.

I also decided I did not want Mace to know I was injured. If he knew I was injured, it might mean I'd have to spend more time in his presence. The last time I'd spent more than a few minutes in his presence was when he'd come to a gig with the Rock Chicks. I ended up singing Hank Williams's "I'm So Lonesome I Could Cry" directly to him. I had no control over it. It just happened. Even the band was taken aback. I did not want a repeat of that moment of weakness.

Unh-unh.

No effing way.

I had a plan. I'd slip into a bathroom, clean up, maybe confiscate a washcloth, then I'd call Floyd to come get me. This was a totally stupid plan, but I wasn't thinking clearly.

Floyd was my pianist, older than anyone else in the band by a decade and a half. Floyd was married to Emily. He had a steady day job, two kids in college and could play and sing Billy Joel's "And So It Goes" so beautifully that if you didn't at least tear up, you had to be made of stone.

His lead on our rendition of "Scenes from an Italian Restaurant" didn't suck, either.

Floyd and Emily would take care of me, I knew it. Especially considering there was a bleeding bullet wound involved.

They were the only ones in my whole life who took care of me, or at least the only ones who did it for any length of time. I didn't call on them often because I didn't want that to end like it had with Mace that night when he stood, shoulder leaned against my doorway, and told me I needed him too much.

That wasn't going to happen to me again. Not if I could help it.

Two men wearing dark suits, white shirts, slim ties and carrying big guns materialized and approached the Explorer as we swung into the drive. I sucked in breath, thinking this was not exactly a welcome party, but they spied Luke and Mace and disappeared in the shadows again.

I had no time to dwell on castles with moats and men with guns because Luke's lights flashed on a limousine that was parked in front of the house. We could see the bullet holes along the side. At the sight, the cab went electric and this electricity was emanating from Luke.

"He should have gone down like a man," Mace said softly.

"Now he'll pay," Luke replied.

"Now he'll pay," Mace agreed.

"Who?" I asked.

Mace turned around to look at me as Luke parked, and I got the gut kick feeling that he forgot I was there.

"You okay?" he asked belatedly, but not, I noticed, answering my question.

No, I've been shot, which could be the definition of "not okay", my brain replied sarcastically.

"Hunky dory," my mouth said.

Luke had turned off the truck and was now twisted to look at me, too. He heard my reply and I saw his half-grin. I grinned back.

"Out," Mace snapped, sounding, for some reason, impatient, and he jerked open his door.

I opened my door, too. Juno trundled over me and hopped down. I gritted my teeth against the pain and hopped down behind her. It took a lot, but I walked normally, and to hide it kept my bloody hand pressed against my belly like a pregnant woman.

Luke had forged ahead, probably keen to get to Ava. Mace walked at my right side, opposite the wounded left side. He walked beside me, but he put distance between us.

When we'd been together he didn't like distance anytime, anywhere. Mace was not a man who shied away from public displays of affection. He walked with his thumb hooked in the side belt loop of my jeans so I was plastered against him. In restaurant booths he sat next to me, not opposite me. He lounged in front of the TV with my head or feet in his lap or me pressed against his side. In bed he was a spooner, the front of his long, hard body curved and pressed into the length of the back of mine. When we kissed, standing up, sitting down, lying in bed, he sought maximum physical contact. He didn't seek it, he demanded it. It was another one of the seven hundred and twenty-five thousand things about Mace that I missed the most.

Juno loped beside us, alternately trotting and sniffing the ground.

After we crossed the little stone bridge over the moat and Mace caught the door Luke was holding open for us, I said, "I'll call Floyd to come get me."

Luke was again moving ahead. Mace fell back in step beside me. I was staring in awe at my surroundings. A long, stone-walled hall, a bright red carpet runner punctuated by shiny brass rods holding it down, crossed swords, wrought iron torches with electrical lights and full suits of armor decorating it down either side. It was unbelievable. It was indescribable. It was like I stepped into a different world.

"You need to wait until we debrief. Then I'll tell you what you can do," Mace replied.

I lost my awe. I forgot about the pain in my hip and my head turned to Mace. I was pretty certain I was pissed-off again.

"What did you just say?" I asked.

"You heard me," he answered, but didn't look at me.

Either in an attempt not to argue or because he was raring to debrief, whatever the hell that meant, he forged ahead, too, his long legs taking him well ahead of me. I scrambled to catch up.

He, and then I, entered a big room with a beamed cathedral ceiling, a massive fireplace and loads of studded leather furniture. There were banners dangling from the stone walls with multiple rows of olde-worlde lions and fleur-de-lis depicted on them. I lost my anger at Mace because I regained my awe.

I stared. It was the kind of room where you stared. You couldn't do anything else.

"Holy shit! Stella! What are you doing here?" That was Indy.

I looked at her and saw the room already held a number of people. Luke and Mace, of course. Also Indy, her neighbors Tod and Stevie (a gay couple I knew from meeting them at Indy's many parties, which I attended back in the days pre-Mace), Ava, Daisy (a new-ish addition to the club; I'd met her too, she looked just like Dolly Parton, but a younger version and yes, she even had the enormous hooters) and Ally. They were all standing and they all turned to me.

"What's on your leg?" Ally asked, her eyes on my leg.

Effing hell, how could I forget about my hip?

"Is that... blood?" Tod's eyes were huge and his hand went to his chest.

"She's been shot!" Daisy screeched.

My eyes flew to Mace. He was standing several feet in front of me, his back to me, and at Daisy's words his head whipped around.

"It's nothing," I told them, backing away.

Mace had turned and was bearing down, gaining ground. I kept edging backward. I ran into something and turned to see a man wearing glasses. Tall, dark hair, some gray, and his hands settled on my shoulders, ending my retreat. I looked into his blue eyes. They were kind, but I also got the impression that he wasn't going to let me go anywhere.

"I'm okay," I told this man I didn't know.

Different hands came to the top of my hip. My gaze swung down and I saw strong, long-fingered hands I knew really well. I looked up from the hands and Mace was in my space.

"Mace, let me go. I'm fine," I said as he bent slightly to the side, tilting my hip gently toward his gaze, and he looked at the wound. I looked, too. There was a lot more blood than I expected. It was everywhere.

When I looked back up, everyone had gathered around.

"I'm totally fine," I repeated.

Mace straightened and his eyes came to mine.

"Hunky dory?" he asked, his voice low and sounding a bit cheesed off.

"Hunky dory." I nodded.

Without warning, I was lifted up. I found myself cradled in Mace's arms, and he started striding back into the big room.

"What the——?" I began to yell.

"Privacy," Mace clipped at Daisy, interrupting me.

"Through here. I'll get a first aid kit," Daisy replied, racing along beside us.

"First aid? Girlie, she needs a doctor." Tod was racing alongside us too.

"She doesn't need a doctor, she needs a hospital." Stevie was on Tod's heels.

"I don't fucking believe this shit. Someone shot Stella," Ally snapped, trailing along as well.

Juno woofed, trotting with the pack, obviously agreeing with Ally.

"We need to boil water. We need clean towels," Ava announced, following, too.

"She ain't birthin' no baby! She's got a gunshot wound!" Indy shouted.

"I know that!" Ava shouted back. "But we need a sterile environment."

Lord save me from well-intentioned Rock Chicks.

Daisy took us to another, smaller room, which had also been decorated with a heavy medieval hand, and Mace stopped and turned.

I saw Luke cut off our followers and declare, "Private," right before he shut the door in their faces leaving Daisy, Mace, Luke and me in the room.

"This is no big deal," I announced.

Mace set me on my feet, but his hands went back firmly to my hips just below my waist, making it clear I was not to move away.

"Should we cut off the jeans?" Mace asked.

"No! These are my lucky Levi's!" I yelled, trying to jerk my hips from his hands (this didn't work).

Okay, so, maybe the jeans weren't so lucky since I'd been shot in them. Still, I didn't want them cut up.

"Would be optimal, but we'll peel 'em off, see how it goes." Luke ignored my outburst.

"I'll get the first aid. I know a doctor who'll come here," Daisy put in.

"Get it and call him," Mace ordered.

"You betcha," Daisy replied and her eyes found mine. "We'll get you taken care of, sugar bunch, not to worry." Then she was off.

Mace's hands were at my fly.

"Hey! What're you doing?" I snapped and slapped at his hands. He caught my wrists and gave them a light jerk so I stopped struggling.

"Stella, we have to get the jeans off and see the wound," Mace explained calmly.

Nope. That was *not* gonna happen.

"No you don't. Let me call Floyd. He and Emily will—"

"You aren't calling Floyd," Mace stated.

"I am," I retorted and shook my hair angrily for good measure.

"You aren't," Mace repeated.

"I am!" I shouted.

I started struggling, got my wrists free and started slapping his hands again.

This went on for half a second before he caught my wrists again and pulled them around my back. The front of my body hit the front of his and I stilled at the shock of it.

"Cuff her," Mace said to Luke.

I unstilled.

"*What?*" I screamed, back to struggling in earnest.

There was a clink and my hands were cuffed behind my back. Luke gripped my waist, holding me still, and Mace worked on my jeans.

Please tell me this is not happening, my brain begged.

Mace unbuttoned the button and I heard and felt the zip going down.

This was happening.

"I'm not wearing any underwear," I lied.

"I'll close my eyes," Mace lied back.

"I won't," Luke put in.

Shitsofuckit!

I decided to stop talking and stop struggling. I also decided this was good. No, this was great. No. This was *absolutely fantastic*. The longer this went on the more I hated Mace, and since I'd spent a year loving him and not having him, hating was a much, *much* better emotion to hold onto.

Mace went into a crouch and, carefully and slowly, he peeled down my jeans. Down, down, just over the wound at the very bottom of the hip, right before my leg started. I sucked in breath between my teeth when he exposed it. He stopped and his hands closed around it, one on my hip, one on my thigh.

I could swear I was blushing. Since his hands and his mouth had been there (and everywhere) and he'd seen me in much less than just my pants rolled down (exposing a pair of plain, white, shorts-style panties with a little pink bow), well, I shouldn't be blushing.

But I was.

"Flesh wound," he muttered.

"Told you," I hissed, powering through the blush.

Mace came up from the crouch, but still close, right in my space.

"We'll clean it and Daisy's doctor can stitch it," he told me.

"Then can I call Floyd?" I asked.

"I told you, not until we debrief."

"I didn't agree to that."

"I wasn't giving you an option."

My eyes bugged out, beyond pissed-off, rocketing straight to angry as hell.

Before I could blow, Luke asked from behind me, "Do you want me to uncuff her?"

"No," Mace answered.

"Yes," I said at the same time.

Not surprisingly, Luke didn't uncuff me.

"Sit down. I'll take off your boots so we can get the jeans off," Mace demanded.

"Stop bossing me around and I'll take off my own boots, thank you very much," I shot back.

"That'll be hard to do with your hands cuffed behind you," Mace returned.

"Uncuff me then," I retorted.

"Stella," Mace said warningly.

"Mace," I returned the gesture.

Mace sighed and looked over my head. I knew he was looking at Luke. I also knew from the expression on his face that he was also looking for patience.

I heard Luke chuckle.

It hit me then that I was standing in a strange house, I had a gunshot wound, my hands cuffed behind my back and my jeans pulled down around my thighs.

Worse than that, Linnie'd had the back of her head blown off and Buzz was out there somewhere without my hand to hold onto.

I looked down at my boots and felt the tears come to my eyes.

"This is humiliating," I whispered, blinking back the tears.

Immediately after I uttered the words, I felt Luke's presence retreat just as Mace got deeper in my space. His hands came to either side of my neck and I sucked in breath at the feel of their warm strength.

God, I missed it when he touched me.

"Kitten," he murmured, and my eyes flew to his.

His eyes had grown soft. I hadn't seen that look in a long time.

I missed that, too.

"Don't call me that," I whispered.

His eyes flashed yet again with something I couldn't decipher, and, still in a voice that was deep, low and sweet, he said, "Stella."

"Take your hands off me." I kept at it, ignoring the flash, ignoring the soft look, at a place in my life where I could deal knowing there was no Mace in it and not about to slide back. "Uncuff me and go away. Send in the girls. They'll help me get my jeans and boots off and clean me up."

"I'm not leaving you," Mace told me.

"Go," I replied.

"No."

I closed my eyes tight and sucked in a breath. Then I straightened my back and opened them again.

In a strong, steady, no-nonsense voice, I stated, "Please. Go."

Mace stared at me a beat. It became two. It slid to three. Then his eyes flicked over my head.

"Uncuff her."

Luke uncuffed me. The door opened and Daisy shot in.

"I called the doctor. He lives around the corner and he's on his way. I got the first aid kit and some cotton balls and some alcohol and some hydrogen peroxide and some clean towels and a whole load of other stuff. I didn't know what you'd need," she announced, bustling into the room, her arms loaded so high you could barely see her head. She peeked around the pile and smiled at me. "And I got you some of my track bottoms so you'll have something to wear." She tossed the whole lot on the couch.

Mace and Luke went to the door.

"She wants you," Luke told the congregation outside, and they surged in, all the Rock Chicks with new arrivals Jules, Jet and Roxie, gay guys and my dog, forcing Mace and Luke to push through the crowd.

Mace kept walking and I watched his departing back.

Luke turned at the door, his eyes hit mine and his chin lifted. I felt the chin lift was an indication of respect. Respect that I didn't freak out when I got shot, or at all. Respect that I let them get on with what they had to do, and maybe a bit of respect that I held my own, even though I didn't win, with Mace. This made me feel funny. A funny I'd never felt in my life, except when I was onstage.

Luke stepped out and closed the door behind him.

"Oh girlie, look at that. That's nothing. Just a flesh wound," Tod declared, head cocked, finger to his cheek, eyes staring at my hip.

"He left," I whispered, my gaze still on the door.

"What's that, sugar?" Daisy was pushing me toward some towels that were now spread on the couch.

"Nothing," I replied and let myself be pushed.

❦

"You okay?" Indy asked.

She and Ally were making up the pull out bed in the room where I'd endured the humiliation of Mace pulling down my jeans. I was putting pillowcases on pillows.

Under strict Lee edict, the Rock Chicks and Hot Bunch were staying the night at The Castle. Apparently they were at war with some guy named Sid and The Castle was out of the way. It had a security system that included camera surveillance outside and was "covered" by an army of men employed by Marcus, Daisy's husband (Daisy and Marcus lived in The Castle, for your information). It had the added benefit of not having its windows shot out in a recent drive-by.

Daisy was in seventh heaven. She was treating this like a co-ed slumber party, not like her big mansion had become a scary-as-shit impromptu safe house. She issued orders to the dark-suited members of her husband's army to go out and buy toothbrushes, contact lens supplies and food so she could serve a "Big Ole Stick-To-Your-Ribs Southern Breakfast" (her words). She handed out nightgowns and toiletries and she assigned bedrooms. She had a goodly number of rooms, but Ally was forced to take a couch, and in deference to my injury, I got a pull out bed. I didn't know where Mace was sleeping, or if he was even staying there, and didn't care. Well, I cared, but I tried not to.

"Yeah, I'm fine," I lied to Indy.

"You are so not fine," Ally muttered.

"I'm fine. It hardly hurts at all," I told Ally.

I was talking about my hip. The doctor came and cleaned it, shot me up with something to numb it and then stitched it. After he was done, he dressed it, gave me some pain killers and took off again, maybe to do another clandestine stitch up somewhere in the early morning dark of Denver. The whole thing took less than an hour.

"I'm not talking about your leg," Indy said.

I threw the pillow at the head of the pull out and grabbed the other one.

"What are you talking about?" I asked.

"She's talking about Mace," Ally told me.

"What about Mace?" I played dumb.

"Chickie, you aren't fooling anyone," Ally replied.

"I'm not trying to fool anyone." This was another lie.

"Yeah you are, most especially yourself," Indy said softly.

Effing hell.

"It was over a long time ago," I explained.

"If it was over, then when the Hot Bunch's women got targeted by a criminal overlord, you wouldn't have been called out, exposed and shot at," Ally pointed out logically.

This was true. This was also something to mull over later, privately, perhaps over some risotto and a nice, chilled glass of pinot grigio.

"Can we talk about this later?" I asked, all of a sudden exhausted. I threw the other pillow at the head of the bed.

Ally opened her mouth. Indy shot her a look. Ally closed her mouth. They smoothed the covers and made to move out.

"Just as long as we *do* talk about it later," Ally said on her way out, not about to be silenced for long by Indy.

"Goodnight," I called, giving no assurances.

"Later," Indy replied and she closed the door.

I carefully took off Daisy's cream, velour, Juicy Couture track bottoms but left on the snug, white t-shirt she'd given me.

"It's new, haven't worn it yet so I haven't broken in the chest area," Daisy informed me, circling her extraordinary bosoms with a pointed, frosty white-polished, ultra long finger-nailed finger to make her point. Ava had seized my

Heidi shirt, which had a bit of blood on it and disappeared, muttering something about stain removal.

I took the pain killers using a glass of water Daisy brought me, got in bed and stared at the ceiling.

My first thoughts were of Linnie and Buzz. Then, for peace of mind, because thoughts of Linnie were too difficult to bear (and because I no longer had my phone so I could call Buzz and see how he was doing because Mace had confiscated it) my thoughts went to the final chapter of the weird and wild evening.

After getting stitched up and changing clothes, the Rock Chicks were called into a Tribe Meeting by Lee.

We all sat in Daisy's big room. The gathering had grown bigger. Jet's fiancé, Eddie Chavez, was there. Roxie's boyfriend, Hank Nightingale, as well. There was a handsome man who I found out was Marcus Sloan, Daisy's husband. Bobby, Matt and Ike, all Nightingale Men, had also arrived. Bobby was a barrel-chested, sandy-blond behemoth. Matt was a fit, also-blond, cute guy. Ike was light-skinned black man, shaved bald with a cool-as-shit tattoo you could see slithering up his neck and down his arm around the sleeve and collar of his t-shirt. The man who stopped my retreat earlier was Nick, Jules's uncle.

There was also a guy I didn't know. He looked a lot like Eddie, but definitely as-yet-untamed-by-domesticity, and by the looks of him, untamable. His eyes came to me when I walked in, I thought because I was the only one injured in the night's proceedings. His eyes didn't leave me, though. They felt hot on me. So hot, they made me feel hot, but in a nice way. A way I hadn't felt under the gaze of a man in a very long time. Eventually, it made me feel so hot I had to look away.

Lee "briefed" us about the situation. Some guy named Sid was under investigation by the police (for your information, when he said, "police", it didn't take a rocket scientist to figure out he meant Hank and Eddie). The police had partnered with the Nightingale Team to hasten the act of bringing Sid down. Mace was overseeing the Take Sid Down Project for the team. Other entities were recruited, and my guess was those "other entities" were Marcus Sloan and his be-suited, big-gun-toting army.

They were close to something. Sid didn't like it, so Sid declared war by going after the girls. Lee knew this not only because it was obvious, but also because he'd had a phone call five minutes after the precisely timed shootings and drive-bys. The caller informed him that he should take this as a warning. Either they backed off or Sid's boys were going to pick off the Rock Chicks one-by-one.

Me getting shot was not planned. I was only supposed to get shot *at*. Again, I would take this opportunity to remind you I was the Queen of Super Shitty Bad Luck.

This information of certain death to the Rock Chicks was met with the vague murmur here and there. For myself, I was totally flipped out, as threats of one-by-one killings of myself and my friends—hell, of *anyone*—was wont to do. Everyone else acted like this was a small bother, like getting a splinter. Irritating but not much more.

Effing hell.

Lee told The Tribe that Daisy and Marcus would be our hosts for the evening and we'd get our orders the next day.

It was then my phone, which I was holding in my hand, rang.

"Sorry," I muttered to the assemblage when all eyes swung to me.

I looked at the display. It said, "Buzz Calling". I flipped it open, but before I could put it to my ear it was pulled out of my hand.

My head shot up and I saw Mace, my phone to his ear, his back to me, walking away.

"Erm, excuse me?" I called, getting up from my perch on the arm of a couch and following him.

"Buzz, she'll talk to you tomorrow," Mace told the phone. "Yeah. She's all right." Then he flipped my phone shut.

Do something! My brain ordered me.

I did something. I poked him in the back. The Tribe had melted from existence (not really, as people can't melt, except in movies like *Raiders of the Lost Ark*; they just melted from my mind) and my pissed-off vibe came back with a vengeance.

"Excuse *me*?" I repeated to his back.

Mace turned. I put my hand out for my phone.

Mace shoved my phone in his back pocket. My eyes followed this action, then narrowed and shot back to Mace's face.

"Give me my phone," I demanded.

"No," Mace replied.

"Give it to me."

"No."

"Mace, give me my goddamned phone!" My voice was rising.

Mace leaned into me and responded calmly, "No."

"I need to talk to Buzz," I explained with rapidly waning patience. "He's gonna need me. His girlfriend had her head blown off tonight, for God's sake!"

"Lindsey's head was blown off by Sid's men. She's the reason they were able to get close to you, watch you, figure you out, find a way to get to you. She's the reason they knew Buzz would call you and knew you'd come running when he did. Lindsey got herself killed so you could be target practice as a warning to me."

My mouth snapped shut and I took a step back. I had not put this together but it made sense, and the idea that I had anything to do with Lindsey's death felt like the gut kick to end all gut kicks.

Mace took a step forward and his steps were longer than mine.

"Stella, I'm not gonna let any of the members of that fuckin' band of yours put you in harm's way. No phone. No communication. Not until we know the lay of the land. Your band wants to talk to you, they do it through me."

Oh no. He did *not* just say what it seemed like he just said.

"Don't call them 'that fuckin' band'," I snapped.

Mace was silent.

"And you can't take my phone!"

Mace remained silent.

"And you aren't going to order me around and stand between me and my boys!" I went on.

"Wanna bet?" Mace asked.

I stared at him. He stared at me.

He didn't look blank and broody, and that emotional flash didn't cut through his eyes. He looked determined and angry, and I got the weird impression that it didn't have to do simply with Linnie being dead, me getting shot and us being sequestered at The Castle.

I changed tactics. "God! Were you this overbearing when we were together?"

"I should have been." Mace fired his shot without hesitation.

My head jerked and my hands balled into fists. I couldn't believe he just said that. I didn't even know what he meant by that.

What *did* he mean by that?

27

Kristen Ashley

"Girlie, hate to break this up—it's great for entertainment value alone—but you *do* know you two have an audience," Tod called from somewhere behind me.

I sucked in breath through my nose, too angry to be embarrassed.

"Thank God we're over," I threw at Mace as my parting shot.

That was when I saw the flash dart through his eyes again. It was there then gone before I could read it.

"I'm keeping your phone," Mace informed me.

"Have at it." I gave up and walked away.

That was it. Daisy got busy getting everyone settled and we dispersed.

Juno put her front paws on the pull out bed, taking my mind from my thoughts.

"You can't get up here. Momma's got a gunshot wound and there isn't enough room."

Juno woofed.

"I know, baby. The floor is cold and hard, but it's all you've got tonight. We'll be home soon."

Juno woofed again.

"Quiet, girl. It's six o'clock in the morning and there's a house full of people trying to sleep."

A soft woof then Juno plopped down. I heard her big dog groan as she stretched out on the floor. Then another big dog groan-slash-sigh as she fell to her side.

"You're such a good dog," I whispered, and I meant it.

I heard an even softer woof and I felt my lips form a small smile.

I punched my pillows, rolled to rest on my unwounded side and laid smack in the middle of the bed. The doctor said the painkillers might make me drowsy. He was not wrong.

Within minutes, I was asleep.

It was an awake/asleep dream. I knew it because I had a lot of them. Always morning, my favorite time of the day when I was with Mace.

For your information, I would have welcomed asleep/asleep dreams of Mace, but I normally dreamed of weird shit like mutant snakes terrorizing Den-

28

ver or being on a road trip with Charo, her shouting, "Coochie Coochie," at passing truckers. I didn't know what these dreams said about me or the state of my unconscious mind, and I didn't want to know.

The awake/asleep dreams were always like this, part-conscious, part-unconscious, right when I woke up but before I was really awake. It was then I would feel Mace's imaginary heat behind me, his hard body pressed to mine, his arm tucked tight around my belly, his breath against my neck.

I went with it as I always did, liking the memory. It was one of the seven hundred, twenty-five thousand things about him I missed most; waking up with him holding me. Feeling safe, feeling wanted, feeling loved. All three of those feelings I'd never really felt in my whole life.

I snuggled into his imaginary heat and hit something very solid and very real.

I froze.

"You're awake," Mace said.

Oh my God. What was going on?

"Mace?" I asked just to make sure.

"We need to talk."

Yep, he was there all right.

Effing hell.

I tried to move away. The tight arm got tighter.

"Let me go."

"No."

Erm, excuse me?

"Let me go," I repeated.

"We're gonna talk."

"Fine, great, wonderful. We can talk not lying in bed." Then it hit me. "What are you doing in my bed?"

"I told you I wasn't leavin' you."

Erm, excuse *me?*

"Yeah, you said that right before you left me," I reminded him.

"I didn't leave you."

"You walked out of the room!"

"I walked out of the room but I didn't leave you."

"You didn't stay."

29

"You were embarrassed. Luke was there. You needed the girls. You said it yourself."

"You still left."

"Stella, I didn't leave."

"You did."

"For fuck's sake," he clipped. "End of topic. We're talkin' about something else now."

Nunh-unh. No we bloody well were not. We weren't talking about *anything*.

I pushed against his arm again. He didn't let go.

"Move your arm," I demanded.

"Why didn't you tell me you'd been shot?"

"Move your effing arm."

The arm tightened and shook gently, shaking me gently with it.

"Answer my question," Mace demanded.

"If you remember, you were a little busy. I was okay. No big deal."

"Not fond of the idea of you calmly bleedin' in the backseat of an SUV that I'm also in, Kitten. In fact, not fond of the idea of you bleedin' at all."

What he said shook me.

I had to ask again, what on *earth* was going on?

Nope, no, I didn't care. Couldn't care. I was over him. Over. Him.

I shifted my focus. "Stop calling me Kitten."

He ignored me. "No tellin' the way this is gonna go down. You're gonna have to get over your attitude and communicate with me."

Erm, excuse me again?

"Get over my attitude?" I asked.

"Yeah."

"Let me get this straight," I started. My voice showing my barely controlled patience, no longer pushing against his arm, I rolled toward him. He shifted. I fell to my back and he got up on his elbow. I glared up at him and tried to ignore how fucking gorgeous he was in the morning. His eyes alone were enough to make you want to wake up and face a new day. "A year ago..." it wasn't a year ago—it was one year, three weeks and three days (not that I was counting), "you broke up with me, walked out of my life. Now someone is shooting at me, using my band to get to you, killing people because of shit you're involved in and you want me to 'get over my attitude'?"

"Yeah," he replied, unaffected by the damning statement I just made.

I got up on both my elbows, which brought me closer to him.

He didn't move.

Then I shouted, "You've lost your mind!"

"Calm down," he ordered.

"Calm? Calm? I was shot last night!"

His jaw got tight. "I haven't forgotten that, Kitten. In fact, that's what we're fuckin' talkin' about."

Something else hit me. Something important, something I wanted an answer to right away. "Why was I shot last night? Why am I involved at all? We aren't together. I'm not your woman. I'm not Indy to your Lee, Jet to your Eddie, Roxie to your—"

"Yeah, you are."

My elbows went out from under me and I fell back to the bed. A weight hit my chest. It felt like it weighed a ton and it took my breath away.

Move! My brain demanded.

I rolled and tried to escape. I had no idea where I was going, but I was going there.

Mace's arm grabbed me around the waist. He threw me back to the bed flat on my back. Before I could do a thing about it, he shifted. Both his hands came to either side of me, he did a semi-push up and landed on top of me, but his weight was slightly skewed to my healthy side.

Okay, so maybe I wasn't going "there".

"*Get off me!*" I screamed, shoving at his shoulders.

"Stella, listen."

"No! Get off!"

"Listen to me, Goddamn it!" he yelled.

For your information, Mace had a short fuse. We argued when we were together, quite a lot. He was a passionate guy, but also, like I said, he had a short fuse. It wasn't always happiness and light. Then again, the make up sex was magnificent.

"Piss off!" I yelled back.

"Sid's boys were there that night you sang Hank Williams to me."

Oh no. I just *knew* that'd come back to haunt me.

I thought back and remembered Linnie was there that night, too, with her bad dudes. Now I knew they were Sid's bad dudes.

Shitsofuckit!

"I didn't sing Hank to you," I lied.

"You did."

"I did not."

"You did. Everyone knew it. Everyone saw it. Even Sid's boys."

"You're a big guy. The bar was dark. You were just a shadow that I focused on. And anyway, I was lost in the song."

"Bullshit."

"Get over yourself, Mace. You broke up with me, I've moved on," I told him.

"Yeah?"

"Yeah."

"You got another man?"

Oh dear. Well, there we were.

"Yes," I told him, and this was not a lie. I was semi-dating a guy named Eric. He was very good-looking. He was into me and he was clear he wanted to be *more* into me if you catch my drift. I was holding back because, first off, he wasn't Mace and second, I wasn't sure about him. There was something about him that I thought wasn't quite right.

I saw Mace's eyes flash again. This was a different kind of flash, an unhappy flash.

"Don't lie to me, Stella."

"I'm not lying. His name is Eric. We've been dating for about a month. We're considering taking it to the next level." Eric was considering it. I wasn't so sure, but Mace didn't need to know this.

Mace stared at me as if trying to assess the validity of my statement.

Then he spoke. "Your relationship progression with Eric just stalled."

I felt my eyes get wide. "Erm, excuse me?"

"He's out of the picture."

At that, I felt my eyes narrow. "He is not."

"He is."

"Who do you think you are?"

"In our current scenario, I'm the guy who's gonna keep you safe. I'm the guy who's gonna keep you alive. And I'm gonna do it however I need to do it, and while I'm doin' it I don't need to have to deal with any of your groupies."

My *groupies?*

Okay, I had groupies. I was in a band. A somewhat successful band, at least locally. Groupies came with the territory.

However, I wasn't a collector of groupies. I had enough to deal with considering Pong and Hugo were both in my band, because they were dedicating their life to perfecting the art of collecting groupies.

And anyway, when did Mace turn into such an asshole?

"He's not a groupie!" I yelled.

"Discussion about *Eric* just ended." He said Eric's name like it tasted bad. If I was smart, I would have read something into that. Instead, I was seething that he was being so bossy. "Now you and I are gonna get things straight—"

"No, we aren't," I interrupted him.

He ignored me. "You and Juno are movin' in with me."

Uh… *what?*

"No, we aren't!" I shouted

"Okay," Mace said amicably. "Then I'm movin' in with you and Juno."

"No, you aren't!" I screeched.

He kept ignoring my outbursts. "You don't go anywhere unless I'm with you or I know where you're goin' and I got a man on you. Got me?"

I decided to extricate myself from the current conversation and start my own.

"You're a jerk."

"I'll tell Pong, Leo, Buzz and Hugo that you're out of commission as their 24/7 babysitter."

What he said pissed me off, but I ignored it in order to stay with my own theme. "You're not a jerk, you're an asshole."

"I'll call Floyd and tell him what's goin' down and he'll back me with the band."

Effing hell, he was pulling out the big guns.

My eyes narrowed again and I hissed, "Don't you dare."

"Floyd knows I can keep you safe and Floyd won't take any shit from the band."

"Don't you dare!" I shouted.

"And when this is all over, you and me gotta talk."

I did *not* like the sound of that.

"This *is* over. I'm not your woman. Just let it be known to Sid's boys that you don't give a fuck about me and I can go about my life—"

"You and I both know that's bullshit, and obviously, so does Sid."

"It isn't bullshit."

"We're over, but that doesn't mean you weren't once my woman."

"I'm not now."

"No, you aren't, but that doesn't stop the fact that I'd care... a great fuckin' deal... if you got filled with bullets."

I had nothing to say to that. Nothing at all. I was trying not even to think of that.

"You fight me, Kitten, I'll take you and them on at the same time. I don't give a fuck, and I always win. Always."

He wasn't wrong. He always won. He'd once been a professional surfer, the best. He'd moved on to become a professional snowboarder and he was the best at that, too. Now he was a PI, and from what I could tell by the respect he got from the tough guys around him, he was pretty damn good at that, too.

I decided it was high time to give up and battle on when Mace and I were not in bed and Mace's body was not on mine.

My eyes slid away from his face.

"Please get off me," I asked, softly, quietly, politely.

"Kitten," he called and my eyes slid back. "Something else you should know."

"What?"

"This is a serious situation. You gettin' soft and sweet isn't gonna work on me, not like it used to."

I decided it was the perfect time to battle on. "Thanks for sharing. Now, get *off!*"

I bucked. Mace slid off.

I rolled off the bed then rounded it, Juno at my heels ready for her morning bathroom break. I grabbed Daisy's track bottoms and tugged them on. I chanced a glance at Mace and he was on his side, elbow in the pillows, head in hand, watching me.

I felt the gut kick. He'd done that before, lots, when we were together. Lying in bed on his side, head in hand, watching me put on clothes, watching me feed Juno, watching me play guitar, the way he looked at me making me feel warm, pretty and interesting.

What I did for a living meant people were always watching me. I was on-stage in front of a crowd a lot, singing and playing. I loved it, fed off it, especially when the crowd found the groove and came along for the ride.

But not even our best groove felt as good as Mace watching me, his eyes lazy, his face soft, his thoughts, I knew, all about me.

Inexplicably, even though we were over, even though I was not his woman, even though he admitted that, I knew the way he was looking at me now was no different than all the times before.

What was going on?

"I don't like this," I told him.

He moved, fast, lithe, graceful, and he was out of bed, standing in front of me wearing nothing but a pair of white boxers. I hated to admit it, but his body was even more delicious than I remembered, and I'd touched it, tasted it, almost every inch of it, and I thought I'd never forget how good it looked... or tasted.

But I forgot.

Effing hell.

His hand came to my hip and his long fingers bit in gently.

"First up for you, this Eric guy gets a call."

I clenched my teeth.

Mace must have seen the clench or just knew it was there. Whatever, for some reason, it made him smile.

Chapter 3

Spill

Stella

"Spill," Ally said to me.

"Maybe she doesn't want to spill," Stevie put in. "You ever thought of that? You know, keeping things to yourself, as in *private?*"

"Listen, Stella and me have been friends for ages," Ally said to Stevie. "She dated one of my brother's boys for months and didn't say a word. Now she's getting shot at like the rest of us. You aren't getting shot at because of the Hot Bunch boys, you can have your privacy. You *are,* you officially become a member of the club. Therefore, it's time to spill."

"The logic is a bit loco, but I have to admit, it makes sense," Indy muttered.

"I think she should spill when she feels like spilling," Jules threw in, sitting across from me. Her hand was on her small pregnant belly bump, her black hair gleaming, her violet eyes on me. They were warm and there was a contentedness behind them that was both beautiful and made me jealous as hell.

"Fuck that. We're not a secret keeping group. It all hangs out with us," Ally stated.

"Except for when Jules kept her pregnancy secret." Daisy's eyes narrowed on Jules.

"Well, you can understand that," Jet noted.

"And when you kept your engagement secret," Roxie said to Jet.

"I only kept it a secret for a few days!" Jet exclaimed.

"Yeah, but you didn't share. We had to call you out, girlie." Tod sounded pouty.

My eyes wandered around the big round table in Daisy's huge, fantastic kitchen, and for your information, I would *love* the chance to cook in that kitchen. Top of the line appliances, plenty of counter space, expensive knives and shining pots on display. It was an amateur cook's nirvana.

Seeing the girls all together, talking about secrets instead of freaking out about getting shot at by fully automatic weapons, it hit me why the Nightingale Men claimed these women.

They didn't seem at all flipped out that they'd been the victims of violence last night. They were just hanging out, doing girl talk over coffee.

Honest to God, it was bizarre.

Indy, redheaded, blue-eyed and built. Ally, dark-haired, brown-eyed and slim. Jet, honey blonde, green-eyed and pretty. Roxie, also blonde but darker, blue-eyed and seriously stylish. Ava, another blonde, totally knockout, bombshell gorgeous with light brown eyes. I'd already described Jules's movie star glamour. These weren't exactly your average women.

But I suspected their attraction for the Hot Bunch had nothing (or if not nothing, then not everything) to do with the fact that their looks ranged from classically beautiful (Jules), to sultry (Indy), to girl-next-door hot (Jet), to sassy-girl-next-door luscious (Ally), to sophisticated elegance (Roxie), to downright sexy (Ava), to in your face stunning (Daisy). I suspected it had more to do with the fact that this crazy, scary life didn't faze them. Not even a little bit.

And if it did, they didn't let it show.

They kept bickering and I looked out the widow, letting them fight amongst themselves and letting my thoughts move elsewhere. My wound was beginning to ache and my mind was filling with thoughts of Linnie. Thoughts such as wondering if her parents had been told yet or if we'd need to do a fundraising gig to pay for her funeral.

Then I decided not to think about Linnie because it might make me cry and thus ruin girl talk, and instead I decided to think about the current state of affairs.

It was early afternoon after a wild-night-late-to-bed sleep in. We'd just finished the Big Ole Stick to Your Ribs Southern Breakfast of eggs, homemade biscuits, sausage gravy, sausage patties and grits.

For your information, I'd never seen so much white food on one plate in my life and never wanted to again.

Now, waiting for our "orders" from Lee (whenever they were going to come), we were finishing up yet another pot of coffee.

Earlier, after letting Juno out, brushing my teeth and washing my face, Mace found me and handed me my phone.

"Eric," was all he said.

"Later," was all I said.

"Now," he finished.

I figured he might leave me alone if I did as I was told, so I called Eric and told him I'd be unavailable for a while. Eric asked why. I told him I wasn't at liberty to say. Eric asked if I was okay. I told him that I was fine. Eric told me I didn't sound fine. I told him not to worry, I was. Eric told me he couldn't help it, he was worried. I told him *please* not to worry, I'd be okay and I'd call him in a few days. Eric said he didn't like it, could he see me now? I opened my mouth to speak and Mace yanked the phone out of my hand.

Then he said into it, "She's done talkin'. She said she'd call you. End of conversation."

Then he flipped my phone shut.

I stared at my phone in his hand because I was relatively certain if I looked in his eyes, I'd scream in his face.

He tucked it in his back pocket, and without a word he turned and walked away.

I stared daggers into his back, and when daggers didn't actually form from the lethal energy emanating from my eyes, I gave up and Juno and I went into breakfast.

The boys were gone. We had an in-house bodyguard standing in the kitchen, wearing a suit, a gun in a holster at one side of his belt and a walkie-talkie at the other side.

Roxie, an animal lover, claimed Juno's attention by lavishing my big dog with pets, kisses and surreptitious scraps of leftover sausage patties.

I ate and then got put on the hot seat.

"Hello? Stella? You in the room?" Ava asked.

"Sorry, my mind wandered," I replied.

"I'll bet." Stevie smiled kindly at me. "After last night there are lots of places for it to wander."

I smiled back at him for his quiet understanding.

"Are you gonna spill or what?" Ally was getting impatient, interrupting our moment and not having the time for quiet understanding.

"Ally——" Jules started softly.

"I'll spill," I suddenly announced.

Everyone's eyes turned to me, and, deciding to get it over with quickly and get them off my back, I started talking.

"It isn't that interesting. Mace and I met, he asked me out. I went and we connected. It went fast, got intense quickly. It was good. No, it was great. Then he broke up with me. The end."

Everyone's eyes turned to everyone else.

Then Ally said, "Give me a break."

"No, really. That's it, in a nutshell," I told her and it was.

"Why did he break up with you if it was great?" Roxie asked.

"I used him up," I explained.

"What?" Jet asked.

"I used him up. I needed him too much. Took too much and didn't give enough."

"These boys have got a lot to give," Daisy replied, sounding confused.

"Yes, I know, and he did give a lot and I took all he gave. The band always calling and me..." I stopped, looked back out the window and started again, "He had a job. He was always working something for Lee, then he'd come to me, someone would call and he'd be out again, doing something for Pong or Buzz or Linnie or whoever. I'd stay home while Mace took care of my business. I was so tired of it."

My gaze swung back to the gang and I continued.

"Don't get me wrong. I love my band, but sometimes, well, let's just say I needed a break. Mace gave it to me. We were together for five months. He always took the calls, dealt with the crises. I slept. I never said, 'You sleep, I'll deal with it.'"

"Or, better yet, tell your band to sort it out their damn self," Daisy cut in.

"They can't," I told Daisy.

"They won't if someone keeps doing it for them," Indy told me, making it sound simple.

I closed my mouth and looked out the window again. She didn't get it. I was the leader of a moderately successful local band. The leader of the band did what they could to keep the band together. It was an Unwritten Rock Band Law. Sometimes it worked. Sometimes it didn't. But if a band was good, especially as good as The Gypsies, you did all you could to make it work before you ever considered calling it quits.

"Seems to me that was something you could talk about, work on," Ava suggested.

"It wasn't just that. It was more," I told Ava.

"More?" Roxie asked.

"Me," I replied then sighed and went on. "It was me. Effing *me*."

"What about you?" Stevie asked.

I saw Jet's back go straight. She'd caught sight of something, but I wasn't paying attention. I'd started and now I couldn't stop, and I was noticing it felt kind of good to get it out, let it go. I was thinking maybe I should have done this ages ago.

Therefore, I kept right on talking.

"My Mom had trouble getting pregnant. When she did, my Dad was over the moon. Totally psyched. He wanted a boy so bad. I know this because he told me, like, every day of my life. Mom never got pregnant again and Dad never got over not having a son. No matter what I did, how hard I worked to gain his approval, his respect, to earn anything, even a little thing that was good from him, I'd never be a boy. Dad was disappointed in me from the minute I opened my mouth, took my first breath and screamed."

"Stella—" Jet broke, in but I ignored her, I was on a roll.

"It wasn't abuse. He didn't hit me. He just said shit to me. Made me feel like dirt. Made me know I wasn't wanted. I don't know how to describe it, it just wasn't nice. What it was was *constant*."

I pulled my hands through the sides of my long hair, held it's heaviness at the back of my head and looked back out the window.

"Mom left me to him. Made it easier for her, kept her out of his sights. He'd turn it on her, make no mistake, and she didn't want it. So she let me take it."

"That's awful," Ava whispered.

I dropped my hands, but kept my gaze at the window. "Maybe, yeah. But I didn't blame her. Still don't. It could get rough. Who'd want that?"

"A mother should protect her child!" Daisy burst out.

I turned my face from the window and smiled at Daisy. "Well, my Mom didn't. I'm not whining. I used to get pissed-off about it, but there's no going back, no changing anything. Not who he is, she is or I am. We are who we are, we did what we did."

"How did you cope?" Jules asked softly.

"I left, soon as I graduated high school. Took off my graduation robes, threw them on the bed, grabbed my guitar and left. I came to Denver, got in a band. You all know Floyd?" My eyes did a mini-scan and everyone nodded.

"Well, Floyd was the pianist. He told me I was good, better than most anyone he'd heard. Until then, no one had ever said anything like that to me in my whole effing life. Definitely not my Dad, and also not my Mom. I knew why. If she did, she'd court the Wrath of Dad. So she didn't."

"Oh sugar," Daisy whispered, and I saw her eyes had tears in them.

"Don't cry for me Daisy," I said softly. "I'm not broken, just scarred."

"Well, I'd think Mace wouldn't ever leave if he knew all this shit. How is this part of why he broke up with you?" Ally snapped.

"Oh, I never told him any of this." I waved my hand in front of me and noticed, in a vague way, Jet's head snapping around and her attention coming to me.

"You didn't?" Jet's eyes were wide. Her face was pale and I saw her gaze slide to the side after she stopped speaking.

"No, and I'm glad I didn't. If he left me because he thought I was needy, heck, if he knew this crap, well, that would have made him leave sooner."

"Stella—" Jet started again, her voice now sounding more urgent.

"Anyway," I kept going, talking over Jet, "after a few years, Floyd and I started another band. Then that band broke up and we started another one. The Gypsies. Then I met Mace. He made me feel good about myself, not just when I was onstage, not only when I had a guitar in my hands and a mic in front of my mouth, but all the time. He made me feel good about just being me. Even when he wasn't with me, just knowing he'd *be* with me eventually felt good. A man like that, a good man... I ate it up. I sucked it out of him. I needed it. No one had ever made me feel that way, not even Floyd. I took all of that I could get, too."

"Stella, girl—" Now Indy had gone pale and she was looking in the same direction as Jet.

"I don't blame him—" I ignored Indy, too.

"Stella, honey bunches of oats—" Daisy tried to cut in. She was looking over her shoulder.

I ignored her, too, and went on, "Not for leaving me. I get it. But he's like my Mom. My Dad, too. I don't blame them, either. But I'll never forgive them. Not ever."

"Sweet Jesus," Jet breathed, and the way she did it made me focus.

I saw that now everyone was looking in the same direction. My head turned to see what they were all staring at, and it was Mace standing in the doorway. He had his shoulder leaned against the jamb, his arms crossed on his chest, his feet crossed at the ankles and his eyes on me.

He'd been there awhile.

Effing hell.

All air evacuated my body and I stared at him.

Do you think he heard? My brain asked me.

"Come here," Mace said to me.

Yep, he heard.

Queen of Super Shitty Luck strikes again!

I shook my head at Mace.

"Kitten, come here." His voice was ultra-deep, low, soft and he was looking at me in a way... in a way...

I closed my eyes tight and shook my head again.

When I opened my eyes again, I saw him uncross his arms and ankles. He pushed away from the door and my body went tense.

"You can come here or I can come get you," he stated.

"I—" I started to say, but didn't move. Apparently my non-movement was answer enough for Mace. His long legs took him across the room in no time. He got close, leaned in and his hand grabbed mine. His hold firm, he yanked me out of my seat to my feet and pulled me out of the room.

"Oh lordy," I heard Stevie say from behind me.

"Sugar, that ain't the *half* of it," Daisy added, and she sounded excited.

Shitsofuckit!

Mace took me through the house and back to the room we'd slept in. I didn't protest or struggle. So, he heard. Maybe a little, maybe a lot. So what? Nothing had changed.

Right?

He hauled me in the room, stopped, closed the door and turned back to me. His hand holding mine drew me near, nearer, *nearer*. He dropped my hand and both of his came to my waist. They slid around to my back and he started to pull me close.

Okay, it was safe to say something definitely had changed.

"What are you doing?" I asked, my voice breathy, my brain rethinking my decision not to protest or struggle. I had my head tipped back and was staring at his face.

His eyes weren't blank but broody. They were intense and active.

I put my hands on his chest and he stopped pulling me close. I figured this was mainly because he couldn't get me closer without me moving my hands. Our bodies were pressed together, Mace looking down at me from his height, six inches taller than me. This, for your information, was another of those seven hundred, twenty-five thousand things I missed most about him: him being so tall. Since I was also tall, it made me feel petite and protected.

I was beginning to find it hard to breathe.

"You remember I told you after all of this was over, we gotta talk?" he asked.

I nodded. For some reason (okay, it was that look in his eyes; he'd never looked at me like that, not even when we were together), I was afraid to speak.

"We're not gonna wait 'til this is over. We're gonna talk now."

Okay, not good. All of a sudden, I didn't want to get this over with.

I found my voice. "I'm not sure I want to talk."

"That's fine. I'll do the talking."

Effing hell.

"I'm not sure I want that, either," I tried.

He dipped his head and his face got closer. "Sorry, Kitten. Enough time has been wasted."

Oh dear. I didn't like the sound of *that*.

I couldn't stop him. That much I knew. When Mace wanted something, Mace got it. I learned that early in our relationship. Like, the first date when he ended up spending the night, being the first and only guy I'd ever dated who I'd slept with on the first date.

However, thinking positively, maybe I could stall for long enough to get my head together.

"Before you start, tell me how much you heard," I demanded.

He didn't even try to screw with me. He just told me flat out, "All of it."

Shit!

"What's the first thing you heard?" I didn't know why I asked. Maybe a form of self-punishment for being such an effing idiot and giving in to Ally making me spill.

"The first thing I heard was, 'Hello? Stella? Are you in the room?'"

Yep, he heard all of it.

I must remind you, my luck was not just shitty luck. It was *super* shitty luck.

"It doesn't change anything," I told him.

"It changes everything, but then, everything changed when you sang Hank Williams to me."

Not this again!

"Mace, I'm not going to say it again. I didn't sing Hank to you."

"Kitten, the place was packed, and still, you and I were the only ones in that room."

Sheesh.

"Please, let me go," I asked, trying a different tactic.

"I didn't leave you because you needed me." Mace saw through my new tactic and didn't think much of it.

I blinked. It felt like it took two days for me to blink. I did it in slow-mo. When my eyes were back to open they were a whole lot wider.

"Excuse me?"

"It wasn't about you."

Ah, so it was this game now.

My lips made a soft noise that sounded like, "poof".

Then I said, "That's what they all say."

"It wasn't."

"So it wasn't me, it was you?"

"No. It was the men who watched you onstage, the ones I'd see gig to gig. Drinkin' beer and adjusting their crotches and likely goin' home and jackin' off, thinking of you singing 'Black Velvet'."

"Right." I sounded sarcastic because I meant to.

His face got closer. "Yeah. That's right. Listen to me, Stella. It wasn't about you. I'm not the kind of man who wants other men jackin' off to his woman. I'm also not the kind of man who wants to share her with four other guys."

My body went solid and my hands pressed against his chest. "I never cheated on you!"

"Yeah you did. Every time you let me take a call from Buzz or Hugo or Pong or Leo."

Okay. Shit. Well.

Um.

I had nothing to say to that because, in a weird way, he wasn't wrong.

He felt my body relax. He knew he scored a point and he took advantage, pressing closer, his face dipping lower, coming to a stop an inch from mine.

"I knew when I got into it with you that I wouldn't be the center of your universe. I was fine with that. I just didn't know I'd be a satellite."

At his words, my body did an involuntary jerk.

I hated it that he thought that. I shouldn't hate it, since I was over him, but I did.

"You weren't a satellite," I whispered.

"I know that now, after hearin' what you said in the kitchen. I didn't know it then." His arms came from around me and his hands went to either side of my neck, his thumbs pressing into the undersides of my jaw to tilt my head further back to look at him. "Kitten," he said softly, "you should have told me."

Hang on a second here.

Was this happening?

And if it was, how was this happening? Why was this happening?

He broke up with me!

"You said I was needy," I accused on a toss of my hair, which, for your information, did nothing to dislodge his hands.

"I said your band was needy," he contradicted.

"You did not," I contradicted right back.

"I did. You heard it the way you wanted to hear it. I hate to break this to you, but Stella Gunn is *not* the Blue Moon Gypsies. There's you and there's the band. Babe, you gotta find where one ends and the other begins."

He was right. I knew he was right. I'd been worried about that for a long time.

But I wasn't going to tell him that.

"You have no right to speak to me this way," I snapped.

"I do."

"And just how do you figure that?"

"Because the minute you sang the word 'whippoorwill' a coupla months ago, your eyes locked on mine, you became my woman again."

I jerked my neck away and took a step back.

Erm, *excuse me?*

"I did not!" I flashed.

"I didn't know it at the time. Maybe didn't want to know it. I definitely fought it. But I gotta say, lookin' back, you did."

"I most certainly *did not!*" I yelled.

He grinned. "Yeah, Kitten, you did."

I could not believe this was happening. I could also not believe he was *grinning* about it.

He kept talking. "It hit me last night after I told you Lindsey'd been murdered. Your face... fuck." I watched his eyes grow soft, a look I knew too well, but this look was magnified, like, by a million, and I experienced a different kind of gut kick. "I knew then we weren't done, definitely not over. Then the bullets were flying around you, and in that instant I became sure."

"Shut up!" I yelled, not being nice nor meaning to be nice, and wishing I could put my hands over my ears, but thinking maybe that was a tad too juvenile.

He didn't shut up. "I thought I'd wait until the Sid business was over, but after what I heard in the kitchen I'm not waiting."

"I have a boyfriend!" I was still yelling. I was getting panicky, somewhat desperate and now kind of lying. I'd never describe Eric as my boyfriend. I didn't know what he was, but he wasn't my boyfriend. I hadn't even slept with him. It had been a long dry spell. I hadn't slept with anyone since Mace.

Mace kept grinning. "You'll have to find a way to let him down easy."

Was he for real?

"Oh my God! You didn't just say that."

"Yeah, I did." He reached forward, grabbed my hips and pulled me to him again. I pushed back. He ignored this and kept talking. "I've been thinkin' and I decided we should stay at your place. Juno's used to it and I miss your big bed."

Wait a second, what was going on here?

"Do you think...?" For some reason my voice was raspy, so I cleared my throat. "Do you think we're getting back together?"

"Getting? No," Mace answered, then continued, "Back together? Yes."

Nope, he was definitely not for real.

This was a dream, but I couldn't tell yet if it was a good dream or a bad dream. I was going with bad dream since I knew how it was likely to end.

"You jerk!" I shouted.

He grinned.

"Stop grinning at me. We are *not* back together!"

For your information, yes, I was still shouting.

"Give me one good reason why we shouldn't get back together," Mace demanded.

I looked at the ceiling and replied, really bitchy, "Oh, I don't know." Then I looked back at him and continued, "You broke up with me, broke my heart, left me alone to put my life back together without you in it. Now I have. My life was just fine until you got me shot at. I'm not going back, Mace. Nunh-unh. No way."

His grin died when I mentioned the "getting shot at" bit.

Then he asked me, "If your life was just fine, why were you singin' to me about how lonesome you were?"

"It's just a song, Mace."

"Bullshit," he clipped, impatient with my lying. "Stella, you told me yourself, none of the songs you sing are just songs."

Okay, he had me there. I couldn't keep fighting that point. I'd definitely lose.

"What about when you can't take my groupies anymore? When you get fed up with the band? What then, Mace? You leave again? Or you ask me to leave the band? Which one would work for you? Because neither one of those options works for me. Either way, I lose something important to me."

"So I'm important to you?"

Effing hell. I walked right into that one. Hell, I'd set *myself* up to walk into that one.

I yanked hard and pulled away from him again.

"You were," I told him. "I'm over it now. My point was—"

I stopped talking because his hand shot out, his fingers cupped the back of my head and he pulled me forward. He leaned into me so close I could feel his breath on my lips and I could see nothing but his eyes.

"This conversation is finished," he announced, and my eyes got big at another demonstration of his sheer arrogance. "I fucked up and hurt you. It won't happen again." His fingers tensed around my head and his deep voice dropped low. "I promise you, Kitten, it won't happen again. You don't trust me now, but I'll make it so you will. You say you can't forgive me, but I'll find a way to change your mind."

I was beginning to get scared. If I was being honest, I was actually shooting straight toward terrified.

"Mace—"

He talked through me saying his name. "But you didn't open up to me so I didn't know how you felt, what I had and what I'd leave behind. That won't happen again either."

"Okay, my new point is, regardless of all that, you *did* leave me behind," I snapped, pulling my ragged desperation close and pushing against his hand.

"It won't happen again," he repeated and he sounded sure.

I was *not* sure. "You're right, because we aren't getting back together."

"Yeah, we are."

"Mace, we are *not*."

"Kitten, it's done." Now he sounded even *more* sure!

"It isn't!" I shouted.

His eyes went even more intense, more alert and he looked…

Oh effing hell, he looked like he looked right before he'd make his move to kiss me with the intent of bedding me: energized, aroused and definitely, *definitely* hot.

I held my breath.

"You challenging me?" he murmured.

I had the distinct feeling I'd painted myself into a corner.

Okay, screw the paint job, Stella Gunn, just exit the effing room! My brain advised.

"No. I'm not challenging you. I'm just saying——"

He cut me off, "Challenge accepted."

Shitsofuckit!

"Mace——"

His fingers tensed, bringing my face even closer, so close, his mouth was nearly on mine.

I stopped breathing.

"Remember, Kitten…" he started.

Effing hell, I could feel his lips moving against mine.

And I liked it.

"What?" I bit off.

I watched his eyes smile. "I always win."

Chapter 4

It's Decided

Mace

"So, it's decided," Lee said.

It was late.

The Nightingale Men were in the down room at the Nightingale Investigations offices with Eddie, Hank, Marcus Sloan, Sergeant Willie Moses, Lieutenant Malcolm Nightingale (Lee's Dad) and Lieutenant Tom Savage (Indy's Dad).

"It's decided," Eddie agreed.

Kai "Mace" Mason was sitting on a chair pulled in from the control room. Mace leaned forward, put his elbows on his knees, linked his fingers and looked at his boots.

Hector was pissed. Mace didn't even have to look at him to know he was pissed.

Then again, Hector didn't have a woman who was targeted for murder, and only Mace had a woman whose blood had already been spilled.

Mace closed his eyes on that thought and the only thing he could see was Stella's thigh, her smooth, soft skin gaping open, wet and bloody.

He opened his eyes again.

"Mace," Lee called.

Mace's head came up. When his attention had been captured, it wasn't Lee who spoke but Lee's father.

"You worked hard on this, son. You 'n' Hank 'n' Eddie got close. But now the girls are on the line. There's no shame in what we're doin'," Malcolm told Mace.

Mace nodded. He knew that. He didn't feel shame.

He felt relief.

He hadn't slept the night before. If he closed his eyes his brain gave him three options. The first, seeing Stella's wound. The second, watching her cover her head when bullets were flying around her. The third, the memory that she was bleeding in the backseat and tried to tell him, but he didn't listen.

It would seem he hadn't paid much attention to Stella, and he thought, when they were together, he'd paid a great deal.

Last night, instead of sleeping, he just lay behind her, listening to her breathe and thinking that sound was sweeter than any song he'd ever heard her sing. And his Stella had a beautiful voice. He'd never heard better.

"You got something on your mind?" Lee asked.

"Yeah," Mace replied.

"Now's the time to talk about it," Lee told him.

Mace didn't speak. He wasn't big on talking through his feelings.

"She's tough," Luke threw in, going direct to the heart of the matter.

Mace's eyes moved to Luke and he went to the heart of the matter too. "Last night, she got shot and a friend of hers got her brains blown out."

All the men in the room were silent. All the men in the room knew that Mace knew better than anyone what it felt like to have someone you cared about murdered. Not just murdered, but their brains splattered by a bullet.

The difference between Stella and Mace was that Mace had actually been there to see his sister's head explode.

"You're gonna have to stick to her," Tom advised.

Mace nodded.

"You two solid?" Vance asked.

"I'm workin' on it," Mace told Vance.

Vance grinned. "By my count, it takes about two weeks to really wear 'em down."

Mace shook his head in amusement. Vance was referring to his and Lee, Eddie, Hank and Luke's wild, dangerous and intense courtships with Jules, Indy, Jet, Roxie and Ava.

"I been noticin' that," Mace replied.

"We're agreed here Mace." Hank cut into the lightening atmosphere. Hank knew Mace, and Hank didn't feel like joking.

Mace's eyes sliced to Hank. "I'm aware of that."

"You go maverick, seeking retribution for what they did to Stella and Lindsey—" Hank went on.

"Going maverick means she's on the line," Mace interrupted Hank.

"Yeah," Hank answered.

"That's not gonna happen," Mace finished, and everyone could tell he meant every word.

Lee's voice cut through the tension. "We got three unsecure homes, and Vance and Monty haven't finished with the surveillance equipment and alarm systems yet. You got a Rock Chick, tonight you stay at The Castle."

After Lee issued his order, Luke lifted his chin. Hank nodded. Eddie sighed. Vance smiled at his feet. Mace looked down at his boots.

"Get good rest. This isn't over until the sit down with Sid," Tom added.

Hector, Ike, Bobby, Darius, Monty and Matt took off. Bobby and Matt had girlfriends, Monty, a wife and five kids. All of them, for some reason, hadn't been targeted the night before, but all were now sleeping while being watched by Brody in the control room.

Lee approached Mace.

"You got something else you wanna talk about?" Lee asked.

"Nope," Mace answered.

"After your sister, this is cutting close to the bone," Eddie put in, coming up on one side.

"That bone's exposed, has been for a long time. Nothing cuts close to it anymore," Mace responded.

"It's different when she gets under your skin." Hank joined the group. "She's under your skin, isn't she?"

"Has been awhile," Mace replied.

"Fuck, you're screwed." Vance came around the other side.

"Have been that way awhile, too. Around about the minute she turned her brown eyes on me," Mace explained.

"The eyes? I thought you'd go for—" Luke came up to the men from behind.

"Luke," Lee cut him off in a warning tone.

Luke half-grinned. "I was gonna say the voice. That sexy, throaty voice. Shit."

"Gotta admit to likin' the voice," Eddie muttered in agreement.

"I fucked it up with her," Mace told them, indulging an extremely unusual moment of sharing.

Luke's hand came to Mace, his fingers tightening around Mace's neck where it met his shoulder. The two men's eyes locked.

"You'll sort it," Luke said.

Luke was right, he would.

━☆☆━

They all drove company Explorers to The Castle, Hank and Eddie riding with Lee. The Ford Explorers in Nightingale Investigations garage were all kitted with tracking devices, communication equipment and bulletproof windows.

Lee's overhead was a bitch.

Marcus was already there when they arrived.

Mace grabbed the workout bag he'd packed with his clothes and a bunch of shit he took from Stella's place when he'd let Vance in to start installing the cameras (he'd never given back her key; she'd never asked for its return), and he went straight to Stella.

She was asleep on her side just like last night. Smack in the middle of the bed, her long, dark brown hair all over the pillows and falling in her face. Her head was tilted forward, her face resting on one of her hands. The other arm was thrown out in front of her, palm up.

She was out, didn't even move when he came in. Likely she'd taken pain killers. She wasn't a particularly light sleeper, but when they were together she'd always woken up when he got home.

Juno rushed him. Mace dropped the bag, sat on the side of the bed and rubbed the big dog down from ears to rump.

"Lie down," he murmured when he was done.

Juno licked his hand, trotted back to the other side of the bed and settled with a groan.

Mace pulled off his boots and clothes and slid in bed behind Stella. He fitted his body to hers, wrapped his arm around her middle and pulled her tight against him.

Then he listened to her breathe until he finally fell asleep.

━☆☆━

Stella

Mace was there again when I woke up in the morning, his hard body pressed the length of my back. I was mostly on my side and belly, my top leg cocked deep, and even Mace's leg was cocked the length of mine.

Yep, that was Mace. Maximum physical contact.

Effing hell.

I didn't move. I needed a battle plan to get out of bed that didn't include me turning around and kneeing him in a place which would make it difficult for him to sire children. I was pissed at him, but not enough to forget that the world would be a poorer place without Mini-Maces roaming it one day.

For your information, the day before had been hectic, even though we didn't leave the house.

First, a lady named Shirleen showed up. She was black, had beautiful skin a shade darker than mocha and the wildest afro I'd ever seen. She kept shouting "oowee" and yelling at different Rock Chicks, for some reason mad as all hell that no one had called her to be a part of the action.

Then a guy named Tex arrived. He was enormous, had blond hair just turning to gray and a thick russet beard. He was louder than Shirleen and even angrier that no one called when bullets were flying. He kept booming "Jesus Jones", and for some bizarre reason he referred to Jet as "Loopy Loo".

Then Duke showed. I knew Duke. He worked for Indy at the used bookstore-slash-coffee house she owned called Fortnum's. I hadn't been there in ages. Tex apparently worked there now, too, and by all accounts (and there were many of them) he was the best barista in the Rocky Mountains.

Duke was a Harley guy. Long gray hair in a braid, thick gray beard, always wearing a black leather vest over a Harley shirt and a rolled, red bandana around his forehead. He was gruff with a velvet-and-stone Sam Elliott voice, but he was a good guy. He walked in, counted heads, muttered, "Shee-it, we're all fucked," and walked out again, not to return.

Then a big black man strolled in. He scanned the room and his eyes hit me.

He looked at Shirleen and stated, "You owe me fifty bucks. I told you it would be the Hawaiian."

My eyes went to Ava.

"They had a bet to see which Hot Bunch Boy would get picked off next by a Rock Chick," Ava explained.

A bet?

These people *bet* on this shit?

Effing hell.

"His name is Mace, you jackass," Shirleen shot back.

"I try not to learn their names. If I know their names, means I know them, and if I know them, I gotta go to their funerals when they get themselves blown to shit," Smithie returned.

I stopped breathing.

"That's Smithie," Jet whispered to me. "He seems tough, but he's actually a very caring person."

Right.

"Smithie! A little sensitivity, if you don't mind," Roxie warned, her gaze sliding to me.

Smithie's eyes came back to me. "Yeah, heard you got shot. Flesh wound. Big deal. These bitches seen worse."

Oh my God! Were these people insane?

"Stop calling us bitches!" Ally snapped.

"Crazy white bitches, the lot of you. 'Cept you." He nodded at Shirleen. "You're a crazy black bitch. Fuck," Smithie finished. He walked out before Shirleen could lose her mind, like she looked like she was about to do.

"He was just here to see if we were all right," Indy assured me.

I was beginning to think the whole bunch of them were beyond insane. They were certifiable.

Then Annette showed. She was Roxie's best friend, just moved to Denver from Chicago and about to open her new head shop called "Head West". She already had one in Chicago, now re-christened "Head East".

"Yo bitches!" she shouted when she arrived.

Yep, these people were certifiable.

"Okay, let me get this straight." Annette stood in the doorway staring at us. "First, you all meet Roxie... now that's *after* Indy got kidnapped a couple times, shot at and car bombs were exploding. And *after* Jet got shot at, kidnapped a couple of times and almost raped. Then came Roxie, and I was around when Roxie was assaulted at a haunted house and held hostage at a society party after, of course, she got kidnapped. I leave and new girl Jules starts a vigilante war against drug dealers and ends up in ICU with two bullet holes in her. Then new *new* girl Ava survives a drive-by, gets kidnapped repeatedly and ends up on a wild ride, exiting a wrecked car right before it explodes. Now *all of you* are getting shot at... at the same time?"

"That about sums it up," Ally told her.

"Denver is cah-ray-zee," Annette announced. "I love this fuckin' place!"

Totally certifiable.

"Oh my God!" Annette screamed making me jump and scaring the beeje-ezus out of me. Her eyes were locked on something across the room. "You got a PlayStation 3? I'm going out right now and getting Guitar Hero!"

Off she went to get Guitar Hero, and when she came back we all stood around playing Guitar Hero, sometimes two of us at a time.

Now I could stand in front of a heaving crowd of hundreds of people playing Ram Jam's "Black Betty". What I could *not* do was stand in Daisy's living room with a toy guitar in my hands and get through the length of Boston's "More Than a Feeling" on beginner level, which meant I only had to master three buttons, without getting "booed off the stage".

What was up with *that?*

Later, Daisy sent one of the be-suited members of the big gun toting army out to get the items on a grocery list I wrote. Jules's uncle Nick came over after he finished work and he helped me as I made herb-buttered salmon wrapped in puff pastry, potatoes dauphenois with cheese and steamed asparagus. None of the Rock Chicks offered culinary assistance, which was cool because it meant Nick and I could get to know each other, and he thought everyone was certifiable, too.

"They may all be kooks," Nick said, "but they're lovable."

Sheesh.

Most everyone loved the food (Annette: "You might be shit at Guitar Hero, but your cooking is *phat*."). Tex declared our meal "fancy-ass nonsense" and went out and got himself takeout chicken burritos (smothered, with lettuce and cheese) from El Tejado.

When Tex got back we all played more Guitar Hero.

By that time my hip hurt, like, a lot.

Indy saw the pain pinching at my mouth and leaned into me. "Lee called and said if I didn't hear from him, we'd be staying here tonight."

This was not good news. I really wanted to go home. However, I also wanted my heart to be beating, my lungs to be working, my blood to be flowing through my veins and my brain to be functioning a lot more than I wanted to go home. Therefore I decided against throwing a hissy fit, going home and likely getting murdered on my way there.

I took the last two pain killers the doctor gave me and Juno and I crashed.

For your information, none of the Rock Chicks asked me about my tête-à-tête with Mace, mainly because they heard my side of it (as I'd been shouting and they'd been eavesdropping).

This brought me up to now.

In bed. Again. With Mace.

I moved cautiously forward hoping he wouldn't notice.

His arm got tight.

Yep, he noticed.

"Mace, let me go."

He didn't let me go.

He buried his face in my hair and murmured in a rough, tired, deep voice, "Christ, I feel like I've had ten minutes of sleep."

This was a toughie. Back in the day (as in, the day before yesterday), if I heard that, I would have barred the door and taken down anyone who dared to disturb Mace's rest unless, of course, they were a member of my band.

But that was the day before yesterday.

"Mace, let me go," I repeated.

His chin moved my hair.

"You still use the same shampoo," he said against the skin at the back of my neck.

"Mace—"

"Smells like mint."

Oh lordy be.

"Mace, I need to get up and see to Juno."

"I wanna see your wound."

Why on earth would he want to do that?

"It's okay," I assured him. "Daisy gave me some ointment that's supposed to make it heal and help the scarring. She cleaned it, treated it and then she redressed it. It's fine."

"I wanna see it."

"It's fine."

His arm got a fraction tighter. "I'm the reason it's there, Kitten, and I wanna see it."

What could I say to that?

Except nothing.

So I said nothing.

I lay there awhile, my new plan being if Mace was exhausted, if I stopped yapping, he'd probably fall back to sleep. When he did, I'd get up and get the hell out of there.

This plan was shit, therefore it failed.

Once I thought he was asleep I tried moving away again and his arm got even tighter.

"Mace—"

"Stella—"

Effing, effing, hell.

"I want to talk to Buzz," I said. I didn't know why (well, I knew why; because I wanted to talk to Buzz).

His body went still for a beat then he rolled away.

I took that opportunity to attempt an escape. I was sitting on the side, ready to push myself up, when one of Mace's arms went around my waist, stalling my progress. His other hand came up in front of me. It was holding my phone.

I pulled in a breath and I took the phone.

"Thanks," I whispered.

He moved as I flipped it open and scrolled down to Buzz. I couldn't get up because he kept his arm around me. He straddled me on a diagonal with one long thigh the length of mine, foot on the floor, his other leg stretched out beside me on the bed.

Juno was up and nuzzling the both of us, in a tizzy of excitement, not knowing who to allow to lavish affection on her. I hit the go button to call Buzz, put the phone to my ear and scratched Juno's head. Mace moved the hair off my shoulder and rested his chin there.

I closed my eyes trying not to feel how good that felt.

"Stella Bella." I heard in my ear.

"Hey Buzz," I said gently. "How you doin'?"

"Not good, Stell." The words were an understatement, which, for Buzz, was a miracle. Let's just say Buzz could be dramatic.

"I figured that," I replied, still using my gentle voice.

Mace pressed closer to my back.

I went on, trying to ignore Mace and how good it felt, his strong presence surrounding me (another one of the seven hundred, twenty-five thousand things I missed about him most of all, FYI), "I wish there was something I could do."

"Nothin' to do. You got your own worries anyway. Mace told us at the band meeting yesterday."

Erm, excuse me?

My back went straight and I didn't have to ignore how good Mace felt anymore.

"The band meeting?" I asked, my gentle voice not so gentle anymore.

Mace's arm tensed.

"Floyd called an emergency meeting. Mace came with him, told us what was goin' on," Buzz answered.

I turned narrowed eyes to Mace. His head came up from my shoulder. He took one look at me and his eyebrows went up.

Buzz kept talking in my ear. "At least it's good you two are back together."

My mouth dropped open and my eyes popped out.

Mace did a heavy sigh.

I looked away.

"Who told you we were back together?" I asked.

"Mace did, yesterday," Buzz answered.

Okay, I was going to *kill* Mace. I just hoped my jury was made up mostly of jilted women, but at that moment I was happy to do my time.

The bastard!

"We are not—" I started to tell Buzz, but he interrupted me.

"Linnie would have been beside herself with fuckin' glee. She loved you two together. Think she was more upset when you two broke it off than you were."

I doubted that.

I again had no way to respond. It was better to think of Linnie beside herself with glee than lying in a bed with half her head blown off.

Buzz finished up, "Keep safe. Don't worry about me or the band. We'll be okay."

I doubted that, too.

"Buzz, I… um…" I didn't know what to say. What *could* you say? "Do you need anything?" I finished lamely.

"Linnie's parents are coming in this morning. They're planning everything. I'll let Mace know what's goin' on."

"You'll let Mace know?" I asked. My eyes went back to narrowed, and this was a different kind of narrowed. A *dangerous* kind of narrowed.

60

Juno caught my look, read my look, knew my look, sat on her doggie heiny and woofed a "What now?" doggie woof.

"Yeah, he told us you were incommunicado and we should talk through him to you. We're cool."

Erm, ex-kah-use *me?*

"Buzz—"

"Later, Stella Bella."

Disconnect.

I flipped the phone shut. I took a deep breath. Then I wondered where the mellow, laidback, I-don't-have-time-to-be-pissed-off Stella Gunn disappeared to.

I tossed the phone aside, shot from the bed breaking free from Mace's arm and turned on him.

"You held a band meeting," I accused.

Mace's leg on the bed came down so he was in a full sitting position. His elbows went to his knees, his hands dangling between them, and he tilted his head back to look up at me.

In keeping the information flowing, Mace often sat like this. This was Mace's way. For some weird reason, I always found it sexy. Now I found irritating.

"Stella—"

"With *my* band," I went on.

"Stella—"

"Without *me*," I kept at it.

Mace decided to keep silent.

You should also know Mace often fell silent when I was in rant mode.

Juno decided to woof then pant, unsure what this turn of events meant to her imminent bathroom break.

"Who happens to be the leader of the band," I reminded him.

Mace kept his silence.

"You told them to communicate with me through you." I was on a roll.

Mace still didn't speak.

I waited. Mace did, too.

I was wearing nothing but a white tank top Daisy gave me and my white panties. Mace was wearing nothing but light blue boxer shorts. I ignored the state of our undress and his utterly fantastic body and put my hands on my hips.

Mace didn't move. I lost patience.

"How dare you come between me and my band!" I shouted.

He started to push off the bed, and I don't know what came over me (maybe temporary certifiable insanity seeping into my pores after a day with the Rock Chicks). I launched myself at him.

Full body.

I hit him in the chest. This surprised him and he took my weight with a grunt. My head connected with his chin, which was kind of painful, and his arms went around me. We fell back onto the bed, me landing on Mace.

Why I decided to wrestle with Mace, both of us barely-clothed and on a pull out bed, would forever remain a mystery for the ages.

But wrestle with Mace I did.

We rolled, we tussled. The bed creaked loudly and frighteningly. We rolled back. We tussled some more. The bed creaked louder and more frighteningly and Juno woofed, now thoroughly confused about the current state of affairs.

I tried to gain the upper hand, an impossible feat. Mace's long fingers wrapped around my wrists, and mostly we tested each other's strength with me losing.

Mace got on top, his face in my face.

His was angry and he clipped, "Damn it, Stella, stop. You're gonna tear your stitches."

"Piss off," I shot back, not caring about my stitches in the throes of undeniable temporary insanity. I pushed off with my foot and rolled him again.

He rolled me back. We tussled some more.

Looking back, it wasn't about the band (not totally). It was about being pissed at him for leaving me. Then being pissed at the way he came back in my life. And taking out on him (even though it wasn't his fault) the fact that I was pissed because Linnie was dead and I was shot. Not to mention him wanting me back and me knowing that couldn't happen because I couldn't live through him walking out on me again.

He somehow got on top with his hips between my legs and my hands pinned above my head.

I was defeated. I knew it and so did he.

We stared at each other, both breathing heavily. Mace, I would realize later, from attempting to hold back, knowing if he used his full strength, he'd hurt me. Me, I knew at the time, because I gave it everything I had.

Eyes locked, we just panted in each other's faces.

Face still angry, that anger warring with something a whole lot different, Mace gritted through his teeth, "Christ, I forgot how fucking good you feel when you're beneath me."

At his words, something shot through me. An electrical current vibrating through every nerve and ending with a sizzle.

Then, do not ask me why, still deep in my insanity, I lifted my head, pressed my lips against his and kissed him.

Without hesitation, his head slanted and he kissed me back, open-mouthed, wet and deep.

Oh dear.

I forgot how good a kisser Mace was.

We then tussled a different way. He let go of my wrists and our hands started bumping into to each other's as they moved, mine over the muscles of his back, his sides, his chest, my fingers sliding up his neck and into his hair. His up my sides, in the tank. He tilted up his abs and ran his hand along my belly, up to cup my breast, sliding his thumb across my nipple.

Lordy be.

I moaned into his mouth.

It didn't take long for it to get out-of-control, mainly because it had been out-of-control since I threw myself bodily at him—a weird, wild foreplay. I was so turned on I was ready. B beyond ready. I'd been waiting a year for this. The feel of his mouth on mine, his sleek skin and hard muscle under my fingers, the taste of him, the smell of him, his touch, his weight.

I started to tug down my own panties. Mace rolled to the side. I lifted my knees and he took over, yanking my underwear down my calves, over my ankles and tossing them away. He rolled to his back, bucked his hips, pulling off his boxers and tossed them in the direction of my panties. Then he rolled back to me, sliding between my opened legs. His hands came behind my knees, he pulled them high and in one smooth, long, hard stroke, he drove into me.

It felt *great*.

"Harder," I demanded, my voice low, my arms wrapping around his back.

"No, Kitten, I'll hurt you," he replied, his voice rough, up on his elbows, his fingers sifting into my hair at the sides of my head, his thrusts firm and fantastic, but controlled.

I kissed him. He took over the kiss, but I got what I wanted. His control slipped and he slammed into me harder.

"Yes," I breathed when our mouths disengaged.

One of his hands went between us, and right where I needed it, his finger honed in. He pressed deep, circled, pressed deeper, circled more.

I felt it. I it was coming.

My mouth against his, I caught my breath, holding back, and then I whispered, "Mace, I'm—"

"Kitten, let it go."

I let it go.

I came, hard and overpowering, my arms tightened around him, my thighs pressed into his sides, his mouth absorbed my moans as it overwhelmed me.

No other way to describe it. It was beautiful. It had always been beautiful. Always.

I took his final strokes, my orgasm still tingling, my head turned to the side. His face was in my neck, his breathing was ragged. I turned my face to look at him. His head came up and his eyes caught mine. They were hot on me, hot and aroused and intense, and I felt like I was the center of the entire effing universe.

Man, he had great eyes.

I slid my fingers into the back of his hair, lifted my head and pressed my open mouth against his, my other hand going to his jaw. The moment I touched his face, he lost control and groaned against my lips.

For some reason, that was even more beautiful.

We were still both breathing heavily, coming down, but he rolled immediately after he was done, taking me with him, resting me on my unwounded side, my leg curved around his waist.

I pressed my face in his throat and held on to him tightly while his hands moved lightly across my back and I made intermittent post-Mace-made-orgasm "mms" in the back of my throat. I never did "the purr" for anyone else, but then no one had given me an earth shattering orgasm like Mace did.

We caught our breath and I tried to catch a thought, but found I couldn't. All I wanted was for time to stop and me and Mace to be there, on Daisy's pull out couch, locked together forever.

Before I had a chance to recover, a chance to remember this was wrong, and more importantly why, his hand slid down my side to my waist, over my hip and then gently pulled my leg from around him. He moved away, sliding down the bed and coming up on his forearm.

I laid there, head on the bed, arms cocked and resting in front of me, staring unseeing as I felt his fingers carefully pull the dressing away from my wound. I kept my head to the bed, but I tilted my chin down to watch him. My eyes focused on Mace and I watched as he looked at the wound, his jaw getting tight.

Then...

No joke.

He gently replaced the dressing, pressing down the tape at is edges.

His head bent to it.

And light as a whisper, he kissed me there.

I stopped breathing.

Effing, effing, hell, hell, *hell*.

He came back to me, his arms moving around me, one hand sliding over my bottom, the other arm wrapping around my waist.

He looked me in the eyes and said softly, "I'm guessin' this doesn't mean I've won."

My sanity instantly returned, just as quickly as it fled.

I retorted, all bitchy (seriously, in my defense, I mean, *hello*, he broke my heart once already. Temporary insanity was one thing, but taking him back was just plain loco), "This doesn't mean anything. As far as I'm concerned, this didn't even *happen*."

For some unhinged reason this made him grin like he found this a fortunate turn of events.

His mouth came to mine, lips still turned up in a sexy smile. His eyes open, his gaze soft as it locked on mine.

I found I was holding my breath when he murmured, "That's what I thought." He touched my lips with his, pulled his head back a fraction, and still smiling, he finished, "Good to know you're not gonna take the fun out of it, babe."

Now what the hell did *that* mean?

No, no. I didn't want to know.

Chapter 5

I Get It

Indy

"Come back to bed," Lee said.

I looked away from the window to see Lee on his side, head in hand, in bed, the sheet down to his waist. I knew he was naked under the sheet and I knew what that naked looked like.

At the thought of it, I started to feel warm all over.

Hmm.

I walked to the bed and sat on the side.

"I don't like it," I told him.

"I don't care. It's decided," he replied.

Boy, he was bossy. After all our time together, nearly a year, I hadn't been able to get the bossy out of him. It was likely I never would. It was also likely I would never stop trying.

I made another attempt. "Maybe we should talk—"

He moved. Quickly.

Hands at my waist, he twisted, taking me over his body, rolling us both to the other side and I ended up on my back, Lee mostly on top of me.

"It's decided," he repeated.

"You didn't ask—" I started.

"Listen to me, honey," he said softly, but his voice was determined. "I got the choice of puttin' on a fuckin' suit in a coupla weeks in order to meet you at the end of an aisle or maybe puttin' on a suit to stand by your coffin. I pick the first."

Okay, he had a point there. I picked the first, too.

"How do the other boys feel about this decision?" I asked.

"Ecstatic. None of us particularly enjoyed the shot at, kidnapped, beat up portions of the Rock Chick Experience the first time around. We're not fired up for a repeat performance."

Okay, he had a point there, too.

"All right," I said.

At my unusually easy capitulation, he smiled at me. I stared.

He had a *great* smile. After a lifetime of witnessing that smile (which I had; his parents were best friends with my parents, I'd known him since I was born) I was still ready for another lifetime.

His mouth went to my neck. A shiver ran across my skin.

"I still can't believe you're gonna give up," I whispered, and I couldn't believe it because it was unbelievable. Lee Nightingale was not a man who gave up.

"It's not givin' up," he murmured against my neck, his mouth moving up to my jaw. "What it is is assessing priorities and not takin' any chances."

I had to admit, it was nice to know I was "a priority".

Still.

"But——"

His mouth came to mine. "Shut up."

My eyes narrowed. "Don't tell me to shut up."

His chocolate brown eyes got melty and I saw smile crinkles form at their sides.

"All right," he agreed.

Then he kissed me and I shut up.

⊸≀⊱

Lee and I walked into Daisy's big room. There were several boxes of LaMar's donuts open and waiting. Smithie was sitting in a chair, eating a jelly donut and talking to Jules, who was drinking coffee and looking pale.

"Morning sickness?" I asked Jules.

"I'm in my fourth month and it's sticking with me," she replied on a grimace. "Can't keep anything down until at least noon. Daisy's breakfast yesterday... not fun re-experiencing *that*."

"Fuck! Don't talk about pukin' while I'm eatin' a jelly donut," Smithie snapped.

"Sorry Smithie," Jules returned on a small smile.

"Where is everyone? We're supposed to have a morning meeting." Lee selected a chocolate-covered donut while I poured coffee.

I looked at Lee. He was ready to get this done. He had other not-so-pleasant things on his agenda that day, like sitting down and giving into the threats of a very, *very* bad guy.

"Well, I heard Roxie and Hank fighting on my way down. Then I heard Eddie and Jet fighting. Didn't hear anything from Luke and Ava. Vance is taking a shower. Daisy's pouting because Smithie brought donuts," Jules answered. "She made coffee, put out the cups, cream and sugar and stomped off."

"Fighting?" Lee asked on an eyebrow raise, completely unconcerned about Daisy pouting, which, given my vast experience with Daisy, I thought took precedence.

I decided not to share this nugget of information. Lee had enough to worry about.

"The girls are not fond of you boys fuckin' throwin' in the towel," Smithie replied. "They like their action. Crazy bitches."

Lee shook his head, clearly agreeing with Smithie.

I glared at him. He stared at me calmly. I gave up the glare and chose an old-fashioned donut.

"I don't want to talk about it. In fact, I don't want to talk to *you*," Jet snapped as she entered the room. She was angry, but this didn't stop Eddie from having her in what Jet called an "Eddie's Woman Hold": arm wrapped tight around her neck, Jet tucked deep into his side.

Eddie seemed oblivious to Jet's rant. Then again, Eddie always seemed oblivious to Jet's rants, which were not frequent but not unheard of.

"Who brought the donuts?" Eddie asked.

Jet rolled her eyes at me. I smiled at her in understanding and took a bite of my donut, which I chased with coffee.

Eddie disengaged and grabbed a glazed cinnamon roll.

"What's up?" I asked as Jet got close. "You pissed that the Hot Bunch are giving up?"

"Yes," she snapped. "Eddie's been working that case for a year, even before he knew me. He's never given up on anything. But we had an Eddie Chat while in bed, and you know what that means."

I knew what that meant. Eddie talked her around. Then Eddie muddled her head by giving her an orgasm. Or vice versa.

Kristen Ashley

It had to be said, the Hot Bunch liked their morning piece of ass, and they weren't afraid to capitalize on the time-saving measure of using sex as a weapon in a disagreement.

"Honestly, I understand he doesn't want to go through this business again. Who does?" Jet continued. "We got over that, but now we're fighting about the wedding. I want something small, in a park or something like that. Blanca wants a full Mass. A full Mass! I'm not even Catholic! And Eddie refuses to referee between me and his Mom," she shared.

"Men don't do weddings," I advised, full of knowledge on *that* subject since mine was just under two weeks away. Lee hadn't lifted a finger except to have Shirleen, his now-receptionist, call a travel agent and arrange our honeymoon. A honeymoon Shirleen wouldn't tell me word one about under threat of retribution from Lee, which even Shirleen took seriously, and Shirleen wasn't afraid of anyone.

Vance walked in wearing a shit-eating grin, which he had trained on Jules. He preceded Luke and Ava, who were holding hands. If you told me two months ago I'd see Luke Stark holding hands with *anyone*, I would have laughed in your face. But with Ava, anyone could see it came naturally. Ava looked a bit dreamy, which meant Ava got herself some.

I smiled to myself. This gave new meaning to the words "Love Shack". If this went on any longer, The Castle was going to have to be re-christened.

They were followed by Daisy carrying a fresh pot of coffee.

"I made coffee," Daisy announced. "Anyone need coffee?"

"Actually, I could use a Diet Coke," Ava answered.

"I need coffee," Jules threw in quickly when Daisy's face darkened.

"Smithie brought donuts. I was going to make pancakes, but Smithie brought donuts. I could still make pancakes. You want pancakes?" Daisy asked Luke hopefully.

He shook his head and grabbed a bear claw, missing Jules nodding her head at him frantically in silent communication.

"Stella makes fancy-ass salmon and potatoes and everyone's in tears of delight. What? I can't even make pancakes in my own damn house?" Daisy burst out.

Uh-oh.

"What kind of salmon did she make?" Vance asked the *wrong* question, grabbing a Bavarian cream and sitting on the arm of Jules's chair.

70

"It was buttered and herbed and in this light as air pastry," Ava rhapsodized, even though Jules was now frantically shaking her head at Ava (who also didn't notice) and Daisy's face was getting pink. Ava went on, "And the potatoes were creamy and cheesy. Sliced so thin, it was *amazing*."

Daisy glared at Ava, plonked down the coffee and stormed out.

"What'd I say?" Ava asked, glancing around in confusion, and Jules smiled at her and mouthed, "Later."

"Let me get this straight. Mace gets the girl who can cook?" Vance put in.

Jules turned from Ava and punched Vance in the arm. Then she covered her mouth, made a gagging noise, shot out of her chair and ran from the room.

"Fuck," Smithie had been reaching for another donut, but after Jules's gag-and-run he sat back instead.

"I'll go home to Brownsburg. Stay with Mom and Dad," Roxie said to Hank, both of them walking into the room.

"No," Hank replied.

"I'll go to Mexico," Roxie continued.

"Roxanne, I said no," Hank returned.

"I'll go to Siberia!" Roxie snapped.

Hank looked at Lee and shook his head.

"Do not shake your head at your brother, Hank Nightingale," Roxie bit off.

"Fucking great. Donuts. Finally, my day has brightened," Hank ignored Roxie.

One side of Luke's lips curled up in a sexy half-grin. Vance's shit-eating grin made a reappearance. Eddie bit his lip to stop from grinning. Lee chuckled straight out.

I was guessing Hank and Roxie hadn't participated in the nookie-a-thon like the rest of us. Then again, maybe they did and the extreme circumstances took the glow off early.

"Do you believe they're giving up?" Roxie asked me on a huff.

"Nope," I replied then took another bite of my donut.

"I don't either," she flopped down on a couch, gave a good glare to Hank then pulled out a chocolate-covered, custard-filled and bit into it so hard the custard splodged out the side.

"Babe, pour me a cup of coffee," Luke said to Ava.

"Please?" Ava said back.

"Beautiful Ava, please pour me a cup of coffee," Luke replied in a soft voice, with a soft look on his face, and absolutely no embarrassment whatsoever.

I stared at him. He looked so hot, his voice so sweet, his face unguarded, my heart stopped beating. I quit breathing and I felt a quiver somewhere only Lee was allowed to make quiver.

My eyes flitted to Roxie, who was staring at Luke mouth open, then to Jet who was staring at Luke mouth open, then to Ava who was pouring Luke a cup of coffee.

"Indy, honey," Lee called.

My head snapped around to see he was standing close to my side. His head dipped in and I saw his eyes were amused.

"Quit drooling," he whispered.

I snapped my mouth shut, gave him a look and shoved in the last bite of my donut.

Jules came back and sat down in her chair again.

"Princess?" Vance asked so quietly you could almost not hear him.

"I'm okay," she murmured.

His hand went to her face, fingers trailing down her hairline and he tucked her hair behind her ear.

Something hit me, sliding all over me like relaxing in a bath of hot water that smelled really good.

I turned back to Lee.

"I get it," I whispered.

"What?" Lee asked, his eyes coming to me.

My gaze did a sweep of the room and came back to him.

"I get it," I repeated and his eyes warmed. He knew what I was saying.

"Good," he replied softly.

"I love you." I kept whispering.

"That's good, too," he said on a grin.

I was about to lean up and kiss him when I heard Ally call out, "I'm gonna have pancakes. I can't *wait* to have pancakes."

I turned around and saw Ally was walking into the room, her eyes huge. She was looking at me with what could only be described as a "Help me!" look, Daisy by her side.

"I bet most everyone has room for pancakes. Nobody really likes donuts anyway, they aren't very filling," Ally declared, going a little over the top, but the determined look on Daisy's face spoke volumes.

Daisy marched right up to Smithie and planted her hands on her slim hips.

"See there, Smithie. *Ally* wants pancakes. Let that be a lesson to you. Do not *ever* bring donuts into a Southern woman's home. Southern women feed their guests, and *not* with *donuts*. Comprende?" she snapped.

"Fuck, woman. You got a screw loose or what?" was Smithie's unwise response.

Before Daisy could retort, we all heard shouted from the other room, "*How dare you come between me and my band!*"

Everyone went completely silent.

Then we heard the creaking of a pull out bed. Not the telltale creaking of morning Hot-Boy-on-Rock-Chick action, but creaking like World War III had just started in Daisy's Den.

"Uh-oh," Roxie breathed.

"Sounds like the Hawaiian has his hands full," Smithie muttered.

"Everyone out," Lee ordered, his voice low, but there was no mistaking he meant to be obeyed, and now.

When the women hesitated, Hank grabbed Roxie's hand, pulling her off the couch saying, "Out."

The bed kept creaking, louder and scarier.

"Let's go," Eddie was guiding Jet out.

"I'll get the coffeepot," Daisy whispered, grabbing both nearly empty pots of coffee.

As quietly as we could, we exited the room and went to the kitchen, leaving the donuts behind.

Upon entering the kitchen, Luke closed the door.

"No one leaves this room until one of those two leaves theirs," Luke announced.

Denied our donuts, Daisy was forced to make pancakes.

⌘

"*What?*" Shirleen shouted.

Lee had just announced that they were giving up, why they were giving up, and that he was going to have a sit down with Sid, and it was pretty clear Shirleen wasn't happy about it.

We were all sitting in Daisy's big room.

Shirleen, Hector, Darius (Lee's other best friend, his now-employee and Shirleen's nephew) and Ike had arrived in time for pancakes, making great strides in improving Daisy's mood. Bobby and Matt were taking care of business. Lee was bleeding money on this venture and someone had to help pay for the wedding.

About half an hour into our kitchen incarceration, Jules had to break Luke's rule because she had to run to the bathroom to hurl.

When she came back to the room, she announced, "Um, they're done. I saw Stella in the hall. Mace too."

"Thank Christ," Lee muttered.

Jules gathered a Rock Chick huddle.

"Whatever you do, do *not* compliment Stella on her outfit," she advised.

"Why?" Ava asked.

"Because it's cute," Jules replied.

"And why wouldn't we tell her it's cute?" Roxie asked.

"Because Mace packed it for her," Jules explained.

"Ah," Jet nodded.

"And he packed her underwear," Jules went on.

"I see," Daisy muttered.

"And it's very sexy. She told me it's the only sexy set she owns," Jules continued.

"Welp, there you go," Ally remarked with complete understanding.

"And he kind of bought it for her when they were together," Jules said.

Oh my. *That* was interesting.

Daisy giggled and it sounded like tinkling bells. I loved Daisy's giggle.

"And he also kind of bought her outfit for her, too, when they were together." Jules's tale of Mace's Wardrobe Decisions Destruction seemed to never cease.

Jet clapped her hands to her on her mouth, her eyes wide and dancing, and Shirleen snorted.

"And it's cute?" Roxie asked with obvious disbelief.

"Super cute, in a Hawaiian surfer kind of way," Jules answered.

"I can't wait to see this," I whispered.

"I can't believe Mace could buy a cute outfit," Roxie responded.

"Is she okay?" Ava asked Jules.

Jules shook her head.

"The stitches?" Shirleen's voice was sharp. She'd been brought up to date with The Battle of Daisy's Den.

"No, I think it's something else. Something that made Stella look pretty pissed and pretty confused at the same time. However, Mace looked *very* pleased with himself when I saw him come into the hall with Juno as Stella went into the bathroom."

"Broody Mace looked *pleased?*" I asked.

We all knew what that meant. Been there, done that, had the t-shirt.

Stella had been laid.

"Dear Lord," Jet breathed.

"This soon?" Ava asked.

"That beats Hank's record, I think," Ally told Roxie.

"Yep," Roxie replied, a small reminiscent smile playing about her mouth.

"Holy crap," I said.

"Shit, I haven't even had time to sort the pool. How am I gonna win any money back at this rate?" Shirleen looked to Ally. "It's gonna have to wait until you get nailed."

Ally opened her mouth to speak but was interrupted.

"You women mind finishing whatever the fuck you're talkin' about later?" Lee asked in a not very polite voice.

My head shot up and I glared at him. "This is important," I snapped.

"Yeah?" he asked on an eyebrow raise.

Oopsie.

Okay, well, maybe his plans that day were a tad bit more important than gossip.

We gave Stella and Mace time to shower and have pancakes, then we all wandered into the big room.

Throughout all this I watched Stella. Her outfit *was* cute. I wanted it. I loved it. It was a black OP tank with a circle of dusky blue hibiscus flowers in a band around the boobs and a pair of dusky gray OP corduroy short shorts. She looked like super-cool, rock-surfer-chick. I was a little surprised at Mace's heretofore unknown shopping abilities and wondered what the underwear looked like.

Stella was being quiet and avoiding all things Mace. Mace wasn't looking straight out pleased, but he certainly wasn't broody or pissed-off, which was mostly what I knew about Mace's inventory of emotions. He didn't look quite happy. Instead he looked energized and alert at the same time he looked mellow, the last new to me in Mace's emotional arsenal.

The Rock Chicks gathered around Stella, acting as buffers in case she needed us, but Mace (breaking Hot Guy Courtship Tradition) wasn't pushing it and he stayed out of her space.

By the time we walked into Daisy's big room, we'd backed off.

That was a mistake.

Stella sat on the arm of the couch next to Ally, Juno sitting on the floor by her side.

Mace walked right in and I watched, mouth dropping open, as he put his hands to her waist, shoved her clean off the couch to her feet, keeping his hands on her. She made an angry, surprised noise and her head whipped around to look at Mace, but I couldn't see her expression.

He sat down where she'd been sitting, slid back, put one foot into the couch and brought her down in front of him, straddling her and doing it close, his hand sliding from her hip to come to rest on the top of her thigh.

Holy shit!

Juno, by the way, took this in stride, clearly used to this type of Mace Maneuver from days of yore.

Mace never struck me as an affectionate type of guy. Like Luke, if you told me Mace would be affectionately demonstrative in a touchy way in public, I would have laughed. But there it was, proof positive.

My gaze shot to Ally. Ally was staring at Mace's long leg by her side and her wide-eyed gaze shot to me. The Rock Chicks darted knowing looks at each other and then our eyes swung to Stella.

Her back was ramrod straight, her face pissed way the hell off, but I could tell she was damned if she was going to blow. Not now. He'd get it later, and boy, was he going to get it.

I wanted to shout, "Atta girl," but I kept my mouth shut.

Lee launched into his announcement, which most everyone knew anyway.

Except Shirleen.

"It's decided," Lee said to Shirleen.

"I don't believe this," Shirleen said back.

Lee had no response.

My eyes moved from Shirleen to Stella. Stella didn't look pissed-off anymore. She looked pale. It would appear that Mace hadn't told Stella, either.

"Erm, excuse me," Stella said, her sexy, rough voice was soft.

Stella's voice, by the way, was something I'd always loved about her, and not only when she was singing. Her voice was, quite simply, the shit.

"You never give up," Shirleen said to Lee, not having heard Stella.

"Too much at stake," Lee replied.

"Excuse me," Stella repeated, and Ally's eyes moved to her.

"I don't fuckin' believe this shit!" Shirleen exploded. "You boys were close to takin' that jackass down!"

"Erm—" Stella started again.

"Yo!" Ally shouted and everyone turned to her. "Stella has something to say."

All eyes moved to Stella.

"I just..." She stopped and looked back at Mace. She still looked pale, but not angry anymore. She turned around and I saw her back go straight again. Then she tossed her dark, glossy hair and said, her throaty voice a lot louder, "I was on a jury once."

Stella quit talking and we all kept watching her.

"Is she goin' anywhere with this?" Smithie, sitting beside me on the opposite couch to Stella, muttered to me.

"Shh," I shushed Smithie.

"Yeah?" Luke prompted Stella.

"A murder trial," Stella went on. "They had pictures of the victim. They showed them to us. It was awful, shot in the chest and the head. Blood everywhere. Effing hell, but it was awful."

Everyone was quiet.

Stella went on, "The prosecution had one witness, this old black lady. She'd seen the whole thing. She came in and she looked at the guy on trial and I knew she was terrified. Her fear filled the room. Everyone could feel it. You could almost... I swear to God, you could almost *taste* it. She lived in this guy's neighborhood. She knew him. She knew he was a bad guy. She knew he could hurt her even if he was in jail. She knew it and we knew it."

Everyone kept staring at Stella. Everyone knew now where she was going with this. Everyone kept quiet.

Stella kept talking.

"The defendant was leaned back in his chair, completely relaxed, staring at her. It was creepy. They asked her what she saw. She kept clutching at her hands, jumpy as a cat, but she answered. They asked her if she saw who did it. She still kept clutching at her hands, but she answered. They asked if that person was in the room. She said yes. They asked her to point him out. Her hands were shaking Effing hell, I'll never forget it, they were totally shaking. But she looked him right in the eye and pointed at him."

"Good God," Jet whispered.

Stella continued, "We found him guilty. They polled the jury. We all had to share our vote out loud, right in front of him as he looked at each one of us. I knew a little of her fear then, but not the half of it. When we left the trial, the victim's family descended on us, crying and carrying on. They made us do a prayer circle. They were so happy it was over. They were happy the man that killed their son or brother or whatever was going to be put away."

"Stella," Lee said softly.

"I want a vote," Stella said.

Mace's arm wrapped around her waist and his head dipped so his mouth was at her ear.

"Kitten," he murmured but we all heard it.

Um... *wow*.

I'd heard it yesterday, Mace calling Stella "Kitten". Still, it shocked me. I mean, how sweet was *that*?

"I want a vote." Stella's voice was louder. "This man killed *my friend*. He shot *me*. He shot at a bunch of my other friends." She stood and Mace stood with her, his arm moving up to lock across her chest. I didn't know what he was trying to do; stop her from talking, give her moral support, but it didn't matter. He wasn't going to succeed at the first and she didn't need any of the second.

"I want a vote." Her voice was definitely loud this time.

"It's decided," Luke repeated Lee's earlier words.

"Okay, but I want a vote," Stella said to Luke, then her eyes scanned the tribe. "If that old lady can put her ass on the line to do the right thing then I can effing well do it, too! If you bunch of badass mothers don't agree, okay. I'm not stupid enough to think I can do anything about this, take this guy down. I know you guys have to do it, but at least I want a fucking vote!"

"I want one, too." Roxie stood up.

Oh shit.

My eyes went to Lee. A muscle in his cheek was working.

Bad sign.

"Roxie—" Hank was walking across the room towards Roxie, but she was backing away.

"No, Hank," Roxie said, her hand coming up to ward him off.

"Stella's right, you know," Ally put in.

"Ally," Lee said in a warning tone.

"You know she's right," Ally said back to Lee, quietly, softly, so un-Ally it was unreal.

Oh crap.

"I do and I don't give a fuck," Lee shot back at Ally, losing patience. "Indy and I are getting married in two weeks and Jules is pregnant—"

"She's right," Jules cut in, standing too. "Stella's right."

"Oh fuck," Luke muttered and looked at his boots.

"Quiet Jules," Vance murmured.

Jules's eyes turned to Vance. "I'll go somewhere."

"No," Vance replied.

"I'll go somewhere safe," Jules went on.

Vance got close to Jules and put his hand on her belly. "You think I'm missin' a minute of this, Princess, think again."

I swallowed, hard.

"Then keep me safe," Jules whispered.

I felt the tears hit my eyes.

Shit!

Shit, shit, shit!

I didn't *do* crying.

I looked at Lee. He was looking at me, the muscle in cheek still working. I got up and went to him. His arm went around my shoulders and he curled me into him. I wrapped mine around his waist.

I put my face into his neck and, right at his ear, I whispered, "You know Stella's right."

Lee's body went solid.

Then he muttered, "Shit."

"We can't give up," I went on.

Lee didn't answer.

"We do this, he wins," I told him.

Lee still didn't answer.

"This isn't who we are, Lee," I finished.

"Somethin' happens to you—" Lee started.

I pulled my head back and looked at him.

"Nothing's gonna happen to me," I promised.

He stared me in the eyes. His weren't hard to read. He was angry, but I could tell he was also relieved.

Like I said, Lee was not a man who gave up.

Then he bent his head and touched his lips to mine.

When he was done kissing me, he said, "Damn straight."

I felt something unknot in me. I hadn't even noticed it was there, but it had been tying me up all day.

Lee moved me to his side.

All the Rock Chicks and their Hot Bunch Boys were in heated conversations.

"Do we need a vote?" Lee asked the group, cutting the conversations short.

Silence.

"I got things to do," Lee reminded them.

"I'm in," Hector said immediately, his eyes on Stella.

"Me too," Darius put in.

"In," Ike added.

"Goddamn it," Luke clipped.

"Luke?" Lee asked.

Luke looked at Lee then turned his head and tilted it down to look at Ava. She licked her lips and shrugged. He touched his forehead to hers, closed his eyes for a brief second then pulled back.

"In," he said.

"Vance?" Lee prompted.

Vance turned his eyes to Jules. She wrapped her arms around his waist from the side.

"Fuck," Vance muttered. "Yeah."

"Hank?"

Hank looked down at Roxie. "You'll go to Brownsburg?" he asked.

"If you want me to," she replied.

Hank did a slow blink and an intake of breath.

"We'll talk about it later," he murmured to Roxie, and in a louder voice he said, "In."

"Eddie?" Lee asked.

"In," Eddie said instantly, and Jet smiled and leaned into him.

"Mace?" Lee asked.

"Out," Mace replied.

The air in the room went still and Stella went rock-solid. They were still standing together, but Stella's fingers were wrapped around Mace's forearm and he was leaned over, his chin on her shoulder.

"Sorry?" Lee asked.

"Out," Mace repeated.

"*Out?*" Hector exploded, obviously not happy, and everyone's eyes turned to him in surprise. Then all eyes went back to Stella and Mace like at a tennis match.

This was because Stella whipped around. Mace jerked back his head, but didn't move his arm so it was wrapped around her shoulders and she was tight against his front. She put her hands to his waist and her fingers curled into the material of his t-shirt.

"He killed Linnie," she said, her head tilted back to look at him.

"Yeah, and he's not gonna kill you," Mace replied.

That was when Stella lost it.

"He murdered my friend!" Stella shouted.

"Yeah, and he shot you!" Mace shouted back right in her face, and the room went still again at his raising his voice to Stella. Clearly angry, super angry, super-tall-muscled-hot-guy angry, but Stella didn't even flinch. Furthermore, Juno didn't move except to roll to her side and stretch out, oblivious to the tension in the room.

"So?" she fired back, completely unfazed by his anger.

"That's not gonna happen again."

"Okay, I'm happy not to get shot again. What I'm not happy about is letting Linnie's murderer get off scot free."

"The cops'll assign someone else, Sid'll fuck up somewhere along the line and someone will take him down," Mace told Stella.

"You sure about that?" Stella asked.

"Not as sure as I am about the fact that you're not gonna be running through machine gunfire again."

Even though she was still plastered front to front with Mace, Stella turned her heard to look at Lee.

"Do I get a vote?" she asked.

"We know your vote, honey," Lee said softly.

"Do I get special dispensation, being shot and all, to cast Mace's vote for him?" Stella asked Lee.

Mace's jaw went tight. He closed his eyes, and when he opened them they were also on Lee, and it didn't take a mind reader to see he was looking for patience *and* fellow Hot Guy understanding.

I very nearly laughed. Poor Mace.

And if you told me two days ago that I'd be thinking *that* I would have laughed in your face about that, too.

Lee shook his head and answered, though I could tell he liked Stella's style, "Sorry, Stella, it doesn't work that way."

"In," Mace ground out, but every single person in the room knew it cost him.

Stella's head whipped back around to look at him.

"Really?" she asked.

"Really," he said to Stella, his deep voice scary, but it was when his eyes sliced back to Lee and he said what he said next that the vibe in the room changed. And if we thought things were tense before, we didn't know the meaning of tense.

"She gets hurt, any of them gets hurt, I go maverick. You understand me?" Mace said to Lee.

Stella froze. Hell, everyone froze. We understood him. He did it for Jet, disappeared and made it his mission to take down the man who was making Jet's life a living hell. Luckily, Eddie, Lee, Hank and Darius had been there when Mace caught up with him.

Bottom line, if Bad Guy Sid hurt Stella or any of the Rock Chicks, Mace, not known for being a mellow guy (at all, even at the best of times), was going to hunt him down and kill him.

Damn, we'd been there, done that and had the t-shirt for that, too. Not only with Mace, but Luke had gone gonzo when Ava got violated too.

Shit.

I looked at Stella and she'd gone pale again.

"Mace," Stella whispered.

"Mace," Hank said louder, his voice full of meaning.

Mace moved Stella to his side. His arm went around her waist, his thumb hooking into the side belt loop of her OP shorts and he held her close.

"Fair warning, Hank," Mace said.

Hank stared at Mace and seconds ticked by.

Finally Hank repeated, "Fair warning."

Not good.

Then again, if something happened to Roxie or Ally or me, or likely any of the Rock Chicks, we all knew Hank would be maverick right alongside Mace.

Shit.

"War," Luke muttered.

"War," Eddie agreed.

"Fuck," Vance bit off.

Hector smiled.

Darius shook his head.

"I'll talk to Bobby, Matt and Monty. It has to be unanimous," Lee announced.

I looked up at Lee. Lee looked down at me.

"I love you," I whispered for the second time that day.

Lee's eyes didn't go melty nor did their sides crinkle. He looked very serious.

Yikes.

"Good," was Lee's response.

Chapter 6

Falling for You Wasn't Either

Stella

I'd fucked up.

Big time.

In my bid to save humanity from whoever this Sid guy was, I put all the Rock Chicks on the line.

I didn't think.

I just acted.

That was happening to me a lot lately, and I was going to have to find a way to stop doing it or I'd get laid again, which I had to admit (only deep down inside) wouldn't suck. Or I'd get killed, which would totally suck.

The Rock Chicks didn't mind. All day they'd been promising me they agreed with me, more than agreed with me, even went so far as telling me I'd saved the day. Their men didn't give up. It was one of the reasons they were with them. Literally, they'd all been kind of hard to win over.

I forced myself to believe them and we'd had a good day. The boys took off to take care of business and the women gossiped, drank coffee, helped Daisy clean out her closets (yes, plural) and played Guitar Hero.

But I was worried. Not that something would happen to me, but that something would happen to one of them and it would be my fault.

Now it was late evening and Mace was taking me home in one of the Nightingale Explorers.

I wasn't talking to him. This, for your information, was my new plan.

It started naturally.

When the Big Meeting was over, I had no chance to talk to him. He just put his hands to my neck, tilted my face up to his with thumbs at my jaw and touched his lips to mine lightly in a brief kiss.

I was too freaked out about what him "going maverick" meant, not to mention the dawning knowledge that I'd put the whole gang on the line, further not to mention a light kiss from Mace was nice, to protest.

Before I could find my voice, he was gone.

Fifteen minutes ago, he walked in while Ally and Indy were dueling through Guns 'n' Roses's "Paradise City", both on advanced, which meant using all *five* toy guitar buttons, which I found utterly impossible.

He looked at me and asked, "Ready to go home?"

I was ready to go home. I was more than ready to go home. Not with him, but I was so ready to go home I wasn't going to quibble. Not because I didn't like spending time with the Rock Chicks, but because I *did*, very much, and every second with the girls made me feel a little bit guiltier and a whole lot shittier.

Mace drove in silence.

This, for your information, was his way. Mace wasn't much of a talker. In fact, we talked a lot more in the last two days than we would in a week when we were together. It was something else I liked about him, that I didn't need to entertain him, and he felt no driving need to dazzle me with his brilliance. It felt comfortable from day one.

As he drove, I watched Denver slide by and my mind wandered to home.

I lived in a huge room in a big, old, gold-boom mansion that had been chopped up into apartments decades ago. The current owners, Ulrika and Swen, were restoring it to its former glory. To pay for this, they first restored the mother-in-law house and rented it out. Then they restored my room and rented it to me.

To get to my room, you entered the mansion at a side door off the Italian-tiled veranda and walked up two semi-private (as in, only Swen, Ulrika, Juno, Swen and Ulrika's three cats and I used them) flights of stairs.

My room was big, airy and painted white (but not harsh white; a soft eggshell). It had hardwood floors with bright-colored rugs thrown everywhere. My décor came from TJ Maxx and Target. On my budget of money from gigs and intermittent guitar lessons for kids of fans of The Gypsies who wanted their children to live their dream (thus, these lessons didn't progress very far because the kids were never really into it, only their parents were, but the kids and I'd have fun anyway), I couldn't afford the good stuff.

It wasn't luxurious but I loved my space.

You walked in the door and to the left there were three steps up to a platform that held my big bed covered in a creamy, eyelet cover with soft yellow sheets. It was shoved in a huge, round turret, windows all around, filmy-white curtains and views of Ulrika and Swen's quadruple-lot garden that Ulrika kept full of flowers and Swen kept tidy as a pin. There were also unadulterated panoramas of the Front Range.

From my front door, to the right and down two steps, was my sunken kitchen, tiny and u-shaped.

In front of the kitchen, up five steps, was a platform holding a worn, moss-green couch, my TV and another big window.

Across from that, up two more steps, was another platform. My ultimate space. Three guitars on stands (two electric, one acoustic), piles of music, two music stands, stacked amps and a big, mauve, overstuffed armchair that had seen better days, but was comfortable as hell.

Behind the partition wall of the kitchen was a stacked washer/dryer, a walk-in closet and the door to the bathroom, which was as big as the kitchen and had a claw-footed tub, a pedestal sink and mosaic tile floors. I kept my wicker laundry hamper in there and a big, glass-front apothecary cabinet that looked like it came from an antique drug store. I found it at a yard sale and Floyd fixed it up for me. Emily and I painted it white and it held my bits and bobs and towels and stuff.

My space was not rock 'n' roll stereotype with rich colors, lots of clutter and tasseled scarves over the lamps. It was tidy and clean, unlittered with junk, which was how my space needed to be because my head was always a mess.

I remembered the first time Mace walked into it when he picked me up for our date. He looked around and couldn't hide his reaction.

"You're full of surprises," he murmured, and I had the feeling he didn't mean to say that out loud, so to be polite, I didn't respond.

I always wondered what he meant. I didn't find myself surprising at all.

After that date, he spent nearly every night with me. We only stayed at his place a few times. He said we needed my bed because of Juno (Mace only had a queen-size), but I suspected it was because he liked my space. As for me, I liked him *in* my space. In the end, too much.

Daisy lived in Englewood and I lived in the Highlands, at least a twenty minute drive if traffic was good (which, it wasn't). My mind moved from going home to its more usual pastime of worrying about my band. Or, at this juncture, them worrying about me.

Especially Floyd.

I sighed and rested my head against the window. Behind me, Juno licked her chops and snuffled the wind coming through the crack where Mace had rolled her window down.

I really needed to call Floyd.

Floyd was talented. He could have done something with his music. He could have gone somewhere if he'd gone after it and moved to NYC or LA. He could have been at least a sessions player, but likely more. A lot more.

He didn't want it. He wanted to live a quiet life with his wife and see his girls grow up happy. So that's what he did. That was Floyd and that's a lot of the reason why I loved him.

At first, he pushed me to be more than I wanted to be, saying not only did I have the talent for it, but I had a stage presence that "knocks your socks off" (his words).

I didn't want fame and fortune, stadium gigs and my picture on the cover of *Rolling Stone*. I didn't write music, I played it. I didn't play music for the money. I did it for my sanity. The only way to escape my shit life growing up was by entering the hundreds of little, dizzyingly cool worlds of notes and lyrics of the songs I played.

Don't get me wrong. I was happy The Gypsies had local success. We demanded top dollar, free drinks, a percentage of the door and our cover charge was nothing to sneeze at. It paid the bills and let me live the music. The whole band knew we weren't going any further because I had no intention of taking us further. I'd been approached by some scouts, more than once, but for me, it was about the band. For the scouts, it was about me.

It was unspoken, but Hugo, Pong, Leo and Buzz all knew the heart of the band was my guitar and my voice, and the soul was Floyd's piano. The other band members were good, but they weren't ever going to be great.

They *looked* great, all handsome guys up there with Floyd and me, and they were better players with the band than they'd ever be on their own. They needed The Gypsies to stay together for them to be anything at all, and part of me knew that was the only reason The Gypsies *did* stay together. We were always fighting and in danger of one of the hot-headed ones (Hugo and Pong) or the dramatic ones (Buzz and Leo) losing it and walking out the door.

I needed us to stay together, and I needed them. At first it had been just about the music, but then they became the only family I had since I'd turned my back on my own. When that happened, it became all about the band.

Mace pulled up the gravel drive at the side of the house and I pulled myself out of my thoughts.

My van was parked by Swen and Ulrika's Volvo.

I didn't have to ask how it got there.

Mace.

I didn't say anything. I was glad I didn't have to go back to Lindsey's to get it. I was also glad I wasn't talking to him or I'd have to say thanks.

He parked and my hand went to the door handle.

"Don't get out until I open your door for you," Mace ordered, bossy as all hell.

I sighed but didn't answer. He got out, skirted the hood, eyes scanning, and he came around and opened the backdoor. Juno bounded out. Mace grabbed the workout bag in the back, slammed the door and opened mine. I exited the vehicle with a lot less enthusiasm.

Mace crowded me in a protective way and didn't waste any time getting Juno and me in the house.

This played havoc with my already tattered guilt. I may not have wanted to be back together with Mace, but it didn't go unnoticed that he was taking care of me and he was being very serious about that task. It also didn't go unnoticed that this was not because I was someone to protect, but because I was *his* someone to protect.

Effing hell.

We walked silently together up the stairs and Mace made me stand in the hall after he unlocked my door. I'd never asked for my key back. This would have necessitated me calling him, which might have descended into me begging him to come back, which was not something I wanted to do, nunh-unh, no way. Therefore I let him keep the key.

He walked in my place. I heard some weird beeping then I heard him doing a walkthrough of the house, and finally he called Juno and me in.

We walked in, Juno turning left, probably to hit the bed in order to take the all-important Big Dog Nap Number Fifteen for the day.

She skidded to a halt on the stairs, stumbled a bit and stared ahead of her in confusion.

I stared, too.

The room was dark. Blinds I hadn't owned when I left two nights ago were pulled low. The bed was moved over to where my guitars were. My guitars were now in the middle, the couch where my bed was.

"What the——?" I started.

Mace closed the door and tossed the bag on the platform where the couch now resided.

I stood staring as Mace went up the platform and turned on a light then came back to me. His hand in his pocket, he pulled out something that clinked.

He got close to me but pointed at the door.

"New deadbolt, chain, peephole. Use the last two when you're in the house. Always use the first one. Not just during this situation, all the time," Mace ordered, handing me a key.

I took the key but stared at my door, which now had three locks and a new peephole.

Effing, bloody hell.

Mace grabbed my hand and pulled me two steps to the side of the door.

"Alarm panel," he announced, dropping my hand, pointing at a new box on the wall and flipping it open. "This is your combination. Memorize it." He handed me a slip of paper.

I looked at the paper, read the numbers, read them again, repeated them in my head and made a wonky, only-understood-by-me mathematical formulation of them (something I did when I had to memorize numbers).

"Got it memorized?" Mace asked.

I looked at him and nodded, not speaking because I couldn't find my voice, *not* because I wasn't talking to him. At that juncture, I kind of forgot about my latest plan.

He took the slip of paper from me, balled it in his fist and shoved it in his pocket.

"You come in, you got thirty seconds to punch in the code then hit this button." He pointed at a button. "You go out, always set the alarm. You got a minute to get you and Juno out the door. You set it the same way, same code, same end button. Yeah?" he asked.

I nodded again.

"See this button?" He pointed to a red button.

Again, I just nodded.

"Panic button. You hit that, a signal gets sent to the police dispatch. They know it, they don't fuck around. They send a car with sirens. Then a signal goes to the control room at the Nightingale offices and we know you've been compromised. Don't hit that button unless you know you got a situation. Hear me?"

What was going on?

"Mace——" I started.

"Do you hear me?" he repeated patiently.

He seemed pretty intense so I decided to nod yet again.

"Both of your phones have the Nightingale control room on speed dial. Hit button one then pound. That way, you can't get to the panic button, you can grab one of your phones. Yeah?"

"Yes," I said.

"The door is alarmed, so are the windows. You hit that code then this button…" he pointed at another button, "while you're in the house. That means the peripheral sensors are activated, but the motion sensors are not." He pointed at sensors with red lights that were in the corners just where the ceilings hit the walls. I looked around and noticed there were a lot of them.

Mace kept talking.

"That means the alarm is set, but if the door or windows are breached, a signal goes to the police, a car goes out and the control room gets the signal, same drill as the other. Got me?"

Oh my God. This was too much. Simply too much. It was insane.

I didn't share these thoughts. My only ability, it seemed, was to keep nodding.

Mace went on, "The room is full of cameras. You won't see 'em, no one'll see 'em. The bathroom has a small window, two stories up. Unlikely to be breached, but it has an alarm sensor. Therefore no camera in the bathroom. The cameras are gonna be on and monitored at the office, 24/7. You need to change, you do it in the bathroom. You still with me?"

I kept nodding.

"There are exterior cameras: the front, back and side doors and the parking area. They're monitored 24/7, too. I talked with Swen. He knows what's goin' on and he's happy with the work we've done. He and Ulrika are set to go on vacation on Saturday. Good timing."

I started to tremble. It was beginning to hit me just how serious this was. Losing Linnie, being shot, knowing the threat, none of that did it.

This was freaking me out.

"Mace—" I started again.

His hand came to my neck, he got in my space and his head bent to mine.

"I'll answer all your questions in a minute, Kitten," he said quietly. "Let me finish explaining the set up and then you can ask me anything you want."

He wasn't finished explaining the set up?

This wasn't already the entirety of the set up?

He kept talking.

"You know Indy's Dad, Tom? He's a detective for the police department?" Mace asked.

I nodded.

So did Mace, once.

"Tom's arranging regular but random drive-bys by squad cars. Anyone watching the house waiting for a chance might either be seen by a car or they'll notice the frequency of squads in the area and they'll be a fuckuva lot more careful or bag the chance to get at you here at all. Every once in a while a uniform is gonna buzz your door. They're gonna wanna see your face, in person, so you're gonna have to show it to them. This could happen day or night. There's video surveillance here."

He pointed to another box with a screen that was situated just above the alarm box.

Then he kept going. "You hit this button, you see them and can talk to them but they don't see you. No plainclothes officers will call up, only uniform, and they'll show you a badge. You only go down if you see the uniform and the badge. By whatever small chance they got, anyone breaches the security and is in the house and on you, they tail you to the door but stay hidden, you got a code word. When you get to him, you tell the officer you're hunky dory. He'll know you're not, but he'll proceed with caution. You got that?"

I was beyond trembling. I was beginning to shiver.

"Babe, you got that?" Mace asked softly.

I nodded.

"Blinds always pulled. The bed was moved away from the windows so they have no shot when we're asleep. Avoid the couch, it's exposed. The walls are brick, you're safe at a wall. Windows aren't safe, don't get near 'em."

"Okay," I whispered.

Mace fell silent.

"Is there more?" I asked.

"Yeah," he replied.

Effing hell.

He kept talking.

"You got safe zones. Fortnum's is covered. The Castle. The offices. Indy and Lee's, Ava and Luke's. And here. That's it. You don't hang anywhere else unless me or one of the boys is covering you. To get to a safe zone you go with an escort. No exceptions. You go nowhere unless you're in a squad car or a company car. Okay?"

I nodded.

He fell silent again.

"Is that it?" I asked.

It was Mace's turn to nod.

"Isn't this all a bit much?"

He shook his head.

"It had to cost a fortune, who paid for it?" I went on.

"Most of the equipment is kept in stock. Any extras were purchased according to the Rock Chick they were meant to protect."

Oh dear.

"What does that mean?" I was afraid I knew the answer before I asked the question.

"I paid for it."

I closed my eyes. That was the answer I was afraid I knew.

Juno woofed in approval.

I opened my eyes.

Juno located the bed. She trotted up and down stairs, made it to the bed, jumped up to it, settled on her belly, put her head on her front paws and watched us.

"How did you get it done so quickly?" I asked, not knowing anything about alarm systems and surveillance equipment, but this seemed a pretty extensive set up to put in place in two days.

"Vance is good and he's fast, lots of practice. Monty, too. They prioritized. Hank, Eddie, Nick and Vance all need windows installed. They're staying at The Castle until the windows are replaced and the clean up done. That meant Vance and Monty could focus on Lee and Indy's duplex, and Lee put in a sophisticated alarm system a few months ago so they just had camera work. Same with

Luke and Ava's loft. It already has high security so they just needed the cameras re-installed. The bulk of the work was needed here."

I wasn't sure how much more guilty I could feel, but I figured I was just about at my guilt limit before my body spontaneously combusted with it.

"How did you arrange so much cover with the cops?"

"Indy and Ally are cops' daughters. Lee's a cop's son. Hank and Eddie *are* cops. To them, this is a family affair. You've been adopted. And Sid is responsible for a lot of shit in this town. Everyone wants to see him brought down, but no one wants collateral damage, especially if it's in the family."

Sheesh.

Well, lucky I'd been "adopted".

Okay, one last thing.

"I've got gigs this weekend, Friday and Saturday nights and Sunday afternoon."

"I know. We've talked to the club owners. We do a sweep before they open. We got men assigned on the inside, and no one gets in without getting their bags checked and they're wanded, including employees."

Wanded?

They were gonna wand people coming to my gigs?

Shit.

After he was done talking, he waited a beat then got closer.

"Any more questions?"

Yes, like, a million! My brain screamed.

I shook my head.

"Now I got one," he told me.

"Okay," I said softly.

"Why're you shakin'?"

I blinked.

"I don't know," I lied. I knew. I totally knew. I was scared shitless.

He got even closer, his other hand came to rest at my waist and the fingers of his hand at my neck gave me a squeeze. For some reason, this made me quit shaking.

"I'm gonna take care of you," he promised, his deep voice low.

"I don't want that," I lied again. I *so* wanted that. I just couldn't allow myself to have it.

Another neck squeeze.

"You should have thought about that before your 'I want a vote' speech this morning."

He was not wrong about that. I should have thought about a lot of things before my speech that morning.

"No, what I mean is, I know I need protection, I just don't want *you* to do it. Assign someone else to me." I thought for a second about my choices and I picked the baddest-ass-looking one of the bunch. "I'll take Hector."

There was an eye flash, but this was not unreadable like the other ones. This one screamed "Anger!" from start to finish.

"Two reasons you aren't gonna get Hector." Mace's voice had an edge.

I ignored Mace's edge and put a hand to one of my hips.

"They are?"

"One, because in about twenty-four hours he'd have you flat on your back, him on top and both of you would be naked."

At his words, my body froze. My eyes bugged out, my hands clenched into fists, but either oblivious or uncaring about the shocking insult he just dealt me, Mace kept right on talking.

"He's itching for it. I can see it in him the way he looks at you. He and I are gonna have words, but bottom line, when it comes to you, that's not gonna happen."

"You've lost your mind," I breathed.

Mace ignored me. "Reason two is because you're *mine*. End of discussion."

Not end of discussion.

I decided to start my battle on the first annoying thing he said and advance right on through the rest of it until he got it into his macho, stubborn, effing head!

"I would not sleep with Hector in twenty-four hours!" I snapped.

"Yeah, you would. He's good. He's better than Eddie was. Better even than Vance, and Vance was a Denver legend."

I'd lived in Denver a long time. I knew a lot of people, half of them women.

Had to admit, I'd heard of Vance. Hell, I'd heard of Eddie (and Lee).

Pre-Rock Chicks, they were all legends.

Focus! My brain shouted at me.

I focused.

"I'm not that type of girl!"

"Kitten, I fucked you on our first date."

He had me there.

"That never happened before. It only happened because it was you," I retorted, too swiftly, thus not thinking my words through, as in not thinking that maybe I shouldn't have said them at all.

He got closer. His hand at my waist slid around my back, his hand at my neck went up and around so his fingers went into my hair, and his palm was warm against the base of my neck. The front of his body was touching mine.

All of that felt really, *really* good.

Oh lordy be.

"Yeah?" he asked, eyes warm and smiling.

My heart began to beat a bit faster.

Shitsofuckit!

I really had to start thinking before I spoke. Or just thinking *at all*.

"Whatever." I blew it off as if it was nothing and the smile in his eyes reached his mouth.

Bastard!

"I'm not yours!" I shouted, advancing on to battle number two.

"You are."

"Am not."

"Kitten, you are."

"Nope. Nunh-unh. No way. Never again!" I ended on another shout.

His head dipped. His smile deepened and his eyes got that I'm-gonna-kiss-you look I liked so fucking much.

"God, I missed you," he muttered, and he said it in a way that, again, I didn't think he meant to say it out loud.

My breath ran away. I didn't know where, maybe to a different state. All I knew was it was gone.

Then there was a pounding on the door.

We both froze.

So much for the fabulous security system. There was someone right at my freaking door!

"Stella!"

Shit! Eric!

The door handle rattled.

"Open the door! Are you okay?"

Oh, this couldn't be happening.

Of all the super shitty luck!

Mace's eyes narrowed on the door and stayed narrowed when they came back to me.

"Who the fuck is that?" he asked.

"Eric," I answered.

Another angry flash then he swore, "Fuck."

He let me go and moved to the door.

There was more pounding as Mace looked out the peephole. I saw his body register something. His jaw got tight and he looked at me.

"You have got to be shitting me," he said.

Okay, now I was confused.

"What?" I asked.

Mace shook his head and opened the door.

Eric stood outside, and I noted somewhat dazedly that he looked good.

He was tall. About three inches shorter than Mace, but still tall. He had black hair with a fantastic wave to it that. If he let it grow long, it would be curly. Not girlie-curly, but man-curly and hot. Instead, he wore it long-ish and it always looked just out of bed messy and, well... hot. He had intense, black eyes and a lean, muscled body. As I mentioned, he was hot, definitely, but in my eyes, no one was hotter than Mace, even hotter than hot Eric.

Eric saw me first, his concerned face registering relief that I was standing and breathing. He started to take a step toward me but stopped and froze when his eyes hit Mace.

Juno lifted her head and woofed her greeting to Eric from the bed, but clearly was too tuckered out from hanging out with the Rock Chicks at The Castle to give it in doggie person. She put her head back down on her paws, but her body shook with her tail just to let Eric know she was totally welcome to him coming to her and saying hello.

Eric didn't have time for Juno just now. His gaze swung back to me then to Mace. Then he walked in. Mace threw the door to and when it caught the frame, Eric exploded, *"What the fuck is going on?"*

Juno woofed again, not entirely sure what to think about this unusual greeting.

"Eric," I said quietly.

"Who's this fuckin' guy?" Eric asked, jerking his head to Mace.

"You know who I am." Mace confused me further by saying.

"I do?" Eric's tone was belligerent.

"He does?" My tone was bewildered.

"You do," Mace answered, his eyes never leaving Eric.

Eric turned to him and something changed in the room. Something lead singers in rock bands wouldn't get. Only hot guys who deal in the world of crime and punishment would get it. So I didn't get it.

"Yeah, I do," Eric replied, his tone now dangerous, and I felt something not happy crawling along my skin at this admission. "What I wanna know is, what the fuck are you doin' here?"

"I could ask you the same fuckin' thing," Mace returned.

This did not give me a warm fuzzy feeling. Most especially because they both looked like they were about to rip each other's head's off, and outside the obvious, there was more to it. I just didn't know what it was.

"Erm... boys?" I called.

Eric tore his gaze from Mace and did a head-to-toe of me, his eyes snapping back to the bandage peeking from under my shorts.

Then his gaze cut back to Mace.

"So she did get hit," Eric said to Mace.

What?

He knew I was shot?

What was going on?

"She got hit," Mace replied.

"And you were there," Eric went on.

Mace's jaw got tight. "Yeah"

"*Fuck!*" Eric exploded again. "Back off, Mason. I've got this covered."

I watched, still totally confused, as Mace zoomed straight from barely controlling his anger to holding on to his anger by a thread, and I knew this was *not* a good thing.

"You got *what* covered, exactly?" Mace asked.

"Stella," Eric responded.

"Why don't you explain that to me?" Mace's thread was unraveling.

"How 'bout you explain to me why you think you deserve an explanation?" Eric shot back.

This could go on all night.

"Excuse me!" I yelled. "I *am* in the room."

"Quiet, Stella," Mace said to me without looking away from Eric.

Oh no.

He was not getting bossy on me again.

"Don't tell me to be quiet. What's going on?" I shouted.

"He's a Fed," Mace answered.

My breath, which had come back, decided to go on vacation again. My guess, Las Vegas.

My eyes slid to Eric.

"A Fed?" I breathed with the last remnants of breath I had.

I *knew* something was not right about him. He told me he worked construction.

Eric's teeth were in a clench.

"That's right," he said between them, his eyes reluctantly leaving Mace and coming to me.

"You work for?" I started.

"Yeah," Eric cut me off.

"He's on assignment," Mace shared.

A muscle in Eric's jaw leaped.

"Assignment?" Now I was sounding stupid, but there was no other way to be.

"Sidney Carter," Eric bit off.

Oh my God. Eric was after Bad Guy Sid, too.

Then it hit me. If Eric was after Sid, then he was with me because...

Effing hell.

I started to back up.

"Stella." Eric turned away from Mace and started toward me.

"Don't fuckin' get near her," Mace warned.

Eric stopped and turned back to Mace. "Do we gotta take this outside?"

"Works for me," Mace replied immediately.

"No!" I shouted and Juno woofed, sensing the degradation of the atmosphere and not pleased that Eric had decided against a more thorough welcome. Juno wasn't used to being ignored. "You two aren't taking anything outside. You're going to tell me what's going on. Starting with you." I nodded at Eric.

Eric turned back to me. He took a step, caught my look, clenched his teeth again and stopped.

"I can't say much," he started, then I reckon he got a load of my *new* look and went on, "Stella, sweetheart, I'm sorry. I can't say much."

"Okay, just tell me what it has to do with me."

Eric glanced back at Mace then to me. "I'm guessin' you know."

"Lindsey," I said.

"And Mason," Eric went on.

What?

"Mace?" I asked.

Eric continued, "We got a guy on the inside. They knew Sid was feeling the heat and was gonna retaliate. We knew who the targets were. We knew you were one of them. We knew why and we knew about the operation the other night."

I went back a few more steps, too stunned by this news to let the heat of anger sweltering off Mace to register on my brain. The backs of my legs hit the edge of one of the platforms and I sat down with no grace whatsoever.

Eric started toward me again, but quick as lightning, Mace moved and got in his way.

Eric stopped and glared at him.

I looked around Mace to Eric. "You knew?"

"Fuck," Eric muttered.

Then, not thinking (yes, again), I jumped up, stormed forward and rounded Mace, shouting, "I got shot!"

Mace's arm tagged me around the middle and pulled me, hard, into his body.

"I know!" Eric shouted back, deciding to ignore Mace's arm, which, my mind crazily veering in wild directions, I thought was wise.

"You didn't do anything about it!" I kept shouting.

"You were supposed to be with me," Eric reminded me.

He was kind of right, I was. He'd put the pressure on, big time, for me to spend the night with him that night, but I told him no.

Mace's hard body felt somehow harder after Eric spoke.

"This is what *I* wanna talk about," Mace said.

"It's none of your fuckin' business," Eric bit out.

"I'm of a different opinion," Mace bit back.

"And why's that?" Eric returned.

"Stella and I are back together," Mace informed him.

Again, not thinking, I twisted my head to look at Mace and cried, "We are not!"

"Stella——" Mace started.

My eyes moved back to Eric. "I want to know why you let me get shot."

"I didn't *let* you get shot. I sat outside. I saw you leave. I followed you to Lindsey's. I saw that Stark and Mason were there, not to mention the cops, and I expected Sid wouldn't be crazy enough to make a move with that kind of coverage. That's when I got a call. Jet McAlister was supposed to be with India Savage and her gang. She wasn't, and Chavez had been called out. I was sent to her house. The drive-by happened before I got there and you were shot while I was in transit."

Well, that made me feel a *little* bit better.

"Now," Eric's eyes narrowed on Mace, "you wanna take your hands off her?"

"No," Mace answered instantly.

"I'm thinkin' that's not the right answer. She was yelling at you earlier. I heard her through the door and she says you aren't back together," Eric returned.

"Yeah, she says that. Then again, I'm pretty sure it was Stella I was fuckin' this morning, it was me she asked to fuck her harder and it was me she was holdin' on to while she purred into my throat after I made her come. That's contradictory information from her and me, but considerin' I intend to be in her bed for the foreseeable future, I figure you understand where the fuck I'm comin' from just about now," Mace shared, his voice utterly lethal.

I stilled and Eric's eyes hit me.

Oh my God, did Mace really just say that? My brain asked me.

"You fucked him?" Eric asked me.

Yep, Mace really just said that.

Oh man, I was gonna *kill* Mace.

"Eric," I whispered. I didn't know why I found this upsetting, outside of what Mace just shared and how he shared it. First, I'd been holding back from Eric. And second, I wasn't his girlfriend, I was his assignment (I didn't know the Feds went *that* far, but there you go).

But I did find this upsetting, mainly because he looked like I slapped him across the face.

Eric closed his eyes and looked to the side; the teeth clench was evident again.

"You need to find another assignment." Mace wasn't in the mood to go with the vibe, which would warn just about anyone (except Mace) to back right the fuck off.

Eric opened his eyes and they were scorching hot with anger. Not just at Mace, but at me.

"Eric, this is complicated," I told him quietly.

"I know it is. I know a lot about you, Stella. I know you fell for him and he fell for you. I know he walked out on you. I also know that there's been no one since him. No one but me. Lastly, I know you were holding back from me, but I didn't think it was because you'd fuck him the minute you got your chance. I thought it was because you figured you'd get fucked over again if you opened up to anyone," Eric explained, not nicely, but it was an explanation.

"Careful with your words." Mace decided to focus on the "not nice" part.

"You didn't open up to me!" I defended myself, ignoring Mace and focusing on the "explanation" part.

"I got a job to do. Opening up to you wasn't part of my directive," he lashed out.

A different kind of imaginary gut kick, this delivered by Eric.

"Thanks a lot," I snapped.

"Falling for you wasn't either," Eric returned.

There it went again, my breath taking off, this time to Wyoming.

Mace's body tensed.

Shitsofuckit!

I opened my mouth to speak, but it was too late. Eric turned, opened the door and started to walk out.

He stopped and looked back at Mace. "Take better fuckin' care of her this time."

Then he slammed the door and was gone.

Chapter 7

Blackbird

Stella

I stared at the door, not sure how I felt about what just happened; only sure it was unhappy and unpleasant, and maybe a little sad.

Mace held on to me.

"Get out," I said quietly, still staring at the door.

"Tell me you didn't fuck him," Mace replied.

I closed my eyes hard and swallowed. This was to obtain a measure of control in order not to scream at the top of my lungs.

Then, again quietly, I repeated, "Mace, get out."

Mace didn't let go. Mace didn't move. Mace didn't speak.

We stood that way, his arm still around me, me still pressed back to his front, both of us staring at the door, both silent, for what seemed like a long time.

Then his head came to my shoulder and he moved my hair away with his chin.

At my ear, he said (now *his* voice was quiet), "First night I was with you, you came hard and you came fast. The night I got back from Hawaii, you did the same. This morning, the same. Every time in between, it took a little more effort to get you to purr for me, Kitten."

I held my breath. His words shook me. Simply what he said, but also how much he remembered. I didn't even think guys remembered shit like that.

"You didn't let him fuck you," he finished softly and he sounded relieved.

"Keep going, Mace, this is great. Pretty soon, I might hate you."

Entirely unaffected by my words, he kissed my neck, let me go and whistled between his teeth for Juno. I heard Juno trundle off the bed and her claws on the wood floors as she approached us.

I watched him take the leash from the workout bag.

"What are you doing?" I asked.

"Juno needs out. We're goin' for a walk. We'll be back."

"No you won't. I just kicked you out," I reminded him.

Mace stopped a foot in front of me. Juno was there so he bent, clicked on Juno's leash and straightened. He leaned into me, kissed my disbelieving mouth lightly, then he and Juno were gone.

I found myself staring at the door again.

Then I found myself wanting to cry.

My boyfriend I didn't want just broke up with me (I was pretty sure that was what just happened), and I was thinking maybe now I was wrong about not wanting him. My ex-boyfriend that I wanted back thought we were back together, and now I was thinking I was wrong about wanting him back (I wasn't sure at all about that). And someone I didn't even know wanted me dead.

Totally Queen of Super Shitty Luck.

I shook my thoughts clear and cleaned Juno's water bowl. I gave her new water, refreshed her food bowl and unpacked *my* stuff from the workout bag, leaving Mace's stuff in as a statement. Then I retreated to the bathroom. I was going to take a long, hot, lavender-scented bath and give myself a pedicure.

I was soaking in the bath, a wet washcloth over my eyes, when Juno and Mace got back.

I heard them moving around.

I heard the bathroom door open.

I prayed to all that was holy that the bubbles were holding up.

"You didn't lock the deadbolt." I heard Mace say.

I was silent.

"You didn't set the alarm," Mace continued, sounding closer, indeed *a lot* closer.

"Sorry, I get an 'F' for the day in security," I replied sarcastically.

The washcloth was taken from my eyes. My hair was up in a knot on top of my head and I had a wide, pale yellow headband holding it back from my face for good measure.

I turned my head, which was resting on a bath pillow on the back of the tub, and looked at Mace. He was crouched down and close. He didn't look angry, but he didn't look happy, either.

"Babe, those particular grades end in 'D', which means 'dead'," he said quietly and in all seriousness.

Shit.

He handed the washcloth back. I took it and put it back over my eyes.

Then I heard his voice come at me.

"By the way, babe, not a good idea to soak with that wound."

Great. He was right.

Obviously, considering he was right, I made no response.

When I heard the door click behind him, I pulled the washcloth off my eyes again and checked the bubbles.

Total body coverage.

Well, thank God for one small stroke of luck.

Hastily exiting the bath, trying not to sound through the door like I was hastily exiting the bath, I toweled off, put on my robe and decided on a self-spa evening. After my pedicure (I went for a deep, violet purple), a nail file and buff and a mini-facial I threw in just because, I was no more clear-headed or relaxed. I was just as confused and just as scared and, additionally, my wound hurt.

I needed my music.

I'd been in the bathroom a long time. By the time I got out, even the summer evening light outside was dimming. I could see it around the blinds.

There was a faint light glowing by my mauve chair. Mace was in bed, surprising me by looking asleep. He didn't move as I walked into the room. Juno gave a soft woof confirming this. Juno was good at being careful when her humans needed rest. It was weird for a dog to do, but it was true.

Mace must have meant it that morning when he said he felt he only got ten minutes of sleep. I'd never seen him go to bed this early. He was always out to all hours, doing whatever crazy shit he did, then doing crazy shit for my band, and then up in the morning, early, usually starting the day going for a run.

I walked to my dresser, pulled out some underwear and put it on under my short robe, careful of the new dressing I'd taped on. Then I pulled out a pair of loose-fitting, peach jersey drawstring shorts and a soft yellow tank top with peachy flowers printed in a strip up the sides. I turned my back to the bed, shrugged off my robe and got dressed.

Then I walked to my acoustic guitar, grabbed it and sat on the edge of my mauve chair, settling the guitar on my thigh, close to my knee, deciding, if I played quietly, maybe I wouldn't wake Mace.

But I had to play. It had been two days and too much happened. I needed it.

And Guitar Hero didn't cut it.

My fingers moved up the neck, feeling the strings, snagging the frets. I strummed a few chords. Then put a few more together.

After a while, I forgot everything. Eric, the way he looked at me, what he said to me and that entire scene. My new alarm system. Police checking in on me. The Rock Chicks in danger. Someone wanting to murder me. That same someone already murdering Lindsey. I even forgot Mace and Juno, who were in the same room with me.

My long-since callused fingers moved along the frets, strummed and plucked at the strings, and, softly, I closed my eyes and began to sing The Beatles' "Blackbird".

And I kept my eyes closed, softly singing and strumming, picking and sliding until I plucked the last two notes. I opened my eyes and saw movement.

I looked to the bed.

Mace was awake, elbow in the pillow, head in his hand, eyes, I could tell even in the mostly dark, on me.

Just like he used to do. Just like always.

"Kitten, come to bed," he said softly.

Just like he used to say. Just like always.

Out of habit, having sunk into living the memory of what we once were, I didn't hesitate.

I put the guitar in its stand, turned out the light and walked to the bed. I rounded it. Mace rolled. Juno moved to accommodate me (such a good dog). I shimmied out of my shorts and I slid under the covers.

Mace's arm wound around my middle and he pulled me deep into him.

"Feel better?" he murmured into my hair, knowing how I needed my music.

"Yeah," I whispered.

He kissed the back of my neck.

"I missed that, too," he told me, talking about me playing and singing and him watching, and I felt a shiver slide across my skin.

I knew not only did he mean to say that out loud, he meant to say what he said earlier out loud, too.

And I didn't know what to make of that at all.

I woke up with Mace's hand under my tank top, not just under it but honing in on my breast.

"Mace——" I said, sounding sleepy.

His hand cupped my breast. The rough pad of his thumb slid across my nipple then back.

"Mace——" I said again, still sounding sleepy, but my voice had dipped lower.

His thumb was joined by a finger, there was a gentle squeeze then a roll.

Pleasant happy tingles shot everywhere and a goodly number of them directed themselves straight between my legs.

Oh lordy be.

I twisted my head to him, my intent to say something, to protest, but he pulled up, leaned in and kissed my open mouth. The kiss was deep, hot and he pressed his hips into my bottom at the same time he did another squeeze then swipe of this thumb. I felt his hardness against my behind and more pleasant tingles, far more intense, scored a path through every nerve.

I kissed him back. I couldn't help it. I didn't try.

We kept kissing then his mouth moved along my cheek, to my ear and his tongue traced its curve. His hand left my breast and trailed down, over my belly, between my legs then he cupped me there.

"Tell me what you want," he murmured in my ear, his deep voice already rough.

"Touch me," I whispered.

He touched me, his fingers pressing in, finding me immediately. I moaned and started to breathe heavily, my mouth open, Mace's lips and tongue at my neck.

I pressed my hips into his lap and nuzzled. He made a noise that came deep from his throat and vibrated against my neck.

I twisted my head again and we kissed, hotter, deeper, his fingers playing me over my undies. I quit kissing and started panting.

His fingers moved away.

"What do you want?" he asked against my mouth.

I didn't delay. I couldn't and I didn't try.

"I want you inside me."

His thumb went into the side of my panties, pulling them up over my bandage and yanking them down to just above my knees. He positioned and entered me.

God, it was beautiful.

My neck twisted the whole time so I was facing him. His hand came back to my breast, his thumb and finger teasing my nipple, our mouths together, alternately kissing and breathing, my hips pressed into his as he thrust into me.

I got close but held back.

"Kitten," he muttered. He felt it, he knew it, he didn't like it.

He never did. He always wanted me to let go.

I always wanted to wait for him.

"Are you close?" I breathed.

He didn't answer, instead he demanded, "Stop holdin' back."

"I want it to happen with you," I told him.

His hand left my breast, went between my legs, his fingers pressed and circled.

I gasped his name. His mouth ground down on mine and he drove into me deep right before I came.

I was dazed and still coming down when, mouth still on mine, his strokes going deeper, faster, I knew he was close.

His voice now hoarse, he said, "Christ, you feel sweet. No one fuckin' sweeter."

It was again something I suspected he didn't mean to say out loud, but I was beginning to think Mace didn't do anything he didn't mean to do. A different kind of warmth spread over me in a thick layer on top of my happy post-orgasm-Mace-still-inside-me feel.

Then his breath caught. He shoved his face in my neck, he slammed in deep and I heard and felt him let out a heavy sigh.

When he was done he settled behind me, his arm wrapped around my belly and he didn't pull out.

I blinked slowly.

Then I realized it had happened again.

Shitsofuckit!

What was I thinking?

When was I going to *start* thinking?

"You okay?" he asked softly.

I nodded my head.

His hand drifted to my bandage, his fingers running whisper-soft along its edges.

"I hurt you?"

I shook my head.

His arm wrapped around my middle again.

My mind was racing to form a plan to get me out of my newest muddle. I mean, I *was* angry at him. He told my now ex-boyfriend he'd fucked me, doing it with a frankness that was just not nice, for Eric or for me. He wasn't listening to me when I told him we weren't together, and he didn't leave when I kicked him out.

This couldn't go on.

Of course, I was lying with him in my bed. A bed I joined him in last night without a peep. A bed where I was lying, my panties at my knees, Mace still inside me.

Perhaps I was giving him mixed signals.

Ya think? My brain asked.

"Babe?" he called.

"What?" I replied, having still not formed a plan.

"What's with black?" he asked.

This question confused me and I forgot all about forming a plan.

"Excuse me?"

"Your songs. 'Blackbird', 'Black Water', 'Black Velvet', 'Black Betty', a lot of the songs you sing have the word 'black'."

His question surprised me. He'd never asked me anything personal and he'd definitely never asked about my music, the most personal thing of all.

I knew he enjoyed it. He came to a lot of my gigs. I saw him standing in the dark, fingers around the neck of a beer bottle, his eyes on me and only me. And just like last night, when we were at my place, even if he was doing something, on a phone call, reading a book, if I started to play he'd always stop and watch, and I knew he'd listen, and I knew further he liked it.

After he came to a gig we had the best sex ever (which put our sex off-the-charts) because I was high from the gig and, I suspected, so was he.

Any time I played when we were alone, after I'd finish, he'd make love to me. I knew it was that because it was sweeter, slower, less energetic; all about giving, always about Mace giving to me.

"I don't know," I answered.

His arm tightened. "Tell me."

I sighed and tilted my chin forward. His head came with me. I could feel his breath on my neck.

I didn't want to get into this with him. It was none of his business.

Even on that thought, I answered. I couldn't help myself, and again, didn't try.

"My life was black. My Dad didn't love me. My Mom used me as a shield against his abuse. I didn't have any brothers or sisters and I didn't share anything with friends. I was too young, I didn't know how. I needed to turn black, my life, into something beautiful or good or cool. Those songs are all good, some of them beautiful, some of them just cool."

I felt a change in his body which translated into a change in the air. It made no sense to me except that I felt different somehow, warmer.

"Does that make sense?" I whispered, for some reason wanting to make certain he understood.

He didn't answer.

I tried again. I didn't know why, but I did.

"In Pearl Jam's 'Black', Eddie Vedder sings..." Then I sang the five most important verses of perhaps the greatest rock ballad in history then I whispered, "Well..." I hesitated then in a low, soft whisper, "That's me."

He moved, disconnected from me, but stayed close, and somehow got closer.

"You aren't black."

"My world is."

He was silent for a beat then he asked, "You ever see any light?"

When I was with you, my brain answered.

"When I met Floyd," I said. "When The Gypsies came together."

"Me?" He went direct to the point I was hiding from him.

"You," I replied honestly.

"Now?"

"We're black," I replied dishonestly. We were as black as the sun and this conversation proved it.

"You really believe that?"

"Yes," I lied.

"You want me to go?"

"Yes," I lied again, and it was hard. My heart was beating and my breath was packing up, enjoying its travels, it was ready to explore Texas.

"You're under my skin," he shared.

There it went, my breath, sitting in first class drinking champagne, straight flight to Texas.

Kai Mason was not a sharing type of guy.

Kai Mason had never shared anything with me, except his presence, his body and his ability to post bond for Pong on occasion.

Who *was* this guy?

No, no, I didn't want to know. I didn't even care.

"Eventually I'll work my way out," I assured him, but I didn't ever want that to happen. I knew it. I just wasn't going to admit it, especially not to him.

"I like you there."

Oh lordy be.

"Mace."

"I'm keepin' you there."

"I don't want to be there."

"You wanna be there."

"I don't."

"You're lyin' to yourself and you're lyin' to me."

"I'm not."

He kissed the side of my neck.

"You are," he said against my neck. "And, Kitten, you should know, I'm good with that. I'll be here when you stop."

Effing hell.

"I'll walk Juno," he offered, clearly done with the conversation.

"Fine." I was done with the conversation, too, and I couldn't walk Juno without a Kevlar vest and a crash helmet, and possibly total body armor.

"Make room for my shit in your closet."

I carefully pulled up my panties as I twisted to look at him.

"Not fine."

His eyes were warm, soft and smiling, which made me feel warm, soft and smiley. Luckily, I kept this on the inside.

Damn his fucking eyes.

"Make lotsa room, babe. Even after this is over, I'm stayin' awhile."

"Piss off," I mumbled and turned back around.

His hand came to the side of my face that was on the pillow. He twisted me to face him again. His head descended and he touched my lips lightly with his.

"I'll be back," he whispered.

Effing, *bloody* hell.

Chapter 8
This One's for Linnie
Stella

"This is, like, 'Beam me up, Scottie'. Fuckin' cool!" Leo shouted.

Leo was staring at my alarm panel and video monitor as if the concept of home security had been invented twelve seconds ago and I was on the cutting edge.

"Gee-zus, but Mace sure don't mess around," Pong added, flipping the door down on the panel and starting to press buttons randomly.

Visions of a dozen police cars and shiny black Explorers screeching to a halt in the driveway, spraying gravel, officers and hot Nightingale Investigation Team members alighting with guns drawn and shooting everything that moved flashed through my head.

I leaped forward and slapped Pong's hand.

"Pong, don't do that!" I snapped.

"What?" Pong asked, looking innocent (or trying and failing).

"No pressing buttons on the state of the art alarm system that cost Mace the moon and the stars and the promised enslavement of his firstborn children," I answered. "Clue in, Pong, this is serious business."

"Jeez, take a chill pill, Stella Bella," Leo said, laidback even in the face of imminent danger (likely because he'd just smoked a doobie), which the band had its share of even before Linnie was murdered and I was scratched onto a hit list. We could just say that we'd seen more than our quota of bar brawls, we'd broken up way too many possible statutory rape scenarios between Pong and/or Hugo and underage groupies, and Leo had been found in possession of illegal substances on more than one occasion.

I looked at the ceiling briefly. When I noted that instructions on how to deal with idiot band members were not written by the hand of God in fancy gold script on my ceiling (as they never were), my gaze shifted to Floyd.

Floyd grinned, knowing my thoughts instantly (as was his way) and shook his head. "Whatever the time, you don't want to do it."

Floyd was probably right. Perhaps I shouldn't kill Pong and Leo.

Still, maybe I wouldn't get into too much trouble if I roughed them up a bit. Anyone would understand. I was under a lot of pressure and my defense attorney could make the jury sit in a room with Pong and Leo for an hour. After that, they'd let me off, no doubt.

The entire band was over to pick up the equipment for the gig that night. Swen and Ulrika let us keep it in an unused room on the second floor. Usually I helped with the lugging and lifting, but seeing as I was on some faceless crazy criminal's hit list, for once I was going to be saved this chore.

"All right, boys. Let's get loaded up so we can set up." Floyd, thankfully, decided it was time to get down to business.

"They really gonna pat down everyone that comes to the gig?" Hugo asked me, ignoring Floyd.

"They're going to wand them," I explained.

Hugo nodded then said, "They go for the pat down, I'm in."

New visions crowded my head. They were visions of Hugo patting down every female who came close to the door. Visions of Hugo's brand of pat down made me shiver and not in a good way, but in the kind of way I shivered every time I had to phone the bail bondsman, whose number, just for your information, was on my speed dial.

"I think they're gonna stick with the wands. They're more accurate at detecting... stuff."

I was making this up. I had no idea which was more accurate.

"I could be pretty accurate with a pat down," Hugo offered.

Sheesh.

"Me too," Pong put in.

Good grief!

Hugo turned to Pong. "We could lose the sax. Half the time I'm playin' the fuckin' tambourine and workin' the crowd. If anyone's gonna get to do the pat downs, it's me."

"Drums aren't that important. They do that MTV Unplugged all the time with just guitars," Pong told Hugo then turned to me. "You could go unplugged tonight. Shake it up a bit."

Unplugged?

Shake it up a bit?

Okay, enough.

I put my hands on my hips, narrowed my eyes and leaned in. "We are not gonna go unplugged and you two are not gonna do *any* patting down of *anyone*. Do I make myself understood?"

"Shit, mama. Be cool," Hugo said, putting his hands up, palms out.

"Man, I thought you gettin' back together with Mace would mean you'd be gettin' it regular again and you'd go back to bein' Sweet Stella Bella, not Stella-on-the-rag," Pong added.

I turned to Floyd but kept my hands on my hips. "Floyd, hit the red button on the alarm panel," I ordered.

"Now, why would I do that?" Floyd asked, still grinning.

"Because it's a panic button and the police will come immediately. I figure they'd appreciate the novelty of being called *before* a crime occurred," I answered.

Floyd just kept grinning. What he did not do was hit the panic button.

Whatever.

"I think that's our cue to go." Buzz, for the first time since they arrived, spoke.

"Man, Stella being targeted for murder puts her in a bad mood," Pong muttered, and fast as a snake, Floyd's hand moved and he slapped Pong upside the back of his head.

"Don't be stupid," Floyd hissed under his breath.

Hugo, Leo and I were staring at Buzz. Pong's gaze swung to him as well. Buzz was white as a sheet.

Okay, maybe I'd rough up Hugo and Leo but I was going to kill Pong.

"Shit, sorry Buzz," Pong murmured.

Buzz looked at Pong a beat, did a little shrug and looked at me.

"You gonna be safe up there tonight?" he asked.

I bit my bottom lip. That was the sixty-four thousand dollar question.

Then I nodded and said, "Mace has it covered," and I prayed to all that was holy that I wasn't blowing sunshine up my own ass.

Buzz shook his head. "Ain't gonna lie, I need the money. We miss this weekend's gigs, I'm up shit creek. I need the music, too. After Linnie…"

We all held our breath.

We knew what he meant. We needed the music just as much as he did. We all loved Linnie and music was what brought her to us.

Buzz continued, "Anyway, it ain't no good if you're not safe."

I walked up to Buzz and put my hand on his neck.

"Mace has it covered," I repeated, this time softly.

Buzz stared at me, then he nodded and the band took off. All but Floyd.

I watched them go, assessing my motley crew. Okay, maybe morbidly memorizing them in case I was shot or poisoned or some such before I saw them again.

Pong was tall and skinny with a mass of thick, dark hair that he kept long, past his shoulders, and teased out in a wild mess for our performances. He also put on eyeliner, which Hugo gave him shit about, but even I had to admit it worked for him, mainly because it made him kind of look like Johnny Depp's Captain Jack Sparrow. He had dark eyes, thick eyelashes, a heavy brow and a personality wilder than his hair, which said a lot.

Hugo was a huge black man with skin like midnight, perfect and smooth. He had broad shoulders and muscular thighs the size of tree trunks. He shaved his afro close to his skull, dressed to the nines even though the rest of the band usually wore jeans and had an easy, wide, white smile that always reached his lazy, dark brown eyes. He had a deep, velvet voice that made Barry White sound like a pansy.

Leo was slight of build, about an inch shorter than me, and had an aversion to shampoo. He had messy, light brown hair, blue eyes and a mellow attitude that was induced through copious amounts of pot smoking. His clothes hung on him and had more than the illusion of being dirty.

This was something for which he took a good deal of shit from both Pong and Hugo.

Pong dressed rock 'n' roll: tight, low-slung jeans, ripped t-shirts, and on occasion, when the spirit of Steven Tyler flowed through him, Pong wrapped thin scarves around his neck.

Hugo, as I already mentioned, dressed like he was torn from the pages of *GQ* magazine.

Leo had no fashion direction and couldn't care less. His grunge look worked for him. The girls dug it, mostly because girls would dig anyone onstage wielding a guitar. Leo, however, was more interested in getting stoned than girls, which was another thing Pong and Hugo gave him shit for.

Then again, Hugo and Pong didn't really look for excuses to give shit. They dished it out regularly.

Buzz was blond, blue-eyed and had a trailer trash Brad Pitt thing going. Tall and lean, mainly because he didn't have enough money to eat, he had a great body, molded not by working in a gym, but by the hand of a benevolent God.

Buzz appearing onstage in a tight t-shirt and faded jeans caused an electric ripple of groupie girl desire to sweep through the crowd every single time.

It helped that he gave off the vibe of a sensitive soul who'd worship the ground his woman walked on. He gave off that vibe because that was who he was, committed and monogamous. He'd given more devotion and energy to Linnie than, in the end, even though now the reminder of it made me feel guilt, many of us thought she deserved.

When the door closed behind them, I turned to Floyd.

Floyd had thick head of gray hair he kept fashioned in a greased back '50s pompadour. He was mostly thin, but sported a slight beer belly. He wore glasses rimmed in black like Buddy Holly's, had a quick grin, a sweet chuckle and long-fingered hands that were magic on a piano keyboard. His sense of contentment for life, family and music glittered around him like an aura. He drew people because he was kind. That kindness was etched into him physically, in the wrinkles around his bright, dancing, hazel eyes and the grooves around his mouth. Floyd was just the kind of person you wanted to know.

"Let's talk about you," Floyd said to me.

Oh dear, here we go.

Okay, I decided in that moment that Floyd was not the kind of person I wanted to know.

I turned away and walked to the platform where my guitars were. "Nothin' to talk about."

"Bullshit, Stella Bella. You aren't pullin' any wool here, girl,"

I stopped on the platform, opened up a guitar case and grabbed one of my electric guitars.

I'd known Floyd a long time and I'd never, not once, been able to pull any wool with him. And believe me, I tried.

"I don't want to talk about it." I tried an evasion tactic.

"Well, I do," Floyd returned. "Not to mention, Emily is scared shitless."

My tactic failed.

Shit.

Floyd had two grown daughters. Therefore Floyd was the Master of the Guilt Maneuver and was not afraid to use it.

"Let's start with Mace," Floyd pushed.

"Let's not," I replied, placing the guitar in the case carefully, and then closing and locking the lid.

I heard Floyd's boots on my floor then I felt Floyd's fingers curl around my upper arm. With no choice, I stopped what I was doing and turned to him.

"Girl..." he said low, his voice both steely and sweet, something which I was sure worked for him with Emily and his daughters. I was sure because it always worked on me.

"He thinks we're back together," I told Floyd and his hand dropped away as his eyebrows went up.

"He thinks?" Floyd asked.

"We're not," I answered.

This wasn't altogether true as I'd been sleeping with Mace for days. Not to mention, I'd had sex with Mace twice. Good sex. Sex some would even define as "getting back together sex," though if I was honest, sex of any kind could be defined as that. And further, not two hours ago, Mace had dropped off two big, stuffed-full gym bags and two boxes of crap at my apartment. Then he grabbed me, kissed me hard and took off saying he'd see me later that night at the gig.

"Why not?" Floyd prodded, cutting into my thoughts.

"How many reasons do you want?"

"How many you got?"

"Seven thousand, two hundred and eleven," I retorted sarcastically.

"Well, I got seven thousand, two hundred and twelve why you should let him back in."

I felt my eyes go round. "Are you loco? Were you *not* around when he broke up with me? Were you *not* there when I went through two boxes of Kleenex in your and Emily's living room? Hello? Mace came into my life, settled in a way I thought was forever and I liked it. I liked it a lot. I liked it too much. Then he ripped us apart and walked away. I'm not going through that again." I shook my head. "Unh-unh. No way."

"Emily left me," was Floyd's reply.

This time, my eyes bugged out and I felt my mouth drop open. I figured my mouth dropped open in an effort to give my body oxygen, but it was an impossible feat. My lungs had turned to stone.

Emily and Floyd were solid. Emily and Floyd were strong. Emily and Floyd were everything. This was impossible.

"Not recently, seventeen years ago," Floyd went on, and I felt the trembling world under my feet grow steady again. Floyd kept talking, "She left me, took the girls, moved in with her parents back in Michigan and was gone for ten months."

"Oh my God," I whispered, thankfully breathing again.

"Don't know why, even to this day, even though she explained it. Whatever it was, we weren't working. Not for her. It didn't matter. Only thing I cared about was she came back."

I staggered back and sat on the arm of my mauve chair, feeling the weight of this news settling on me like a boulder. I'd always thought that Emily and Floyd were the end-all-be-all of relationships. I couldn't wrap my mind around this information.

Juno trundled over to me and butted my hand with her nose until I started scratching behind her ears.

Floyd crouched in front of me.

"What I'm sayin' is shit happens to couples. In any relationship there's ebbs and there's flows. You want that relationship to work, you put on your life jacket and ride it out."

I shook my head, not feeling much like going in the conversational direction he felt like taking me, but Floyd kept talking.

"You gotta learn to give, Stella. I'm not sayin' this to be ugly, but you're bound up tight. That boy walked into your life and you didn't give him a fuckin' thing, 'cept your music. I watched—hell, we all watched—and we knew he was ready to lay the world at your feet. All you had to do was let him in. You never let him in."

I felt a queer sensation, like someone had reached a hand in and started squeezing my heart.

"I let him in," I said softly, but I knew that wasn't altogether true, either.

Floyd put his hand on my knee and looked into my eyes.

"You got more to give than your music, girl."

Direct shot, right to the gut.

But he was wrong.

"I don't."

"You do," Floyd said firmly.

Okay, wait just one damned minute.

I wasn't going to take the fall for Mace giving up on me. That was not going to happen.

"He wanted it, he should have asked," I said to Floyd. "He never talked to me. Looking back, we didn't know each other at all."

"You ever ask him? Did you ever talk to him? Did you ever try to unlock whatever demons that boy has trapped in his mind?" Floyd asked.

This threw me. It threw me so much, to hide it I gave a sharp laugh, a laugh that didn't even sound like it came from me, and I shot up from the chair. Floyd came up from his crouch.

"Mace? Demons?" I asked.

Hardly.

Mace was...

Well, just Mace. Supercool, superhot, super job, super good at every-thing he did, just all around *super*.

Floyd was staring at me, doing it so intensely it made me uncomfortable.

My body prepared for another blow because something weird was hap-pening here.

Super weird.

And I didn't get it.

And furthermore, I didn't want to get it.

"You don't see it?" Floyd asked.

"See what?"

Floyd's face shifted, and I could swear for a moment he looked disap-pointed right before he hid it.

Then Floyd got close.

"Stella, I wouldn't..." He stopped, shook his head, and I could tell he was warring with something. Then his hands came to my upper arms, his long fin-gers curling around them and he squeezed. "I wouldn't have expected this from you. But here it is, right in front of me. So I'm gonna say it straight. Get out of your fuckin' head and look around you. First thing, look in Mace's eyes. That boy's got pain there, plain as day and deeper than anything you've experienced in your whole fuckin' life."

All of a sudden, saliva filled my mouth and I feared I might vomit.

Quickly, I swallowed it down.

"What?" I asked, but that one word sounded shaky.

"You're so busy wrapping yourself in cotton wool so no one will hurt you that you don't see the world around you. You got a reason, I know. Your Dad was a schmuck, your mother... worse. Ain't nothin' worse than a woman who uses her own child as a shield."

My body got tight.

"You don't know how it was, Floyd," I said somewhat sharply.

"I don't *care* how it was. You blame your Dad. You make excuses for your Mom. They're both guilty as sin for doin' what they did to you. But now, *you're* guilty for letting them control your life years after you left them behind, built something good and became a decent person. Not everyone is like them, Stella Bella. Not even close. You know that. You gotta realize that in the battle of your early life, you won. But you aren't lettin' yourself enjoy the victory. You just keep preparin' for the next battle, a battle that might not come."

I pulled away and put distance between us, to get away from Floyd, but also to get away from his words.

"Floyd, you're telling this to a woman who got dumped *for no good reason.* Okay, I didn't let him in, but he didn't let me in either. And he didn't talk to me about it. And he left because of all the things I *am.*"

"Goddamn it, girl, you're not the band," Floyd shot back, losing patience.

"I *am* the band," I shouted.

Because, let's face it, it might not be right and it might not be good, but it was true.

I went on, "And, let's not forget, if people are so loving and caring and deep and giving, why is Linnie dead? Hunh? Why? Why do I have to live in fear of being murdered even though I didn't do a damn thing but fall for Mace, like, ages ago? Why do I have to worry about more of my friends getting murdered? A battle that might not come? It's not only going to come, it's here Floyd! This is my life. It's always been my life. Battle after battle. Time after time. Day after day."

I threw my hand up when Floyd opened his mouth to interrupt me.

"No. No, don't say it. I see where you're coming from, but you aren't me. You don't know. You don't have to live in my head. I have to take care of myself, you, the band, the music. It's all I've got. It's all I ever had. Anything good came in, like Mace, it went away. I can't reach for more. I tried but couldn't keep hold. I learned my lesson. I can live with what I've got and be happy."

For a second Floyd looked like he was going to say something more. Then his face went soft. He closed the distance between us and leaned in, putting his forehead to mine.

"I'm happy," I repeated quietly, putting my hands on Floyd's shoulders and giving him a squeeze to make my point.

Floyd lifted his head.

"I want to believe that," he said, his voice had lost the steel and was now just sweet. "But, Stella, you break my heart."

That hand wrapped around my heart squeezed tighter so my fingers on his shoulders gripped harder.

"I don't want to break your heart," I whispered. "Please, just let me do what I have to do," Then, even softer, I said, "I need you, especially you, to support me."

A smile played about Floyd's mouth, but he shook his head.

"Love you, girl. Love you like you were my own."

I felt another heart squeeze, another gut kick, both at the same time. Somehow, though, these didn't hurt.

"But, I'm rooting for Mace this time. I ain't standin' by lettin' him slip through your fingers again."

I reared back, but Floyd leaned in close.

"I'm gonna do what I have to do to help him break you."

Oh my God!

"Floyd!" I shouted.

He put his hand on my cheek, grinned then said, "It's for your own good."

I'd heard him say that to his daughters, dozens of times.

I stared at him, speechless and shocked, as he moved away. He grabbed my guitar case and walked out without another word.

Juno and I watched him go then Juno looked at me and woofed.

"You got that right, girl," I said to my dog, feeling distinctly like I was sinking. "My luck *sucks*."

Juno woofed in agreement.

I stared back at the door.

Then I asked my dog, "What do you think he meant by pain in Mace's eyes?"

I looked to Juno and a big string of drool plopped from her lip to the floor. This I decided to take as a Juno shrug. Then I decided to do a mental shrug and not think about pain and Mace and, most especially, not his eyes.

⧽⧼

The Palladium was an old movie theater on Colfax that had been turned into a huge club fifteen years ago. The bloom had long since gone off the rose. It was filthy and smelled of beer with hints of smoke and the occasional waft of vomit.

But the acoustics were perfect.

You could get five hundred people in there without the fire department getting antsy, but the owner, a man strangely named Monk (who was anything but), pushed the fire code limits every time The Gypsies came to play. We were pure gold to him. We could pack the place at top dollar on the door with lines down the sidewalks waiting to get in, and tonight was no exception.

We loved playing there. The stage was big and gave us room to move, and all of us preferred the big crowds. We were happy doing the more intimate gigs at Herman's or The Little Bear, but we were on fire when we had a full house at The Palladium.

And tonight was no different. The place was shoulder to shoulder.

Seeing as it was an outside possibility that this would be my final performance, I wasn't holding back. I'd even dressed beyond the pale just in case I was going to die. I didn't want my corpse to be anything but full on rock 'n' roll.

I'd scrunched out my hair to maximum, wavy volume. I'd done smoky, just short of slut-o-rama, makeup. I'd pulled on faded jeans, a black tank with silver sequins and rivets stitched on the front in the shape of a coiled, striking snake and a racer back so you could see my black bra straps. I'd threaded a black, tooled-leather belt with a huge, intricately filigreed silver buckle through my belt loops.

Completing my ensemble were black cowboy boots with a higher than normal heel and kickass designs etched into the leather, huge, wide, silver-hopped earrings, silver rings on every finger (sometimes more than one) and a kickass, wide, battered, silver band was shoved up my arm, hugging my bicep.

We were at the end of our second of four forty-five minute sets and I was beginning to loosen up.

I was loosening up because I knew four Nightingale men, wearing black windbreakers with the word "Security" in huge yellow letters on the back, were manning the four sets of double doors. Ike, Jack, Bobby and Matt, each paired with one of Monk's bouncers, all of them wanding everyone that came in and searching backpacks and purses.

Luke was floating between the doors, not wearing a windbreaker, but being generally badass, thus not inviting killer intentions.

Eddie, Hank and Willie Moses were all drifting through the crowd, badges and guns on full display on their belts, further dampening any nefarious mood.

I knew Hector was outside because I saw him briefly when Luke brought Ava and me to the gig. Hector emerged from the shadows, gave Luke a nod, me a once over with his black eyes, and then he slid back into shadows again.

Vance was stationed at the door that led backstage.

Lee was *on* the stage, at the back, in the dark, watching the crowd.

If this wasn't enough, I noticed that Indy's coffee man, Tex, had planted himself at a stool, back to the bar, and I could see when my glance strayed to him that the big man's eyes were rarely on the stage.

Duke, on the other hand, had planted himself in front of me, moving up and down the front of the stage whenever I moved. Even though his back was mostly to me, I suspected from the looks on the faces of the crowd closest to him that he was glaring them down, squashing the happy vibe. All except the Rock Chicks, all of whom (except Jules) were front and center. Happy vibe secure, Indy, Ally, Jet, Roxie, Daisy, Shirleen, Ava and Annette were singing along with me at the top of their lungs and screaming like freaks after every song.

As far as I could tell, Mace had not yet arrived.

I figured even Madonna didn't have this caliber of security so it was unlikely tonight was my night to die.

And that made the gig all the more sweet.

My glance slid to Floyd and I gave him the nod.

It was time.

We were going to deviate from the set list. Everyone in the band knew about it.

Everyone, that was, but Buzz.

Floyd caught Leo's eye and Leo lifted his chin just as Hugo caught on and grinned, stepping toward a microphone.

Buzz was looking at his boots.

The band might be on fire, but Buzz was only swept up in the flame; he wasn't participating much in building it higher. His mind was on other things.

I took my eyes off Buzz, looked at the crowd and wrapped my hand around the microphone with a toss of my hair.

This was Pong and Leo's cue.

Pong's sticks clicked on the drums, Leo started the first chords, and I knew without looking that Buzz had clued in. He couldn't help but clue in. We all knew what those clicks and strums meant.

"This one's for Linnie," I told the crowd.

Everyone screamed. The wave of sound hit the band, firing us up all the more even though most people probably had no idea who Linnie was. They didn't care. Any song that was for someone was going to be *something*. And this song, a song we rarely ever played, they knew would rock the whole fucking house.

I glanced at Buzz and found his face was pale, but his eyes were on me and they were shining. I looked away, knowing if I kept looking at him I'd lose it, just as Hugo's deep voice started smoothly delivering the lyrics.

And the lyrics were to ZZ Top's killer, kickass "La Grange".

Hugo sang.

A few more strums, a few more clicks.

I felt it in my belly, like I always felt it in my belly just like I knew Linnie always felt it in her belly.

Wait for it... my brain breathed in anticipation.

Pong's drums went wild and Leo's soft guitar went solid. The crowd surged in and my stomach plunged.

This is what it's all about. This is what Linnie lived for, my brain told me what I already knew, because I understood Linnie. I lived for it, too.

Hugo's velvet voice slid back in, "Have mercy..." then he smoothed through the "haw haws" and delivered the lyrics.

When it was time, Pong rounded out the beat and I went front stage and started to blow the lid off.

"Have mercy," Hugo finished.

He stepped back with a big, white smile at me and I rolled.

I walked the stage, eyes on the crowd, Leo and Pong setting the rhythm. I watched the crowd throb, the heads bob, the bodies sway, the hands in the air jacking out the beat. I smiled wide at them. They were asking for it, and as usual, I gave it to them. It was the only good thing I had to give. I was generous with the gift and they sucked it right up.

Leo stopped. Pong and I took turns. Leo cut in and I cut out, leaving it to Leo and Pong.

Then Pong exploded, Leo came back, and finally, so did I.

Floyd joined the fun, scooting across the stage, crouched low, jaw jutting back and forth, playing air guitar like he was a white Chuck Berry.

I watched Floyd's antics and only I could hear my laughter over the music. My eyes moved to Hugo who was doing a weird, super fly black man dancing to rock 'n' roll dance, shoulder's moving up and down, hands tucked tight to his chest, head bobbing, feet moving around in a wide square.

The crowd was there, feeding us, but they'd also somehow melted away.

The band was all on its own. We were the only ones in the club and we were tight, most ev'ry night, and there was no mistake about it.

Buzz, his bass not needed in this part of the song, was jumping up and down, a wide smile on his lips, tears streaming down his face, his bass flipped around so it was at a slant along his back.

I was working the stage, working the band, following alongside Floyd as he made another crazy crouch-walk back across the stage.

I tossed my hair, throwing my head back to do it and just kept playing.

I stopped, leaned forward at the hips and laughed open-mouthed in the direction of Leo, who was moving his hips and shaking his head, his dirty hair in his eyes, grinning like a loon. I looked to Pong who was banging on the drums, swinging his wild hair around so much it was like a living thing.

Linnie would love this, my brain told me.

Linnie always loved this, I told my brain, and she did. Linnie's favorite was always ZZ Top's "La Grange". She begged us to do it, every gig.

Here's to Linnie, my brain whispered.

"Here's to Linnie," I whispered back.

I smiled at Buzz. He smiled at me and went to the microphone as the notes started to fade.

"*Long live rock 'n' roll!*" he screamed.

The crowd roared.

I nodded at the lighting guy.

The stage went black.

◥◣◢◤

A bottle of Fat Tire beer was shoved into my hand by Duke when I came down the steps at the side of the stage.

"We got trouble," Duke growled, but I'd already felt it. The high from "La Grange" disappeared in a flash, and my eyes moved to the source of the trouble just as Duke plastered himself to my side and the band came clattering down behind me.

"What's goin' on?" Floyd asked.

I moved toward the back wall where Lee, Vance and a newly-arrived Mace had Monk pinned to the wall, using nothing but their collective badass presence to hold him there.

"And lighten the fuckin' crowd," I heard Mace finish on a snarl when I stopped several feet behind his back.

I didn't have to see his face to know Mace was *not* in a good mood. I just had to look at the straight line of his back and the tight way he was holding his powerful body.

"*Have you lost your fuckin' mind?*" Monk screeched, eyes huge and riveted on Mace.

"You don't close down the door and lighten the crowd, I'm *gonna* lose my fuckin' mind, make no mistake," Mace returned, and honest to God, there was no mistake to be made in the tone of Mace's voice.

Lordy be.

"What's happening?" I asked.

Four sets of male eyes moved to me, but it was Monk who spoke.

"Stella, beautiful, call off your man."

I felt the band settle in behind me and Duke was still close to my side.

"What's happening?" I repeated.

"You don't call off your man, we got problems," Monk threatened.

I never liked Monk. I suspected he skimmed from our take on the door. I knew he watered down drinks. I also knew he didn't card pretty young girls, nor did he serve them the watered down booze. He also got too close when he talked to me and he had bad breath. All this was not conducive to me liking him, so I never did.

I shoved in between Mace and Vance.

"What... is... happening?" I asked, speaking slowly and sounding as pissed-off as I was.

I mean, no one messed with a ZZ Top vibe.

No one.

Especially not someone like Monk.

Monk had dark, thick, bushy hair around the sides of his head, but he was bald and shiny at the top. He was shorter than me, rounder than anyone I knew and had weasel eyes. He looked like a weird, scary clown without the makeup.

"He's over code for maximum capacity," Lee answered for Monk. "And his boys aren't doing thorough searches."

This was not good.

Monk often went over code. This wasn't a surprise. But thorough searches were kind of important if I wanted to be breathing in the morning. And equally important for all the Rock Chicks to be safe.

"You know how long it takes to wand someone and look through their shit? It'd take hours to get people in here," Monk flashed at Lee then lost his bravado and visibly quailed when Lee's angry eyes sliced to him.

"Monk, do you have any idea what's at stake here?" Floyd had shoved in between Lee and Mace, and he looked even angrier than Lee (but not more than Mace). One glance at Mace said very bad things for Monk's immediate future.

Before Monk could answer, Lee cut in and said to Monk, "You agreed to the procedure."

"I agreed but I had no idea it'd be this tight, take that long at the door. The Gypsies are a solid act, but there were people leaving the line and goin' home. That's me losin' money. I don't like losin' money." Monk, stupidly, wasn't backing down.

"You still got a line outside and you're over capacity. You aren't losin' shit," Vance threw in.

"Turn 'em away, close the door and thin the fuckin' crowd. I want fifty people ejected before the next set," Mace demanded.

I watched Monk and it was like in the cartoons when dollar signs rolled in character's eyes. You could see Monk calculating the loss at the bar, not to mention the cover charge he'd have to return if he ejected fifty people.

"That's not gonna happen," Monk told Mace.

Mace leaned in and it was not a friendly, shiny-happy-people lean.

Definitely not good.

Okay then, time for me to intervene.

I pushed in front of Mace and pressed my back into his front in an effort to hold him back.

"You don't do it, we don't go back onstage," I said to Monk.

"You don't go back onstage, you don't get paid," Monk said to me.

"You don't pay, I break your legs," Mace joined the exchange.

"Awesome," Pong muttered from behind us.

Pong had always liked the idea of us employing muscle so we wouldn't get cheated by club owners, which happened a lot. Unfortunately, we'd never been able to afford it, and even though Hugo had volunteered to kick some ass, I was worried he'd break a finger or something doing it. We needed his fingers; fingers were kind of important for a saxophone player, so I forbade it.

Lee got closer to Monk.

"You eject fifty people and you shut down the door. We got five cops in the club and they'll call in the code violation if you don't. Then they might feel inclined to call the TTB, just for shits and grins."

At this, Monk paled.

"What's the TTB?" I heard Leo whisper from behind us.

"Fuck knows," Pong muttered.

"Alcohol and Tobacco Tax and Trade Bureau," Hugo answered.

"Oh jeez," Leo breathed with more than a hint of panic.

"Relax, it ain't the DEA," Buzz threw in.

"Thank God for that," Leo said with relief.

"And anyway, that bag of grass you got in your guitar case ain't shit to the DEA," Pong declared.

"Yeah, they got bigger fish to fry," Hugo pointed out sagely.

I made a quick prayer for deliverance from a band who would talk openly about one of their members in possession of a bag of marijuana after having just heard five cops were in the crowd.

When no deliverance was forthcoming, I twisted and looked around Mace's body to the boys in my band.

"Would you guys *shut up?*" I snapped.

They all just stared at me with expressions that said, "What?"

My effing band.

I turned back around to Monk.

"So?" I prompted when Monk didn't speak.

Monk's expression twisted into one that made him look like he'd just sucked on a lemon. It was not attractive. At the best of times Monk was not attractive, so one could say this was more like *really not attractive*.

"I'll close down the door and thin the crowd," Monk gave in.

I looked at the ceiling. "Thank you, God."

My eyes came back to Monk when he started speaking again.

"Stella, you continue to be this big of a pain in the ass and this asshole stays connected to the band," Monk jerked a thumb at Mace, "I'll have to rethink my schedule."

Okay, there it was again.

Proof that my luck sucked.

We had three gigs scheduled in the next two months at The Palladium. Even with him skimming off the top, we got our biggest take from Monk. Hell, Leo and Buzz could live for weeks off one night's take at The Palladium. We couldn't lose The Palladium.

Before I could retort, Mace moved. One second, I was between him and Monk. The next second, *nothing* was between him and Monk and Monk had miraculously grown six inches. This was because Mace had him off his feet, pressed to the wall partly with Mace's body, partly with Mace's hand at his throat.

"Do I have to explain my point?" Mace asked from between his teeth.

Monk's eyes were bugged out and he was staring down at Mace. He shook his head as best he could with Mace's hand wrapped around his neck just under his jaw.

Mace dropped Monk but stayed close.

"You give the band's take of the door and pay to me tonight. I count it and I don't like what I see, we're gonna continue that conversation," Mace told Monk.

Effing *hell*.

Did Mace just say that?

Monk glared at Mace, but he nodded. Then he scooted out and lost himself in the crowd.

I watched Monk go.

Yep, Mace just said that.

Mace just took care of me and the band.

Again.

Effing, blinding hell.

"I fuckin' love that guy," Pong said. His eyes were on Mace.

Effing, effing, blinding, blinding, hell, hell, *hell.*

"Don't you have groupies to tag for post-gig festivities?" I asked Pong.

Pong's body jerked at the realization that he was standing around with me and a bunch of men when he could be working the girls in the crowd, setting up that night's action.

"Oh shit, yeah." Pong turned and punched Hugo's arm. "Time's a-wastin', black man."

Hugo looked down his nose at Pong. "Don't call me 'black man'."

"Why not?" Pong was on the move. He didn't actually care why not. He always called Hugo "black man" and Hugo always told him not to.

"A black man can call me 'black man'. An eyeliner wearin', hair-spray sprayin', skinny white cracker can't call me 'black man'." Hugo was on the move, too.

"Don't call me 'skinny white cracker'." I heard Pong say as he disappeared into the throng.

"You *are* a skinny white cracker." I heard Hugo respond as he disappeared, too.

"I need a beer," Floyd said to no one and he headed toward the bar.

"I need my weed." Leo headed backstage.

Buzz came up, eyes avoiding mine, and he gave me a brief hug. Buzz was often affectionate, but after all the drama, this still took me off-guard.

Before I could respond, he disappeared in the crowd, too.

I watched the space where I'd last seen Buzz.

I knew what the hug was for—Linnie and "La Grange".

I pressed my lips together so I wouldn't cry.

Duke, Vance and Lee melted into the shadows, leaving me with Mace.

I took a swig of my beer. I was too emotionally charged to deal with Mace at that moment.

No, strike that, I was too emotionally charged to deal with Mace at all, ever.

"I need some alone time," I told him, even though I should have been thanking him. Yet again, he was taking care of me *and* my band.

To avoid looking at Mace, I was looking at the crowd. Duke, Lee, and, I noticed, now Hank and Willie, were holding back some people who wanted to get to me. They were creating a little pocket of solitude in the crowded club.

I could have kissed them.

"You had a year of alone time. That time's up," Mace replied, and my eyes shifted to his, then they narrowed.

Erm, pardonnez moi?

"Excuse me?" I asked.

He got close.

I retreated.

My back slammed against the wall. His hand came up to rest on the wall by the side of my head and his body curled around, fencing me in.

"Mace, please…" I asked softly, hoping he'd give in as he often did when I went soft.

"You're magic up there," Mace clearly wasn't in the mood to give in, and I knew then that he wasn't newly arrived either. He'd likely been there all night, in the shadows, watching.

This made me shiver.

In the dim light of the club, I saw he'd gone soft, too, and his soft was a heckuva lot more powerful than mine.

Oh dear.

"Stop it," I said.

"You think you're good, but you're not good. You're fuckin' magnetic."

"Stop."

"You could light up arenas."

I closed my eyes tight.

"Stop," I whispered.

I felt him get even closer, the heat from his body hitting mine.

It felt good. It felt safe. It felt right.

"What you're not is black."

My eyes flew open, but even so, there was only time to see him melt into the crowd.

Effing, bloody, fucking *hell.*

I knew I was going to do it, right after our never-say-die, always-up-on-always, burning-down-the-house, gig-ending, band-defining version of "Ghostriders in the Sky".

I knew I was going to do it, break precedent, maybe even shift the entire center of the band, maybe even pound a crack in our foundation just in order to do it.

Because I had to do it.

Mace had to get it.

If he didn't get it, I was lost. I already felt myself veering off the path.

And I'd just found my way again.

I wasn't going back.

I couldn't.

Nunh-unh.

No way.

It was the end of the night, the crowd was screaming for an encore that the regulars knew they were never going to get. They knew this because they never got it.

Never.

No matter how much they screamed and clapped and stomped their feet, after we sang "Ghostriders", The Gypsies were, without fail, done.

Until tonight.

The band had had their fill of applause, saying "thank you" into their mics, raising their hands to the crowd and feeling the love. They were turned away and getting ready to pack it in. The house lights were already up. The crowd was just beginning to come to the realization that they'd have to climb down from the high where we'd taken them. I felt the desperate urgency sift out of the applause as it downshifted to appreciation.

That was when I started strumming my guitar.

Buzz's head jerked toward me and I felt Floyd's eyes on me. I noticed Leo glancing around in confusion. Hugo froze to the spot, his eyes on the strumming fingers of my right hand, the contorted fingers of my left pressing the frets.

I didn't even look at Pong.

I ignored them all as I strummed.

Then I stepped up to the mic.

133

I gave a soft, "oh yeah," into it, letting it snake into the quieting crowd, listening to the hum die as I played the chords.

As if rehearsed, Buzz, Leo and Pong came in right on time which it most definitely was not rehearsed. It was a song I played at home, alone, but never allowed myself to sing, never allowed the band to play. A song so deep in my soul, I *couldn't* sing it. I was afraid I wouldn't do it justice.

By that time, the crowd was totally still, deathly silent and staring in fascination toward the stage.

I was known for never changing lyrics, never changing the words of a song sung by a man to fit it to myself as a woman. This gave me a subtle edge because lesbians thought I was one of them when I sang about women and that was my code to tell them I was a member of the club. This didn't affect me. I was happy for the additional fans, and lesbians always gave a good vibe at a gig.

They didn't know that I didn't change lyrics because they weren't my lyrics to change. In my head, a song was a solid thing, rendered from marble by its maker, and it wasn't up to me, Stella Gunn, to take my unqualified chisel to it for my own purposes.

But tonight, I was going to make another unprecedented exception.

I was going to change Vedder's lyrics, fit them to myself and Mace.

My eyes found him. He wasn't hard to find. Throughout the last two sets, I always knew where he was.

Just like before we broke up, when I always but always knew where he was at a gig.

He was standing head and shoulders above the crowd, five feet from the bar, his eyes on me.

Our gazes locked.

That was when I sang to Mace.

Yes, again.

And I felt it as the crowd pulled in their breath.

And then, through giving it to Mace, I gave them Pearl Jam's epically beautiful ballad, "Black".

After I finished the lyrics, I held out the "be" and shouted my "yeah" just as Mace came unstuck from my spell and started to push through the crowd, making his way toward the stage.

The band played behind me with a power and certainty that made it sound as if we'd played the song millions of times rather than just this once.

The chords I played sounded angry, as if sliced from my guitar. Floyd's fingers were pounding out the notes on the piano, notes to a song I didn't even know he knew.

The crowd was still silent, stunned, watching, enthralled.

I let the final words to the song rush out of me, hoarse and filled with scratching despair, just like it rushed out of Eddie Vedder on Pearl Jam's world-rocking, genre-defining album "Ten".

As I sang, Mace was nearly at the stage when I closed my eyes to shut him out as if closing my eyes could shut him out of my life forever.

Still playing, my head dropped and I rested my forehead on the mic, the vision of Mace, eyes never leaving me, pushing through the crowd toward me, burned on the backs of my eyelids.

I played lead, Floyd's piano thundering around me, matching the same notes that came from my guitar. The band began singing their "da-do-do-do, do-do-do's" and before my fingers could strum the angry riff and I could shout my anguish like Vedder, I was pulled roughly from the mic.

My eyes came open and I stared, frozen to the spot in disbelief.

Mace was there, onstage, right in front of me, right in front of five hundred people.

I stayed frozen as his hand wrapped around the neck of my guitar. He yanked it over my head and then jerked me forward so that my body slammed against his.

His free arm sliced at a slant around my back, crushing me to him. His head came down, his mouth finding mine, and he kissed me, right there. Right onstage. Right in front of five hundred people. Open-mouthed, hard, wet and full of *everything*.

His body bent forward, pushing mine back so I was arched over his arm, my torso and hips pressed deep into him.

He kissed me and kept kissing me as the band played around us, pushing the song longer, longer...

I heard the cheers, the shouts, the stamping feet, the applause. The crowd was wild, my subtle edge as a possible lesbian was forever obliterated.

And through it all, Mace kept kissing me.

When he finally tore his mouth from mine, he didn't move away. He kept me bent over his arm, his face less than an inch from mine, our eyes locked and we were both breathing heavily. My heart was beating like a hammer. I could feel it in my chest, in my throat, and dear God, I could feel his, too.

"You didn't get it," I whispered.

I could taste the acid of tears in my throat, the sting of them at the backs of my eyes.

I really, *really* needed him to get it.

But he didn't understand that he turned my world to black and he didn't get it that I couldn't go through that again.

"No, Kitten, you don't get it," he whispered back.

My hands were clutching his shoulders. I started to try to push but I realized I couldn't. I couldn't push and keep control of my tears and my terror and my shaky belief in the fact that what I was doing was right. Not all at the same time.

So I just held on.

"Let me go, Mace."

He didn't let me go.

Instead he spoke.

And what he said, with the background soundtrack of the repeating end notes of a soul-destroying rock song, changed my fucking life.

"I can't be the star in your sky when you're the only star left shining in mine."

This time, my breath took the Concord out of retirement and shot to Paris.

That was right before the gunshots rang out.

And the gunshots rang out just seconds before Mace and I went down, Mace's big, hard body landing on mine like a dead weight to the sickening, discordant sound of the strings of a crashing guitar.

Chapter 9

Sex Wax

Jet

I was smiling at Daisy, still high from Stella and The Gypsies' "Ghostriders", which always lasted at least ten minutes (if not more), and no matter how many times we heard it, which was every time we saw them play, they made it fresh and full of energy, and it always brought the house down.

But tonight it was more. The band was on fire and that fire blazed through the crowd, white-hot. It was enough to make us forget our troubles, the danger again confronting us, and just enjoy some good ol' rock 'n' roll.

Daisy grinned back at me and shouted, "Yippee kay yay!"

So, of course, I shouted it right back at her.

Over Daisy's shoulder, I saw Annette and Roxie doing a high five, then they bumped hips, and seeing that, I giggled.

It was great being a Rock Chick.

Only thing better was being Eddie's Woman.

Lucky for me, I was both.

My eyes slid through the crowd, looking for Eddie (not finding him, by the way) and coming to stop on Tex.

Like he had been all night, Tex was sitting at a stool, his back to the bar. But now, his narrowed eyes were locked on something as if that something was something he did *not* like.

Since there were a lot of things Tex didn't like, I didn't think much of this.

Then, to my surprise, I heard the first notes of Pearl Jam's "Black" coming from Stella's guitar.

Good God.

I felt, as well as heard, the tremor of surprise go through the crowd and my stunned body slowly turned. On my way around, I saw that Indy, Ally,

Roxie, Daisy, Ava and Annette were no longer Post-"Ghostriders" high. They were all staring, mouths wide open, at the stage.

The Gypsies never did an encore.

As in… never.

When my eyes hit Stella, I instantly became transfixed. She was at the mic and singing a slow, "Oh yeah".

Her eyes moved, then locked on someone in the crowd, and I knew without looking where her gaze was directed. I knew without looking that she was going to sing to Mace.

Like she did a few months ago when she sang Hank Williams.

And, just like then, after she started singing, it hurt to listen.

But it was a beautiful pain.

I knew it hurt her to sing it just as it hurt me to hear it. She poured feeling into every song she sang, but that song… that song, she poured her soul into it and the entire club felt it. And, in a club-wide moment of shared, stunned reverence, we were all dead silent while we watched her communicate her pain.

It was arresting. As the song wove through the crowd, the lyrics a gentle assault, we all stood frozen and watched.

Then, as if from nowhere, Mace was onstage, his long legs eating the distance as he came at her. We watched as he pulled her away from the mic, tore her guitar from her hands, and then he was kissing her.

I sucked in breath at the sight of it.

It was a hungry kiss, a hard kiss, a kiss meant to be private, but instead it was very, *very* public. I felt the kiss stirring in my belly even though I knew I should look away.

I didn't look away.

I couldn't.

The crowd started to cheer, to scream, to stomp their feet.

I didn't want to cheer. I wanted to cry, but bizarrely, I also wanted to laugh.

Before I could give in to either of these emotions, I saw the little red dot dancing between Stella and Mace's bodies.

Someone had a laser light.

Through the music-induced stupor I felt annoyance claw at me.

Who could witness this passionate emotional display and jack around with a laser light?

Then I heard Duke's gravelly voice shout, "Gun!"

Um… gun?

It came to me that wasn't a laser light and my body jerked. As if I wasn't in control of my own actions, instead of running or throwing myself to the ground, both of which would have been smarter, I turned to look behind me and saw Tex throwing people out of his way as he lumbered through the crowd toward a target.

"Down!" Shirleen yelled.

I whirled back to face the stage and saw the laser light go up sharply to a point several feet over Pong's head. Then I was on the floor, Shirleen's body on top of mine.

Gunshots rang out.

I heard screams, shouts, running feet. It was pandemonium at the Palladium.

The gunshots stopped. Shirleen's weight left me and she got up, leaned down, her fingers wrapped around my wrist and she pulled me to my feet.

"Rendezvous!" I heard Eddie shout, and my eyes flew in the direction of his voice. I saw him, gun out, other hand pointing to me. I also saw a man on the floor, Tex over him with a knee in his back. Tex had the man's arm twisted behind him, the crowd giving them a wide berth. Further, I saw Luke had a rifle. He tossed it to Willie, then his eyes sliced to the Rock Chicks and focused on Ava.

That was all I saw. Hector's arm was around my waist and he was pulling me away. Vance was there; so were Duke, Ike and Bobby. All of the boys had their guns in their hands and they were herding the Rock Chicks toward the back of the club.

This was not easy. There were still tons of people fighting, pushing and running, trying to force their way out but in the opposite direction. The Hot Bunch, big, strong and carrying guns, cleared a path, often resorting to tossing people out of the way to do it.

"Stella and Mace!" Indy shouted and my eyes flew to the stage.

Mace was up, Stella flung over his shoulder, and he was striding to the stairs, the band on his heels.

We hit the stairs as Mace made it to the bottom. He bent and put Stella on her feet.

Stella looked pale and shocked, but luckily alive and not covered in blood. Her wild eyes took a sweep of Mace as if searching for bullet holes. She looked up at him, opened her mouth to speak, but Mace got there before her.

"Rendezvous," he barked at Hector, and without hesitation, he turned in the direction of Tex, Luke and Willie.

"Mace!" Vance clipped, his tone urgent, but Mace didn't stop.

"Fuck," Hector snarled. His head turned and he shouted, "Lee!"

I looked to where Hector's eyes were aimed and saw Lee jump off the stage and push through the crowd on a trajectory that would take him to Mace.

"Let's go," Duke said, shoving us toward the back.

"What's he gonna do?" Ally asked, her eyes on Mace.

"Move! Now!" Duke shouted and started shoving harder.

We moved. We didn't want to, but we moved.

We knew the drill and we'd wasted enough time.

They herded us into Explorers and we went to The Castle.

~·~

"*Chiquita*, get away from the window," Eddie ordered.

I turned from watching Stella and Mace drive away in an Explorer and looked at Eddie.

His feet were bare, his chest was bare, his belt was undone, and so were two buttons of his faded jeans.

As usual, Eddie looked fucking hot. Definitely worth the f-word.

And also, Eddie was obviously ready to go to bed.

Even after our adventurous night, including rock 'n' roll in the face of certain danger, that danger coming at one of us in the form of gunfire and the Rock Chicks' fast getaway in bulletproof SUVs, Eddie was already wound down.

This was because Eddie was a cop. Eddie's job was dangerous, not to mention he'd survived five Rock Chick/Hot Bunch Courtships, including our own. This was just another night for Eddie.

"Is Mace okay?" I asked, dropping the curtain I had pulled back from the window.

I asked because Mace could be a little intense and we hadn't had time to debrief downstairs. Eddie came in before Mace and took me directly upstairs.

He looked exhausted so I didn't argue, even though I wanted to know what happened. As in *really* wanted to know.

If Mace made it to the man who shot at Stella before someone talked him down from going berserk, Stella and the rest of us would be visiting Mace at the local penitentiary for as long as they put people away for manslaughter.

I was taking it as a good sign that he was driving off with Stella in an Explorer.

Though they could be driving to Mexico as fugitives from the law for all I knew.

"Yeah. Lee controlled it before we had to lock him down," Eddie replied, finishing with the buttons on his jeans.

Well, that was a relief.

I walked toward him and picked up the t-shirt he'd discarded. I tossed it on the bed and started to undress.

"I can't believe they opened fire in a crowded club," I said, pulling off my tee.

"Sid's crazy," Eddie replied, his voice like a verbal shrug, but there was an edge to it.

No doubt about that. Sidney Carter was definitely crazy.

And maybe Eddie wasn't wound down. Maybe Eddie just wanted to think about this later, as in, while telling crazy stories to our grandchildren when we were retired and living in Arizona.

I sat on the bed and yanked off my boots.

"You okay?" Eddie asked, and I looked up at him.

Then I quit breathing.

He was standing there totally naked, arms crossed on his chest, eyes on me.

Eddie had no problem with nudity.

Also, it should be said, I had no problem with Eddie's nudity.

I shrugged off thoughts of how little problem I had with Eddie's nudity and nodded.

I was okay.

I'd learned a long time ago that if you were still walking and breathing, it was best just to get on with it.

I got up, pulling off my jeans then taking off my bra as Eddie got into bed. I grabbed his t-shirt and was about to tug it on when Eddie stopped me by saying, "Don't think so."

My arms through the sleeves of his tee but not yet having pulled it over my head, my eyes moved to him.

"What?" I asked.

"Drop the shirt, *mi amor*," Eddie demanded in a soft voice. His eyes, I could see from the length of the bed, were liquid.

My belly melted.

I dropped the shirt.

Then I put hands and knees to the bed and crawled toward him, his body between my limbs. I watched his face as he watched my progress, a smile playing about his mouth as I made my way up his length. When we were face-to-face, I stopped and lowered myself full on him.

His arms wrapped around me, one hand going into my panties at my behind.

"You okay with staying here?" I asked, and watched Eddie's liquid black eyes start glittering.

Eddie hated Marcus. Marcus hated Eddie. Our current arrangement was not an optimal situation. Both men put up with each other for the sake of the friendship between Daisy and me. This was a tentative truce. *Very* tentative.

Before he met me, and before I met Daisy, Eddie had spent some time trying to bring Marcus down. Marcus was not clean, not by a long shot. Somewhere along the line, Eddie had pulled back from his pursuit of Marcus, and Marcus, Eddie told me, had pulled out of some of his more villainous ventures. But Marcus wasn't ready to go clean, and Eddie wasn't ready to give up.

If Marcus slipped up, Eddie would nail him.

Eddie and I being houseguests of the Sloans went against Eddie's grain.

In a big way.

Not to mention Eddie told me last night that the Denver Police Department told him they also frowned on our current arrangement. This meant Eddie wasn't going to win Detective of the Year. Since Eddie frequently went his own way, he'd likely never even be nominated (not that they actually had a Detective of the Year award). I knew Eddie was okay with that. He wasn't big on politics and working the system. He preferred to focus on the job, or at least his way of doing it.

Eyes still glittering, Eddie answered, "Willin' to do just about anything to see you safe."

I knew what he said was true. He'd proved it more than once.

This earned him a smile, and when he saw my smile, as always, his eyes went soft. This was because Eddie liked my smile, like, a lot.

I felt warmth spread in my belly. This time it was a different kind and I dropped my head and nuzzled my face into his throat.

Eddie did an ab crunch, lifting us both. He yanked the covers from between our bodies and I swung my legs around to help him. Then he laid back, me still full on top of him, and he flicked the covers over us.

His hand went back into my panties, this time with intent, and his other arm wrapped tight around me.

My face still in his throat, I whispered, "Tell me about Mace."

His hand stopped.

"Not a good idea, *cariño*."

He sounded serious so I snuggled in closer and kissed his neck to soften him up. And I liked to kiss his neck. He smelled good everywhere but especially his neck.

I had to soften him up because, for whatever reason, all the Rock Chicks had an alternate Hot Bunch guy. Indy's was Eddie. Roxie's was Vance. Jules's was Luke. Ava's was Lee.

Mine was Mace.

Mace and I had a connection. A connection Eddie didn't like, but he no longer tried to stand in the way. I knew that Mace had witnessed his sister's murder. Our connection started when Mace saved me from getting murdered in the same way.

At first, Eddie thought Mace wanted to move in on his action, but this proved not to be the case. After my trauma was over, Mace and I stayed connected. This meant, every once in a while, Mace came over to our place for dinner, sometimes when Eddie was there, other times when he wasn't.

Mace didn't talk much and he never shared, but I knew he liked listening to me and he definitely liked my chili and my meatloaf. But his favorite was my roasted chicken and cheesy-garlic mashed potatoes.

Mace and I were a weird kind of friends. Because of what we shared (him saving my life, me being alive), he obviously meant a lot to me, and for some reason, I knew I meant a lot to him.

When you knew those kinds of things, you didn't have to talk about it.

Eddie had told me about Mace's sister, but he didn't go into detail.

Now, seeing as Mace was my alternate Hot Bunch Guy *and* next in the Rock Chick Firing Line, I needed to know, and I knew I could never ask Mace.

So I asked Eddie.

"I'd like to know," I pushed.

"No, you wouldn't."

I lifted up on a forearm and looked down at him.

"Yeah, I would."

"Jet—"

"His sister got murdered, Eddie. I know the story doesn't have a happy ending."

He watched me a beat, then two, then he sighed and I knew he was giving in.

I didn't smile. Since my drama was over, living with Eddie, my sister back in Denver after spending years in LA, my mother happy and healthy again after her stroke and dating Tex; I had lots of smiling moments, not counting, of course, being the target of a killer.

But this wasn't one of them.

Eddie rolled, forcing my arm out from under me, until we were on our sides, face-to-face.

His hand came out of my panties, but his arm stayed tight around my waist.

Then he started talking.

"Mace comes from money. Lots of it. His Mom and Dad divorced when he was young. His Dad had the money, kept it, didn't share and went on to acquire a string of trophy wives. Mace stayed with his Mom. They moved from LA to her native Hawaii and their standard of living changed in a serious way. His Dad had another child, Mace's half-sister, with wife number three of five. He moved on to wife after wife, leavin' the women and kids behind with less than they were used to havin'. Mace was close to his Mom and established a long distance bond with his sister, but he didn't have much to do with his father."

I wasn't surprised. By the sounds of Mace's Dad, I wouldn't have much to do with him, either.

Eddie had stopped and I watched his face, knowing from his look that what he had to share was unpleasant. My hand moved up his belly to lie flat on his chest. When I did this, he started talking again.

"The Dad was loaded. We're talkin' *loaded*. Not millions, billions. Even so, when he moved on to a different woman, he left the life he had behind, which meant he didn't have much to do with his kids. This meant that even though it wasn't a significant threat, with that kind of money, there would always be a threat, and he left his kids unprotected. Because of that, the sister got kidnapped, held for ransom."

"Oh my God," I breathed, stunned by this, even though I, too, had been kidnapped. So had Indy. And Roxie. And Ava. None of our kidnappings had been enjoyable, but most of them didn't last very long. We'd all gotten away or been rescued, and none of us had been held for ransom.

"Mace's Dad's a jackass. Strong man. Wouldn't pay the ransom, wouldn't get the police involved. He hired his own team of commandos. They had no clue who they were dealin' with. They fucked it up, botched the mission, and after, Mace's Dad got his sister's hand delivered to him in a box."

I felt bile rise up my throat, but I swallowed it down and closed my eyes tight.

Okay, so maybe Eddie was right. Maybe I didn't want to know.

It was too late. Eddie kept talking.

"At that point, Mace was done. He went against his father, got the police involved. They cornered the kidnappers and started negotiating. For some fuckin' reason, the kidnappers asked for Mace to be the go-between, demanded he make the approach. The police refused until they heard her screamin'. Mace lost it, demanded to be sent in. Without much choice, her still screamin', they suited him up with vest and helmet and sent him in, but the SWAT team was ready to go in right after him and put an end to it. The kidnappers knew they were fucked. They had no intention of negotiating. The minute Mace hit the room, before SWAT could make their move, they blew her head off and pumped eleven rounds into Mace's vest. One through his shoulder, one through his thigh, two into his helmet before they turned their guns on themselves. It was a bloodbath. Mace was the only one to come out alive."

This knowledge settled in my brain, then entered my bloodstream, and it burned like acid.

I opened my eyes and felt the wetness leaking out the sides.

"Mace was twenty-five when it happened," Eddie continued. "His sister was sixteen."

I tilted my chin down and pressed my forehead against Eddie's collarbone, unable to process the idea of a sixteen year old girl enduring that before her life was cut short. Further unable to process the idea of her brother living with that knowledge for the rest of his life.

Mainly because it was utterly un-processable.

"I got this from Lee. Mace doesn't talk about it. And this is where the story gets fuzzy," Eddie went on.

My head tilted back, the tears still in my eyes, and I looked at him.

"It isn't done?" I whispered.

Eddie shook his head.

"There's more?" I asked.

Eddie nodded his head.

"What?" I prompted, not wanting to know, but needing to know all the same.

"Don't know who they worked for, the kidnappers, but it was a big operation. The Dad was involved. Could be guns. Could be drugs. Could be deeper, uglier. It may be just because he's an asshole that the Dad didn't call in the police or the FBI. It could be he was hidin' somethin'. The kidnappers could have been after the ransom, but them callin' Mace in with the intent to kill him smacks of retribution. Odds are the Dad did something that required payback. That's my guess, but I don't have a clue, and Lee won't give me one."

"What are you talking about?"

"Lee doesn't want me lookin' into it. Not that I would."

"Looking into what?"

"How Mace learned his skills."

"What skills?"

"The skills he uses for Lee."

I blinked at him in confusion and my silent tears cleared. "What?"

Eddie sighed then he stated, "He was a snowboarder, Jet. A good one, one of the best. If you go back seven years, look at boarder magazines, you'll see his photos in ads. He had endorsement contracts. He was in commercials aired on ESPN. Go back before that, same thing with his surfing. He was famous. He still is in that crowd."

"I knew he——" I started, but Eddie interrupted me.

"Now he's a PI."

"Yes, I know but—"

"A good one."

"I know, but—"

Eddie interrupted me again, "One of the best. Lee was trained by the Army. Monty was trained by the Navy. Luke, I don't know, but it was an official operation and he's definitely had training. Specialized training. Vance is an ex-con. He'd lived a life of crime since he was thirteen years old, would likely still be in that life, he was so good at it. He only got caught because his buddy was shot while they were stealin' a car and Vance didn't leave him behind. Lee channeled his natural abilities, trainin' him in other shit, and he took to it. Mace is self-taught. Lee didn't have to do any training with Mace."

"Self-taught?"

"Self-taught."

"What does that mean?"

"That means between his sister gettin' murdered and Lee recruitin' him, he'd gone from a surfer and snowboarder to acquirin' skills that had nothin' to do with sex wax."

I blinked again. "Sex wax?"

"Yeah, you use it on your surfboard for foot traction, on the bottom of a snowboard to reduce friction."

My brows drew together. "How do you know that?"

He grinned. "Been boardin' with Mace."

I blinked (yes, again), mainly because this was insane. Eddie and I had been together for over nine months. We were getting married in a little over five and this was news to me.

"You board?"

His grin deepened to a smile. "I live in Colorado, *chiquita*."

So did I, but I didn't snowboard. Or ski, for that matter. That took money, something I'd never had.

"You didn't board last winter," I commented.

"I had somethin' to keep me at home last winter."

This time I didn't blink, but my stomach did a happy curl.

I ignored it and got back to the subject.

"So, these skills—"

He rolled into me so he was mostly on me. "What I'm sayin' is somethin' went down after the bloodbath. Mace disappeared off radar. No more competitive boardin', reneged on his endorsements. The kidnapping and murder made the news, big story. It happened in LA. Mace was famous, his Dad well-known. But, after it was over, there was nothin' from Mace. He vanished. He didn't resurface until Lee recruited him, and he recruited him for a reason. All Lee's boys have a specialty. Mace's is one you don't need to know."

"But—"

His hand came to the side of my face and his eyes got serious.

"You don't need to know," he repeated in a way I knew he wasn't going to tell me. And I knew, no matter what I tried, he wouldn't tell me.

His hands started roaming and his head moved so his mouth was at my neck. I knew he was looking for a way to turn my mind to different, far more pleasant things, but I pulled my neck away and wrapped my fingers around one of his wrists to stop his hands from roaming.

"Eddie."

"Shit, I know *that* 'Eddie'," he muttered into my neck with more than a little frustration. Eddie, by the way, had quickly become an expert in all the ways I could communicate by just saying his name. Therefore, this time, he knew it was my turn to be serious. His head came up and he looked into my eyes.

"Is he okay?" I asked.

"No," Eddie answered bluntly. "But he will be, soon as this shit's over and Stella gives in."

"Pardon?"

Eddie sighed then touched my mouth with his and dropped his forehead to mine, his thumb stroking my jaw.

When he spoke, he did it softly.

"Lotta wounds don't heal, Jet. Seein' your sister's head get blown off, I suspect, is one of 'em. Havin' a Dad, and not havin' one, I'm thinkin' you understand, is another. You got a good woman in your life, even though the wounds stay open, you move on, live life. The pain doesn't go away, but life has a different focus. A better one."

He was right. I had a Dad, but didn't have one most of my life. That wound had never healed. My Dad was an inveterate gambler. He was around a lot more now, getting his life sorted, but he could fall off the wagon at any time.

My sister and I lived with that knowledge and the fear that went with it, and it was no fun.

Finding Eddie and believing in us had given my life a different focus.

A better one.

However, with the recent, newly acquired knowledge that my fiancé, Detective Eddie Badass Chavez, snowboarded and his innate understanding of Mace's wounds, worried me.

My hands slid up the sleek, muscled skin of his back, one stopping at his shoulder blade, the other one sliding up his neck, my fingers sifting into his hair.

"Do you have a wound that won't heal?" I asked quietly, and braced myself for his answer.

He lifted his forehead from mine and his eyes dropped to my mouth.

"Lived a lucky life, *mi pequeña,*" he muttered. His eyes came back to mine and they were again liquid, but this time also filled with tenderness and affection and I felt my heart skip a beat. "And, *alabado sea Dios,* it keeps gettin' luckier."

Then he was done talking and he kissed me, deep and wet, and I was done talking, too.

His mouth slid down my neck to my chest where he murmured, "You're about to get lucky, too."

His mouth slid down further, then further, then he spread my legs and his mouth was *right there,* and he was very right. I got lucky, too.

After Eddie made me lucky with his talented mouth, he came up over me. He slid inside me, pounded deep and he got even luckier (and so did I).

When we were done, he turned out the light, rolled me so my back was to his front and he wrapped both arms around me. One went tight around my midriff. The other one went low, to cup me between my legs.

This was a new thing of Eddie's, holding me this way after we'd made love. It started a few weeks ago after I agreed to marry him. It was intimate, possessive and somehow claiming, even though I was already his.

I had to admit, I liked it.

"*Chiquita?*" Eddie called when I was just about ready to fall asleep.

"Hmm?"

"It's likely Stella doesn't know any of this shit."

My eyes opened.

Eddie went on, his voice holding a gentle warning, "It's Mace's to tell her."

I didn't say anything.

Eddie kept going. "You women talk. I'm askin' you not to talk about this."

"She should know," I replied.

"She should, but when he's ready to tell her."

"Eddie—"

He interrupted me, his voice firm, his arm and hand both tensed and I sucked in breath. "No, Jet."

I bit my lip.

Then I nodded.

I wouldn't tell Stella.

Unless I had to.

Chapter 10

Demons

Stella

"Fuck," Mace swore under his breath as we drove down the graveled drive next to Swen and Ulrika's mansion.

I knew why he was cursing. It was four o'clock in the morning and I'd been shot at (again!). Mace had just spent the last hours of his life being held back from murdering the guy who shot at me (this made him unhappy, me relieved) and talking to police. Now, upon arrival home, we both could see Eric, his arms crossed on his chest and his feet planted wide, standing illuminated in the outside light that hung over the side door to the house.

I sighed.

Loudly.

Eric watched our approach and I saw that his hair was even messier than normal, probably from running his fingers through it. Even though the light wasn't great, you could still tell he was pissed.

I figured he knew what went down that night.

Effing hell.

This was not a good situation. I knew Mace was not in a chipper mood. He was wired and he was angry, and Mace's brand of angry was pretty effing scary.

I didn't have the energy to deal with Mace's scary brand of anger, or Eric's for that matter. I had a lot going on in my head. I hadn't had a chance to process what happened onstage, considering the fact someone nearly shot me (again!). I also hadn't had the chance to avoid Mace in order to get my head together because I was too busy making calls to check on the band who, by the way, were all freaked way *the hell* out, but they were breathing, which in my crazy-ass life at the moment I took as a boon.

Further, when Mace came to The Castle, I took one look at him and I knew it would be beyond stupid to pour oil on *that* fire. So when he ordered me (without a greeting; just walked into Daisy's big room and said it) straight out to get to the car, instead of mouthing off, which I really wanted to do, I went to the car.

Now this.

Just in case you forgot, I'll remind you. My luck sucked.

Eric was approaching my side of the Explorer before Mace came to a full stop. Once the car halted, he yanked my door open, reached in, released my belt and pulled me out of the cab.

And now this!

As my boots hit the gravel, I started to say something. What, I did not know, but I didn't get the chance to get anything out.

"Hands off," Mace growled, rounding the hood of the SUV.

"Fuck you," Eric replied, clearly and insanely not reading Mace's scary-unhappy body language.

Lordy be.

"Eric," I said softly, trying to pull my arm free (and failing), and thinking I should defuse the already-heated situation.

Again, I didn't get the chance. Mace spoke before I could.

"I'll say it one more time, Turner. Hands off."

"And I'll say it one more time, Mason. Fuck you," Eric returned, yanking me toward his metallic-granite-colored Chevy Trailblazer.

Shitsofuckit!

Before I knew what was happening or I could utter a word, both men moved.

Fast.

I was thrown free of Eric. There was a scuffle and Mace and Eric ended the scuffle face-to-face, fingers curled into each other's tees.

"Stop it!" I shouted, rushing forward and shoving between their bodies to separate them (this failed, too, for your information). Still, my intervention kind of worked. They both pushed off with their hands, each taking a step back, but they continued the stare down.

Effing men.

I opened my mouth to speak, but to my increasing frustration, Eric got there before me.

"I'm taking her into protective custody," he announced.

Oh dear.

"The hell you are," Mace shot back.

"You aren't keepin' her safe," Eric returned.

"Yeah, and it's safe standin' out here fuckin' dealin' with you," Mace clipped, throwing his arm out to the night to make his point.

Eric switched subjects. "She got shot at."

"I know that," Mace retorted.

"Again," Eric pushed.

"I know that," Mace repeated, visibly losing what was left of his patience.

"Pong nearly got his head blown off." Eric kept at it, and I wondered how he knew that, but didn't have a chance to process that, either, because Mace lost his patience.

Leaning toward Eric, he roared, "*I fucking know that!*"

"I can keep her safe!" Eric shouted back.

"Yeah, like you kept Skinny Blackburn safe?" Mace returned, his tone shifting smoothly to quiet and dripping with sarcasm.

I blinked in confusion.

Skinny Blackburn? Who the eff was Skinny Blackburn?

I watched Eric wince and knew Mace scored a point.

Before I could butt in, Eric recovered and informed Mace, "I'll see to Stella personally."

Uh-oh. I was thinking that wasn't the right thing to say.

Mace, already tense, went solid, and his voice was now dangerous when he said softly, "I bet you will."

"Stop thinkin' with your dick, Mason, and be fuckin' smart," Eric warned.

That, I suspected, wasn't the right thing to say either.

"You got a minute to get the fuck out of here before I rip your goddamned head off," Mace snarled.

Yep, I was right. Not the right thing to say.

Eric ignored Mace, turned to me and ordered, "Get in the Blazer, Stella."

Oh shit.

I didn't have a chance to speak or move before Mace, not taking his eyes off Eric, said to me, "Stella, don't go near that fuckin' Blazer."

"For fuck's sake, get in the goddamned Blazer!" Eric yelled, also now talking to me while glaring at Mace and also losing patience.

Hmm.

Conundrum.

See, Eric was a Fed and I figured the federal government had the resources to make it unlikely that I would be riddled with bullets. And this was something which was looking uncomfortably more and more like it might happen in my near future.

But Eric also had a thing for me that I didn't have the emotional capacity to explore at the present moment, considering my life was in danger, not to mention a complete mess. One thing I knew, I didn't need to owe him.

Unh-unh.

No way.

On the other hand, Mace was a badass, hot guy. He and the Nightingale Team knew what they were doing. What happened tonight wasn't his fault. It was Monk's and it was mine. First, the boys wanted to give in and I didn't let them with what I now considered my immensely idiotic "I want a vote" speech. Second, we played the gig knowing the danger and the security challenge it represented. I knew Mace felt it was his fault, which I found upsetting. I didn't want to find it upsetting, but I couldn't help myself. I was over Mace (kind of, or at least I was still going with that thought), but I wasn't *that* over Mace.

However, I was trying to steer clear of Mace, and Eric was giving me a golden opportunity.

Shit.

What to do?

When I hesitated, Mace, his eyes still locked on Eric, spoke low. "Stella."

"My luck sucks," I declared, because I hadn't made a decision and I was stalling for time, and, of course, it was the truth.

"Stella, sweetheart, get in the Blazer," Eric coaxed, eyes still on Mace.

"You call her 'sweetheart' one more fuckin' time, I'll shove your teeth down your throat," Mace growled.

Oh no. It appeared the impossible was happening and things were degenerating.

Eric grinned a humorless grin and jerked his chin at Mace.

"Let's go," he invited.

Yikes!

Mace took a step forward. Eric stood his ground but brought up his fists.

"Oh for goodness sake, stop it!" I shouted, getting between them again and putting a palm on each of their chests.

I made a split-second, scary-as-shit decision and turned to Eric.

"What happened tonight wasn't his fault, Eric. They had tons of men there. Monk's an asshole, you know that. He was worried about the money. He didn't do thorough searches so he could get people in the door."

Eric looked down at me. "You shouldn't have been up there in the first fuckin' place."

He had a point.

"No, maybe not," I allowed. "But we don't play, Buzz and Leo don't eat. We had no choice."

"You're dead, so are The Gypsies, then they *really* don't eat," Eric returned.

Another excellent point.

I pressed on, "Eric, I have people who count on me. The band... my dog." I petered out because that was kind of it and it sounded lame. Still, I kept going. "I have responsibilities. I can't disappear. The other Rock Chicks are on the line and I'm the one who put them there."

Eric took a step back. I felt a moment of relief that he was backing down and I dropped my hands. Mace took a step forward so we were close. Eric's eyes narrowed on us and my relief was swept away, but unusually luckily, Eric let it pass.

"How in the fuck did *you* put them there?" Eric asked me.

"Don't answer that, Stella," Mace broke into our conversation, and Eric's brows snapped together in annoyance. But before he could say anything, Mace continued. "You need to get inside."

Mace was right. I'd been shot at twice in less than a week and hit once. It was a graze, but still. I felt exposed and I didn't like it.

I moved away from Mace and got in Eric's space, attempting some form of damage control.

"Thank you for coming tonight and wanting to help, but I'll be okay," I told him quietly.

He looked down at me and his face went soft, his eyes went warm and I realized, unfortunately belatedly in our relationship, that he wasn't just good-looking. He was *really* good-looking.

And maybe he was a nice guy.

Sheesh.

My fucking luck.

"Yeah, you will, because I'll be keepin' an eye on you," Eric replied, his voice as soft and warm as his eyes. Then he leaned toward me and went on, "You need anything, Stella, you know how to get me. Anytime, you call."

"Thank you for that, too," I whispered.

"We're done," Mace announced on a growl, and my mini-moment with Eric ended when Eric's eyes sliced angrily toward Mace. "Inside," Mace continued.

"I'll be keepin' an eye on you, too," Eric warned Mace, all softness and warmth out of his voice.

Mace put his hand in the small of my back and pushed me toward the door.

What he didn't do was respond.

❦

I woke up to Mace's mouth at my neck, his hand trailing whisper-soft along my belly.

Against my sleepy volition, my body shivered.

Effing hell.

"Mace," I breathed, my voice throatier than normal with sleep and other things besides.

He didn't respond. Instead, his other hand slid under my body, going up to cup my breast, the trailing fingers of his hand at my belly starting to move downward.

Both felt nice.

Really nice.

Shitsofuckit!

Last night, after the Eric Fiasco, Mace had taken Juno out for a bathroom break while I got ready for bed. When he returned, he got on the phone and Juno and I hit the hay. To my surprise, even after all the drama, I crashed almost immediately, falling asleep listening to what I suspected was Mace debriefing with who I assumed was Lee.

Now, I was laying partially on my belly, partially on my side; my leg crooked deep, Mace's body pressed tight to me, his leg crooked into mine.

"Mace," I repeated, my sleepy-weak resistance already flagging.

We needed to talk about a lot of things and I needed *not* to have sex with him again. I was beginning to think I was giving him the wrong impression.

Hell, who was I kidding? How could he *not* have the wrong impression?

"Quiet, Kitten, I wanna listen to you come," Mace murmured into my neck as his hand pushed into my panties.

His words made my body shiver again.

"We need to talk," I told him, holding on to my failing resistance, but his finger honed in on the target and pressed deep.

Oh lordy be.

My hips jerked and involuntarily, I started purring. I couldn't help myself, it felt nice.

What was the matter with me?

Did I have *no* willpower?

"We'll talk later," Mace declared, his deep voice smooth as velvet.

"We need to talk now," my mouth protested even as my hips pressed into his hand.

"Later," Mace returned, and I wanted to say something, honest I did, but there was some lovely circling at the target. Then his hand moved lower and his finger slid slowly, *deliciously* inside.

"Oh my," I whispered, my eyes closing and my head tilting back until it hit his shoulder.

All of a sudden, I didn't care what impression I was giving. I just wanted his finger never to stop what it was doing.

I turned to face him and he didn't hesitate. His mouth was on mine and he was kissing me, hard and deep, as his finger moved slowly in and out and my hips moved with it.

It felt effing *great*.

"Sweet, wet, silk," Mace whispered against my mouth. His words trembled through me and I purred against his lips.

It was then the sound of a buzzer I never heard tore through the room.

Erm, what was *that*?

Mace's finger stopped. My eyes opened slowly and he muttered, "Fuck."

"What's that?" I asked just as the buzzer went again, this time for longer.

"Fuck," Mace repeated, his finger sliding gently out of me. I felt his heat leave me as his body moved away.

"Sorry, babe, door," he said as explanation.

He kissed my shoulder, threw the covers back and knifed out of bed.

Juno, who was standing by the door staring up at the alarm panel, woofed in doggie confusion. She'd never heard the buzzer, either.

I watched Mace stalk naked to the door and tried to get my body back under my control.

This was difficult, mostly because I was seriously turned on, but also watching Mace's naked body doing anything only managed to make me more turned on.

Okay, this was ridiculous. Somehow, I was going to have to get control of my Inner Mace Slut.

Mace hit a button and bit out, "What?"

I saw Hector's face fill the video screen. "We got a problem."

My body went tense as I watched Mace's do the same.

"Everybody okay?" Mace asked.

"Yeah, this is a different problem," Hector answered.

Beautiful.

Just what we needed.

A *different* problem.

"Shit," Mace cursed, obviously agreeing with me. "Come up." Then he hit a button and turned to me. I watched, my breath catching as his hard face grew soft and his voice dipped low. "Kitten, you need to get dressed."

The soft face/sweet low voice thing was another one of those seven hundred twenty-five thousand things I missed about him most of all.

I ignored how that made me feel and kept my eyes on him while I threw the covers back.

Juno woofed again, just to remind us of her presence, her need for a bathroom break, and probably, her desire to have breakfast. I got out of bed as Mace ruffled the fur on Juno's head then walked to the edge of the platform, grabbed his jeans and pulled them on commando.

There was something very sexy about Mace going commando.

Very sexy.

Down, Mace Slut! My brain commanded.

I shook thoughts of Mace going commando out of my head and went to the closet. I yanked on a pair of jeans, a bra and a purple t-shirt that read "Olde Town Pickin' Parlor" over the headstock and neck of a guitar. While I was dressing, I heard Mace open the door and greet Hector.

By the time I came out of the walk-in closet, Mace and Hector were in my small kitchen and both were standing, hips against the counter. Mace had pulled on a white tee, had a copy of the *Denver Post* in his hands and he was reading the front page.

"Hey Hector," I said, speaking to him directly for the first time in my life.

His hot black eyes came to me and I felt their scorch like a physical touch on my skin.

"Stella," he replied.

Wow.

It must be said, Hector had great eyes.

Mace's head came up from the paper and he looked between Hector and me. Hector didn't take his eyes off me nor did those eyes cool.

My body did another involuntary shiver.

Mace's mouth got tight right before he said, "Could you make coffee, babe?"

At that moment, I thought coffee was an excellent idea, even better than I normally thought of the idea coffee, and let's just say I liked my coffee a lot. Making it would give me something to do other than think of Mace *and* Hector.

I nodded, mumbled, "Sure," and scooted toward the coffeepot through what small kitchen space was left with two tall, muscled men in it.

I started to prepare coffee and heard the paper rustling.

"What's going on?" I asked.

"Front page news," Hector answered what I thought was nonsensically.

I turned to him, empty coffeepot in my hand, my mind on how to get to the sink Hector was leaning against without coming into contact with him, and I asked, "What?"

He jerked his head to the paper Mace now had opened and I saw the front page.

I looked at it and my eyes widened in shock when I saw *me* on the cover.

It was a half-body shot from the hips up, guitar in my hands, the mic in front of me, my head tilted down and to the side to look at my guitar, a small smile on my face. The photo was taken at a gig that, I suspected from the t-shirt I had on (which I hadn't worn in ages), was at least a year ago.

Next to my photo was the same size picture of a younger-looking Mace at the bottom of a snowy mountain in full-snowboarder gear, hair tousled and wet with sweat, board under his arm. Other photographers surrounding him, he was ignoring them and caught on the move by the cameras.

The headline read, *Local Celebrities under Fire.*

"Effing hell," I breathed right when the phone rang.

"Dammit," Mace muttered, tossing the paper on the counter and reaching up to the ledge where I kept my phone. He put it to his ear and barked, "What?"

I was too much in a dither to mind Mace being rude while answering my phone. I was focused on being front page news *and* being referred to as a "celebrity".

I knew Mace had been famous, but when did *I* become a celebrity?

"She has no comment," Mace said into the phone. He hesitated then continued, "I have no comment either," then he beeped it off and put it on the counter.

I stared at him a beat, letting the words "no comment" permeate my stunned brain, and with effort came unstuck, handed the empty pot to Mace and snatched the paper off the counter.

I was beginning to feel weird. Way weird. Panic weird. I didn't know why, but it didn't feel good.

"Stella…" Mace started to say but I wasn't listening.

I wandered out of the kitchen area. Juno got close and gave a little whine.

"In a minute, Juno," I mumbled, my eyes scanning the page.

"I'll take the dog out." I heard Hector say, but I didn't pay attention.

I arrived at the end of the bed platform and sat. I no sooner got my ass on the platform when the paper was snatched from my hands before I'd been able to read a single word.

My head snapped up.

"Hey! I was reading that," I semi-lied to Mace who was standing over me.

The door closed behind Hector and Juno.

"Fuck it, Stella. We need to stay focused," Mace replied.

I stood. 'Focused on what?'

When I stood, it brought me close to Mace. He didn't move out of my space, just kept looking down at me.

"Focused on what's important," he answered calmly.

"Being front page news isn't important?" I retorted, not calm at all.

I'd never been front page news. I didn't know how it made me feel. It was both weirdly thrilling and scary-as-shit. But also, that strange panic was still encroaching. I still didn't get it and I didn't want to. I had enough to panic about as it was.

"No," Mace broke into my thoughts.

"Then what's important?"

"Keepin' you alive. Workin' out our shit. Movin' on together. That's what's important."

I shook my head at his words, not awake enough or together enough after last night's drama and this morning's position on page one to go there.

I changed subjects. "Who was on the phone?"

"Doesn't matter."

"Who was on the phone, Mace?" I asked again.

He opened his mouth to speak and the phone rang again. My eyes moved to it. Mace's upper body twisted and he looked over his shoulder to look at it, too.

It rang a second time and Mace turned back to me just as I launched myself, moving quickly around him, toward the phone.

I was almost there when Mace hooked an arm around my waist, hauled me into his body and reached around me. I was reaching, too, but his effing arms were longer and he tagged the phone.

He beeped it on and put it to his ear.

"Yeah?" he clipped just as I shouted, "Mace!"

He listened for two seconds then said, "We have nothing to say," then he beeped it off again.

"I cannot believe you just did that! It's *my* phone!" I yelled, struggling against his arm, which was still tight at my waist.

He shook me. "Stella, calm down and listen to me."

"Let go!"

He did but only so I could take a step forward. Once I did, he grabbed my hand, twirled me and brought me back to him, front to front.

He placed the phone on the counter, put both arms around my struggling body and tilted his head down to look at me.

"Listen," he ordered.

I stopped pulling away from him and looked at his face.

"This is unreal," I stated the obvious.

"Reporters are fuckwads. We don't talk to them. Ignore it. Don't read it. Say nothing. Don't pay any fuckin' attention. This'll be over and they'll move on to new meat."

"I can't ignore it!" I snapped.

"Why the fuck not?"

I didn't know why not. My life was so out-of-control, it didn't feel like I knew anything anymore.

"I know you have experience with this, Mace, but I don't," I told him.

"That's why you need to listen to me," Mace returned.

Then it came out. It came from someplace buried deep. Someplace I thought was locked away for good, never to be opened again.

The panic overwhelmed me and my body started trembling. It was so huge I quit fighting and melted into Mace. My head tilting back further, I put my hands to his chest and my shaking fingers curled into his white tee.

I heard the tremor in my voice when I asked, "What if my mother sees that?"

Mace's face had been hard with determination, but at my words his face and his green eyes went soft.

"Kitten," he murmured.

"I'm not big news, but maybe you still are," I told him. "What if it makes the news where she is? I need to talk to the reporters, tell them I'm okay, tell them you and Lee and the boys know what you're doing. Tell them the police are involved. The Feds, too. Tell them that Sid's a prick and he killed Linnie and we're doing the right thing."

"Stella, we can't tell them any of that shit."

My fists grew tighter on Mace's shirt.

"She has to know we're doing the right thing."

Mace studied my face a beat and his head dipped closer to mine.

Then, quietly, he asked, "Your Mom does or your Dad does?"

I blinked.

"What?"

"You want your Mom to know you're doin' the right thing? Or you want your Dad to know?"

I shook my head. "I don't care about Dad."

"Kitten—"

My body went still and I shouted, "I don't!" right in his face.

I didn't know why I shouted, I just did.

I also didn't know why I was trembling and feeling panicked, I just was. Big time.

I started to pull away again, thinking only of escape. Where to, I had no idea, but I had to get there, right... effing... now.

Unfortunately, Mace was ready for me.

He turned us, picked me up with his hands at my waist and planted my ass on the counter. Then he moved in with so much determination his hips forced my legs open at the knees and he kept coming until he was ultra-close. We were chest to chest, privates to privates, nose to nose. He put his hands on the counter on either side of me.

"Talk to me, babe," he demanded softly.

I turned my face to the side and stared at the counter.

Something was happening to me, something very frightening, and there was only one thing I knew—I couldn't deal.

I needed to lock it down.

Mace didn't feel like letting me lock it down. His hands came to my neck and he moved my head to face him. His thumbs at my jaw, he forced me to look up at him.

"Talk to me," he repeated, and his eyes looked strange. He was looking at me in a way he'd never looked at me before. It was a warm look, but if I was reading it right, it was filled with concern. So much concern it looked a lot like worry. And all that was mingled with such tenderness, at the sight of it, my breath didn't take a flight, it beamed to another galaxy.

"I can't," I whispered.

The phone rang again and we let it, staring at each other.

Mace didn't move. Neither did I.

The phone stopped ringing and Mace's face came closer, his forehead resting on mine.

"They don't know where you are," he said, and it wasn't a question.

I didn't answer, but my non-answer was an answer.

"You don't want them to know where you are." Mace made another statement and I kept quiet. "You don't want them to know," he repeated. "You don't want them to know so much that you'd sabotage your career by turning down the scouts. Keepin' yourself secluded here, doin' small-time gigs rather than lettin' yourself be what you're supposed to be."

I swallowed.

He was digging deep into a place he wasn't allowed to be. A place I didn't let anyone visit, not even myself, and my trembling body started shaking.

I put my hands to his chest and pushed.

He didn't budge.

"Move away, Mace," I whispered.

"You lied to Daisy. You aren't just scarred. You're broken."

I was beginning to breathe heavily.

"Move away."

Mace changed tactics. "They can't hurt you anymore."

I felt them then, the tears sliding up the back of my throat, my sinuses tingling.

I swallowed again. This time it hurt.

"Please, move away."

"I won't let them. Floyd won't let them. Fuck, if Hugo heard them say one nasty thing against you, he'd tear them apart. You have people who care about you now, Kitten. They can't get at you. You can let it go. You can shine."

For some reason, I said, "They can get at me."

"Kitten."

At his soft, deep voice uttering his sweet, special name for me with his face so close, his eyes all I could see, I exposed myself in a way I'd never exposed myself to anyone. Not friends, not bandmates, not even Floyd.

"*He* can get at me," I said so softly I could barely hear myself.

Mace closed his eyes and his hands moved from my neck, down my back and he wrapped his arms around me, but he didn't take his forehead from mine.

I hated to admit it, but his arms around me like that felt good.

No, if I was honest, they felt *great*.

I couldn't deal with that, either.

His eyes opened again and they drilled into mine. "He can't."

I nodded my head.

Mace shook his.

I put my hands on either side of his neck and squeezed gently.

"You don't get it," I whispered.

"I get it."

"You can't."

He pressed even closer. His voice got lower and I watched in horrified fascination as something tremendously frightening happened.

Earth-shatteringly frightening.

World-rockingly frightening.

I watched, my breath held, as the guard I never knew Mace kept firmly in place faded clean away.

"Babe," he murmured fiercely. "I *can*."

That was when I slid out of my pain, out of my panic, and I saw them, clear as day, dancing malevolently behind his beautiful eyes.

Demons.

Mace had demons.

And they were far worse than anything I could even imagine.

Sinister tingles slithered down my back as a savage, steel-toed boot hit me straight in the gut. It was so savage, my body jerked with it and I sucked in breath, staring speechless at the open torment in Mace's eyes.

Before I could say anything (not that I knew what to say), the phone rang and the buzzer went on the door.

The moment was lost.

The guard slammed down over his features and he stepped away. Snatching the phone off the counter, he stalked to the door.

What was THAT? My brain asked me.

I was still trembling, now for a different reason.

I have no idea, I told my brain.

Juno bounded in before Hector and Mace muttered, "No comment," into the phone again while I watched.

What are we gonna do? My brain asked.

I swallowed, more scared now than when bullets were pounding in the dirt all around me. More scared than I'd ever been in my whole fucking life.

I have no effing idea, I answered.

Chapter 11

First World Tour

Stella

I had no time to figure it out.

Juno butted my calf with her nose with such strength my whole body shifted to the side, telling me in no uncertain terms it was breakfast time.

I'd already left her in the clutches of an unknown, but hot (not that "hot" factored in Juno's choice for companions, but still, it must be said) Hispanic guy for her morning bathroom break. I was heading for Worst Doggie Mom of the Year if I didn't at least take care of the bare necessities.

"All right, baby," I murmured, jumping down from the counter.

Juno knew what my motion meant. She wagged her tail in response and her whole body went with it.

"We gotta roll." I heard Hector say as I nabbed Juno's bowl from the floor.

"Yeah," Mace replied. "Give me a second."

I looked up to see him coming my way.

I straightened and backed up two steps, still in the throes of a jumble of strong emotions, none of which I could process at the moment considering my dog was starving.

"I got things to do," Mace told me, stopping close, and I tilted my head back to look up at him.

"Okay."

Mace going was good. No, it was *great*. It meant I could nap. It meant I could play my guitar. It meant I could call Ally and process every second of the last twelve hours. Or, better yet, pull together a clever disguise and skip town.

Mace took the bowl from my hand and put it on the counter.

Juno whined, unhappy with this turn of events.

"I have to feed Juno," I informed Mace.

"In a second."

My poor Juno.

Mace continued speaking. "You answer the phone, it's a reporter, you say 'no comment' and hang up. Got me?"

"Mace—"

"Stella, no comment. I don't want that shit in my life. Not again."

My head jerked a bit to the side and I felt a mini-gut kick at his words and the harsh undercurrent with which he said them.

I wondered what he meant, but I didn't ask because I was telling myself I didn't want to know (when, in reality, I did).

Do you *see* how messed up my head was?

"Stella, tell me you got me," Mace pressed.

"I got you," I muttered, giving in so I could feed my dog and because I didn't want that in Mace's life either (and, unfortunately for Juno, not in that order).

It seemed my luck was going to be even shittier than normal that morning because we weren't done.

Mace got closer and shifted. He did this so his back was to Hector and I was hidden from him. Mace put his hand to my neck and dipped his face toward mine.

His eyes were back to guarded, but they were still warm when they looked deep into mine.

"We good?" he asked softly.

I didn't know if he was asking if we were good about what happened on-stage last night. Or if we were good about what happened with Eric. Or if we were good about the interrupted bed action that morning. Or if we were good about the crazy-scary shit that happened in the kitchen five minutes ago.

Since the answer was the same for all of them, I said, "No."

This made him smile.

Which made my toes curl.

He bent in, touched his lips to mine, giving me a neck squeeze at the same time. Then, lips still on mine, he promised, "We will be."

That gave the toe curl the addition of a full body tremble.

He gave me another neck squeeze then walked away and I stood motionless in the kitchen watching him move toward one of his bags. For some reason my skin started to feel hot, so my eyes shifted toward Hector who was standing, arms crossed on his chest, gaze on me, mouth curled in a sexy grin.

Sheesh.

I came unstuck and did the only thing I could do (legally) at that moment.

I got down to the business of feeding my dog.

Mace was sitting on the edge of the bed platform tugging on his boots when the buzzer went.

"Jesus Christ," Mace muttered and Hector moved toward the panel.

I bent to put the bowl of food on the floor and Juno shoved her face in it before it was settled. I was rubbing down her body when I heard the disembodied voice of Hugo in the room.

"We gotta know a secret password or what?"

"It's the band," Hector told Mace.

I will note he told Mace, not me.

"Let them in," I said.

"I'll talk to them," Mace said at the same time, getting up and walking toward the door.

Erm, what?

Now wait just one effing minute.

"You can just let them in," I told Mace as I followed him.

"Stay here with Stella. I'll be back with the band." Mace ignored me and spoke to Hector.

"Mace!" I snapped. "Just let them in."

Mace turned to face me. "We'll be right up."

My eyes narrowed on him. "What's going on?"

"I just want to get a few things straight with the band."

I did not *think* so.

"About what?" I pushed.

"About 'no comment'."

Oh.

Okay.

I could see that.

Mace and I both knew everyone, including the grieving Buzz, would be happily loose-lipped with reporters unless warned. Especially if they thought they could get The Blue Moon Gypsies and any of our gig dates in print.

"You can talk to them up here," I told him.

"I'm talkin' to them downstairs."

"Mace."

"Stella."

"Jesus, is someone gonna let us in or what?" Pong's disembodied voice didn't come through the panel. We could hear him shouting from outside.

"Two seconds," Hector said into the speaker, and before I could say another word, Mace was gone.

I looked at the door then at Hector and remarked angrily, "He's annoying."

"He's probably got his reasons," Hector replied.

"And I should care about those reasons because...?" I prompted.

Hector didn't hesitate. "You don't have to care about 'em, you just gotta understand he has 'em."

I glared at Hector for a beat.

Whatever.

It was then I realized I was alone with Hector and it was then I remembered to feel uncomfortable.

I stared at him.

He grinned at me.

All of a sudden I didn't know what to do or say. All I could think about was Mace telling me that in twenty-four hours, Hector would have me flat on my back, him on top and both of us would be naked.

And this didn't seem like a bad idea.

Oh my God, you are SUCH a slut, my brain remarked.

This was all communicated to Hector on some Hot Guy Secret Wavelength and his grin turned to a wolfish but highly effective smile.

Effing hell.

Thankfully, he threw me a bone.

"You were makin' coffee?" he reminded me.

"Oh yeah, right," I muttered and then scooted into the kitchen.

I grabbed the pot, filled it with water and turned to the coffeemaker while Hector joined me in the kitchen. I would have preferred him to stay further away (say, Alaska) but I didn't have a choice, and I didn't want to ask him because he'd think I was a slutty wuss.

I poured the water into the coffeemaker and tucked some hair behind my ear.

"So..." I searched desperately for conversation, wondering how long it would take to tell the band they had two words they could say to reporters and other than that they had to keep their mouths shut, and I figured, with my band, it would take approximately eighty-two hours.

I was going to have to make a lot of conversation.

I glanced at Hector. "Do you have a girlfriend?"

Now why did I ask that?

Why, why, why?

"Nope," Hector replied.

"No one special?" I went on.

Shut up! My brain screamed.

"Didn't say that," Hector answered.

Interesting. My brain was no longer screaming.

I shoved the pot under the spout, flipped the switch and looked at him fully.

"There's someone special?" I asked.

He didn't answer.

"But she's not your girlfriend?"

He crossed his arms on his chest, leaned a hip against the counter and again didn't answer.

"Who is she?"

"She's not a Rock Chick," he told me. "She's rich. She's unbelievably fuckin' beautiful. She made the first move and then shut me down so she's gonna have to make the second move, too."

I blinked.

This seemed a lot of sharing for a badass tough guy. A badass tough guy I barely knew.

I was curious to know what shutting Hector down entailed and why any woman in her right mind would do such a ridiculous thing, but I was too much of a scaredy-cat to ask.

"And what do you do until she makes the second move?" I asked because she would make the second move, no doubt about it. She'd be crazy not to.

He was back to grinning and he answered, "I have fun."

Oh lordy be.

I knew what Hot Guy Fun consisted of. I'd had a dose of it that morning with Mace's hand in my panties.

Whoever-she-was, she better hurry up.

All of a sudden, Hector said, "You're good."

I stared at him. My mind still on whoever she was and hot guys' hands in my panties, I wasn't following.

"What?"

"I've seen you play, at The Little Bear, Herman's, The Gothic. You're good."

I had compliments before, even compliments from hot guys, even compliments from hot guys who wanted to get in my panties. Likely, they were complimenting me *because* they wanted to get in my panties.

But something about the simple way Hector shared his opinion felt different, more honest. I knew innately that he wasn't the type of guy who threw meaningless compliments around for the eff of it.

I felt my cheeks getting warm, turned away to look at the filling coffeepot and muttered, "Thanks," hoping he'd move on to a different subject. This one was even more uncomfortable than the last.

I felt his body heat and it was both immense and close.

I looked up to see he'd closed the distance and was inches away.

Yikes!

Before I could say anything, he spoke.

"What I wanna know is," he started softly, "what the fuck you're still doin' in Denver?"

I was finding it hard to breathe, seeing as he was close. His heat was hitting me, he was seriously good-looking and I had nowhere to retreat.

I persevered, "I live here."

"No, I mean you and the band. Anybody who sees you play knows they got a bargain. They should be payin' top arena prices to watch the likes of you."

I was no longer finding it hard to breathe. I was just not breathing *at all*.

Did he really say that?

He kept going. "You need a decent manager. You should be on the road. You should go to LA. You should get under the nose of some scouts."

"I've talked to scouts," I broke in.

"And?"

"I like where I am."

I watched as surprise crossed his features and he muttered, "You're shittin' me."

"No, really, this is good."

He shook his head. "You're better."

I felt that weird panic edging into me, but it was connected with the same thrill of being on the front page of *The Denver Post*.

"This is good," I repeated, ignoring the panic and the thrill.

"You're better," he repeated, too.

"You don't understand." I sighed and pressed myself against the counter to get a little space, but this didn't work because he leaned in. I stared in fascination as his face grew hard.

"No, I don't. I don't have a gift. Been watchin' yours for a while now and wonderin' why you don't share it with more people." He paused and got even closer before he asked, "You wanna tell me why?"

"Not really," I answered, and it was the truth.

Not only was it the truth, it was none of his business.

I barely knew this guy!

Granted, he told me about whoever-she-was, but this wasn't share and share alike.

Unh-unh.

No way.

He stared at me.

I stared back.

He stared at me some more.

I stared back some more.

Then he moved away an inch and said, "I fuckin' hope Mace can talk some sense into you."

"Once this is done, so are Mace and I," I informed him bitchily.

I watched his brows go up right before he burst out laughing, throwing his head back and everything.

I crossed my arms on my chest.

"What's so damn funny?" I snapped.

When he stopped laughing, his face was still warm with it, and if I thought he was good-looking before, I was wrong. *Now*, he was just plain beautiful.

"You are, *mamita*. You're fuckin' hilarious."

"Am not," I returned, sounding like a six year old and also not caring. He was freaking me out!

Hector leaned in again. "You are, and I'll want fuckin' backstage passes when you're on your first world tour."

"Right," I muttered dismissively, but feeling the panic and thrill slice through me again.

"Right," Hector replied firmly.

The door opened and I was saved from further discourse with Hot Hector by my loud band storming in, led by Mace.

It took Mace a millisecond to notice Hector and me in a close squeeze in the kitchen and it took another millisecond for his temper to flare.

"What the fuck?" he asked.

"I was making coffee," I explained immediately, sounding stupid.

"Thank God. Coffee!" Leo exclaimed, making a beeline toward the kitchen.

"Be cool, *hombre*. We were just havin' a chat," Hector put in, exiting the kitchen as Leo entered.

"I hope that fuckin' coffee's strong," Hugo grumbled.

"A chat?" Mace asked.

"Yeah, nothin' to get excited about," Hector replied, but I watched and Mace didn't look like he believed Hector.

"Is there gonna be enough coffee for everyone?" Buzz asked.

"It's not even finished brewing yet!" Pong shouted like the coffee was going to take three years to brew and that was the only sustenance he was allowed.

Juno shifted her big dog body out of the small space as the male, human, Blue Moon Gypsy bodies pressed toward the coffeepot. I took my opportunity and followed her.

I was done.

D-o-n-e, done.

I stomped straight to the bed, Juno leading the way, and when we made it there, she jumped up on the bed and I looked at her.

"Why me?" I asked my dog.

Juno woofed.

"Why can't I be a lesbian?" I continued.

Juno sat down, her tail sweeping the bedclothes in a wide arc, her tongue lolling out the side of her mouth, her inability to speak English hindering our counseling session.

"Why couldn't I form an all-girl band like The Go-Gos?" I went on.

"The Go-Gos! Surfer-girl music? Shee-it. You crazy?" Hugo called from behind me.

I turned so my back was to the bed and flopped down. I threw my arm over my eyes and tried to pretend I was on a beach. A deserted beach. A deserted beach thousands of miles away from civilization.

Juno got down on her belly and snuffled my neck with her big, wet nose.

Well, okay, a deserted beach thousands of miles away from civilization, but with Juno with me.

I dug my fingers in the fur of her head, scratching behind her ears.

Juno licked my face.

I felt something on either side of my knees, which were bent at the edge of the bed. Then the bed depressed and I took my hand from Juno's fur and lifted my arm from my face.

Mace was in push up position, his body looming over mine, bent at the waist, his hands in the bed on either side of my body.

I could see the bunched-up muscles in his upper arms and I felt a warm rush between my legs.

Down, Mace Slut! My brain cautioned.

What was the matter with me?

"Babe, I gotta go," Mace said softly.

"Okay," I replied.

"Remember, no comment."

I sighed, then said, "I remember."

"When I get home tonight, we'll have dinner and talk."

Mace referring to my place as "home" caused that panicky feeling to emerge again, right along with the thrill.

"Fine," I said.

"Use the alarm," he went on.

"Gotcha."

"I'll call sometime today."

"Mace, are you gonna go or what?" I was losing patience and my ability to hold back the panic, thrill and the warm rush at his proximity.

He grinned and bent his elbows until his chest was brushing mine. He kissed me hard but closed-mouthed, then did a push-up and he was gone.

I closed my eyes and wondered what to do next.

I didn't get a chance to form a plan. Something big hit the bed and both Juno and I bounced with it.

I opened my eyes as I heard the door open. Pong had jumped on the head of the bed, flat on his back. I looked toward the door and saw Mace and Hector were leaving.

"Later, Hector," I called and watched him casually lift a hand in response, total cool.

"Is the coffee ready yet?" Pong yelled to Leo, who was standing in my kitchen staring at the nearly full pot.

"We're close," Leo answered.

There was more movement on the bed when Floyd sat down.

I looked at him.

He looked concerned.

He also looked something else. Something frightening. Something I sensed had to do with Mace's demons. Something that was somewhere I *did not* want to go.

"You okay?" he asked softly.

"No," I replied honestly.

"Is anyone gonna ask *me* if I'm okay? It was my fuckin' head that nearly got blown off," Pong demanded.

"They were aimin' at Stella Bella," Buzz commented, throwing himself on his side lengthwise at the foot of the bed.

"So?" Pong snapped.

My eyes moved to Pong. "Are you okay?"

Pong looked at me, lost his annoyance and grinned. "Sure. Bitches were all over me last night. Bein' in mortal danger appears to be an aphrodisiac."

I rolled my eyes back in my head.

"You're a fuckin' idiot," Buzz said to Pong.

"A fuckin' idiot who had a foursome last night," Pong shot back.

Oh lordy.

"I'm too old for this shit," Floyd muttered.

The phone rang and I got up on my elbows and watched Hugo move toward it.

"No comment, Hugo," I reminded him.

"I speak English not Swahili, mama. I heard Mace. I hear you. Jesus," he paused, beeped on the phone and greeted, "Yeah?"

I flopped back down on the bed, re-thinking my career path. Then re-thinking my romantic path. Then my careening thoughts conjured up a sketch of a woman who would be silly enough to shut Hector down. Then the look in Mace's unguarded eyes flashed before mine and I got a full body shiver.

I heard Hugo say from above me, "Stella, it's Monk."

I opened my eyes to see Hugo standing at the side of the bed.

Effing hell.

I did an ab curl and reached a hand out for the phone.

I wasn't looking forward to this conversation.

Monk had had someone with a rifle in his club last night. Worse, that someone fired the rifle. Even worse, Monk had missed out on post-gig last call due to a frenzied stampede. Even *worse*, Monk would have no entertainment tonight. We were set to play there again and there was no way in hell we were going to do that.

"Monk," I said into the phone.

"Stella, beautiful," Monk gushed exuberantly, not sounding angry at all.

Erm, what?

"Monk, I'm sorry about—" I started.

"Did you see *The Denver Post?*" Monk interrupted me.

"Um, no," I told him. "Not exactly."

He didn't care if I saw it or not and I knew this when he announced, "The Palladium was mentioned five times in *The Post*. Best advertising you can get, fuckin' free! This is shit-hot." Monk continued speaking happily in my ear. "We're gonna double the cover charge tonight. We'll make a killing."

He wasn't serious.

"Monk, we can't play tonight," I said.

Silence then, "Why the fuck not?"

I looked around at my band. They were all watching me.

"Well, because we got shot at last night," I explained.

"So?" Monk asked.

"With a rifle," I went on.

"And?" Monk pressed.

"Pong nearly got his head blown off," I continued.

"Last night, Pong had women drippin' off him," Monk returned. "That boy hasn't been that lucky since the University of Colorado women's volleyball team came to see your show."

I remembered the night the volleyball team came to see the show. That hadn't been a good night, at least not for me, and definitely not for Mace. It had ended in a five o'clock in the morning phone call that saw Mace extricating Pong from a situation where Pong lost all his clothes (but his black bikini briefs) in a game of strip poker. When he tried to get them back, he'd learned how strong a gaggle of college-aged female athletes could be. And let's just say that Mace hadn't been all that thrilled to have Pong sitting in the front seat of his silver Chevy Avalanche wearing only his black bikini briefs.

"Even so—" I continued to try to convince Monk of the seriousness of the situation, which kind of pissed me off, considering there should be no convincing to do.

"Stella, you're playin'," Monk broke in.

"Monk, you can't think—"

"I can and I do. You don't play tonight you never play the Palladium again," Monk threatened.

My body got tight.

"Monk!"

"Not only that, Stella, you don't play tonight, I start talkin' to the other club owners. Talkin' about shit like wandin', searches and that fuckin' Mace guy gettin' in my face and puttin' his hands on me."

Effing hell.

"Monk, listen to me, we can't play tonight. It's too dangerous."

"No, Stella, you listen to me. You play tonight or you don't play in Denver. Anywhere in Denver. Ever again."

"Are you threatening me?" I snapped.

"It's not a threat. Trust me."

My luck sucked!

Before I could retort, the phone was ripped from my hand and I watched Hugo put it to his ear.

"Monk, you got Hugo," he said into the phone, his deep, velvet voice an angry purr. "Yeah," he went on. "No, you listen to me, you circus freak cracker. We play tonight, you double the cover and we get the take."

I stared in shock at Hugo's words as Hugo paused for a few beats then kept talking.

"Quiet, you're listenin' to me now, motherfucker."

The angry purr got angrier and I held my breath.

"You open the doors an hour early to get folks in. You follow the security protocol to the letter. The… fuckin'… letter. You understand?" Hugo paused again, nodded his head once then went on, "We play thirty minute sets, not forty-five. You put signs up that say no bags, purses or backpacks allowed." I heard yelling come from the phone, but Hugo forged ahead. "No one wearin' bulky clothes, either. No jackets, no sweatshirts, nothin'. The minute you hit code maximum, you close the doors. No one gets in unless someone goes out. We clear, motherfucker?"

There was more yelling coming from the phone and I glanced around at the band. Leo was in the kitchen, three empty coffee cups dangling forgotten from his fingers. Floyd had angry eyes narrowed on the phone. Pong was grinning. Buzz was biting his lip.

I looked back at Hugo when he started speaking again.

"You try to fuck The Gypsies, we got problems. You don't want problems with me, motherfucker. I know you like toot, I know who you get your toot from and I know you're tappin' his piece. He's a serious guy and he don't like sharin', 'specially with a circus freak cracker. You want him to stay in the dark and you to stay supplied with blow, not to mention your piece of ass, you keep your fuckin' mouth shut. Now, are we clear?"

Silence from Hugo and the phone.

Then Hugo said, "Damn straight, motherfucker," he beeped off the phone and tossed it to me. "We're good," he told me calmly.

I blinked.

"We're... good?" I asked hesitantly.

"Monk's on board," Hugo replied.

I threw out my arms. "Hugo, are you nuts? We can't play tonight! We can't play until this shit is over."

"Be cool, mama, we'll be all right," Hugo responded.

I stared at him, mouth open.

Everyone was nuts. Everyone, that was, but me.

"You're nuts," I told Hugo.

"Anyone want eggs? I'm cooking," Leo called from the kitchen.

"I'd kill for some eggs. You got bacon?" Pong asked me, entirely unaffected by all the scariness happening around him.

"You're nuts, too," I said to Pong, who just grinned at me and pushed off the bed.

"Toast. I need toast. With grape jelly. And loads of butter," Buzz said, exiting the bed as well.

"There's bread. There's bacon, too," Leo announced, head in the fridge.

I looked at Floyd.

Floyd didn't look happy.

Finally, one sane person!

He stared at me and shook his head.

I waited for him to intervene, to bring sanity into our crazy world.

Then he shrugged.

"Is the coffee done?" Floyd asked as he got up and walked to the kitchen.

Shitsofuckit!

I flopped back on the bed.

Beautiful.

This was just beautiful.

"You better call Mace, get him to set up the security detail," Hugo said from his place leaning against the kitchen ledge.

Even more beautiful.

Mace was going to have a shit fit.

And here I was, pulling him in to help me and my band.

Again!

"Stella Bella, you want eggs?" Leo asked.

I looked at Juno.

She blinked at me then panted a bit. I watched as she gave up the fight against consciousness, rolled to her side and groaned as she stretched out, preparing for her doggie nap.

Eyes still on Juno, I answered, "Yeah, I want eggs."

Chapter 12

Set List

Stella

"Denver, let me hear you make some noise!" I shouted into the mic, still playing my guitar, the music roaring from the amplifiers.

At my demand, the crowd went nuts.

I looked to Buzz and smiled. He smiled back while jacking his head up and down. My gaze moved beyond Buzz to see Floyd's head swinging back and forth, his shoulders bunched up, his fingers crashing on the piano keys. I stepped back and looked behind me to see Pong's hair was flying out wild as he shook his head and banged the drums. My gaze moved to Leo, who had his head bent, staring at the stage, but his feet were hopping up and down to the beat.

Hugo was playing the keyboards, something he rarely did. He said this was because it gave him bad flashbacks of the organ lessons he'd taken at church, lessons forced on him by his ball-buster of a grandmother.

I felt badly about giving Hugo flashbacks of his ball-buster grandmother because I'd met her and she *was* a ball-buster.

But we needed the keyboards.

We were ending our third set on our fourth encore of Bob Seger and The Silver Bullet Band's "Get Out of Denver". Keyboards were paramount. You didn't do "Get Out of Denver" without keyboards.

Hugo had had to suck it up.

He hated it, but he did it for the band.

I executed the finishing riff with the drums, keyboards and piano crashing all around me. Then, as the keyboards and drums kept the excitement going, I put my arm up in the air, finger pointed to the ceiling, bounced my head and shoulders with my finger slashing the air, one, two, three, four and then we all jumped high one last time as I brought my arm down in a wide swipe and the music stopped.

I turned to the mic, wrapped my hand around it and smiled to the crowd.

"That's rock 'n' roll!" I yelled, and a wall of sound hit us as they screamed back.

"We need a beer. Give us fifteen minutes and we'll be back," I told them and they screamed again.

I grabbed the neck of my guitar and swung it in an arc, moving my hair out of the way with a shake of my head and disengaging the black leather strap (that had killer, tiny, daisy flower silver rivets running up each edge, a double threat, girlie but still rock 'n' roll) from around my shoulder. I placed my guitar in its stand and walked between Buzz and Leo to the stairs that would lead offstage.

The crowd had moved from fanatic screams to clapping and stomping rhythmically, chanting the word "Gypsies" over and over again. They were hoping for encore number five, and I had to admit, I was high enough to give it to them.

But seriously, as high as I was, as much as the music and the crowd were feeding me, I needed a fucking beer.

***

My day had started out shit and didn't get better.

Let's just say Mace hadn't been happy that our evening plans had changed from a quiet dinner and a talk about our future to his having to pull together a security detail for a death defying rock gig.

After the band left, I called Mace and managed to talk him around. Okay, so it could more appropriately be described as yelling him around. But once he gave in, to my shock, Lee phoned and started yelling at me, too. Then Luke phoned. Then Hector. Then Eddie. I hung up on Hank and then had Roxie phoning me, yelling at me for hanging up on Hank.

The Hot Bunch weren't all that excited about me getting shot at again, but more, if I was putting myself out there, the Rock Chicks were coming for moral support. And that they *really* didn't like.

As for Roxie, she just didn't like me hanging up on Hank.

I was in a pickle. I couldn't make the Rock Chicks stay home. I couldn't let down the band.

Either way, I was screwed.

So, I stuck with the program.

These calls were intermingled with calls from reporters and friends, both wanting to know what was going on. Since I wasn't allowed to talk to reporters and since I didn't really know what was going on, these calls were short and annoying.

So I decided to quit answering the phone and Juno and I cleaned my house, top to bottom. Well, Juno didn't clean. Juno watched me clean part of the time and snoozed the other part.

Then I worked on the set list. This took a while, considering it might be the last gig I'd ever play. I told myself I wasn't being morbid, just prepared, but I knew whatever it was, it had to be special.

What I didn't do was nap, play my guitar to soothe my troubled soul or come to any conclusions about my effed up life.

I should have done all of those, or at least some of them, or, at the very least, the last one. But I didn't have it in me.

☙❧

I harbored hope that people would stay away from the show considering the cover was doubled, the security was fierce and bullets were flying.

This hope was dashed.

By the time Vance took me to The Palladium, the doors were closed because the club was already at maximum capacity. I could see there was still a line straggling all the way down the sidewalk (half a block!) and curling around the corner. All of this and the show didn't start for thirty minutes, or as it turned out, fifty, as the band gave me trouble (because they always gave me trouble).

Crazy Rock 'n' Roll Denverites.

The good news was there were also a couple of squad cars and uniforms out front, providing what Vance called "presence", which did double duty of helping to control the crowd and making bad guys think twice.

My being "adopted" by the Denver Police Department definitely had its perks.

☙❧

The other good news was that, once we starting playing, the band was hot. We were on fire the night before, but we were an inferno tonight.

We'd never played this good.

Never.

※

I got to the side of the stage and Mace shoved a Fat Tire in my hand.

"Tomorrow, we'll talk about your set list," he growled.

I looked at him, noticed right off he was ticked and had an instant buzz kill.

I'd been creative with the set list. We were playing songs we'd rehearsed for the hell of it but rarely, if ever, played. These included Son House's "Death Letter", Blue Oyster Cult's "Don't Fear the Reaper", Billy Joel's "Only the Good Die Young", Benatar's "Hit Me with Your Best Shot", AC/DC's "Thunderstruck", and Warren Zevon's "Lawyers, Guns and Money".

Furthermore, we played two songs that we'd never played at a show and no one had ever heard outside of rehearsal.

The songs were written by Buzz and Leo. I wasn't a songwriter but they were, and they were pretty good at it. We'd never played them. Not because I didn't let us but because Buzz and Leo weren't comfortable with it.

I decided that, seeing as all of our asses were on the line, it was now or never.

Buzz and Leo disagreed.

Floyd, Hugo and Pong thought it was a great idea.

The band fought.

My side won, but this meant we were twenty minutes late taking the stage.

And so it goes with rock 'n' roll.

The crowd loved the new songs. They loved all of it. They were fucking eating it up.

Mace, however, clearly did not appreciate the irony.

"It's my band," I told Mace. "I write the set lists and I don't take any lip."

This was a lie. I took lip all the time.

Mace glared at me, and he was so good at it I felt it prudent to snap my mouth shut. So I did.

As with each break, Mace put a hand in my back and steered me backstage.

184

They were taking no chances tonight. All the Hot Bunch, Tex and Duke were there again. The same drill as the night before. The difference was, while the boys of the band worked the groupies or the bar, I spent my breaks sequestered in the dressing room with the Rock Chicks.

"Holy crap! That was great!" Indy shouted when I entered the room.

I saw that this time around Vance was playing bodyguard. Last break, it was Luke.

Vance gave Mace a nod, Mace accepted it with a return chin lift, glared at me one last time and shut the door behind him as he left.

"I loved your version of 'Don't Fear the Reaper'. That was fantastic!" Roxie yelled, not holding any grudges from our earlier throw down.

I smiled, took a pull from my beer and threw myself on the ratty couch Monk should have replaced twelve years ago.

"They ain't wrong. You are *hot* to-*night,*" Shirleen hooted. "Shirleen likes her some hip-hop and every once in a while, the blues, but the way you play it, girl, I'm thinkin' of claimin' back rock 'n' roll."

"You can't have it, Shirleen." I smiled at her. "Tonight, I think it's mine."

"Damn tootin'," Daisy put in on a tinkly-bell, girlie-giggle and she knocked her beer bottle against mine.

"So, how are things with you and Mace?" Ally asked, bored with the Stella Accolades and wanting to get to a juicier subject.

"Ally," Ava said and then rolled her eyes at Jet.

"I'm just asking," Ally retorted.

"Non-starter," I answered Ally after taking another swig of my beer, not about to share about Mace's demons, not yet. I hadn't even dealt with them yet. I didn't even know if I *could* deal with them. "I don't have time to deal with Mace and the band and my dog and the front page of *The Post* and my gigs and the idiot Monk and getting shot at and Eric—"

"Eric?" Jet asked.

"My boyfriend," I answered.

There were some gasps. Unfortunately, Ally was taking a sip from her Fat Tire when I answered and thus spewed it across the room, forcing Ava and Roxie to jump wide of the beer spray.

"Your *what?*" Ally semi-yelled, still spluttering.

"Well, he wasn't my boyfriend, but he was, kind of. We were seeing each other," I explained.

Kristen Ashley

"Were?" Indy asked.

"After Mace and I, erm," I bit my lip and my eyes slid to Vance who was studying his boots then I looked back to Indy. "*Did it,*" I whispered to the girls and then went on talking in my normal voice. "We all had a showdown, Mace, Eric and me. During the showdown, Mace told Eric he fucked me. *Bluntly.* Eric didn't appreciate that."

"I bet he didn't," Shirleen muttered, making eyes at Daisy.

"Why didn't you tell *us* about Eric?" Ally demanded to know.

I shrugged. "Well, Eric and I were together, but we weren't. It's hard to explain. Then I found out he was a Fed—"

"*What?*" It was Daisy's turn to splutter through a defunct swallow of beer.

"Yeah, a Fed. He's investigating Sid, too, and got close to me to do it. But he said he fell for me. Told me straight out, right in front of Mace, right after Mace told him he fucked me." I paused, not wishing to share further because sharing meant reliving. I was still nursing a mini-buzz and I needed to keep it going for the last set, and reliving that particular memory would kill the buzz dead. "It's complicated," I finished.

"It ain't complicated, it's fucked up. That's what it is," Shirleen commented, and she was not wrong.

"I can't believe Mace told him he fucked you. Did he use those words?" Ava asked, and at my nod, she went on. "That's just rude."

"That's just the Hot Bunch. They're all straight-talkers," Indy reminded her.

"Still, this Eric guy has a thing for Stella. He could at least *try* to be sensitive," Ava continued.

This made Shirleen, Ally and Indy burst into gales of laughter and Daisy, Roxie and Jet started giggling.

Shirleen wiped an eye. "Mace? Sensitive? Ava, girl, you are too much."

Ava gave Shirleen a look.

I gave Vance a look, wondering what he thought of all this.

Jules, again, had passed on the night out with the Rock Chicks, preferring to stay home and keep herself and her unborn baby safe.

This, I thought, was a good decision.

Vance had given up on his study of his boots and was now wearing a shit-eating grin and watching me.

186

Apparently what Vance thought about all of this was that it was highly amusing.

I rolled my eyes.

His grin got wide.

Whatever!

There came a knock at the door and Vance went tense.

"Scout," Hector's voice said from the other side of the door and it was my turn to go tense.

"Scout?" Roxie breathed, her huge eyes swinging to me, and all the Rock Chicks swayed with the excitement filling the room.

"I'm unavailable," I said to Vance quickly, but he ignored me and opened the door.

Damn it!

Monk walked in with Hector and a balding, middle-aged man who still managed, even thin on the top, to look cool wearing jeans, a light blue collared shirt and black boots.

"Stella, beautiful, you're on fire tonight," Monk raved, clenching his hands together like a greedy, maniacal banker in a bad movie.

I stood and murmured my thanks, my eyes on the scout. My eyes being on the scout had the added benefit of allowing me to avoid Hector, Vance, Monk and the Rock Chicks.

I took a pull from my beer, swallowed and asked, "And you are?"

"Dixon Jones. A&R. Black Fat Records," he answered.

Oh.

Wow.

I'd heard of Black Fat Records, even though they hadn't been around very long. They were small and they were choosy. They found good talent, they took good care of them and they had a killer marketing department.

If I'd ever wanted The Gypsies to be signed, it would be with an outfit like Black Fat Records.

"Enjoying the show?" I asked like I didn't care, which I didn't. Not really.

But then again, I did.

What the eff was wrong with me?

Dixon Jones smiled at me. It was genuine and it threw me.

"You write the new material?" he asked, and this threw me, too.

I shook my head. "That's Buzz, my bass player. He writes the music. And Leo, my rhythm guitar. He writes the lyrics."

"Those songs were tight. It's good to see you branching out of covers," Dixon commented, and this threw me most of all.

"You catch a gig before?" I asked, doing my damnedest to stay outwardly calm.

"Anytime I'm in Denver, The Gypsies are playing, I come," Dixon replied.

Oh my Lord!

"So why haven't you ever met my girl here?" Monk pushed in and clapped Dixon on the back. It gave me the creepy-crawlies to be referred to as Monk's girl, so much so, even though I tried to stop it, my lip curled.

Dixon looked down his nose at Monk and replied, "Except when they're playing The Palladium. I usually avoid The Palladium."

Monk got a little pale and stepped back.

I couldn't help myself, I smirked at Dixon Jones. All of a sudden, I liked him.

"Couldn't miss tonight," he said, lifting a copy of *USA Today* I hadn't noticed he was carrying. "Rock 'n' roll in the face of certain danger. I figured it'd be good but shit. Gotta tell you, Stella, you and your boys delivered beyond expectation. Your set list is inspired."

Then Dixon snapped the paper open and turned a page to face me.

On the page was a grainy photo of me and Mace making out last night onstage. I didn't look at the caption. I was too busy staring at the photo. I, of course, had never seen myself kissing Mace (or anyone) and I was weirdly fascinated.

The photo was probably taken by a cell phone camera. It didn't look great, but it didn't look bad, either. In fact, the way I was bent over Mace's arm, the drums in the background, Mace's fist wrapped around the neck of my guitar, my hands clutching his broad shoulders, our lips locked, it looked hot.

Smokin' hot.

Shitsofuckit!

"Holy crap," Indy whispered.

"*USA Today*?" Jet breathed.

"I didn't see that one," Daisy muttered.

"Great fuckin' picture," Ally observed.

I took a step forward, my hand coming out to take the paper, but I didn't make it. Vance got there before me, tagged the paper and took a step back.

"You need to focus on the show," Vance said to me, folding the paper and tucking it under his arm.

I stared at him, shocked. So did Dixon Jones. The Rock Chicks all looked at each other, and they did it knowingly.

Not good.

Something was up.

I turned to Vance. "What are you? My manager?"

Vance looked at his watch then back to me. "For the next two minutes, yeah."

"Are not," I snapped.

"Focus, Stella," Vance shot back.

"We need to talk," Hector said to Dixon, and I turned angry, confused eyes to Hector.

Dixon was also looking confused.

I looked back at Hector and read his intent.

Oh no.

This was *not* going to happen!

"Don't talk to him," I said to Dixon.

Now Dixon was looking at me and he still appeared confused.

The Rock Chicks huddled closer except Shirleen. She approached Dixon.

"Yeah, Hector and me and you, we *all* got to talk," Shirleen said to Dixon.

Oh dear.

This was getting worse.

"And me!" Daisy pressed forward.

Oh no!

Even worse!

"No!" I shouted, trying to move, but for some reason Ally and Ava had me in a death grip.

Dixon swung his gaze from me to Daisy to Shirleen.

"Who're you?" he asked Shirleen.

He asked Shirleen, but Daisy answered.

"Managers. We *all* manage The Gypsies. Just like any real good, smokin' hot rock band, they're a handful, comprende?"

"They're not my managers," I told Dixon.

Shirleen had her fingers curled around Dixon's upper arm and was leading him to the door. She leaned in toward his ear and lied, "She says that three times a day."

I looked to the ceiling and silently said a short, pointed prayer.

My prayer went ignored, and with a bemused glance over his shoulder at me, Dixon Jones disappeared behind the door.

I turned woodenly and looked at Ally. "What just happened?"

"Ask me no questions, I'll tell you no lies," Ally replied.

My eyes narrowed and I could actually feel my pulse beating in my throat. Then I shouted, "What the eff does that mean?"

"That means," Jet materialized in front of me, "you have to trust us."

This was not good.

Not good at all.

They were up to something.

And I was pretty certain I knew what it was *and* I didn't like it.

I shook my head at Jet. "Not with a scout I don't."

"Trust us," Indy said, coming to stand by Jet.

Eff that!

"You all are fucking nuts. Everyone is fucking nuts! The world is fucking nuts!" I yelled just as the door opened and Mace walked in.

Completely oblivious to my tantrum, Mace looked at me with still angry eyes and announced, "Time for your last set, and Stella, if there's one fuckin' song about death or guns, *I'm* gonna shoot you."

Effing... bloody... *hell*.

⁓⁂⁓

We were scorching through our gig-ending "Ghostriders" when it happened.

I'd managed to put everything to the back of my head and the last set, if possible, was better than the first three. We'd started the set easing the crowd into the vibe by doing America's "Ventura Highway". We could burn the house down with chest-thumping rock 'n' roll, but between Floyd, Buzz, Leo and me, we could also sing a powerful harmony, and even if I said so myself, our "Ventura Highway" was sweet.

We followed that with two more of Buzz and Leo's new songs. When I introduced the songs, the crowd shouted their approval so loud, they missed the first thirty seconds of the first song because their cheers were drowning out the music.

I got a warm fuzzy feeling watching the crowd's approval wash over Buzz and Leo. My two boys glanced at each other, their faces an obvious mixture of the panic and thrill I'd been feeling all day. But, with them, I could see the thrill part was definitely winning.

Then we were done messing around. It was time to rock and we slid back into the theme of the night (Mace was just going to have to shoot me) with REO Speedwagon's "Ridin' the Storm Out", Molly Hatchett's "Flirtin' with Disaster", The Doobie Brothers' "Dangerous" and finally "Ghostriders".

We were closing out the song. The crowd knew it and they were frenzied, hands up in the air, bodies swaying, catcalls piercing the air.

And it was then, riding the high of a great show, heart racing, blood pumping (thankfully), skin tingling, lips in a permanent happy grin, I saw him.

A scruffy man wearing a beat-up army jacket over a t-shirt, hair a mess, hands in the pockets of his jacket, he was making his way with determination toward Jet.

Through my buzz, two things hit me.

It was a warm end of May evening and jackets weren't allowed.

Effing Monk!

Duke was again working the front of the stage, but he didn't see the guy and he had his back to me so I couldn't catch his eye.

There were Hot Bunch men in range. In fact, the guy pushed right by Vance, who was looking in the opposite direction.

Like last night, Lee was on the stage with the band. I kept playing but twisted my torso to look at Lee. I tried to catch his eye but he was on alert, not paying attention to me, his eyes were scanning the crowd.

Getting desperate, I twisted back around and tried to get Vance's attention, but for some reason, he turned and pushed in the other direction, away from the Rock Chicks.

Eff it, there was nothing for it.

My eyes glued on the guy, I went to the mic and tried to offer a warning by saying "Jet..." but just as I uttered her name, I watched in horror as a pocket of people opened behind Jet.

The guy had easy access.

Effing, holy, hell!

He made it to Jet in a couple of steps, his hand started to come out of his pocket and it was then I freaked.

"*Jet!*" I screamed into the mic.

Her eyes were already on me, but there was no time to warn her; the man was right behind her.

I whipped the guitar off, dropped it to the stage with a loud crash of the strings, ran to the edge and executed a stage dive, jumping off and aiming my body at the bad guy.

I vaguely heard the crowd give a shout of approval at my stage dive just as I hit the guy, full body.

"What the—?" he shouted, caught unaware, with one hand out, one hand still in his jacket. His free arm went around me. He staggered when my weight hit him, one, two, three steps, and then we both went down, him on his back, me on top.

Unfortunately, we careened into others and they went down with us.

It was all arms and legs and bodies and what seemed like a million feet, most of them kicking, as we rolled into others and took them all down.

I stayed focused and struggled with the guy, trying to get a firm hold on his wrists. He was strong and he was wiry, and even though not exactly young, he still was a guy so I found this a difficult task.

I heard Floyd's voice asking for calm but I ignored it, too busy grunting and wrestling with the bad guy.

"Jesus, girl, what the fuck's the matter with you?" he asked, on the defense, wrestling back and also grunting.

For some reason, I shouted, "You're wearing a jacket!"

"So?" he shouted back.

"Jackets... are... not... *allowed!*" I yelled right before an arm sliced around my waist and lifted me clean off him.

I struggled, twisting around to see Vance had hold of me. He set me on my feet in front of his body, but he kept me close with the arm around my waist.

Since he was a member of the Hot Bunch, I quit struggling, pointed at the guy still on the floor and shouted, "*Get him!*"

Vance's eyebrows went up and he asked, "Get who?"

"The guy with the jacket," I yelled.

Vance's gaze shifted to the guy on the floor and mine went with it. I saw Luke was now there. Hand extended to the guy, Luke pulled him to his feet.

"You okay, Ray?" Luke asked and my body froze.

"She's fuckin' loco," "Ray" answered, brushing off his jeans and straightening his jacket, his eyes on me.

I stared, noting distractedly the Rock Chicks had arrived, and with them a goodly number of the crowd. All were pressing in and watching.

"You know him?" I asked Luke.

"He's my Dad," Jet answered.

Oh dear.

"Oh," I mumbled, feeling stupid.

"You okay, Dad?" Jet asked, moving toward him.

"Yeah, but it's a miracle," he replied to Jet and then glared at me. "What's the matter with you? You jumped on me! From the stage!"

I felt the need to defend myself. "You're wearing a jacket!"

"What's the fuckin' deal with the jacket?" Ray snapped at Luke who had his eyes on Vance behind me and his mouth cocked in a sexy half-grin.

Then Luke's eyes dropped to mine. "Since Ray's not likely to murder his own daughter, or any of her friends, we figured it was okay to let him in with his jacket."

"Oh," I repeated and looked at Ray. "Um, sorry about that," I muttered.

"You're loco," Ray told me.

I bit my lip and sliced an apologetic look to Jet who, thankfully, appeared to be fighting a grin.

"Can't be too safe," Vance said from behind me, but I could swear he sounded like he was trying not to laugh.

I twisted in his arm and watched his mouth twitch.

Shitsofuckit!

My eyes caught on Shirleen and Daisy, who were sandwiching Dixon Jones, all of them on the edge of the crowd, all of them looking at me. Shirleen and Daisy were smiling. Dixon Jones again looked confused.

My effing stupid shitty luck!

"I'm not usually like this," I told Dixon.

Dixon's body lurched like he was in a trance and my words snapped him out of it.

I noticed the band pushing in close, Vance's arm dropped from around my waist and I took a step away.

"Holy shit, Stella Bella. We're calling you Ramba from now on! You the wo-man!" Pong yelled.

"Guess we don't need Mace as muscle anymore," Leo noted. "We got Stella."

"Next time, pick a girl to jump on," Hugo advised.

I rolled my eyes to the ceiling.

"One thing you can say, Stella Gunn," Dixon remarked, now *his* mouth was twitching. "You're pure fuckin' rock 'n' roll."

I didn't know if that was good or bad.

Since pure rock 'n' roll, to me, was a positive thing, I decided to take that as good.

I tossed my hair and smiled at him.

His eyes shifted to my hair and watched it move then they came back to mine and he lost the fight with his smile and it went wide.

"Show's over," Mace, all of a sudden there, announced.

"Fuckin' A, but *what* a show!" Tex boomed, also all of a sudden there. He got close to me and dropped a huge hand to top of my head. "Girl, you are *the shit!* You can burn through Molly Hatchett *and* take care of business. Fuckin' A!" he repeated, taking his hand from my head, and, not done, boomed, "God *damn!*" Then, obviously in the throes of a Rock Moment, he turned to the crowd and shouted, "Do we love The Gypsies?"

The crowd, mostly watching in bewilderment (I'd never done a stage dive to end a show so they were uncertain at the state of affairs), gave a feeble cheer.

"*Fuck that!*" Tex roared, throwing his arm up to punch the air. "*Do we love The Gypsies?*"

Catching on, the crowd cheered back, stronger now. There was some scattered applause that started to grow, then grow some more. A few shouted "Yippee kay yay" and then the chants of "Gypsies" began.

Oh dear.

"Awesome," Pong breathed from beside me, his eyes moving over the chanting crowd.

Mace's hand tagged mine. I looked up at him and knew in an instant he was done.

"We're outta here," he declared, proving me right, and started shoving his way through the crowd, pulling me along with him.

As we went, people pressed in. Wound up by the show, its bizarre ending and Tex, they were in a tizzy. So much so, I felt hands on me. People were grabbing at my t-shirt, trying to tag my belt loops. I felt fingers slide through my hair and I watched the same thing happening to Mace.

They were closing in, caught in the moment, making it hard for even Mace to shove his way through.

I felt fear begin to seize me, scared silly at a new threat. My fans, rocked by the show, reading the papers, knowing the danger, wound up by Tex, all of that pushing them to the brink. I feared they'd tear us to shreds.

Mace stopped. He turned, bent, put his shoulder in my belly and then I was going up. I ended bent double over his shoulder, his arm wrapped around the backs of my thighs. Using his other arm and shoulder to push his way through the crowd, people went flying as I saw the flash of cameras coming one right after the other.

Beautiful.

I wondered if those pictures would make front page, too.

Luke, Lee, Vance, Hector, Eddie and Duke all moved in to flank us and Mace didn't stop until we hit the backstage door. With my head lifted, I watched the Hot Bunch close ranks behind us, stopping the crowd, right before the door closed behind Mace and me.

That was how we made our dramatic exit.

Mace put me down in front of the backdoor to the club and shoved it open. Darius materialized from the shadows, did a chin lift, a scan of the area and vaporized into the shadows again.

Mace pushed me in the passenger seat of one of the four black Explorers parked in the alley. He got in the driver's side and we took off.

I held myself stiff, wondering at his mood, which, figuring this was Mace, was probably not happy.

I glanced to the side and saw he was smiling full on, white teeth and all.

"Why are you smiling?" I asked.

He looked at me then back at the road, his smile not wavering.

Then he answered, "I've decided I like your set list, Kitten."

"You do?"

"Yeah," he said then expanded on his answer. "Not one fuckin' song you played tonight had anything to do with the word 'black'."

Shitsofuckit!

I totally forgot!

Chapter 13

You Want In Here?
Stella

The minute we got back to my place, Mace took Juno out for a bathroom break.

I took the fastest shower in history.

I did *not* need to be naked with Mace in the house.

Further, Mace and I needed to talk.

It was time. No more effing around.

It was three o'clock in the morning and I was exhausted, coasting on fumes from the high of the gig, not to mention my ridiculous, gig-ending stage dive, a memory which I knew would be cringe-worthy for the rest of my effing life.

But Mace and I still needed to talk and we were going to do it.

I jumped out of the shower and toweled down. I wrapped the towel around my hair, put on my robe and hightailed it out of the bathroom just as I heard Juno and Mace return.

Mace was activating the alarm when I left the bathroom. I ignored him and moved quickly toward my dresser, seeing to priorities, as in getting dressed. I had a pair of sky-blue lace hipsters in my hand when I heard him approach. I was about to bend over and put them on when I saw his hand come around me. He snatched the panties from my fingers and tossed them on my chair.

I whirled around. "What are you doing?"

I didn't need to ask. I knew what he was doing.

He grinned, his hand coming up to yank the towel from my hair.

I planted my hands on my hips and tossed my head to get my hair out of my face as he threw the towel in the direction of my panties.

"Mace, what are you doing?" I repeated.

"Gonna fuck you, babe."

Oh dear.

He had that look about him. That look I liked. That look that turned me on.

That look that said he was, indeed, gonna fuck me.

Nope.

Unh-unh.

No way.

I stood my ground, hands on hips.

"No, you're not. We have to talk. We have a lot of talking to do and we're going to do it. Now."

Mace moved around me and I had to pivot to stay facing him.

Suddenly, he stopped, and then started walking forward. As I was in front of him, I had no choice but to walk back.

I put a hand to his chest. "Stop. Listen to me—"

He didn't stop and he was clearly not listening to me.

His hands came to my waist right before I would have fallen down the stairs. He lifted me and I was forced to throw my arms around his shoulders.

"Seriously, Mace. This isn't gonna happen. I'm too tired and we have a lot to talk about. We need to talk about it."

"Seriously, Kitten. This is gonna happen. We can talk later," he returned and put me on my feet beside the bed.

I did the hands on hips thing again.

"You're beginning to piss me off," I informed him.

He put a hand in my belly and gave me a shove, gentle enough not to be rough, rough enough to send me flying.

I bounced on the bed and tried to whirl, but he got hold of my ankles and twisted me back. Then he pulled my legs wide and came down on top of me, his hips sliding between my legs, his jeans rubbing against the insides of my thighs.

I had to admit, I liked that.

Like, a lot.

"Mace!" I shouted.

His mouth came to my neck as his hands started moving on my body. They felt nice, warm and strong.

Effing hell!

"You gonna yell through this or what?" he asked my neck.

"Yes," I snapped.

"That'll be new," he muttered, and then I felt his tongue behind my ear.

That felt nice, too.

Hello? Inner Mace Slut? Take a hike! We have talking to do. We have to get our head together. We have to get our life back into our control, my brain reminded me.

I turned my head to disengage Mace's mouth from my neck.

"Honestly, Mace—" I started to say, but he lifted his head and looked in my eyes as his fingers slid into the wet hair on either side of my face.

I saw his eyes were alert, energized, aroused.

It was then I knew he was gonna fuck me.

I knew this because I wanted him to fuck me.

Like, a lot.

Oh screw it.

⌖

Just for your information, I will mention that I could swear he looked like he was about ready to laugh right before I lifted my head to kiss him.

⌖

"Babe."

When I heard Mace's voice, I opened my eyes and stared at the wall. It was light outside, and I suspected it was late morning.

I felt delicious, cozy and relaxed. I could feel Mace's hard body behind me, his arm around my waist, his face in my hair.

I loved waking up to a bed warm with Mace. It was one of the seven hundred twenty-five thousand things I missed about him.

Shitsofuckit!

I'd done it again. I'd had sex with Mace. I'd let him spend the night with me. I'd even let him (mostly) move in with me!

What was I doing?

Mace's arm tightened and his body got closer.

"Stella, wake up." I felt his deep voice rumble against the back of my neck making goose bumps rise along my skin.

"I'm awake," I told him.

His arm tightened further, wrapping around my belly, and he kissed my neck.

199

"It's late. Sorry to wake you, but I got shit to do."

I thought this was good. Mace having shit to do meant I'd have time to think, to plan, to get my head together.

"Okay," I replied.

He nuzzled my hair with his nose, but other than that, he didn't move.

When his not moving lasted more than a few seconds, I called, "Erm, Mace?"

"Yeah?"

"You have shit to do," I reminded him.

"Yeah," he answered, but still didn't move.

"Well, are you gonna do it?" I asked.

"I thought you wanted to talk."

Oh, right.

I wanted to talk.

This was true, I wanted to talk.

And something about him reminding me I wanted to talk and giving me that opportunity, even though he had "shit to do", made me feel even cozier and more relaxed.

However, in the cold light of day but waking up in bed with warm Mace, I forgot what I wanted to talk about.

I was searching my foggy brain for clues as to what I wanted to talk about when Mace's arm moved, his hand splayed on my midriff, his body slid away and he pushed me to my back.

He leaned in, the front of his body pressed against my side. He got up on his elbow and looked down at me. His green eyes were warm and alert and I remembered again how much I liked the look of Mace first thing in the morning.

As I looked into his eyes, my brain still foggy, still feeling cozy and relaxed, my thoughts on Mace's eyes (then they careened off in the direction of about seven thousand of the seven hundred twenty-five thousand *other* things about Mace I liked), he looked into mine. This lasted for a beat that turned into two, then three, then his mouth moved and he looked like he was fighting a smile.

"Kitten, I don't have all day," he told me, and my head jerked, pulling me out of my Mace Happy Thoughts Reverie.

Shit!

Okay.

Concentrate.

The Talk with Mace...

It came to me.

"You're screwing with my head," I informed him.

There was no doubt about it and I had the last five minutes as evidence. He was definitely screwing with my head.

His reply was instantaneous. "Yeah. And?"

I blinked with surprise at his ready answer.

Then I stared.

He didn't even try to deny it.

All fogginess left me and my mind became clear. I did an ab curl to sitting position, dislodging his body and twisted to face him.

"Well, stop doing it!" I demanded.

He did an ab curl, too. His hands came to my waist and he lifted me over his body. Then he yanked my knees to bent so I was straddling him and his knees came up, caging me in as his arms wrapped around me.

I pushed against his bare chest and pressed into the bed with my knees.

This didn't work.

"Mace, let me up."

He didn't let me up.

"Stella, I got about ten minutes then I gotta get going. You got more you want to say?"

I quit trying to get away, stunned at his arrogance and annoyed that he was ignoring my wishes (yet again) and snapped, "Hell yes!"

"Then say it."

"All right. I'll say it. Or, I should say, I'll *repeat* it. I want you to move out. I want this to be over, whatever this is, right effing now. I want you to quit screwing with my head. And I want you to stop interfering with my band."

"No."

I waited for him to say more, but, apparently, that was it.

"No?" I asked.

"No," he repeated, like that was that, then he went on. "That all you got?"

I was back to my stunned, annoyed staring.

I just could *not* believe him.

Kristen Ashley

He waited then leaned up to touch his mouth to mine and made a move to shift me off his body as if our talk was over, all was hunky dory. He was going to exit the bed and get on with the rest of his day.

Erm... no.

We were not done.

I put my hands to his shoulders and pressed down, locking my thighs at his hips.

"Hang on a second," I said.

Mace stilled and started to look impatient.

Amused, but impatient.

"Stella, in case you forgot, I got a bad guy to catch."

"I know that, but we aren't done talking."

"If that's what you want to talk about then we are."

"We aren't!"

"We are."

"Dammit, Mace!"

His hands on my waist got tighter and his face came closer and that face had lost its amusement and was now very serious.

"This is how it's gonna go down," Mace stated, his voice firm.

Effing hell.

I don't think I want to know how it's gonna go down, my brain sounded kind of scared.

I don't either, I told my brain.

"You're obviously gonna fight it and that's fine, I already told you I'm happy to take you on. We both know where we stand with this. We're goin' over old ground. You gotta know, though, that this kind of fight, there aren't any rules. If it means I gotta fuck with your head then I'm gonna fuck with your head. You don't like it, tough."

Did I say he was unbelievable?

In case I didn't, he was just *unbelievable!*

"I don't like it," I returned. "As I already told you, I'm not going there again. Not with you."

"You're already there," he informed me.

"I am not!" I snapped back.

The amusement returned. "Babe, you're sitting naked in my lap on the morning after a night where you begged to suck my—"

I put a hand over his mouth to stop his words and drowned out the muffled noise with a sharp, angry scream that came from the back of my throat.

I thought back, and I *had* begged, and then he'd let me, and it was nice, for both of us.

Shit, I was so weak!

I took my hand from his mouth, shut my eyes tight, lifted my arms and grabbed my hair in both of my fists.

This, I decided, was not going my way.

At all.

And it was all my fault.

Then it hit me, something else we had to talk about.

I dropped my arms, opened my eyes and looked right into his.

He was full on amused now.

I ignored his amusement.

"Tell me about yesterday morning in the kitchen," I said quietly.

The amusement disappeared instantly.

Oh dear.

"What about it?" he asked, his voice was guarded.

"You know," I answered, my voice still soft.

His hands still at my waist, he made to move again, but I did the hands-pressing-on-shoulders, thighs-locking-on-hips move again and he stilled.

His eyes came back to mine and now *they* were guarded. No warm amusement, no determination, no impatience, nothing.

Blank.

Hidden.

He didn't say a word.

And that's when I knew.

Mace was going to do whatever he had to do to win me.

Except what would actually work.

"I get it," I whispered.

I watched his eyes flash with anger.

"I don't think you do," he replied.

"No, you're right. I don't. And you aren't gonna give it to me," I retorted, knowing he wasn't going to share. Knowing he was willing to take, but he wasn't willing to give. This hurt. It shouldn't hurt. I didn't want it to hurt. But it was a kick to the gut all the same.

Kristen Ashley

Then I said softly, "Same shit, Mace. Just a year later."

It was my turn to try to get away, but he twisted and we ended with me on my back. He was on top of me and we were face to face.

"You think you got it figured out, Kitten, but you don't. Bottom line, you aren't ready for it," he told me.

I probably wasn't ready for it, if the look in his eyes yesterday morning was anything to go by.

But I had to know. I knew I shouldn't want to, shouldn't need to, but I had to.

"And you get to decide when I'm ready?" I asked.

"Yeah."

"And when's that gonna be?"

"I'll tell you when it's not gonna be. It's not gonna be when you're trying to push me away because you still don't trust me," he returned.

"So you get to screw with my head, fuck with my life, take what you want and you give me nothing?"

"You got it," he answered, totally calm.

He could not be serious.

"I don't *believe* you. You're just... *unbelievable,*" I spat my earlier thought out loud.

His hand traveled down my arm, locked around my wrist and pulled it up. When he had it between us, his hand shifted, pressing mine flat against his beating heart.

"You want in here?" he murmured, his eyes intense, so intense I felt my gut clench with fear. This was a fear I didn't understand. It wasn't even logical, but it scared me all the same. It was the same fear as yesterday morning, huge and uncontrollable.

"No," I lied. Except for the ability to play my music, being in his heart was the only thing I'd ever wanted in my whole effing life.

He shook his head. "Until that answer changes, babe, you get what I'm willin' to give you. My protection, my attention and my cock."

I gasped at his frankness and my body went solid with fury.

"Unbelievable," I hissed.

"When the time comes where you give me somethin' without me havin' to pull it out of you, where you give me a piece of you without me havin' to take it, then I'll give you a piece of me."

204

"That time's never going to come," I snapped back, though I wanted a piece of him. I wanted more than a piece of him. I wanted all of him. I even wanted a chance to help him battle those demons. In fact, I wanted the chance to take them on all on my own if it meant Mace wouldn't have them anymore.

I knew it, I hated myself for my weakness, but it was the truth.

I might not be able to be honest with him, but I had to be honest with myself, or at least this once.

"It'll come," he promised, breaking me out of my thoughts.

I glared at him to hide the emotional tumult in my head.

He calmly returned my glare.

"Don't you have shit to do?" I reminded him, my voice sharp.

I was done.

Done, done, *done!*

He kept watching me for a few beats then his gaze went soft. Instead of moving away from me, his head came down and his face disappeared in my neck.

I pushed at his shoulders. "What are you doing?"

"Don't wanna leave it this way."

"There's no other way to leave it," I informed him, and his face came out of my neck. He rolled off me to his side, taking me with him, his arms around me. Both hands slid up my back, he pressed the area between my shoulder blades so my torso was tight against his and he threw a thigh over mine, pinning me.

I didn't fight this. I was beginning to learn (belatedly) that fighting him physically was detrimental to my abilities to fight him emotionally.

One of his hands tangled in my hair, giving it a gentle tug so my head tilted back. He dipped his chin down to look at me.

Then he said, "All right, Stella, I'll give you one."

Uh-oh.

One? One what? My brain asked.

"One what?" I said out loud.

"A piece of me."

Oh dear.

He kept talking. "The worst part of breaking up with you was you lettin' me walk away."

My breath packed up and took a shuttle flight to the moon.

"What?" I whispered.

205

"It was so good between us, I didn't think in a million fuckin' years you'd let me walk away," Mace went on.

"What?" I asked. Yes, again!

His arms got tighter, his hand fisted gently in my hair, right before he said, "It was a test."

His words hit me like blows. My body froze rigid then I shouted, "*What?*"

"You failed," he continued.

Effing hell. Effing hell. Effing bloody *hell*.

"You… are… joking," I breathed, carefully enunciating each word.

"Babe, I hope you get that I'm prepared to fight for you, but I gotta know you'll fight for me, too. This shit goes both ways. This doesn't end until I know you won't walk away, but also you won't let me walk away. Never again."

What he was saying wasn't quite penetrating my brain.

"What you're telling me," my voice was both quiet and weirdly scratchy, "is that if I'd asked you back, you would have come?"

The fingers of his hand not in my hair started to stroke my spine.

"I needed you to make a statement, Kitten," he said softly. "You didn't."

All of a sudden, I felt like crying.

I fought it and persevered at trying to understand what he was telling me.

"What you're saying is you didn't break up with me because you wanted to break up with me. What you're saying is you broke up with me to test me?"

"Yeah," he replied.

Simple as that.

Yeah.

A year of heartache and a simple "yeah".

It all boiled down to that.

Tears filled my eyes. I didn't want them to, but I didn't fight them either. I was *way* beyond fighting. I wasn't sure what I was feeling. I just knew none of it was good.

"Okay," I started, my voice now croaky and his hand left my hair, his other hand stopped stroking my spine and his arms got tight. "I just want to be sure I have this straight. You came into my life, gave me the first something good I had outside of music and took it away as *a test?*"

"Kitten—"

What he said and what it meant finally penetrated my brain.

"You jerk," I whispered.

His arms grew tighter. "Stella, listen to me——"

"You jerk," I repeated, my voice breaking, the tears sliding out the sides of my eyes. I didn't even try to control them because I knew I couldn't.

"I didn't know how you felt. You didn't tell me——" he started.

"You didn't ask," I reminded him.

"Babe, if I'd have asked, would you have told me?"

"Yes," I said immediately and watched his head jerk back in surprise, but I ignored it and went on. "I would have told you. Back then I would have given you anything."

He watched my face as if assessing my honesty then his hand went up. His fingers sifting into my hair, he tilted his head back and shoved my face into his throat.

"Christ, Stella," he said, but it sounded more like a groan.

"Mace, next time you feel like 'giving me one', you should reconsider," I advised. My voice had turned cold, my eyes had dried and I knew, somehow, my heart had gone hard. "Now, let me go."

I meant the words with a double meaning.

Of course, he didn't let me go.

Instead, he muttered, "I fucked up."

He was right about that.

"Yes, you did. Now let me go."

"I fucked up," he repeated, then used my hair to pull my face out of his throat and his head tilted down to look at me. "Kitten, I'm sorry," he whispered.

I knew it took a lot for him to say that.

I knew it.

But it hurt so much I didn't care.

"I'm sure you are. And I'm just as sure that I don't give a fuck," I lied.

But it sounded good, it sounded real, and I watched him wince as I scored the point. I knew that seeing his wince should register somewhere, but it didn't. "Now let me go."

He still didn't let me go. Instead, he said, "You need to get it."

"Oh, I get it," I told him, even though I didn't and I never would.

"No, babe, you don't. Yesterday morning——"

I shook my head.

"Oh no you don't," I snapped.

He was *not* going to fuck with my head anymore. He didn't want to share until he got his piece of me, so be it. I was keeping all my pieces all to myself.

Fuck that!

His arms got so tight they made it hard for me to breathe and I watched as his face morphed from soft remorse to the beginnings of hard anger.

"Listen to me," he growled.

"We're done talking," I interrupted him. "I don't want to talk anymore. Go find the bad guy, Mace, so this can be over."

"You need to understand where I'm coming from," he told me.

"I don't care where you're coming from," I shot back.

Morph complete, Mace was straight out angry. "Stella, I'm warnin' you, you got one shot at this. You throw it back in my face, you won't get another one."

Hard-hearted or not, that scared the snot out of me.

Regardless of the fear, self-preservation took firm hold and answered for me. "I'll take that chance."

His face stayed angry, but I could swear I saw pain flash in his eyes, sharp and fierce. The sight of it made bile climb up my throat, but I had no chance to take back my words.

He let me go.

Then he exited the bed.

The loss of his body felt like a cold slap.

I sat up and pulled the sheets around me as he walked to his jeans. His body was taut, his movements jerky. It didn't take a body language expert to know he was pissed.

And what was even scarier, maybe even hurt.

Shitsofuckit!

Now what had I done?

I felt my heart start racing and swallowed the bile in my throat.

I opened my mouth to call to him when the buzzer went.

"Jesus," he muttered.

He yanked on his jeans and walked to the alarm panel.

"Mace," I called, but it came out more quiet than a whisper and he didn't hear me.

Mace hit the button on the alarm panel.

Ally's face filled the video screen and Mace said, "Yeah?"

"Open up!" Ally demanded. "Rock Chicks!"

He took his finger from the button, muttered, "Jesus," again and then hit another button, buzzing them up.

He unlocked the doors, turned to me and said, "I'll take the dog out."

Then he went to his bag, pulled out a navy blue henley, yanked it on and was sitting on the platform, pulling on his boots when the Rock Chicks stormed the door. Ally, Indy, Jet, Roxie, Ava, Daisy, Shirleen, Annette and even Jules was there.

"We hit the news!" Ally shouted, holding up a copy of the paper. "This time all of us." Then she snapped her mouth shut and her eyes swung from me, to Mace, back to me.

I sat, still frozen, still naked, still in bed, staring at my friends as they all stood, silent, realizing from the heavy air that they'd interrupted something.

"Um, is this a bad time?" Jules finally asked.

In answer, Mace got up, stalked to the leash hanging by the side of the door and whistled for the strangely-attuned-to-her-human's-emotional-turmoil-thus-silent Juno.

As he did all of this, the Rock Chicks and my eyes followed him.

Mace did one more (very weird) thing before he left.

He yanked the paper out of Ally's hand, ignoring her surprised, "Hey!" and he shoved it under his armpit.

Then he was gone.

I stared at the closed door.

The Rock Chicks stared at it, too.

Slowly, Shirleen turned to me.

"Shirleen's not thinkin' good thoughts," she announced.

"You got *that* right, sister," Jet muttered.

Effing hell.

Chapter 14

Maybe in a Towel

Stella

I wrapped the sheet around my body and then shuffled on my bottom to the edge of the bed.

"You okay?" Ally asked.

"I'll make coffee," Ava muttered and headed into the kitchen.

My feet hit the floor and I headed toward my robe. "I think something bad just happened," I said softly, not certain I wanted to share, but too scared at what I was feeling to keep it inside.

"You think?" Shirleen asked. "Air was so heavy you could cut it with a knife."

I looked at her as I struggled to put the robe on over the sheet. Her eyes were sharp but her face was soft, and that combo eloquently showed her concern.

I felt the tears hit the backs of my eyes again. I pulled breath in through my nose and decided maybe I shouldn't share.

"What was in the paper?" I asked, changing the subject and dropping the sheet.

"Unh-unh, girl, what just happened?" Daisy was standing, hands on her slim, faded denim-covered hips.

I took a moment to peruse Daisy's ensemble, which was faded denim from head-to-toe, literally. She was wearing a billed, slouchy, denim cap on her platinum blonde head, pigtails peeking out from under it at the back, wispy bangs at her forehead. She had on a tight, faded, buttoned up, denim vest, so much cleavage bulging forth from the v-neck that she was forced to leave one button undone, taking the vest from indecent to mildly pornographic. Completing her look, she wore jeans, skintight all the way down to her ankles, and denim covered, pointed toed, spike heeled mules.

I allowed myself another moment to marvel at her ability to pull off this ridiculous outfit as if it was the height of couture before she snapped, "Well?"

I grabbed my sky-blue lace undies and pulled them on while saying, "I think I just did something stupid."

"More stupid than not just lettin' Mace back into your life without this idiotic rigmarole? Bullets flyin'. Hot Bunch boys puttin' their asses on the line. Threats against all you all…" Shirleen whirled her finger around to take in all the Rock Chicks. "Still, you all act like getting a booty call from one of the Hot Bunch was like being tortured. I just don't get it."

"It's hardly a booty call, Shirleen. They get in your head, move into your house, push you around, tell you what to do, so damn bossy," Indy sprang to my defense heatedly as I walked toward the kitchen. In fact, Indy's words were so heated it seemed she was having a flashback.

Shirleen put a hand to her chest and reared back. "Oh, is that it? Well excuse me! You poor child!" Then she made a snorting sound. "Shee-it, any one of those boys wanted to push me around, I'd say bring it on. Hell, I'd pay for one of 'em to move into my house. They don't even have to do me. Just walk around so I can watch. Maybe in a towel."

Jules looked at me and rolled her eyes.

"You don't understand," Roxie put in.

"Nope. That's right, girl, Shirleen *does not* understand. So what trauma are we up against now?" Shirleen's eyes moved to me. "You havin' too many orgasms or what?"

"Is there such a thing as too many orgasms?" Annette asked before I could answer. Even though I barely knew her and she'd never been to my house in her life, she was opening and closing my cupboard doors, searching for I didn't know what.

"No, child, that's the point," Shirleen replied with barely restrained patience.

"For what it's worth," Annette went on, giving up on her search and turning to the group. "I'm with Shirleen on this one. Jason ain't no slouch in the orgasm department but we got a deal, him and me. It's like those lists you make with movie stars. If, say, you got a chance at The Rock, you could take it without getting in trouble with your partner. Me and Jason got a list, me, the Hot Bunch, Jason, the Rock Chicks."

Everyone went silent and stared at Annette.

All except Shirleen.

She said, "Mm, girl, you got good taste. That Dwayne Johnson is one shit-hot black man."

"He's Samoan," Annette informed Shirleen.

"That boy is black," Shirleen shot back.

"Half and half," Annette, clearly a bevy of The Rock Information, went on.

"I want the black half," Shirleen returned.

"Oh my God, can we stop talking about The Rock?" Jet yelled.

"I don't mind a short conversational switch to The Rock," Daisy said. "Have you seen *Walking Tall?*"

"Yeah, about seven thousand times," Annette replied.

"I prefer *Faster.*" Shirleen shared her opinion. "There was no sex scene, which was a minus. But the role required two hours of him bein' broody. Him bein' broody for two hours is a definite plus."

"I made a DVD of half an hour, continuous loop of him fighting Vin Diesel over and over and *over* again in *Fast Five,*" Annette shared. "You wanna come over and watch it? I'll make popcorn."

"Oowee, Vin Diesel," Shirleen breathed.

"I am *so there,*" Daisy stated.

"Count me in," Shirleen said after recovering from visions of half an hour continuous loop Johnson vs. Diesel action.

I sat on the edge of a platform, fell to my back and stared at the ceiling.

Were we really talking about The Rock?

He was, of course, hot, but I had other, slightly more important things on my mind.

Ally's face filled my vision.

"You with us, Stella?" she asked.

"No," I replied.

"Okay, maybe we should quit talking about The Rock." I heard Shirleen give in.

My eyes moved to Ally. She was on her hands, leaning over me.

"What was in the paper?" I asked.

Her head came up and she looked over her shoulder. There was a weird noise made by one of the Rock Chicks. Which one I didn't know.

Ally moved out of my eyesight but sat down beside me as I lifted up to sitting position.

Everyone was again silent.

Oh dear.

Finally, Daisy answered, "Well, the whole thing is out. Indy and Lee, Jet and Eddie, Roxie and Hank, Jules and Vance, Luke and Ava. Someone talked. I don't know how they flew under the radar this long, but it's out now. The whole thing. There's a three-piece exposé about the whole Rock Chick on Hot Bunch experience. Today's piece was the first one. They did Indy and Lee, Jet and Eddie. They're gonna follow you and Mace as it goes along."

I stared at her.

She caught my stare and went on, trying to make me feel better (but failing). "If it's any comfort, sugar, they got a great picture of Mace carrying you out of the club last night. You can't see much of you but your ass, but Mace sure looks good."

That was when I said, "You... are... fucking... *shitting*... me."

"I still wanna know who spilled," Ava noted, clearly not recognizing my immense freak out.

"I'm guessing Tex," Ally said.

"Uncle Tex wouldn't talk. I'm thinking Duke. Duke can have a big mouth," Roxie replied.

"No way it's Duke," Indy put in.

"Tod?" Jet asked hesitantly.

"Tod's a definite possibility," Indy said, crossing her arms.

I was looking from one to the other, thinking that they were focusing on the wrong thing.

"How about May, do you think May might say something?" Ally asked Jules.

Jules sighed then nodded.

I'd had enough. "Who cares who did it! We have enough to worry about. Someone wants us all dead. And Mace and I just had a very unhappy conversation, *very* unhappy, where he was about to let me in and instead of getting a piece of him, I threw it in his face. And he told me that was the only chance I was going to get. And, I repeat, I threw it in his face! I don't want a chance, but I do! I don't want to care that I might have hurt him by not listening to what he had to say, but I think I did, and furthermore, I think I care. Effing bloody hell, my life's a shambles. I don't know what to think! What the hell do I do now?"

"He was going to let you in?" Jet asked softly, her eyes on me were intense, and they scared me a little bit.

I nodded.

"And you didn't let him?" Roxie went on.

I tore my eyes away from Jet's scary-intense ones and nodded again at Roxie.

"Sugar, why'd you do a fool thing like that?" Daisy demanded to know, hands back to hips.

"I don't know! People are shooting at me. Mace is effing with my head. Linnie's dead. I'm on the front page of the paper. A journalist I don't even know because I still haven't seen a paper is going to follow this fucked up shit between Mace and me. And a scout from a very good label told me he's been coming to my shows. I'm not thinking straight," I replied.

"Oh, speakin' of that scout, Dixon Jones comin' to the gig this afternoon," Shirleen put in.

I felt my heart seize as my eyes cut to her.

"What?" I asked.

"Yeah. He's into you. *Way* into you. We're talking deal," Daisy informed me.

Deal?

Daisy and Shirleen were talking *deal?*

With *my* band?

They couldn't talk deal.

Only I could talk deal.

Effing hell.

My eyes moved to Daisy and my breath moved to Idaho.

"What?" I repeated, a word that I beginning to hate.

"Deal," Shirleen took over. "Hector knows someone who knows someone who knows what he's talkin' about in the music business. Hector talked to him and he's got the lingo. This Dixon Jones guy thinks Hector's the shit because, well, he *is* the shit. You shoulda seen him. It was like he did it for a living."

I opened my mouth, then closed it, then opened it again and said, "I met Hector a few days ago."

"Well, Dixon Jones thinks we're your managers with Hector being Top Dog," Daisy explained.

My brain thought about the idea that an A&R man from Black Fat Records would think The Blue Moon Gypsies needed *three* managers, with two of them being Shirleen and Daisy, and swiftly rejected that idea as seriously unpalatable and spit it right back out.

"Hector's a private detective," I said stupidly, going for denial.

"We know that and you know that, but Dixon Jones thinks he's a shit-hot music biz type. We're lookin' at studio time," Shirleen replied.

Oh.

My.

God.

"Studio?" I whispered.

"Yeah, recordin' studio," Shirleen told me, like I didn't know.

"That is fuckin' *phat!*" Annette shouted.

I turned to Ally. "Do you think, if I walk outside, someone will shoot me?"

"It's a possibility," Ally told me.

"Then that's my next move," I replied and stood up.

"*You can't get shot!* Dixon is meeting with you and the band after your gig at The Little Bear," Daisy screeched.

It was then my brain thought about the idea of any scout having a meeting with my band, who were likely to do something immensely stupid, and it regurgitated that thought, too. Fast.

"He's not meeting the band," I said.

"He is, and you are, too," Shirleen returned.

"Okay, you think maybe I can have a moment to process all that is fucked up with my life before it gets fucked up even more?" I snapped at Shirleen.

"Ain't no time to process, girl. This is life. Roll with the changes," Shirleen retorted.

"Don't quote REO Speedwagon at me!" I yelled.

"This page is done, sugar, you got to turn the page," Daisy got close.

"Okay, now you're quoting Bob Seger," I clipped. "And you're not allowed to do that, either."

Daisy turned confused eyes to Indy. "I thought I was still quoting REO."

"Maybe we should stop talking in Rock Speak and help Stella to deal with this issue with Mace," Jet cut in.

"Ain't no time for that, we got a gig to get to," Shirleen said, as if she'd been going to gigs with me for years rather than a few days. "And anyway, Vance and Matt are waitin' outside and Vance ain't gonna be happy if we hang out forever. He was doin' Jules a favor, bringing us over here. He said he's got shit to do."

"No, Shirleen, really, we should deal with—" Jet pushed, but I interrupted her.

I did this by shouting, so loudly I didn't hear the door opening and Mace coming in. "Oh shit! The gig! The equipment's still at the Palladium. Mace has to set up the security detail. Effing hell!"

"It's covered," Mace's deep voice announced.

I jumped in surprise and everyone turned their eyes to him.

He unhooked the leash from Juno's collar and Juno moved to me slowly, giving head butts and sniffs to Rock Chicks as she passed.

I looked at Mace and knew with a glance he was still pissed.

"What's covered?" I asked cautiously.

His eyes came to mine. "Everything. Shirleen's got Roam and Sniff helpin' the band move the equipment. Luke's in charge of the security detail and he's already arranged it with The Little Bear. You're good," he told me. I took a moment to wonder who the eff Roam and Sniff were, then he finished, "Now, I'm takin' a shower."

Shirleen got a huge grin on her face at the idea of Mace taking a shower. The rest of The Rock Chicks shuffled uncomfortably because they knew they shouldn't be there, but in a one room apartment, there was nowhere else to be.

I moved toward Mace as he came at me to get to the bathroom.

I put out my hand, caught his forearm and said, "Mace, we need to talk."

He stopped, looked at my hand then at me, face hard, voice low and vibrating with anger. "Done talkin', babe."

Sharp, hard gut kick.

Effing hell.

My hand dropped. He kept moving, entered the bathroom and shut the door behind him.

I stared at the door.

The Rock Chicks stared at the door.

We heard the shower go on.

"Oowee," Shirleen whispered reverently.

"Time to go," Jules announced.

"Stella—" Jet said.

"Time to go," Indy was staring pointedly at Jet.

Jet stared back.

Indy jerked her head once toward the door.

Jet jerked hers back, but this looked like it was to communicate a negative.

I got the feeling they were having a conversation without words, but I didn't want to know what they were saying.

What I wanted to know was what Mace was thinking.

Shitsofuckit!

He was screwing with my head without even *trying* to screw with my head.

Or maybe I was screwing with my own head.

Juno shoved her nose in my belly, a hard-to-miss doggie cry for breakfast.

"Okay, baby, breakfast," I told her, giving her a behind the ears scratch.

Her tongue lolled out happily.

On that, Ally gave me an arm squeeze. "Later, Stella."

"See you at the gig," Ava called on a wave.

"We didn't get any coffee," Annette noted. Then, at a look from Roxie, she gave up on coffee, smiled at me and gave me a peace sign.

"We'll talk later," Jet promised on her own wave.

"Knock 'em dead," Jules said.

"Don't forget the meeting," Shirleen warned.

"Bring the band," Daisy reminded me.

"Hang in there," Roxie called before blowing me a kiss.

Only Indy got close and gave me a hug.

"You'll be all right and he'll be all right. I promise. No bullshit. Everything will be all right," she whispered in my ear then pulled away and looked in my eyes. "Yeah?" she finished softly.

"Yeah," I replied. Even though I didn't believe her, I wanted to.

She touched her cheek to mine and whispered, "Later, girl."

Then all the Rock Chicks were gone.

I made my dog breakfast and poured myself a coffee, but all the while I did it, my head was in the shower.

Therefore, when Mace got out of the shower, I was standing in the kitchen, a half-drunk cup of coffee in my hand, Juno's heavy body lying on my feet, and my eyes were on the door.

I watched as he moved toward his bags, pulled out some fresh clothes and then yanked off the towel. I held my breath at the sight of him, but I didn't get a very long look. He dressed in record time and walked back to the bathroom.

I stayed where I was, a feeling of dread stealing over me.

Something was not right and it was more than its usual under-threat-of-being-murdered not right.

Mace came back out, tossed his boots by the platform, shoved his clothes in his bag, pulled out a pair of socks and then zipped the bag closed.

Oh yes.

Something was not right.

That feeling of dread grew.

He sat on the platform again to put on his socks and boots.

"Mace—" I started. What I was going to say I didn't know, but I didn't get the chance.

"The boys'll cover you today," he told me, not looking up from what he was doing.

"Mace—"

"I'll have my shit outta here by the time you get back."

I felt my mouth fill with saliva, that feeling of dread building and spreading so fast I was paralyzed.

I fought the paralysis and whispered, "Mace—" yet again.

"I'll call Turner and tell him he's up."

My hand not holding the coffee cup came down and gripped the counter.

"Eric?" I asked.

Mace stood and looked at me. "You know another Turner?"

I shook my head, even though I probably did. I knew a lot of people.

Mace put his tongue to his teeth and gave a sharp whistle.

Juno shot up and trotted to him. Mace bent over and gave her a full doggie rubdown.

A final, *farewell* full doggie rubdown.

This isn't right, my brain sounded panicked and confused.

"Mace—" I started again.

Mace stopped rubbing Juno down and headed toward his bag.

"Stay well, Stella," he said, not looking at me.

He bent to his bag and lifted up, throwing the strap over his shoulder and turning to the door.

Oh my God, this isn't right! My brain screamed.

I had to do something. Anything. And I had to do it quick.

"I broke my arm when I was twelve. Fell off my bike," I blurted.

Mace stopped on his way to the door. His side to me, he only turned his head when he looked at me.

I swallowed. "When I got home, my Mom was gone. I don't know where. My Dad was the only one there."

Mace didn't move and didn't speak.

My breath wasn't taking a hike, it was coming fast and scared. All thoughts of wanting Mace out of my life were gone.

Poof.

Vanished.

"Dad didn't—" I began, but Mace interrupted me by shaking his head.

"Too late," he told me, and my stomach clenched.

"Let me finish," I whispered. Mace shook his head, but I kept talking. "My arm was hanging funny. It hurt so much I thought I'd pass out from the pain. You'd think that's all I would remember—"

"Too late," Mace said again.

"But it wasn't what I remembered." I pressed on. "He was so pissed. Dad was. He was watching some golf tournament on TV and he was pissed at me because he had to take me to the hospital instead of—"

Mace interrupted me again. His body turned toward me and his voice was back to low and vibrating in that scary way. "Too fuckin' late."

"Don't go," I whispered, changing tactics, my head coming together, my thoughts, for the first time in days, finally clear and focused.

I knew what I was doing, letting him have sex with me, sleep with me, move in with me. I knew I was doing it because I wanted it. I wanted him. Actions speak louder than words, but I'd so wrapped myself in that cotton wool Floyd told me about, I didn't hear the muffled communication.

I held my breath.

Mace stared at me.

I stared back.

"Please, don't go," I said again.

Part of me expected him to grin in triumph, come forward, pull me in his arms and kiss me.

I decided I'd have to act pissed-off for a while and then, once I gave him a load of shit, I'd let it go.

Instead, his mouth got tight, he turned on his boot, and he muttered, "For fuck's sake, arm the alarm."

Then he was gone.

My body was twisted in order to look over my shoulder at the closed door.

What just happened? My shocked brain asked.

I didn't answer.

I knew what just happened.

I slid down the cupboard, put my coffee cup beside me on the floor, closed my eyes and pressed my forehead into my knees.

I felt Juno pushing her nose into my neck, giving doggie comfort as best she could, but I didn't turn to her.

Instead, I slid straight into the place that knew me well.

I slid directly into black.

⟞⟡⟝

The gig was almost over.

The Rock Chicks were sitting at tables up front and center, all of them looking subdued and a little worried.

The Hot Bunch, Tex and Duke were all on duty, guarding the doors, the stage, wandering the crowd. I'd seen them all.

All of them.

But Mace.

Even though the show was shit (all my fault and I knew it), the crowd was preparing for "Ghostriders".

Instead, I pulled my arm in a sweep in front of me, disengaging my guitar strap from my shoulders. I set my guitar in its stand and walked across the dusty, faded rugs that covered The Little Bear's stage. I sat next to Floyd on the piano bench. He was staring at me, his eyes startled.

For the past four hours, the entire band and The Rock Chicks had all tried to get through to me. I was so deep in black I just went through the motions like an automaton. I didn't know what they asked. I didn't know what they said. I didn't even know my own replies.

I leaned in to Floyd and whispered in his ear.

He put his hand over the microphone. "Stella, girl—"

I closed my eyes tight then opened them and looked into his.

"Just do it," I begged.

He gave me a long look, nodded to the band then started playing.

The room went silent in shock.

I looked at the rafters, blindly taking in the trademark Little Bear bras nailed to them, then I pulled Floyd's microphone my way, closed my eyes and started singing.

And what I sang was Billy Joel's, "And So It Goes."

I sang it for Mace, who wasn't even there, but I did it anyway, because nothing said what I needed to say better than those beautiful, heartbroken lyrics.

Floyd played the final notes to the song and I kept my eyes closed, waiting. Waiting and hoping.

I opened my eyes and looked at the crowd.

The minute I did, they roared with applause.

But it didn't hit me the way it normally did.

Because Mace wasn't there.

He didn't charge up to the stage, taking me in his arms and telling me beautiful things.

"Stella, girl—" Floyd whispered, but that was it. I was done. I'd done it to myself this time. I had no one else to blame.

For some insane reason, I got up and ran across the small stage, jumped down and started pushing through the crowd. I felt nothing. I knew nothing. I just knew I had to go. Where, I had no idea. I just had *to go.*

I could feel hands on me, tugging at me. I heard my name called in familiar voices. I knew one was Hector's, the other was Duke's.

But I was gone. Through the crowd to the doors. I felt freedom, but it was far from sweet. Then I was caught, my momentum meaning I was lifted up, swung around and put down. I looked behind me and up to see I'd been caught and was now held by Bobby, one of Lee's men.

"Shit, woman, what're you thinkin'?" Bobby's voice was annoyed.

I didn't answer.

I struggled to get away, kicking and grunting, and then something happened.

Bobby was no longer struggling with me. He let me go and he was struggling with someone else, a big bulky man, bigger and bulkier even than Bobby, and Bobby was enormous.

Then Luke was there and he barreled into another man. With a shoulder to the other man's belly, Luke lifted him clean off his feet and slammed him against the wooden railing outside The Little Bear. The man flipped feet-over-head over the railing, landing on his back and cracking his skull with a sickening thud against the pavement. Luke turned toward me, but there were more men. One came at him, then more people were there, including Hector, Lee and more suited men, and all of them were engaged in hand-to-hand combat.

Before I could get my wits about me, I felt hard, firm fingers attach on my upper arm. I gave a surprised cry right before I was yanked down the wooden plank steps, and before I knew what was happening, I was thrown into the backseat of a waiting, long, sleek, black limousine.

The door closed behind me and the limousine shot away.

I realized I was holding my breath and I turned to see there was someone in the backseat with me.

He was very tall, lean, well-built, on the other side of middle-aged. Black hair peppered with silver and wearing in an expensive suit, expensive cufflinks and an expensive watch.

Oh, and last but not least, he had clear, sharp, achingly familiar jade green eyes.

I stared at him with my mouth open while he spoke.

"Hello Stella. I'm Preston Mason, Kai's father."

Oh dear.

Chapter 15
I'm Not Good Enough for Him
Stella

"I'm supposed to be in a meeting," I told Preston Mason because I couldn't think of anything else to say.

I had actually been half-assedly planning to get out of the meeting with Dixon Jones by feigning a migraine or a heart attack or something, but now I kind of wish I'd made the meeting with Jones. I figured he'd be a lot easier to deal with than a surprise kidnapping by Mace's apparently super-wealthy Dad.

"You'll need to reschedule," he replied.

I decided to push. "It's kind of important."

He calmly adjusted the cuff of his impeccable light blue shirt under the sleeve of his equally impeccable dark blue suit jacket.

"I'm afraid you'll have to reschedule."

I sat back as the limousine took a curve on the mountain road.

The Little Bear was in Evergreen, a mountain town that managed to be hip, cool, exclusive and a Harley boy hangout all at the same time. It looked just a smidge shy of being the type of place where gunslingers would still have showdowns at high noon.

I effing loved Evergreen. It was as rock 'n' roll as you could get (according to me).

"Erm," I ventured carefully. "Did you just kidnap me?"

His jade eyes came to me. "Yes."

Wow.

Well one thing was certain, even if I didn't have the eyes as proof, Preston Mason was as straight talking arrogant as his son.

"Why?" I asked.

"We need to talk about Kai."

"I don't want to talk about Kai."

And I didn't.

Furthermore, I didn't want to call him "Kai". It felt weird. I felt weird enough as it was. I didn't want to feel weirder. If I felt any more weird, my mind might spin off into an alternate reality and live there the rest of my life, my body still in real reality, lying in a coma, confounding doctors who would eventually turn off life support, and then where would I be?

"How well do you know Kai?" Preston Mason took me out of my crazed thoughts and my eyes focused on him again.

"Um…" I hedged because this was a good question.

Biblically, one could say I was a Kai Expert. All other ways it was up for debate.

"I feel I should warn you, my son is not a good man."

I sat and stared at him in complete and total shock.

Then I said the hated word, "What?"

"He's responsible for his sister's murder, amongst other things."

Gut kick.

So huge and savage my body jerked with it.

Mace's sister was murdered?

Visions of Mace's face swam in my head, the demons dancing in his eyes. Mace telling me he could understand what I meant about my father.

And meaning it.

Holy effing hell.

Mace's sister was murdered.

"Mace's sister, your daughter, was murdered?" I whispered.

He studied me and it made me uncomfortable. The eyes were familiar, but they were also completely different. There was nothing behind them, no emotion, even when he was talking about his daughter's murder.

For your information, this creeped me way the hell out.

"Don't you read the papers?" he asked me.

"I haven't had the chance," I replied.

"It's all lies," he said.

"What's lies?"

"All of it."

"What, exactly?"

He changed the subject. "I want you out of his life."

This threw me because I hadn't come to terms with the last mental blow he'd dealt.

"Out of whose life?" I asked stupidly.

Preston Mason's eyes narrowed. "Kai's."

"Why?"

"Do you know who I am?"

I shook my head but said, "You're Mace's father."

I watched his lip curl right before he asked, "How stupid are you?"

Now I was getting angry.

What was with this guy?

He kidnaps me and then he's mean to me?

What was up with that?

"What's with you?" I snapped.

"I know how stupid you are. 2.5 grade point average. You skipped just enough school so you could graduate, too much to learn anything. You didn't go to college. Your father's a welder. Your mother's been a waitress for twenty-five years. Neither of them went to college either."

"So?"

"So, Kai graduated with honors from the University of Hawaii with a bachelor's in civil engineering."

Yowza.

Civil engineering?

That sounded hard.

I shook off thoughts of Mace beavering away at his studies using a protractor (or whatever they needed for civil engineering), forged ahead and clipped, "So?"

"So, the last girl Kai got serious about was the daughter of a senator."

Yikes.

Really?

A senator?

I hid my surprise and repeated, "So?"

"My God," he muttered. "You really are stupid."

Now totally pissed-off, I leaned forward and hissed, "Stop saying that."

"You don't get it, Stella. What I'm saying is that you aren't good enough for my son."

He was not for real!

I sat back, crossed my arms on my chest and threw one leg over the other, bouncing my brown, dusty cowboy-booted foot.

"Let me get this straight, big man. First you tell me your son is responsible for your daughter's murder and he's not a good man. Then you act like a poorly-written character out of a formulaic romantic comedy and tell me I'm not good enough for him. I gotta tell you, it's not me being stupid. It's *you* that's not making any sense."

"Maybe I should have had a picture book drawn up so you could follow along," he returned.

"Yeah, too bad you didn't do that so I could take it away from you and beat you with it, you crazy loon," I snapped back, leaned forward and pounded on the smoky partition that separated us from the driver. "Take me back to the bar!" I demanded.

"Sit back, Stella, I'm not done with you yet."

I looked over my shoulder at him. "You might not be done with me, but I'm done with you." I turned around, banged on the partition again and shouted, "Take me back to the bar!"

"Sit back!" Preston Mason's voice had risen and he sounded pissed-off.

I again looked over my shoulder. "All right, Mr. Mason. I'm having a *bad* day. And I mean *bad*. You do *not* want to mess with me. Not today. Seriously." I turned back around and banged on the partition and shouted, "Take me back to the goddamned bar!"

"Your father has fallen behind on his mortgage payments," Preston Mason said and I stopped banging.

This, I knew without a doubt, was not a fortunate turn in the conversation.

Slowly, I turned around and looked at him.

"How do you know that?"

"Because I own his mortgage."

Shitsofuckit.

"Mr. Mason, you know a lot about me, so I'm guessing you know I haven't spoken to my father in years. So I have to ask, this would mean something to me because...?" I prompted.

"Because your father has a lot of debt. Your mother's been ill. He didn't have insurance and she certainly didn't. Chemotherapy costs a great deal when you're too proud and too stupid to take Medicaid."

Oh no.

No.

I didn't just find out my mother had cancer and my father was too proud to help her out with government funded healthcare (which the stupid jerk would be) from Mace's asshole father.

Did I?

I stared at him.

And, for some reason, I knew he wasn't lying.

Okay, it was safe to say my bad day just got worse.

My... fucking... shitty... luck.

I tilted my head back and looked at the ceiling of the limo.

Then I closed my eyes.

Then I sat back, crossed my arms and legs and looked out the window.

"Take me back to the bar," I said quietly.

"I'll foreclose," Preston Mason warned.

"No you won't," I told the window.

"Oh yes, Stella, I will."

My head turned slowly and I looked at him. "No. You won't. This morning Mace broke up with me." I flicked out my hand. "Your whole scene was a waste of time. It's over between us."

He watched me closely, likely assessing my honesty.

I stared him straight in the eye.

I watched his face relax.

"Well, that's good news," he said softly, the tips of his lips going up in a humorless smile.

How on this earth did Mace come from this man's loins?

"Promise you won't foreclose," I demanded.

It was his turn to sit back, but he looked relaxed and at-ease.

"Money's money. They don't pay, eventually, they'll be—"

"You foreclose, I go after Mace."

His brows drew together. "You just told me Kai broke up with you."

"*Mace* broke up with me, yes. We had an argument. It was bad. But I'm under his skin. He told me so his damn self. You leave my parents alone, I'll just be a scar. You turn them out of their home, I'll start itching." I uncrossed my arms and leaned toward him. "And, Mr. Mason, I'm an itch he likes to scratch."

Mace's father's eyes moved over my face, my hair and down my torso. It took a lot out of me not to squirm, but I held my body and gaze steady.

Finally, he said, "As long as I own the loan, I won't foreclose."

I wasn't *that* stupid.

"You keep the loan for as long as my mother's alive," I returned.

"Stella."

"Something happens to them while she's still alive, you'll be staring at me during Thanksgiving dinner."

He muttered under his breath and I was pretty certain it was a curse word.

He hit a button and said into the car, "Jon, we're taking Ms. Gunn back to the bar."

It was my turn to smile a humorless smile.

───※───

We hit the outskirts of Evergreen before either of us spoke again.

And it was me who broke the silence.

"You're wrong," I said, again staring out the window and not facing him.

"Yes? And how's that?"

"Mace is a good man."

I heard him laugh. It was as humorless as his smile.

I watched Evergreen slip by and saw The Little Bear. There were black Explorers everywhere and my heart hurt a little to see Mace standing, hands at his hips on the wood walk outside the bar with Tex, Lee, Hank, Hector, Eddie and my entire band standing with him.

Lee saw us first and jerked his chin at the limousine. I watched Mace turn and I noted two things immediately. The first, he was the most handsome man I'd ever seen in my life. The second, he was furious.

"You're also right," I went on quietly.

"And how's that?" Preston Mason's voice was also quiet, and as I was turned away from him, I didn't notice his eyes were also locked on Mace.

The limousine slid to a stop, but before it did, Mace was already at my door.

"I'm not good enough for him," I whispered.

The door opened and Mace leaned in, his hand wrapped around mine and he yanked me out. My hand held firmly in his, he kept me at his side as he leaned back into the limo.

He pointed at his father and he said in a tone that sent chills up my spine, "We're not done."

"Kai—" Preston Mason started, but he didn't get any further.

Mace slammed the door and pulled me toward an Explorer.

I yanked at my hand. "Mace."

He kept going.

I yanked again. "Mace."

He stopped us at the passenger side door and pulled it open. "Get in."

I looked up at him then I noticed movement and saw that the limousine was still there. Preston Mason had alighted and was watching us.

I felt my heart skip, squeeze then stop.

It wasn't a good thing for your heart to stop. It hurt your whole body.

"Get in the car, Stella," Mace ordered.

I looked at him again and his voice rumbled in my brain.

This shit goes both ways. This doesn't end until I know you won't walk away, but also you won't let me walk away. Never again.

I could get him back.

I needed you to make a statement, Kitten. You didn't.

If I made a statement, I knew, I just knew, I could get him back.

Then his father's voice came to me.

He's responsible for his sister's murder.

I didn't believe that for a second.

What I did believe was that whatever happened with his sister, Mace believed it.

At that moment all I needed to do was make a statement.

And making a statement put my Mom and Dad on the line. I sure as hell didn't have the money to help them out.

And I wasn't about to make Mace take care of yet another of my problems.

Which would only be another in a long line of problems, of the past and undoubtedly well into the future.

Yep, Kai Mason was too good for me.

Mace got closer to me.

"Babe," he said softly. "Get in the car."

His voice washed over me like soothing elixir.

I knew I had my opening. His father gave it to me. Mace didn't like it when I was in danger. He didn't like it at all. He didn't like it enough to get over being mad at me for being stupid.

I allowed myself to feel it for only a beat then I asked. "Are you taking me to Eric?"

Mace's eyes narrowed. "No, I'm not fuckin' takin' you to Turner." I shook my head. He let go of my hand, his fingers wrapped around my upper arm and he leaned in. "We'll talk at your place. Now get in the car."

"Take me to Eric," I said softly.

I felt his fingers tense spasmodically on my arm, but that was the only reaction he allowed me.

I could take no more.

"Goddammit, Mace, take me to Eric!" I shouted.

He stared at me.

I held my breath, kept my outward calm as my insides were shivering and stared back.

The pain slashed in his eyes again.

This time, it also slashed through my heart.

He let go of my arm, turned and walked back to the doors of the bar.

"She wants to go to Turner," he told Lee as he tossed Lee the keys in his hand. Lee caught them, but in turn Hector lobbed some keys at Mace. Mace nabbed them and went straight to another Explorer. I watched as he swung in, started up the SUV and drove away.

"Get in the car, *mamita*." Hector's heat all of a sudden was close, beating into my side, and he was talking to me softly.

"You'll take me to Eric?" I whispered and, with Mace gone, I didn't fucking care that Hector could see plain as day the tears in my eyes.

"I'll take you wherever you want to go," he replied.

Without further hesitation, I got in the car.

⊰⊱

I felt the bed depress.

Then I felt the weight of my hair being lifted away from my neck.

"You all right, sweetheart?" Eric's voice came at me in the dark.

No.

No, I was definitely not all right.

I didn't know what time it was, but it had to be late. I'd been lying in that bed for hours. It was coming on summer and the days were longer, but the light had faded and night was pitch black.

"Yeah," I lied.

"You need to eat something," Eric told me.

The very thought made me want to hurl.

"I'm not hungry."

"Stella, that tells me you aren't all right," Eric said. He waited for my response that didn't come then he went on, "What the fuck happened with Mason's father?"

"He's a jerk," I told Eric.

Eric laughed, but it was short and I got the feeling he didn't think anything was funny.

"Preston Mason is a definitely a jerk."

I tried to focus on him in the dark, but he was just a shadow so I focused on where I thought his head was.

"Do you know him?"

Eric was silent a second then his voice came at me and it was heavy with surprise. "Everyone knows Preston Mason, Stella. The man's famous."

I got up on an elbow.

Just so you know, I knew I was doing wrong. I wasn't only playing Mace, I was now playing Eric.

Earlier, I had thought for a brief moment to ask Hector to take me to his place, but Hector had to work with Mace. If Hector took me in Mace would freak out. Their working relationship would deteriorate and I'd be to blame for that, too.

No, the only way to make a surgically clean, never to be healed break with Mace without dragging anyone into it that mattered was to be where I was right at that moment.

In Eric Turner's bed.

Mace wouldn't ever forgive that.

Ever.

"Famous for what?" I asked.

Eric moved. Leaning forward, he turned on a lamp that lit the room with soft light.

It was a decent room. An impersonal room. The room of a man who probably didn't live there, but was staying there for an assignment.

Eric had wanted to put me into protective custody, but I wouldn't let him. I had a life to lead. I would go back to my ultra-safe apartment, but only when I knew Mace couldn't get in anymore.

That was a phone call I was *not* looking forward to.

My mind went from the phone call to Eric, who was watching me.

His hand came to my jaw and he murmured correctly, "He's on your mind."

I closed my eyes and bit my lips.

Then I opened my eyes and whispered, "I'm sorry."

Eric got up and grabbed my hand. "Come to the living room."

Not letting go of my hand, he led me to the equally impersonal living room. He sat on the couch then he pulled me down on his lap.

I should have resisted, but I didn't. I also didn't resist when he pushed me so my back was to the couch, my head was on the padded arm rest and he was on his elbow at my side. My ass was still in his lap, my legs over his thighs, his other arm lying loose across my belly.

Somehow this intimate position felt more comfortable and reassuring than sexual and predatory. I figured it had a lot to do with the worried, gentle look on Eric's face.

"I'm tryin' to figure out how you spent so much time with Mason, fell deep for the guy and don't know who his fuckin' father is," Eric said to me.

I was trying to figure that out, too.

Though, if I was honest, I knew the answer.

Because I was a big, screaming loser.

When I didn't say anything, Eric went on, "Preston Mason is loaded. Stinking rich. He's got shitloads of money."

"I kinda guessed that with the limo and the suit."

Eric smiled. It was a good smile, and some girl someday would be super-lucky when he smiled at her like that. Unfortunately, that girl was not going to be me.

"As rich as you think anyone can be, sweetheart, he's richer."

That was a little surprising considering I could think of being filthy rich.

"Yeah?" I asked.

"Yeah. And he didn't get where he is because he's a nice man, either."

I pulled in breath, and before I could reconsider or even think of what a bitch it made me that I was laying on Eric's couch with Eric and playing at his feelings for me in this whole fiasco, I said, "He told me Mace was responsible for his sister's murder."

Something in Eric's eyes flashed and I didn't like it, mainly because his face got tight along with the flash, and he looked supremely pissed-off.

"What?" I used the hated word again, but Eric stayed silent. Then, as humiliating as it was in outing how shallow my relationship with Mace had been, I shared, "I didn't even know Mace had a sister, much less that she was murdered."

I knew this, too, surprised Eric. The anger went out of his face and he shook his head. Then his face went soft again.

"Figure I had you, warm and willing in my bed, I wouldn't talk about my sister's kidnapping and murder either."

My breath felt like exploring the coast of Maine and I felt my eyes go huge.

"Kidnapping?" I breathed.

"Oh fuck," Eric muttered before he looked at my knees.

My hand went to his face and I turned him to look at me.

"What the fuck happened to Mace's sister?"

Eric watched me, then he did it some more, then he sighed and it was heavy.

"I'm gonna let Mason tell you this story."

"Mace and I are done," I replied quickly.

His mouth formed a smile that didn't reach his eyes.

When he spoke, his voice was sweet but weirdly sad. "Sweetheart, as much as it kills me to admit it, you aren't done. And it's his story to tell." I opened my mouth to speak but he shook his head. "It's his to tell, Stella. It isn't pretty and if he didn't share it with you, he didn't for a reason. But I got no doubt he'd planned to get around to it eventually. The time's got to be right for that kind of shit. The time isn't right when you find a good woman. You don't want to lay your shit on her up front and freak her out."

This made sense.

And any story that involved a jerky asshole of a father and a kidnapped and murdered sister was *definitely* shit you didn't want to lay on anyone, good woman or not.

I was already freaked out and I didn't know what the eff happened!

What I did know was that I would have known because Mace was going to tell me that morning.

I closed my eyes and turned my head away from Eric.

"I'm such an idiot," I whispered.

Eric moved, stretching to lie by me full out on the couch. His arms moved around me to pull me full frontal, his legs tangled with mine, and I pressed my face into his chest.

After a few minutes of holding me, Eric asked, "You want me to take you back to him?"

I did.

I definitely did.

And I definitely knew that I'd been wrong about Eric.

He was a good guy.

A good guy I was using, and another good guy I'd never have because I was thinking I was exactly as stupid as Preston Mason thought I was.

I answered, "Mace and I are over."

Eric's arms got tighter and his voice got lower, and I could swear I heard a hint of anger when he asked, "What did Preston Mason do to you in that car?"

"Nothing."

"Bullshit."

I tipped my head back to look at him. "Seriously, Eric," I lied through my teeth. "Nothing. We just talked." At least that last part wasn't a lie.

He wasn't buying it. "Preston Mason doesn't make a move without an ulterior motive. He didn't kidnap you from a gig to have a chat."

"I'm not saying it was a pleasant chat. I'm just saying he didn't do anything to me."

Eric's brows drew together. "Stella, you're keepin' something from me."

"No, I'm not. You know I didn't want to be back together with Mace. I just decided to make it clear," I lied.

Yes, I lied.

Yes, again.

And no, I didn't mind going to hell. It couldn't be much worse than my life was at that very moment.

Eric watched me again. It did, of course, occur to me that he was a federal agent and likely could read the body language and facial expressions of much more accomplished liars than myself, but at that moment I was too tired to care.

"I need to sleep," I told him.

"You need to eat then you need to sleep," Eric returned.

"I'm not hungry."

He pushed up, rolled over me, got to his feet and then pulled me to mine.

"Then you get a bowl of cereal," he decided.

"Eric."

"No argument." His voice was firm, so was his grip on my hand, which led me straight to the kitchen.

⌦⌫

Eric

Eric forced a bowl of cereal on Stella.

Then he sat on the couch and watched a movie with her, which she fell asleep halfway through.

He carried her to his bed, pulled a blanket over her still-clothed body, left the room, closed the door and walked into the living room.

He made a couple of calls and got the number he needed.

He dialed Lee Nightingale's cell.

"Yeah?" Nightingale answered.

"It's Special Agent Turner."

Lee's voice went on alert. "Stella?"

"She's fine," Eric responded. "You still got that boy wonder at your computers?"

Lee didn't reply.

"You do, you get him to work on Preston Mason and whatever the fuck he's holding over Stella. Something happened in that car. She's not talkin'. There's gotta be a link."

"We're already on it," Lee responded.

"She doesn't know about Caitlin Mason," Eric went on.

"I know," Lee replied. "You said 'doesn't'. You didn't share?"

"Not my place."

Silence. Then, realizing from Eric's words the lay of the land, Lee went on, "Mace wants the papers kept from her."

Eric thought about the papers the last two days, rehashing every last, juicy, devastating detail of Caitlin Mason's kidnapping and murder and Kai Mason's involvement as part-martyr, part-hero. Worse, his now very public relationship (making out onstage with a local rock star, for fuck's sake) was quickly becoming legend. Stella was cast in the dual role as balm to soothe the wounded soul alongside damsel in distress. A dual role that would only be intensified after her version of "And So It Goes" (Eric didn't see it; the agent he'd assigned to watch her had reported to him about it, in detail) and her post-gig kidnapping complete with the Nightingale Men publicly (and therefore open to cell phone cameras) engaged in pretty fucking brutal physical skirmishes in an effort at her protection.

"I don't blame him," was all Eric said, but his point was made. While she was with him, Eric wouldn't let Stella see the papers.

"You get more—" Lee started, and as much as Eric hated it, he interrupted.

"I'll call."

He beeped off his phone, set it on the end table. He went to check the house alarm, looked out the window in the door to check for the car on the street, two houses down, two agents sitting inside. Spotting the car, he got his gun and put that on the end table, too. He grabbed a blanket, yanked off his boots, lay down on the couch and finished watching the movie.

Chapter 16
Squirtable Cheese
Hank

The next morning, Hank and Mace walked into Lee's office. Lee was sitting on the front edge of his desk, his head bent toward a file in his hand. It came up when they entered. He closed the folder and dropped the file on his desk.

"What did George say?" Lee asked.

George Riverside was a prosecuting attorney. Hank, Eddie and Mace had a meeting with him that morning to discuss the Sidney Carter case. Primarily, the discussion centered around if it was strong enough to arrest him.

"He says we don't have enough," Hank replied and Lee's eyes narrowed.

"You are fuckin' shittin' me," Lee muttered.

Hank shook his head.

George Riverside was a good attorney. He was also ambitious. He knew the Sidney Carter case would make headlines. It could even make careers. George liked headlines and he had big ideas about his career. He wanted people to remember his name, especially come election day.

He also liked to win cases.

What he didn't like was headlines about cases he didn't win. Even though Hank, Eddie and Mace had a tight case, George was being cautious with Carter. He wanted the case locked down, a sure thing, which was impossible. That kind of sure thing didn't exist. It was not only impossible, it was fucking frustrating.

"Eddie get anything out of the shooter?" Lee asked as Hank stopped at the side of the desk.

Lee was referring to the man who shot at Stella and Mace Saturday night.

Mace moved to a chair in front of the desk and sat down, putting his ankle on his opposite knee.

"Nope, shooter's closed tight," Mace replied.

Hank watched as Lee shook his head in surprise, and he knew why.

Eddie was known to be particularly good in the interrogation room.

Hank had watched, though, and Eddie got nothing.

Hank also knew why that was.

The shooter was on a semi-suicide mission. He didn't expect to get away with shooting Stella in a crowded club. He expected to get the job done, but get caught and then get rewarded. Likely, Carter made a deal and was doing good deeds for the shooter's family. It was Carter's MO. He bought allegiance, one way or another, and paid well for it. So well, the chain was buried under money so deep, no one along the line was willing to break it.

On this thought, Hank took in Mace. Even after yesterday and their bad news from George this morning, Mace looked calm and relaxed. Hank had known Mace long enough to know Mace was neither calm nor relaxed. His body, even at rest, was alert, his eyes stone-cold.

Hank knew why this was, too. Hank knew about Mace's sister. Lee had told him about it in detail, including the fact that Mace was incorrectly shouldering the responsibility for what happened in the end game. Hank also knew that Stella didn't know about it. Mace had told the team he wanted it to remain that way until he was ready to share. Finally, Hank knew that any conversation Stella had with Preston Mason was likely to reveal that information. Following this thread, Hank could only assume that Stella's actions after her conversation with Mace's father were an indictment. Or, at least, Mace thought they were.

"I've lost patience with this shit," Lee said, cutting into Hank's thoughts. "We're gonna have to dismantle Carter's army."

It was Hank's turn to shake his head.

"Lee—" he started.

Lee turned to his brother. "I'm gettin' married on Saturday, Hank. I don't think Indy'll like walkin' down the aisle wearin' a flak jacket and a helmet."

No, Lee was right. Indy wouldn't like that. She'd have a shit fit.

"Maybe you can postpone the wedding," Hank suggested.

Lee's eyes went hard. "I'm not postponing my fucking wedding."

Hank watched his brother.

Strike that idea, he thought.

"Maybe you shouldn't be here for the rest of this conversation," Mace put in, gaze on Hank.

Hank's body went tight and his eyes cut to Mace. "I didn't give a year of my life to this investigation to have you guys fuck it up when we're this close."

Both Lee and Mace tensed, but Hank ignored it and went on, "You boys aren't goin' commando and screwin' the pooch. It's not gonna happen."

"Hank—" Lee started, and Hank moved his gaze to Lee.

"It's not gonna happen," Hank repeated. "We play it by the book."

Hank knew his brother didn't like playing by the book. In fact, it was half a miracle Hank had managed to keep them clean this long. Mainly because not only did Lee not play by the book, Kai Mason had made an art of pissing all over the fucking book.

"We're close," Hank reminded them. "And we've been clean so far. Don't fuck it up."

"The girls—" Lee began, but Hank interrupted him again.

"I know what's at stake, Lee," he said quietly. "But Carter goes down, he's gotta stay down. This isn't under radar. We got reporters watching our every move now. You know it and I know it. We gotta play it by the book."

Lee looked at Hank.

Hank returned his stare.

Lee's eyes flashed angrily and Hank knew he had him. He also knew Lee didn't like it. Lastly, he knew he'd only bought some time. They didn't bring Carter down soon, Lee, Mace and Lee's men were going to toss the book out the window.

"Fuck," Lee muttered, giving in as Mace's phone rang.

Hank watched Mace fish his phone out his pocket and look at the display. Whatever it said, Mace didn't like reading it.

He flipped open his phone and clipped, "Yeah?" as a knock came at the door.

Lee called out a terse invitation to enter as Mace said, "Fortnum's. In an hour," then flipped his phone shut and shoved it back in his pocket, mouth tight, body tense.

Hank didn't have a chance to question Mace. Brody, Lee's computer guy, came in and shouted, "I found the link!"

All the men turned to look at Brody.

Brody's pale face under his dark-rimmed glasses was full of excitement. He bounced in, probably wired on copious intake of energy drinks and over-processed food, and threw his doughy body in the other chair in front of Lee's desk as he shoved the glasses more firmly up his nose.

Brody was a computer genius and looked the part. He could do anything with computers; hardware, software, wiring, programming, troubleshooting, searching and, most important to Lee, hacking.

He was dark-haired and goofy as all hell. He was in his early thirties, but he acted like he was twelve. Still, you couldn't help but like the guy.

"Did you guys see it? We made front page again today. Totally awesome!" Brody was still shouting. "Fuckin' great picture of Luke tossin' some guy over a railing. Man, I wish I was there."

Hank moved to the side of Lee's desk, crossed his arms on his chest and rested his thigh against it, his body turned mostly to Brody.

"What'd you find, Brody?" Mace asked, but either Brody didn't hear him or he chose to ignore him and his eyes swung to Hank.

"They did you today. You and Roxie. All about your thing, which people knew about, kind of, as it made the news after Vance blew off Roxie's ex's hand at Daisy's party," Brody informed Hank unnecessarily as, early that morning, Hank, sharing coffee with a sleepy, seriously grumpy (but still cute) Roxie, had read the whole thing. "Got a great picture of her from some beauty pageant when she was in high school. Dude, she was hot even back then," Brody proclaimed.

Hank took a deep breath and settled in. Brody was on a roll and they'd just have to ride it out.

"And they did Jules and Vance, too. It was killer. They made her sound like a superhero. I forgot how good she was at kicking ass. Too bad she's into this mom-to-be shit, she was awesome!" Brody went on.

"Brody, did you find the link?" Lee cut in, and Hank could tell by Lee's voice he was losing patience.

"I wonder who's feedin' them this shit. They got *everything*," Brody ignored Lee and kept at his theme.

"The link," Lee repeated, voice firm.

"What link?" Mace asked.

"They're doin' Ava and Luke tomorrow," Brody continued with excitement.

"Brody, shut the fuck up about the paper and focus. The link." Lee had lost his patience and now his voice was not only firm, but low and vaguely threatening.

Brody clamped his mouth shut and stared at Lee in confusion for a beat.

Then he said, "Oh, yeah. Right. Sure, I found it. I got the link."

Brody stopped talking and all three men stared at him.

"Well?" Lee asked, now crossing his arms on his chest.

"It wasn't that deep, but I had to call Kim in on it," Brody started.

Kim was another employee of Lee's who worked the computers. She ran searches mostly, but also did some phone investigation.

Brody kept going. "See, The People's Bank is owned by Canault Limited. Canault Limited is owned by SunPower. SunPower is owned by—"

"Cut to it," Lee interrupted Brody, having, from experience, learned how to deal with Brody's exuberance, but never having learned to have patience with it.

"APM Holdings!" Brody finished on a shout, the room went hostile and that hostility was coming entirely from Mace.

Everyone in the room knew that Preston Mason was the man behind the multi-national, multi-billion-dollar APM Holdings.

"What the fuck?" Mace asked, his voice low and unhappy, his eyes on Lee.

Hank knew that after Stella was kidnapped by Mace's dad, Lee had ordered both Brody and Vance to look into it. Brody could find a computer trail, amongst other things. Vance could find everything else. Lee was protective of his team, and seeing as Preston Mason could pose a significant threat and had made a move, Lee wasn't taking any chances.

What Hank hadn't known, until now, was that Lee hadn't shared this with Mace.

Lee ignored Mace, eyes still on Brody. He prompted, "Let's go back, Brody, this all means…"

Brody blinked then said, "Oh yeah. The People's Bank owns Travis and Sherry Gunn's mortgage."

"Stella's parents," Lee guessed, and the hostility in the room increased.

Mace's calm and relaxed posture started to disintegrate. He hadn't moved, but his entire body had become visibly tight.

"Yeah," Brody confirmed.

"Explain," Mace growled at Brody, and Brody's eyes moved to Mace. With one look at Mace, Brody's face lost even more color.

"Well, they're behind on their mortgage. Like, seven months behind. The bank has already sent foreclosure notices."

Any trace of calm and relaxed was history. Mace unhooked his ankle from his knee, sat forward and put his elbows to his knees, body leaning toward Brody.

Brody took this in and swallowed, but pressed on, "It gets weirder."

"Yeah?" Mace's voice was deceptively light.

"Yeah," Brody replied. "See, Stella's folks've been having problems for some time now. That's what Kim looked into. Stella's Mom's got cancer and they don't have insurance. They're in debt out the ying yang, drowning in it. They were already behind on payments when The People's Bank bought the mortgage. It was a bad purchase, but that shit happens all the time. What's weird is that even though they weren't current on their payments and fallin' behind on their other bills—their credit rating is in the shitter, by the way—they went to the bank and borrowed more money against the house and the bank gave it to them."

"Goddammit," Lee muttered.

"It gets weirder," Brody went on, and Hank watched Mace close his eyes for a second, sit back in his chair again, then train his gaze on Brody as Brody carried on. "This isn't new. This all started to go down a year ago." Brody turned back to Mace. "I wasn't here then, but Kim said it was when you first started to see Stella."

Hank watched as Mace traced his teeth with his tongue behind closed, tight lips. Hank knew this wasn't a good sign.

"Mace—" Lee started, but Brody was still talking.

"It gets weirder."

Mace's jaw got tight.

"Brody, just finish it," Hank put it quickly.

"Well, I found out all this shit about Stella's folks in, like, an hour. Kim's good at asking questions, and friends and neighbors talk, especially when someone's sick, so we had the story real quick." Brody stopped, swallowed, turned to Mace and said, "Ovarian cancer. That's where it started. They thought they caught it but it spread." He paused again and shared quietly, "It's not looking good." Mace sucked breath into his nose, but nodded at Brody to go on and he did. "Well, I don't know why I did it." Brody shrugged and fidgeted. "I'm no detective like you guys, but it was weird. I mean, why would anyone fuck with a sick woman? Kidnap her daughter?" More hostility from Mace but Brody soldiered on, "So, I started to look deeper and this is where it gets really weird."

"Fucking hell, Brody, just——" Lee cut in.

"I'll finish, I'll finish," Brody said, putting a hand up to Lee then dropping it. "You know that guy who came around a while ago? Out of the blue, makes a meeting with you, wants to invest in Nightingale Investigations, tryin' to talk you into expanding?"

"Yeah," Lee answered, but Hank was watching Mace and he didn't like what he was seeing.

"You shut him down, but I got a hunch. I looked into him. That trail was deeper, harder to track, but I got it eventually, and that guy, and his money, is linked to Mace's dad, too."

Lee's eyes sliced to Mace and he muttered, "Power play."

"What?" Brody asked.

Lee's gaze moved back to Brody. "Anything else?"

Brody shook his head. "That's it so far."

"You feed this to Vance?" Lee pressed.

"Yeah," Brody answered.

"Keep diggin'," Mace ordered, and Brody's head turned to Mace as Mace kept talking. "Everything. Look into Stella, me, Lee, Nightingale Investigations——"

"Luke," Lee said.

"Fuck," Mace mumbled.

Hank closed his eyes. He knew about Luke, too. It would be a long shot. Luke's past associations were buried in a lot of folders where black marker was undoubtedly used heavily. Still, you had enough money, you could find out anything. And Preston Mason had more than enough money.

Hank opened his eyes again when Lee started talking.

"Anything, Brody. Anyone, any member of the team, any one of the Rock Chicks. This is your mission. You sleep it, you eat it, you fuckin' breathe it. Find out if Preston Mason has uncovered anything or tied himself to any of us. Even you," Lee demanded.

"Me?" Brody asked.

"You," Lee replied. "And while you're diggin', you're buryin'. Anything you can find, they can find. They haven't found it yet, you bury it so deep it'll *never* be found."

"Seven years," Mace put in, and Brody turned wide eyes to him. "Go back seven years."

Hank tensed and so did Lee.

"Mace," Lee's voice held a warning.

"Got nothin' to hide," Mace replied.

"You do," Lee returned bluntly.

"Not from him," Mace went on.

Lee was silent.

"He knows I know," Mace said, his voice filled with soft menace. When Lee didn't reply, Mace went on, "I got the upper hand, Lee. He knows it. He wants it back. Or, at least, he wants my silence."

"What are we talkin' about here?" Hank asked.

"Caitlin," Lee replied, and both Hank and Brody pulled in breath.

Mace never talked about his sister.

"I know who took her. I know why," Mace told them both, straight out. "My fuckin' father was involved in some bad shit, fucked over the wrong people and Caitlin paid the price. He doesn't want that out and he doesn't like that I got it to hold over him. He's playin' me and he's usin' Stella to do it. He's demonstratin' his power, his reach. He wants to ensure my silence. He wants me to know he can control me. He wants me to know, I talk, he can make it hurt."

Lee looked at Brody. "Find Preston Mason's weakness."

"I got his weakness," Mace reminded Lee.

Lee's gaze cut to Mace. "I want more."

Mace and Lee locked eyes. Mace nodded and turned to Brody. "What'll it take to bring the mortgage current?"

"Around six K," Brody replied.

"I'll get you my bank details, you do the transfer to bring it current and I want details on their other debt," Mace demanded.

Brody's eyes bugged out. "I have the details and you can't have that kind of money. Nobody has that kind of money."

Hank hitched a leg and settled on the desk, one foot on the floor, one foot swinging.

"Collection," Hank said.

"No fuckin' way." Mace's voice was terse.

"I'm in. I'll talk to the boys," Lee added.

"This is my problem," Mace clipped.

"It's not your problem. It's Stella's problem," Lee returned.

"Like I said, it's my problem," Mace shot back.

Lee, nor Hank, nor even Brody could answer that. It was just the flat out truth.

"Dudes, even if everyone puts in, it isn't gonna touch it. When I say they got debt, I mean *they got debt*," Brody informed them.

"Get Kim on the phone again, talkin' to friends and neighbors, the local church," Hank ordered Brody.

"Holy crap," Brody said.

Mace did not like the turn of the conversation.

"Don't piss me off," Mace warned.

"We're not tryin' to piss you off, Mace," Lee bit out, his voice hard. "I'm guessin' Stella sat, alone and unprotected, in the back of that limo and Preston Mason threatened her and that pisses *me* off. She's yours, and you're a member of my team, which makes her mine. Anyone messes with you, or her, they mess with me. No one fuckin' messes with me. We got enough on our plates with Carter. We don't need your Dad havin' a way in. I'm cuttin' off all his routes. That costs money, fuck it. Bottom line, a woman's dyin', and that woman is Stella's mother and your father is leanin' on them. Suck it up, we're all steppin' in."

Without waiting for a response, Lee turned to Brody.

"Find me something on Preston Mason and if he's got in anywhere, I want to know." When Brody sat staring at Lee and not moving, Lee leaned forward. "Do it, Brody. Now."

Brody nodded. He jumped up and actually ran out of the room.

"I don't like this." Mace was back to sitting, apparently relaxed although anything but. His eyes were sharp and angry and they were trained on Lee.

"I know you don't. I was in your spot, I wouldn't either. I'm sorry, Mace, but you got no choice," Lee replied.

"Don't like that either," Mace told Lee.

"We gonna have a problem about this?" Lee asked.

"Yeah," Mace responded instantly.

Hank intervened. "Mace, you know Luke took a bullet for Roxie."

Mace knew immediately where Hank was heading and shot back, "Flesh wound."

"Lucky chance. It could have been worse," Hank returned, and Mace pressed his lips together because he knew Hank was right.

Hank went on, "You know what Eddie and Darius did for Indy. You know that gets out, Eddie's fucked. His career in the toilet. Eddie's also pulled back from Marcus. He hates it but he's done it, for Jet. And you watched Jet get shot and we all know what that meant."

"Hank—" Mace broke in, but Hank kept going.

"We all know what Darius had to do to disentangle himself from the shit swirling around Jules, too. We know what Hector's livin' with because he fucked up and nearly got Jules killed, tryin' to protect Roam's street cred, of all fuckin' things."

"I get it," Mace snapped.

"You don't," Hank replied. "You're new to this so I'll tell you, bein' tangled up with a Rock Chick means makin' certain sacrifices and livin' with your decisions. The time to make yours is now."

The vibe in the room stayed hot as the three men stared at each other.

Finally, Mace muttered, "Fuckin' hell."

Hank glanced at Lee. Lee returned his look, took in a breath and Lee's gaze moved back to Mace.

"Turner called last night."

As Mace's head snapped toward Lee, the vibe in the room shot back to hot. So hot it was combustible.

"He's on side," Lee finished.

"What the fuck does that mean?" Mace asked.

"That means he quizzed Stella. He didn't find out dick and encouraged me to look into your Dad. He told me she didn't know about your sister, but I'm guessin', since they obviously had the conversation, she knows the basics now and she's curious. He's on board with keepin' her in the dark. I know you don't like it, but you got an ally in that guy. He'll take care of her."

"I'm gettin' her back," Mace returned.

"Hold off," Lee advised.

"No fuckin' way," Mace responded.

"You get her back, you'll force your father's hand. We don't need that right now."

Mace hesitated a beat then he shot out of his chair and exploded, "*Goddammit!*"

Hank winced then he went tense. Mace, angry, could be practically uncontrollable, even double-teamed by himself and Lee.

"Calm down, Mace," Hank said low.

"Fuck that. I don't play by his rules," Mace growled, his entire body visibly tight, such was the hold he had on himself.

"That isn't smart," Lee warned.

Mace stood there, straight, taut and furious. Then, out of nowhere, his body relaxed. He took another breath in through his nose and a slow grin spread on his face.

His voice was quiet when he said, "I'll be smart."

Without another word, Mace moved to leave and Lee glanced at Hank before calling, "Where the fuck you goin'?"

Mace didn't turn when he replied, "Gotta get some keys cut."

Then he was gone.

⌁

Roxie

I was sitting on the couch in the television room, my monogrammed stationery on my lap, a half written letter to a friend in Charleston lying there forgotten. Shamus, Hank's and my chocolate lab, was curled into himself on his huge, denim doggie bed in front of the wood-burning stove.

It was the first evening I'd been home in days. The front windows had been replaced. There were cameras everywhere and the new alarm system on all the doors and windows was armed the way Vance, who brought me home, showed me how to do.

I was sitting there staring out the window, or, more accurately, staring at the drawn curtains over the window. Vance told me to do that, too, and I wasn't thinking about my letter.

I was thinking about Hank.

Or, more to the point, about what Hank said to me earlier that day.

Then, because if I thought about it any longer, my patience at waiting for Hank to come home would run out, I let my mind wander to Mace.

Or, more to the point, Mace walking into Fortnum's late that morning under the direct gaze of all the Rock Chicks (except Shirleen, who was fielding calls at the office and Jules, who was at work at the Shelter), Tex and Duke.

Stella was there, too, with her new hot guy, Eric and, I had to admit as much as I didn't want to, Eric was definitely hot.

I was thinking about how Mace, without a word, handed Stella the keys to her apartment.

Or, even more to the point, Stella's face when Mace turned around and walked away.

Or, even *more* to the point, Ally losing it and following Mace in order to scream at him on the sidewalk outside of Fortnum's in clear view and easy hearing of everyone inside, who stood watching the show.

Ally went on about Mace being a "fucking macho idiot" and quoting the lyrics of Billy Joel's "And So It Goes", informing Mace that Stella sang it to him the day before, even though he wasn't there to see it. Then taking her life in her hands by going so far as to shove his shoulder and asking him, in a near shriek, *"What the fuck's the matter with you?"*

At that, clearly done, Mace put a shoulder to her belly, picked her up, carried her back into the bookstore, set her on her feet, and again, without a word, turned on his boot and walked away.

Stella, frozen through all of this, had gone pale as a ghost when Mace returned and then left without glancing in her direction.

Ally stared angrily at the door and then declared, "Electric shock treatment. That'll bring him around."

At Ally's words, Stella came unstuck, turned to Eric and murmured, "I'm sorry," and she bolted into the back of the store.

Daisy and Indy took off after Stella.

Ava and Jet laid into Ally.

I watched Eric, who was staring into the bookshelves after Stella.

I walked to him and explained, "We're kind of a nutty bunch."

Eric's dark eyes tilted down to mine, and that was when I realized I had to admit he was definitely hot.

"I know," he replied and his mouth formed a small grin, "I read the papers." Then he went on, "Miss Hendrick's County?"

Jesus.

I was going to *kill* whoever was talking to the reporters.

"That was a long time ago," I told him.

"They have a swimsuit competition?" he asked.

My eyes narrowed and my hand went to my hip.

"It was a teen pageant. They didn't do swimsuits, just fitness."

His eyes got a pleasant, warm look about them, which made him even hotter and he muttered, "Shorts then."

Good grief.

"Um, don't you have a thing for Stella?" I rudely reminded him.

"No shot," he returned, without hesitation or apparent bad feeling.

"So, you're feeling like branching out?" I asked, cocking my head angrily to the side.

"Nope. Just lookin' for happy thoughts. You in a teen pageant fitness routine, wearin' shorts, is a happy thought," he returned.

Holy cow.

I decided right then and there that he might not be a member of the Hot Bunch, but he could join the team in a shot.

His eyes lost their flirty warmth and went hard and serious (yep, definitely could be a member of the Hot Bunch). "Call one of your boys. I got things to do and I gotta go. They need to know Stella's lost her bodyguard." I nodded, he turned to leave then twisted back to look at me. "Keep her away from the papers."

With that, he was gone.

The door had barely closed on Eric when Uncle Tex boomed at Duke, "Well?"

Duke growled back, "Well what?"

Uncle Tex threw his meaty paws up in the air and boomed (again), "Well, it's time to lay the truth on Stella!"

Duke nodded his head and his eyes went to the door. "Damn straight. But it ain't me that's gotta lay the truth on her."

"I'll agree with that," Jet put in firmly, and everyone looked at her.

Jet had shared with all of us the crazy, intense and heartbreaking story about Mace and his sister. We'd all been told to keep quiet. Direct orders from Mace, who told Lee, who told Indy, who told the Rock Chicks. But Jet didn't like it, not one bit. She looked like she'd just lost patience with keeping Mace's secret.

"You don't say shit, Loopy Loo," Tex warned Jet.

"Someone has to—" Jet started.

"Ain't gonna be you," Tex went on.

"But—" Jet pushed.

"No lip. Get to work," Tex ordered, even though, freakishly, considering the crush of people Fortnum's had seen the last several days due to all the newspaper coverage the Rock Chicks and Hot Bunch were getting, they were in a lull and only had a few people hanging out at tables.

Jet glared at Uncle Tex.

Uncle Tex glared back.

Jet had a quiet attitude that usually worked really well.

But no one had enough attitude to out-attitude Uncle Tex. He was a crazy man.

"Oh, all right. But he's got one more day," Jet gave in.

"Jet, darlin'—" Duke started his soft warning.

"One. Day," Jet finished and flounced behind the espresso counter.

I caught Duke giving Uncle Tex a look and I figured Mace was going to get a head's up call, but I was worried Mace wouldn't care.

I went to my bag to get my phone. I flipped it open, hit the side button, put it to my ear and said Hank's name. It rang once before he answered.

"How's it goin', Sunshine?" His deep voice said in my ear, and like always, I got a full body shiver.

I set the shiver aside and answered, "Not good. We just had a scene. Stella got to Fortnum's a little while ago, telling us she called Mace and asked for her keys back, and he told her to meet him here. Mace came in, gave Stella her keys, barely looked at her, didn't say word one and took off. Ally went nuts, caught him before he left and started yelling at him. Mace didn't even blink. Stella got upset and ran into the books. That Eric guy just left. Told me to let you know he went."

I paused and then went on, my voice dropping to a whisper.

"I can't believe it Whisky, but it looks like it's over. Mace isn't giving her anything. I don't know what's happened and she's slid back to wherever she was yesterday during the gig. It isn't a good place for her to be and I'm worried."

"He gave her keys back?" Hank asked.

"Yes, without a word. He's not a demonstrative guy, but he's pretty big on PDA with her. He didn't touch her. He didn't even get near her. It's so un-Hot-Bunch-like, it's unreal," I replied.

"Don't worry about it," Hank told me, sounding supremely unconcerned.

I tried to get through to him. Why, I didn't know. Probably because I thought he could get through to Mace. I thought Hank could do just about anything.

"You don't get it, Whisky. Something bad happened. Stella told us that—"

"Don't worry about it."

"Hank!"

"Sunshine, don't worry about it and don't tell anyone, especially fuckin' Ally, what I'm gonna tell you right now."

I went silent.

Hank correctly assessed this as my agreement and went on, "I spent the morning with Mace. He's got the full picture about Stella. When he left Lee's office this morning he told Lee and me that he was goin' to get some keys cut. Everything's fine."

I let out a relieved breath.

Mace didn't give her back her keys.

He gave her back *a set* of her keys.

I smiled at the phone.

Hank kept talking. "I'm gonna be late, but I want you to wait up for me. Boys are busy, but they're doin' drive-bys. I still want you checkin' in occasionally."

"Okay."

"Don't let Shamus out. I'll see to him when I get in."

"Okay."

His voice went soft and I got another shiver when he said, "Later, sweetheart."

"Later," I replied.

"I love you," he finished.

My body went solid, but before I could make a noise I heard the disconnect.

I stood still with the phone to my ear, eyes staring unseeing at the floor in front of me.

"Roxie, you okay?" I heard Ava ask.

I didn't answer.

Hank had never told me he loved me. I knew. Or at least I thought I knew. But he'd never said it.

And, because he never had, I hadn't either.

Good God.

"Roxie? Are you okay?" Ava repeated and she was now close.

I lifted my eyes and focused on Ava.

"Hank just told me he loved me," I whispered.

"Yeah? So?" Ally asked and she got close, too.

"He's never said that before," I told Ally.

Both Ava and Ally reared back in shock and looked at each other.

"Jeez, he's not a very fast mover, is he?" Ally asked no one.

"He didn't give me a chance to say it back." I kept sharing.

"Have you ever said it to him?" Ava asked.

I shook my head.

"You don't move very fast either," Ally informed me.

My eyes went to her and I felt them narrow. "I'm sorry Ally. The last guy I said 'I love you' to took a sledgehammer to the door and eventually beat the shit out of me, kidnapped me and stalked me. Maybe I'm a bit gun shy about this love business."

"Hank'd never do that to you," Ally returned.

"I know that," I shot back.

"Then what's your problem?" Ally enquired.

My body got tight. "What's *your* problem?" I asked back. "You've been in a bad mood all day. You upset Stella!"

"Well, excuse me. But I'm beginning to understand where Shirleen is coming from with all this shit. My brothers and my friends got a load of shit on their plate on a regular basis, mind you. They don't need Rock Chick shit thrown at them all the time. It's getting ridiculous."

"Just you wait until it's your turn, Ally Nightingale," Ava, being a Rock Chick, went on the defensive.

"It isn't going to happen to me. No fuckin' way," Ally retorted.

"What makes you so sure?" I asked.

"Because there's only one left, not including Darius. And Darius doesn't fuck white women and is like a brother to me," Ally answered. "And nothing is gonna happen between me and Hector, 'cause I've known him since we were kids. He's like a cousin or something."

"So, what you're really saying is," Jet came up to our huddle and entered the conversation, "that you're pissed-off you *aren't* gonna get your shot at a Hot Bunch guy."

I smiled at Ava and Ava smiled back.

Ally turned angry eyes to Jet. "No, what I'm saying is I wouldn't get myself into a shitload of trouble. And if I did, I'd take care of my own business. I wouldn't let some guy stick his nose into said business. I wouldn't put up with that shit for a second. Some fuckin' macho badass telling me what to do and fucking with my life and my head. I wouldn't play those games. Some guy tried to do that to me, I'd put an end to it, pronto."

I couldn't help myself, I laughed. So did Jet. So did Ava.

"Seriously, chickies, not gonna happen," Ally said into our laughter.

"I *cannot wait* for some guy to rip into your life and make you eat those words," Ava told Ally.

"Not gonna happen," Ally repeated.

"You are so going down," I said to Ally.

Ally turned to me and snapped, "Can we stop talking about this?"

"Sure," I replied breezily.

"Who do you think it'll be?" Jet asked Ava.

"We're not talking about this anymore," Ally reminded Jet.

"That Eric guy is hot," Ava remarked to Jet.

"Fuck you," Ally said to Ava and stomped toward the espresso counter. We watched as she stopped halfway there, saw Uncle Tex grinning at her like a loon, then she turned on her heel and stomped into the books.

We all looked at each other and burst into laughter.

We didn't have time to enjoy our hilarity. The bell over the door went and Tod stormed in, eyes wild.

I didn't have to guess why Tod looked wild. He was Indy's officially unofficial wedding planner and it was T-minus five and a half days to nuptial takeoff. Because of this, Tod was clearly in a state.

"Do you think because you're all the possible targets for murder and mayhem that you can get out of this wedding business?" he screeched upon entry just as Stella, Daisy and Indy came back up front. Tod's eyes narrowed on Indy and he went on screeching, "Girlie, there's shit *to do!*"

"I know, Tod. Calm down," Indy replied.

Tod threw up his hands. "Calm down? I will not calm down! We need to confirm numbers with the catering company. We need to finalize seating arrangements. We need to box and bow the handmade truffles for wedding gifts.

Somebody needs to learn calligraphy in, like, an hour so we can handwrite the place cards."

"I thought we decided I was going to do them on my computer?" Ava, unwisely, put in.

"*You* decided. I *did not* decide. Place cards need to be handwritten! *Everyone knows that!*" Tod shrieked.

The door opened again, the bell ringing over it, Annette came in and shouted, "Yo bitches! Anyone get kidnapped or shot at today?"

Before anyone could answer, Tod turned to Annette and snapped, "What're you wearing to the wedding?"

Annette's head jerked in response to his attitude slapping her in the face upon entry and replied, "Don't know, Toddie Hottie. I figure I'll smoke a doobie and it'll come to me."

Tod's face got red and I feared his entire head would explode.

"You come to Indy's wedding stoned, I'll shoot you," Tod threatened.

"Dude, I only do weddings stoned. It's the only way to go. Weddings are boring. Snooze-a-rama," Annette shot back then turned to Indy. "No offense."

"None taken," Indy smiled.

Tod gave up on Annette and turned his glare back to Indy.

"We need a Full Wedding Briefing. Now," Tod declared. "Somebody call a Hot Bunch escort. We're all convening at Indy and Lee's in half an hour."

"Excuse me, but Jet, Ally and Indy are working. We got a breather, but any second we could get a crowd," Tex threw in.

"Who cares!" Tod shouted back. "Weddings take precedence over *all*."

"Not when sellin' boatloads of coffee pays for 'em, motherfucker," Tex boomed in return.

"Don't call me motherfucker," Tod threw down.

"Motherfucker," Uncle Tex boomed.

"Oh lordy," Daisy muttered.

"Okay, before there's bloodshed, I just wanna make sure you're all comin' to my store opening tomorrow night," Annette put in. "You gotta come. We're gonna have crackers and that squirtable cheese stuff and everything."

Unimpressed by squirtable cheese, Tod informed Annette, "No one is going to your opening. Not unless every single response card has been counted, the caterers have been called, we know where every ass is seated at the reception and those places have *handwritten* place cards and boxed and bowed truffles on their goddamned plates," Tod snapped then pointed at Indy. "Thirty minutes. Your house."

Then he was gone.

"Oh dear," Stella breathed.

"Divide and conquer," Daisy charged in. "Indy, call Lee. Tell him we need an escort. Jet and Ava, stay here, see to business. I'll call Jules, tell her to bring May as soon as they're done at work. Indy, Ally, Roxie, Stella, Annette and me'll go to Indy's place and get Tod sorted out." Daisy turned to Annette. "And we wouldn't miss your opening for the world, sugar."

"Phat," Annette smiled.

Daisy's gaze moved to Stella. "We'll talk about rescheduling with Dixon Jones at Indy's. He was cool about you missin' the meetin' seein' as you were kidnapped and all, but we don't want that lead to go cold."

Stella's eyes slid sideways to Indy who reached out and gave Stella's hand squeeze.

"Let's get crackin'!" Daisy finished.

I'd spent the afternoon boxing and bowing truffles and arguing with Tod over seating arrangements.

Stella spent the afternoon alternately arguing with Daisy and Shirleen (via the phone) about Dixon Jones.

A little after five, Jules and May arrived to help.

Around six, Roam and Sniff (two of Jules's runaways from the Shelter who'd moved in with Shirleen after Jules's drama was over) showed up with three big Famous pizza boxes.

At about seven, Shirleen arrived with a guitar case in each hand and announced that Roam and Sniff were now officially getting guitar lessons from Stella.

Until around eight, Stella and the boys were upstairs in Indy's TV room and we heard them plunking away at the guitars.

At eight thirty, Vance showed up to escort us home.

We had, however, managed to get all the wedding work done and have a Wedding Briefing, going over every last detail, before Vance showed up.

Throughout the evening, I'd checked in with Hank a couple of times, and then, restless and hoping writing a few letters would settle my mind (and my heart), I'd tried it.

It didn't work.

Now it was after eleven o'clock and I was wired.

I heard the front door open and my body jerked at the noise. I grabbed my stationery, tossed it and my pen on the coffee table and headed toward the front of the house as I heard Hank give a whistle.

He had Shamus's lead in his hand when I rounded the door to the kitchen and his gaze came to me.

Upon seeing me, his eyes warmed with a smile.

"Hey, sweetheart," he said like he normally said every day if I was awake when he got home.

"Hey, Whisky," I replied like I normally replied every day if I was awake when he got home.

When I moved in with him, I thought I might have trouble falling into anything normal. I thought my ex, the crazy Billy, would have ruined me for normal. A normal routine. A normal relationship. A normal life with a normal (but hot) guy, in a normal neighborhood with a normal dog. I thought that kind of normal would be lost to me forever.

But normal with Hank wasn't your average kind of normal.

It was the extraordinary kind.

And I took to it, no problems.

He came to me, curled an arm around my waist, leaned down and kissed my temple. But when he was done with his kiss, he left his lips where they were.

"How was your day?" I asked softly, my face tilted up, my eyes open and looking at his dark hair curling into the back of his strong neck.

I decided I should remind him he needed to make an appointment to get a haircut, especially right before his brother's wedding, but I wasn't going to. Hank had great hair, soft, thick and wavy, and I liked it a shade too long. I liked it a lot.

"Over," he replied and gave my waist a squeeze. "Takin' Shamus out," he murmured against my temple before giving me another kiss. "I'll meet you in bed."

I nodded, feeling my stomach melt, my head sliding against his jaw. He stepped away, hooked the leash on the quivering-with-pre-walk-ecstasy Shamus, and they were gone.

I washed and moisturized my face and put my hair up in a messy knot on top of my head. I put on a stretchy, pale pink, lace nightie, got in bed and waited.

Incidentally, I was still wired.

I heard the door open again and then Shamus's nails on the wood floors in the front room then through to the kitchen. There was silence for a few beats as Shamus hit the carpet in the television room before he rounded the door to the bedroom. He burst through, galloping toward the bed. He jumped up and came at me, licking my face while he got an ear rub.

This, too (if I wasn't in on the walk), was normal.

Hank followed much more slowly.

"Shamus," Hank said low and Shamus backed off. He started to roam the bed, even though he had to know the lay of the land by heart since he roamed it nightly. He lay down at the foot facing Hank and he panted.

"Hank…" I started then stopped.

For the first time in months with Hank, I didn't know what to do.

You didn't just blurt out you loved someone for no reason.

Well, you did, but you didn't.

Good God.

"Yeah?" Hank asked, yanking off his tee.

"Um…" I hedged then asked, "You wanted me to be up?"

He dropped the tee to the floor and sat at the edge of the bed to pull off his boots.

"Yeah," he replied.

"Why?"

He dropped one boot and went after the other, back still to me, he answered, "Felt like fucking you."

All the breath went out of my lungs.

Over the months of living together, Hank and I'd had a lot of sex. That had never been normal. It had always been extraordinary and that had never changed.

What wasn't normal was Hank making me stay awake in order to do it.

"You don't normally have any problem waking me up if you're in the mood," I reminded him.

He'd already taken off his other boot and socks and now he stood, turned to face me and went after his belt. This gave me a full on view of Hank's chest, which was my favorite part of his body. If you didn't count his eyes. And his lips. And, um, other parts.

"Want you awake and alert tonight, Sunshine," he said before he grinned.

259

Kristen Ashley

"Why?"

He didn't answer. Instead he said softly, "Take off your nightie, Roxie."

I felt my body tremble, but other than that I didn't move.

I was feeling weird. It was a good weird, a scary weird, an expectant weird.

"Why do you want me awake and alert tonight?" I repeated.

"Roxanne. Take off your nightie."

"Hank—"

"Do it," he ordered then he dropped his jeans.

I got a good look at some of the other parts of his body that were my favorite, one in particular, and I took off my nightie.

Hank watched me do this.

Then he moved.

I was straddling Hank, knees in the bed, my head thrown back. Hank was deep inside me, his face pressed in my throat, his hands moving up my back.

I slid up, then down, and I tilted my chin to look at him.

His head went back. I put my mouth on his and kissed him.

He kissed me back, tongues tangling. His hands went to my hips and he moved me up. My mouth disengaged then his fingers dug in and he slammed me back down.

It felt so damned good with my lips against his, I gave a soft moan.

Now was definitely the time.

I ground my hips into his, flexed certain, secret muscles and felt his soft groan.

"I love you," I whispered.

His fingers tensed at my hips and his eyes caught mine.

"Glad to hear you say that, Sunshine," he whispered back.

I smiled.

He fell to his back, arms around me, taking me with him.

Keeping us connected, he twisted us to the side. He opened the drawer on his nightstand and pulled out a dark blue, velvet box.

260

I stared at the box, my body going tight, as his thumb flicked it open and I caught sight of the diamond before he shoved his index finger in, pulling the ring out of the blue silk.

He tossed the box to the nightstand, sat back up, still keeping us connected. His right hand skimmed down my left arm, captured my hand, positioned it and he slid the ring on my finger.

I sat frozen, staring at the diamond solitaire on my finger.

It wasn't huge, it wasn't small.

It was a normal, diamond engagement ring.

It was *just right*.

"If you let Tod plan our wedding, I'm takin' that back," Hank told me, and my eyes flashed to his.

I stared at him, one beat, two, then three, and whispered, feeling the tears sting the backs of my eyes, "You're never getting this back."

I watched him smile right before he kissed me.

Then he rolled me to my back and he finished what we started.

When we were done and recovered, he slid off to my side, but wrapped an arm around my belly, threw a thigh over mine and nuzzled his face into the side of my head.

Shamus, who'd exited the bed when the fun began, returned. He did a little roaming and settled where he always settled; down my length, the opposite side to Hank.

Both the canine and human Nightingale boys, like they normally did, pinned me down.

I flicked my thumb against the base of my ring finger, making sure I didn't imagine it.

I felt cold, solid, honest-to-goodness gold.

I didn't imagine it.

I turned my head to the side, found Hank's mouth with mine and smiled.

"Happy?" Hank muttered against my lips.

I didn't answer verbally, I nodded.

He gave me a light kiss.

I felt the tears I hadn't shed earlier slide out of my eyes.

So did Hank.

"Jesus, you're a nut," Hank mumbled, his arm going tighter.

"Don't call me a nut," I whispered, my voice sounding scratchy.

Kristen Ashley

"Sorry Sunshine, you're a nut," he replied. "But that's a good thing."

I decided to ignore that. Hank called me a nut nearly every day.

And for some insane reason, he *did* think it was a good thing.

"I need to call my Mom," I told him.

"It's two o'clock in the morning in Indiana," he reminded me.

"Trust me, Hank, she won't care."

And she wouldn't.

Trish Logan would be over the moon.

Trish Logan would call an emergency church meeting so the whole congregation could praise the Lord that her daughter, Roxanne Giselle, had finally landed herself a good, decent, honest man.

"Call her in the morning," Hank demanded.

"Whisky—"

His arm got super tight. "Roxanne, call her in the morning," he repeated. "Tonight is yours and mine."

I sucked in breath.

Then I said, "Okay."

He turned my body to face his, lifted his head and buried it in my neck.

I wrapped my arms around him and held on tight.

Shamus got the hint and exited the bed.

Chapter 17

We're Good

Stella

I was drifting back and forth between awake and asleep.

In my waking moments I was visualizing my bank balance and wondering how much I could afford to send home to Mom and Dad (the answer I came up with... not much).

In my sleeping moments, I was dreaming of flying truffles, exploding confetti, Dixon Jones laughing maniacally, Preston Mason showing me a picture book with gruesome caricatures of murders in it and Mace's face filled with pain.

I came fully awake when I heard the scrape of a key in the door.

Juno's body jerked, confirming I wasn't hearing things. I felt her come up to her belly. As she was at the foot of the bed I couldn't see her, but I figured her head was up, facing the door, ears perked.

I assessed my situation, which was pretty much effed. I'd fallen in bed then into a fitful sleep without the phone close by. I had no weapons and I wouldn't know how to use one anyway. The house was on a huge plot, no other houses close by, and Swen and Ulrika were on vacation.

No one would hear me scream.

The alarm beeped when the door was opened. Juno moved again, the bed shaking with her bulk and she jumped down.

My body was rigid with fear as I listened in terrified confusion to buttons being pressed and the beeping stopped.

I was so panicked I didn't realize after the beeping stopped that I didn't hear anything else except soft movement and Juno's tags jangling on her collar.

In other words, my dog didn't bark.

This should have told me something.

Instead, I was visualizing myself lying in bed, one of the Nightingale Men, maybe Mace, finding me there looking like I was sleeping, but instead the back of my head would be blown away.

On that thought, I heard rustling like someone was taking off their clothes. I knew this to be true when I heard the clank of a heavy belt buckle hit the floorboards.

Lordy be.

They were going to rape me before shooting me.

Okay, so I'd die. My luck was shitty enough that was a possibility.

But I was *not* going to be violated first.

Unh-unh.

No way.

Eff *that*.

I felt the presence approach the bed. I lay still, waiting for my moment. The covers moved, drifting slowly off my shoulder. I felt the bed depress as weight hit it and I twisted and whirled.

I got to my back, perpendicular to the bed, lifted my knees and aimed at the huge shadow that looked like it had a knee to the bed. I kicked out with both legs, hitting him right in the gut.

I heard his pained grunt. His body went back and I rolled the other way, off the bed, and started to run toward the alarm panel with its panic button.

"*Help! Help! Somebody, help!*" I screamed even though I knew no one would hear.

But maybe my luck would change.

Maybe an ex-Marine sergeant with super good hearing who had an extensive collection of medals was taking a middle of the night run to chase away the battle nightmares. He'd hear me, charge in and save the day.

On this thought, I leaped off the platform toward the door, my body in mid-air when an arm sliced around my middle. I emitted a loud, "Oof!" and I went flying the other way.

I landed on the bed with a bounce, but before I could twist, a heavy body landed on me.

"*Get off!*" I screamed in the shadowed face of my attacker as I twisted, bucked and pushed.

"Jesus, Stella, cool it," Mace growled back, his voice sounding weirdly guttural.

My body went still and I stared at his shadowy head.

"You cool?" Mace asked.

I didn't answer. I was too surprised.

Instead, I nodded.

He must have seen it or heard it because he rolled off me and lifted his knees so the soles of his feet were on the bed.

"Fuck, but you've got lower body strength," he grunted.

I turned to my side and got up on an elbow. My eyes becoming accustomed to the dim light, I saw he had both hands to his belly.

"I thought you were going to rape me," I told him.

His head twisted to the side and the air in the room went funny and not in a good way. I felt his eyes on me in the dark.

"Why the fuck would you think that?" he clipped, voice still low with residual pain.

"I thought you were a bad guy coming to kill me. Rape me then kill me."

The air in the room went back to normal.

"The bad guys don't have your alarm code, babe."

Hmm. He was right about that (I hoped).

He continued, "You got cameras everywhere. We'd know he was here before he got the outside door open. You'd have had a call to warn you."

Hmm again.

In my freak out, I forgot about the cameras.

"And he wouldn't have a fuckin' key," Mace went on.

"You don't have a key, either," I reminded him.

"Kitten," his voice was back to normal, now soft and gentle, but normal, "you think I'd give you back your key?"

My breath went on a road trip down Route 66.

What was he saying?

"You handed them to me today in Fortnum's," I told him.

"I handed you a set. I had another set cut."

My breath checked into a motel with a pool.

So when I asked, "Why'd you do that?" it came out all wispy.

"So I could get in when it was time to come home at the end of the day."

I lay there on my elbow, on my side, looking down at his big shadow.

My mind was awhirl, multiple thoughts twirling through it all at once.

Then it settled on just one.

Mace was back.

That was when I pounced.

At first he wasn't recovered, or he was surprised that one second I was lying there, the next second I was all over him, so he didn't move much.

This had the benefit of me getting my hands, lips and tongue on him. This had the added benefit that, when I discovered he was still wearing boxers, I could rip them off him.

Then he recovered and it got heated. It became the tangling of arms and legs, the sliding of lips, the tasting of tongues, the gliding of fingertips and the dragging of nails.

He tore my panties down my legs and whipped my tank over my head.

I got my mouth between his legs then he got his between mine.

Then I rolled him over, got on top, wrapped my fingers around him and guided him inside.

I was in control for three glorious strokes before he rolled me and pounded deep.

I wrapped my calves around his thighs and begged him to do it harder.

Mace complied.

He was kissing me when I came, moaning into his mouth.

It took him longer and my eyes were on the shadowy column of his throat when his head reared back, he drove into me one last time and let out a deep, long sigh.

His weight settled into me after he finished, and I liked it, the heaviness of him, even though I couldn't breathe.

I took it as long as possible. When I made an audible gulp for air, Mace heard it and immediately rolled to his back, taking me with him so I was on top.

We were both still breathing hard, me alternately purring. I tucked my face into the space between his shoulder and neck and cradled the back of his head in my hand.

As my breathing slowed, the purring breaths stopping, I realized something was happening to me. Something thrilling and frightening. Something like being on the front page of the paper and referred to as a "celebrity".

But bigger.

And better.

Something that made me think, for the first time in my life, that my luck was about to change.

I didn't want to test it but I had to.

"Mace?"

"Yeah?"

I didn't know what to say.

Then I did.

"You walked away."

His arms had been loose around me but they got tighter.

"I was pissed, Kitten," he said softly.

He *was* pissed. And Mace pissed was like a natural phenomenon, a tornado or a hurricane or a volcano exploding or something.

"I was a bitch," I whispered.

One of his hands came up and tangled in my hair.

"You got reason. Lots of shit happening to you. You can't keep it inside, it'll fuck you up. So you gotta be able to take it out on someone. That someone is me." He twisted his head and kissed my shoulder before he finished quietly, "I gotta learn to handle you with more care."

My throat made a noise I couldn't control, soft and low, like a moan of pain. But it wasn't that I felt the pain. It was that I was letting it go.

His head settled back, his hand twisted softly in my hair and his other arm wrapped tighter around my waist.

"Why'd you give me back my keys?" I asked.

"You told me to."

"Yeah, but—"

My body tensed when Mace interrupted me by saying, "For now, whatever my father told you to do, he's gotta see you doin' it."

Oh my God.

How did he know?

"How did you know?" I breathed.

Mace didn't answer me, instead he went on, "What we're not gonna do is play by his rules. He won't know I'm comin' home to you."

"Do you think he's watching?"

"Yeah."

Effing hell!

How creepy!

"Why?" I asked.

"Because he's an asshole."

It occurred to me that Mace was talking about his Dad but I didn't go there, mainly because I agreed with him. His Dad was The Supreme Asshole of All Time.

"If he's watching, he'll see you come in," I pointed out.

"No, he won't."

"Yeah, he will. Swen and Ulrika have motion sensor lights outside and—"

"He won't see me."

"Mace—"

His arm gave me a squeeze. "Babe. Trust me. He won't see me."

The way he said it, I trusted him. I decided not to go there later. I didn't want to know how Mace learned how to get into houses without being seen.

He moved us into the bed, flicking the covers over us. We settled in and he pulled me so our fronts were touching, my hands against his chest, his arm resting at my waist. His fingers started to move whisper-soft of my back. I decided this felt really nice when Juno joined us and the bed rocked with her movements before she collapsed at our feet.

"You know about your Mom bein' sick and the mortgage, don't you? That's what he got you with, isn't it?" he asked quietly.

I didn't ask how he knew that. He was a private investigator. The question would be stupid, and whatever Preston Mason thought of me and my grade point average, I wasn't stupid.

"Yeah," I answered.

"How much did he share? About your Mom?"

"Not much. Just that she had cancer and they were behind on their mortgage, which he owns, by the way."

Mace sighed then he said, "They were. Today they became current."

My body froze. I had a mind to protest, to scream and yell, not at him, but at the world and maybe his effing asshole father.

Instead, I burst into tears, loud and obnoxious.

But I had reason. The tears were triple-fold. I was sad about my Mom. I was grateful to Mace for taking care of yet another one of my problems. And I was pissed as hell at his father.

Mace gathered me in his arms and held me tight.

I cried for a long time and he held me the whole way through.

When I started to recover, I lifted my head and yelled, "I'm sorry Mace, but your father is a *dick!*"

Then, for some stupid reason, I burst out crying again.

As my second crying jag commenced, Mace pulled away and knifed off the bed. I sat up and watched his shadow move, still gulping with tears. He jumped off the platform, went into the bathroom and came back, getting into bed again and stuffing Kleenex in my fist.

I took a few deep breaths to control my emotion, an effort that was luckily successful. When I was done wiping my face and blowing my nose, Mace took the Kleenex from me and tossed it on the nightstand.

Juno had come to her belly to watch all of this. After Mace tossed away my Kleenex, she made the doggie assessment that the most recent drama was over and settled on her side with a groan. Mace stretched out in the bed on his back, pulling me into his side. I rested my head on his chest and draped my arm across his abs.

"After that, I hate to tell you, but you gotta know," Mace started, and I sighed into his chest, heavy and huge and nodded so he went on. "It's ovarian cancer, Kitten. It's spread. We got info that it's not lookin' good."

I bit my lip for a beat then whispered, "I'll call her tomorrow."

His arm, curled low around my back, gave me another squeeze.

"There's more to talk about, but we'll do it in the morning. You've had enough for tonight. Yeah?"

I nodded again.

Then I instantly reneged and said in a voice, so low you could barely hear it, "I know about your sister getting kidnapped and murdered."

I felt his body go solid.

It was my turn to give Mace a squeeze.

"Please don't go away, please." I was still speaking super softly.

"I'm right here," he replied.

"You were going to tell me."

Hesitation then, "Yeah."

"I'm *such* a bitch." My voice was louder now and harsh even to my own ears.

"Kitten."

I got up on an elbow and looked at his face. "Did I miss my chance? I don't want to miss my chance. You said you're supposed to be there for me, but I also have to be there for you," I explained before whispering, "Please, Mace, give me another chance."

His hand came to my neck, his thumb sliding along my jaw, then up to follow the bottom edge of my lower lip.

"Tomorrow."

"Mace—"

"Tomorrow."

"I want to—"

What he said next, or more importantly, admitted, rocked my world.

"I can't talk about it in the dark, Kitten. It'll fuck with my head all night. It's gotta be talked about in the light."

I understood that.

Effing hell, but I understood that.

I would have never guessed Mace had a weakness but there it was.

And without hesitation, he gave it to me, a piece of him.

That piece was the fact that he lived in black, too.

It was right then I knew I loved him.

And that my luck had finally changed.

And that come hell or high water I was going to pull him out of black.

This made me happy, but I kept my smile to myself. My head went back to his chest and my body relaxed into his. I felt his relax under mine and listened to his breathing go even.

When I thought he was asleep, that was when I allowed myself to smile.

Therefore, my body gave a start when he asked, his voice husky. "We finally good?"

I pressed my body further into him and whispered, "We're good."

I noticed his chest moving, shaking in a strange way. It took a few moments to realize he was silently laughing.

I came up to an elbow and looked down at him again.

"Are you laughing?" I asked, thinking maybe he'd gone temporarily insane with lack of sleep or something.

"Yeah," he answered.

"Why?"

He did a mini-ab-crunch and twisted so he was on his elbow, too, his face in my face. So close, it was the only thing I could see.

"I win," he murmured and his words were full of triumph and arrogance.

For a millisecond, I considered giving his shin a good kick.

Instead, I rolled my eyes and muttered, "Whatever."

At that, his arms shot around me, he dropped to his back taking me with him, me mostly on top, and he burst out laughing.

⇥⇤

It was a long time later when I knew definitely without a doubt that Mace was asleep that I thought he was wrong.

It was me who won.

⇥⇤

It was after ungodly-hour-in-the-morning sex. After Mace took Juno out. After a slightly-later-but-still-ungodly-hour-in-the-morning couple's shower that I was making eggs benedict from scratch.

Mace was hindering these efforts because he was in the tiny kitchen with me, sipping a mug of coffee, his big body leaning against the counter and getting in my way.

He was wearing faded jeans, no belt, no shoes, hair still slightly damp. He was also wearing a bit greener than olive green short-sleeved henley. It was a sweet henley mainly because it had been made for a normal man; a man without large, defined, muscular biceps. Therefore, the sleeves fit tight, drawing your attention to Mace's large, defined, muscular biceps.

My attention on Mace's biceps was also hindering my cooking efforts. Hollandaise sauce required concentration or it would split and when it split you had to throw it out and start all over, which sucked (I knew this because it happened to me a lot).

I was wearing a pair of cutoff jeans shorts and a black racer-back tank with a skull entwined with vines emblazoned on the back in charcoal gray. Like Mace, my hair was wet and my feet were bare.

"The boys'll know I'm comin' to you at night," Mace told me.

"How?"

"Babe, the cameras," he reminded me.

Effing hell. How was I always forgetting about the cameras?

Mace went on, "The Rock Chicks need to be kept in the dark."

I was whisking the sauce like my life depended on it, which was the way with hollandaise sauce, and I looked over my shoulder at Mace in confusion.

"Why?" I asked.

"They got big mouths, that's why."

He was not wrong about that. The Rock Chicks definitely had big mouths.

"Okay," I repeated. Then something about the cameras hit me. I saw the sauce had thickened and I pulled it from the burner, trying to keep my cool as I began to feel uncomfortable. "Mace, those cameras—"

"Yeah?"

I set the sauce aside, fished the poached eggs out of the water and put them on the waiting toasted English muffins and grilled Canadian bacon while I said, "They don't watch when we, um… you know. Like this morning?"

"Internal cameras are shut down when the men are home."

I let out a sigh of relief.

Thank God for *that*.

I poured the sauce over the eggs and set the pan aside. I handed Mace a plate (three eggs, three thick pieces of bacon, three muffins. It was a lot of food but he was a big guy) with a fork and knife and turned my attention to my own plate (one egg; I wasn't a big breakfast type of person).

We stood in the kitchen, plates on the counter, bodies sideways, eating standing up.

I really needed to consider investing in a dining room table. How I was going to do that and send money home I had no idea, but I figured it was time to start pushing the guitar lessons gig.

I was busy eating and my mind was busy thinking. Instead of feeling relaxed and happy that Mace was there and we were "good", not to mention we'd had great sex (twice), I was tense and slightly freaked out. I couldn't shift from what had gone down the last week, my despair of the last year, straight into back together with Mace all is hunky dory.

First, I was worried about our conversation this morning, not only the "more" Mace told me we had to talk about, but also I was worried for him and whatever he was going to tell me about his sister.

And second, my life was still a shambles.

With my head filled with these things, it took a while for me to feel the pleasant warmth sweeping up the back of my neck.

I lifted my gaze to see Mace's eyes were on me. They were warm and sweet and his lips were turned up at the ends.

"What?" I asked.

"Missed your cooking, Kitten," came his soft answer. "Don't know any-one who can whip up eggs benedict like she was makin' toast."

I was guessing he liked his eggs.

There it went, freak out obliterated.

I smiled at him.

He smiled back.

He had a great smile.

Why did we spend a week fighting with him? My brain asked me.

Oh, shut up, I told my brain.

Mace's attention went back to his plate and he forked into another egg. "Hank's started a collection."

I was chewing so I swallowed, chased the eggs with some coffee and asked, "A collection?"

He didn't answer my question, instead he said, "Everyone's in, including Marcus, Malcolm and Tom. Hank'll go after Tod and Stevie and Shirleen when you and I come out. They got about fifteen large so far."

I was confused and not following. "Fifteen large what?"

"Fifteen large dollars."

I stared at him.

"Sorry, Mace," I explained. "I'm not following."

His eyes went from his plate to me. "For your folks."

Gut kick. It wasn't unpleasant, but for a moment it was paralyzing.

I jerked out of my temporary paralysis and asked, "Hank did a collection for my Mom and Dad, and in one day they've got fifteen thousand dollars?"

Mace nodded.

Eyes back to his plate, he kept talking. "Luke's loaded, so is Lee. Darius has got money put away. Before Vance met Jules, he kept his overhead low, lived tight, didn't spend much. Even though they're lookin' to put money down on a house, Jules has got some huge account that's supposed to be her Uncle Nick's, but he's demandin' she put it down when they find a place. I don't get that, don't care. Bottom line, Vance was generous. Marcus said that once Daisy found out about it, she'd want to be top the heap so he doubled the highest kick in."

My mouth had dropped open.

Finally, I said, "Fifteen thousand dollars?"

Mace went back to eating after he said, "Yep."

"And you?" I asked. "How much did it take to bring them current on their mortgage?"

"Six K. Marcus doesn't know about that," Mace replied calmly, forked up the last of his eggs, grabbed his plate and walked it to the sink.

I was not calm.

The freak out had returned with a vengeance.

He was running hot water on his plate when I told his profile, "That's twenty-one thousand dollars."

"Yep," Mace repeated.

"Twenty-one thousand dollars in... one... day," I went on.

Mace turned off the water and shifted to face me. His eyes were alert and he watched me closely.

"Yep," he said again.

"That's..." I started then stopped then started again. "That's *insane*."

"Their debt tops a hundred K, or it did. I looked over your parents' shit last night. Your Mom's not workin'. Your Dad barely makes enough to cover the mortgage and household bills. They doubled up on the mortgage to take care of the first round of treatments. This round is bringin' them low."

Another gut kick. This one *was* unpleasant.

"One hundred thousand dollars?" I whispered.

"Yeah," Mace replied softly.

I looked at him.

He returned my stare.

Then I shouted, "Oh my God! That's... I can't... oh my God! I can't wrap my head around that!"

"Stella—"

I shook my head, dropped my fork in my plate, put the plate on the counter and raised my hands then dropped them.

"Not counting the money from the last three gigs—which, by the way, Monk hasn't paid yet, though The Little Bear paid Floyd I just don't have my take—I've got seven hundred and fifty dollars in savings, just over a thousand in checking and maybe a thousand in the savings bonds Mom used to buy me for Christmas," I told Mace then walked out of the kitchen, whipped around on one foot and walked back to see Mace had turned to watch me. "Oh my God. I can't help them. I can't... even fifteen thousand dollars can't... and we can't take that money!"

"Kitten—"

"It's too much!" I yelled.

He smiled, which, for your information, I thought was totally insane in a world that was *completely* insane.

"You try talkin' Hank and Lee out of givin' your folks that money."

I considered this.

I didn't know Hank all that well. He seemed really nice. A little less intense and more laidback than the other Hot Bunch boys, but not *that* much less intense and laidback.

Lee, on the other hand, sometimes just plain scared me. He was bossy and, you could tell, used to getting his way.

Shitsofuckit!

When I was about to come to terms with all this, Mace spoke again. "My father's gonna pay off the rest and give them a nest egg. Whatever happens with your Mom, it'll happen with her feelin' comfortable."

My mouth had dropped open again and I was staring at him like he'd just announced his intention to spend the next six years traveling to Mars so he could set up a colony of super-Mace-humans.

"What?" I breathed.

"My father is gonna make your family comfortable. He's gonna give them a million dollars. That'll pay off their bills, pay off the house and pay for whatever lies ahead."

I still hadn't stopped staring at him.

"You're crazy," I breathed.

He shook his head.

I put my hands to my hips and leaned toward Mace before I spoke. "First, I don't want his money. I know he's your Dad, Mace, but he's a jerk. Second, he's mean. He's not going to give my parents one million dollars. Third, I don't want his money!"

I ended this on a shout, my body so tense I could feel the muscles in my neck pulsating.

Mace, however, was calm. "It isn't his money."

"What do you mean, it isn't his money?"

"I mean it's mine and it's my Mom's. It's also Caitlin's and Caitlin's Mom's. He owes us all, and the time for him to pay has come."

I blinked and asked, "Caitlin?"

"My sister."

My tense body froze solid.

It was time.

Effing hell, it was time.

I didn't know what to do. I wanted to go to him, but I didn't think that was right. It also wasn't right to hold my ground. I was at least three feet away from him. It seemed a mile. He still seemed calm, but he couldn't be. There was no way.

I made a decision, stayed where I was and forced my body to relax.

Then I asked softly, "Her name was Caitlin?"

Mace stayed where he was, too, and replied, "Yeah."

I took in a breath then let it go. I tried to find something innocuous to start with, settled on an idea and continued, "Did she look like you?"

Mace watched me a beat, shook his head once and answered, "No. She was blonde. Blue eyes. Tiny."

I kept my silence and my distance; only my eyes were on him. But my brain was emanating comfort vibes as hard as it could, and I hoped like crazy he was receiving them.

He put a hand to the counter and leaned into it.

Then he repeated on a tortured murmur, "Tiny."

I knew in an instant the conversation had changed.

Something about the way he said that word made my heart squeeze.

I waited, eyes on him. He kept his eyes on me.

When he didn't say anything, I whispered, "Tiny?"

When I said the word, his eyes closed. When they opened the demons were there. I saw them, clear as day.

Effing bloody hell.

I held my breath but kept my distance, and I hoped to all that was holy I was doing the right thing.

He spoke again. "She was a dancer. Ballet. Good at it. So petite, Christ, so fuckin' small. But graceful. Just the way she moved was like a dance." He stopped and started again, "She was pure elegance. All she had to move was her hands. She had exquisite hands." He stopped again then went on, his voice quiet, "Jesus, I'll never forget the way she moved her hands."

He stopped again and I thought there was something important about this, but somehow I knew it wasn't the time to push it.

"You were proud of her." My voice was soft.

Mace didn't answer. He didn't have to. I knew the answer was an affirmative.

Instead he said, "She wanted to move to New York."

I nodded.

He kept talking and his voice was getting low and rough, and my heart squeezed again at the sound of it. "I took her there when she was fourteen. She fell in love with the place."

I pressed my lips together and nodded again. This was hard. I wanted to go to him. It hurt to hold my ground, but I stayed away.

"You guys didn't have the same Mom?" I asked.

Mace shook his head.

"Half-sister," I went on.

Mace just looked at me.

"You were close," I guessed on a whisper.

"I called her Tiny," Mace shared.

Understanding the importance of that word, I felt the tears hit my eyes and thought about having a cool, tall, handsome, surfer dude brother who took me to New York, loved the way I moved my hands and called me Tiny.

It was an immensely happy thought at the same time it was devastatingly sad.

Softly I said, "I bet you were a good brother."

"Not good enough," he returned, his voice now unbearably rough and so low it was barely a mumble.

And his eyes were haunted.

I couldn't help it. It hurt too much to keep looking at him. I closed my eyes.

I felt a streak of wetness roll down my left cheek, opened my eyes again and whispered, "Tell me."

I held his gaze for a beat, two, then he muttered, "Fuck, Kitten..."

He stopped speaking. His head dropped, he stared at the floor and that was when I moved.

I went right to him, fit myself into his body, the top of my head under his face, my arms tight around him. All the while I did this, he didn't move, not a muscle. Didn't even put his arms around me, just kept leaning against the counter.

I pressed my cheek into his chest.

"Tell me," I whispered again.

I heard his cell ring and his taut body went tighter.

"Ignore it," I said.

He didn't.

His head came up, he pulled the phone out of his pocket and I leaned back to look at him.

It was over.

The guard had slid down over his eyes.

I lost him.

Shitsofuckit.

Even so, he wrapped an arm loosely about my waist as he flipped open his phone with his thumb, put it to his ear and muttered, "Yeah?"

I turned to face his chest and put my forehead there so I felt his body give a small jerk as his fingers flexed into my hip with such strength, it caused a little bit of pain.

My head snapped back. I saw his jaw was clenched and I felt a coldness start seeping through my veins.

"I'll be there in ten," he clipped into the phone. He flipped it shut, and without hesitation let me go, on the move to something urgent.

I turned to watch him nab his belt and boots, the oxygen burning in my lungs.

"What's going on?" I asked, scared shitless whatever it was was about the Rock Chicks.

He dumped his boots on the edge of the platform and started to slide his belt through the loops.

Then his eyes came to me.

"Carter branched out," Mace's voice was hard. "With the Rock Chicks protected, this morning he went after Shirleen."

I took a step back as if he'd dealt me a physical blow.

Effing hell.

Chapter 18

La La La

Stella

Mace took off after he put a gentle fist under my chin, tilted my face to his and brushed his mouth on mine, muttering a promise that he'd let me know as soon as he knew anything.

He called twenty minutes later (a *long* twenty minutes) to tell me a squad car with two uniformed officers would be at my house to pick me up "in five". He also told me I was not to let the cops in unless they said the code words. As he was talking, I heard angry, male shouting in the background, but Mace disconnected without giving me an update.

When my buzzer went, I saw a uniform on the video display who showed his badge and said, "Hunky dory."

At that, Juno and I headed out.

The officers balked at Juno taking a ride in the squad car but I held my ground, and since that ground was outside and exposed, Juno went with me to Nightingale Investigations.

No way in hell I was leaving my dog behind.

If Sidney Carter was branching out, how soon would it be before he went after pets?

Even if my luck had started to turn, I was taking no chances.

The not-very-informative officers didn't update me about Shirleen either, except to say they were still sorting things out "at the scene".

The only scenes that involved my friends that I liked were the ones we created ourselves, and for your information, I didn't like those much either.

The officers escorted me to the outer office door of Nightingale Investigations. We were greeted by a silent, tight-faced, angry-looking Jack, and an angry Jack scared me enough to stay silent, too. Jack took over, walking Juno and me to the down room.

The down room was where the boys had meetings and hung out if they were on call. It also had a variety of fitness and weight lifting equipment. There was a couch, but in the few times Mace had taken me to the offices the last time we were together, I'd never seen anyone sitting on it. The boys were usually on the treadmill or the weight bench.

In other words, if you hadn't already figured this out, the Nightingale Men didn't really know the meaning of "down time".

As Juno and I entered the room, I saw Jules, Ava and Jet had their asses planted on the couch and they were sipping coffee. Daisy was sitting in a chair, leaned back, filing her nails. Ally had lifted up the back of the weight bench and she was lounging on it, legs straddling the bench. Indy and Roxie were seated at a table, playing double solitaire, mugs of coffee beside the cards.

In case this had not been proved irrefutably, their mellow demeanors were verification they were all effing nuts.

"Is Shirleen okay?" I asked upon entry, Juno loping toward Roxie, who had leaned to the side and was snapping her fingers at my dog.

"She's fine, but she's pissed. She has to buy a new couch," Ally replied.

I stared at Ally.

This answer both relieved and confused me.

"Thank God. Looking at that old one gave me a migraine," Jet muttered.

I turned to stare at Jet.

"I liked it. All those big swirls, black against white. Drama. It was pure Shirleen," Indy commented.

My gaze swung to Indy.

"Maybe Luke and I should get a new couch," Ava put in thoughtfully. "I'm not sure I'm into all that leather."

I looked to Ava.

"I like Eddie's couch," Jet was still muttering. When my eyes moved to her, I saw she had a small smile on her face and it didn't take a mind reader to know why she liked Eddie's couch.

"Sugar, how you doin'?" Daisy asked, and my gaze went to her to see hers was sharp on me.

I was pretty happy we weren't talking about couches anymore that was how I was doing.

I opened my mouth to speak then clamped it shut.

Mace told me the Rock Chicks needed to be kept in the dark.

Effing hell.

So instead of sharing, I said, "Hanging in there," and it wasn't a total lie.

Things were good with Mace and me, which I couldn't tell them; it was shit everywhere else, but that wasn't news. However, I had a feeling that I had one more trial to get through when Mace finally told me the whole truth about Caitlin. And after what happened that morning, I preferred someone shooting at me to whatever Mace had to say.

I walked deeper into the room, and in order to get off the subject of me, I asked (against my will, taking the conversation back to couches), "What's this about Shirleen's couch?"

Daisy waved a hand in the air. "Oh, she just shot the guy who broke in this mornin'. Used her .44, which means mess, comprende?"

It was Daisy I was staring at now.

Shirleen *just* shot the guy who broke in?

With a .44?

Why did Shirleen have a .44?

Strike that, I didn't want to know.

When it appeared Daisy was waiting for me to confirm this information had sunk in, I nodded and Daisy continued, "He reeled back, landed on her couch, blood everywhere. She's pissed. She loved that couch."

"Did he shoot at her?" I asked.

"Yeah, she ain't stupid," Daisy kept talking, but her attention went back to her nails. "With her history, no way she'd shoot someone, even an intruder, without him shootin' first. Got three bullet holes in her wall, but that's okay, just needs a little spackle."

Her history?

A little spackle?

Effing hell.

"He dropped the gun when she nailed him," Daisy went on. "Problem is, she'd disarmed him, but she was so pissed about him bleedin' on her couch, she coldcocked him with her gun butt anyway. She's gonna have a bit of a problem explainin' that."

Oh my Lord.

"Anyway, they'll be here soon," Daisy said, her eyes moving from her nails back to me. "And you and me got to talk about Dixon Jones."

Nope.

No way.

Not gonna happen.

I pulled a chair toward the couch and sat down. Juno decided to make the rounds and began doing person-to-person greetings. That was to say sniffing everyone.

"Maybe we can talk about Dixon Jones when people aren't breaking into houses and bleeding on couches," I said to Daisy.

"Life goes on, sugar," Daisy returned on a shrug. "I called him last night. He had to leave town after your last gig. He's comin' back to Denver, gonna be at your gig on Thursday. He wants a meet then. I suggested we do it beforehand, seein' as most of the times you get kidnapped or shot at or jump audience members is after the gig. When I explained this to him, he agreed."

I decided to ignore Daisy reminding Dixon Jones about the mayhem in my life, considering he'd witnessed most of it, and even if it wasn't hard to forget, it'd been in the papers.

I was saved from having to retort when the door opened and Shirleen stormed in.

The girls weren't wrong. She was fine, but she was pissed.

"Who's gonna pay for my couch, hunh?" She was yelling at a man who was walking behind her. He had light brown hair, the cut expensive, and he was wearing a suit, which also looked expensive. He was tall-ish and slight but still fit, maybe late thirties, early forties. His face was tight, and if anything, he looked even angrier than Shirleen. "Who's gonna pay for therapy for Roam and Sniff?" she demanded.

Roam and Sniff, her teenaged foster kids, followed her in. Roam was a handsome, tall, gangly black kid, the gangly part beginning to fill out well. Sniff was a small, skinny white kid whose acne was healing and who was hilarious, something I'd learned during their first guitar lesson yesterday evening.

Neither of them looked like they were in need of therapy.

"Hey, Stella," Sniff called, his face forming a goofy grin as he waved at me.

Roam gave me a chin lift, his eyes shifted to Jules and he muttered, "Hey, Law."

Jules got up to greet the boys as the room filled with the Hot Bunch (all of them, every last one), Tex and Duke.

Body language, incidentally, screamed unhappy.

I looked at Mace, but he didn't look at me. I knew this was an act for the benefit of the Rock Chicks, but it still sucked.

The brown-headed man stopped and his eyes pinned Shirleen.

"I'm glad you reminded me. Why don't we talk about those boys, Miz Jackson? Tell me again how *you*, of all people, became a foster parent?"

I didn't even know the guy and I knew that not only was he angry, what he'd just asked was not so vaguely threatening. I knew this because the air in the room went heavy.

"The boys were in my caseload at the Shelter," Jules said to the man. "I did the background checks on Shirleen."

The man turned to Jules. "Your dedication is impressive, Mrs. Crowe, considering you were in Intensive Care when these two were placed with Miz Jackson."

Uh-oh.

My eyes moved back to Mace. He had his arms crossed on his chest and his feet planted wide. He also had a look on his face that said if this guy didn't stop being such a jerk, Mace was going to rip his head off.

"That's enough, George," Hank said quietly.

"Yeah, Nightingale, it's enough," George replied, voice still angry. "I've had nothing but shit from you and your men all fuckin' morning."

Hank's eyes narrowed, and I took back my earlier thought that he was less intense and more laidback then the rest of the men. At that moment, he was even scarier than his brother.

"We went through three boxes yesterday morning, George," Hank clipped. "Not to mention six days ago, there were four drive-bys and Stella fuckin' got shot."

"That wasn't reported," George shot back.

When Hank spoke again, his voice was vibrating he was so angry. "It sure as fuck was. Mace and Luke made statements and we had three squads on the scene while the incident took place. Furthermore, we got five hundred witnesses to rifle fire at a fuckin' club on Friday night."

"None of that was linked to Carter," George returned.

"For fuck's sake, George," Eddie exploded. "Lee got the call before the drive-bys!"

"Hearsay," George replied.

"You've got to be shittin' me," Vance snapped.

George's gaze swung to Lee. "You get the call on tape?"

Lee's eyes were on George and I changed my mind again. Perhaps he *did* scare me more than Hank.

Not taking his eyes off George, Lee said low, "Hank..." and I got it immediately that if Hank did not handle this George guy, Lee would, and it might get messy.

But Hank was already talking and he wasn't paying attention to Lee. His eyes were also on George.

"We're done," he said.

George turned back to Hank. "I'm tellin' you Nightingale—"

Hank interrupted him.

"A week ago, the windows of my house were blown out by an AK-47, my fiancée in the house at the time," Hank snapped. "And I've known Shirleen since I was ten fuckin' years old. She's family. And someone broke into her house this morning and drilled three rounds into the wall of her livin' room, but they were aimin' *at her*."

George had the grace to look a might uncomfortable but still hanging on to stubborn and angry as he glared at Hank.

Thus began a tense staring contest that went on until Hank broke it.

"Done," he repeated then, without another word, he walked out of the room.

All the men and women stared at George.

George stared at the door.

Then he looked at Eddie. "He wouldn't be that stupid."

It was Eddie's turn to cross his arms on his chest, and with one look at him, he went to the top of the list of Hot Bunch Boys Who Scared Me Most.

"We played your game, you fucked us, and this mornin' Shirleen nearly got her head blown off," Eddie said, his voice tight. "Now, *hombre*, we're gonna fuck you."

George looked around the room and his lip curled before he hissed, "You think you're untouchable."

Luke's body moved slightly right before he said, "Don't play that game, George."

"You're messing with the wrong man," George replied to Luke.

Lee's eyebrows went up and he entered the exchange. "You think?"

284

George, in my opinion, took his life in his hands and pointed at Lee. "The days where the Nightingale men have carte blanche to waltz through Denver are over."

"You don't back down, your dream of sittin' behind the Governor's desk is over," Lee returned.

"Fuck you," George spat at Lee.

Oh dear.

Lee leaned forward, maybe an inch, but it was a scary inch. "Now it's you who's bein' stupid."

George glared at Lee.

Lee calmly returned his glare.

Then George made a weird, angry, scrunchy face. His glare traveled the room, taking us all in before he stomped out.

Everyone stared at the door.

Beautiful.

I didn't even know what was happening, but it was pretty obvious we had a new problem.

My eyes went back to Mace and saw his were on me. He moved his head in a short, nearly imperceptible jerk then he walked out, too.

"You boys okay?" Jules quietly asked Roam and Sniff.

"Fuck yeah, it was great. Shirleen's the shit," Sniff replied, throwing himself in a chair. "It was like the movies."

"Black bitch can move fast," Roam muttered.

"Don't call Shirleen a 'black bitch'," Jules snapped, her voice no longer quiet.

"Be cool, Law. She don't care," Roam returned.

"I *do* care, boy, and you just lost this week's allowance," Shirleen broke in, hands on hips, narrowed eyes on Roam, who kept belligerent eyes on Shirleen. She, apparently, didn't like his belligerent eyes so she continued, "*And* you bought yourself bathroom duty."

"Shee-it," Roam mumbled, his gaze sweeping the room, his shoulders hunching as if he wanted to disappear.

"I got three and a half bathrooms," Shirleen informed me. "Boys take turns each week cleanin' 'em." She turned to Sniff. "You got the week off."

"Killer," Sniff's goofy grin returned.

Roam was saved any further embarrassment when the door flew open and Smithie stormed in, a pretty black woman in tow.

His eyes moved through the room and he was mumbling under his breath.

"Hey, Smithie. Hey, LaTeesha," Jet greeted, but Smithie waved at her with impatience and his eyes went back through the room, his mouth still moving silently.

Then he yelled, "Where's the fuckin' Hawaiian?"

"Mace is fine," Roxie told Smithie, and I caught Indy rolling her eyes at me.

Smithie's gaze sliced back through the room and stopped on Roxie. "Where's your man?"

"Hank's fine too," Roxie smiled.

"*Oo, girl!*" LaTeesha suddenly screamed, making me jump before she surged toward Roxie. "When'd you get that ring?"

My body went still as my eyes moved to Roxie's hand which, I noticed, now sported a sparkling diamond engagement ring.

My stomach pitched in a happy way when Roxie's gaze found mine and she smiled at me.

I smiled back.

"She and Hank got engaged last night," Ava shared, and I looked at Ava, who was also smiling huge.

LaTeesha's happy face turned back to Roxie, who had her hand in LaTeesha's, ring pointed skyward.

"Was he sweet?" LaTeesha asked.

"Oh yes," Roxie said softly.

"It wasn't sweet. It was *hot*," Daisy put in.

Ally placed her hands over her ears and chanted, "La-la-la, not-listening-to-the-story-of-my-brother-proposing-while-doing-the-nasty-one-more-time, la-la-la."

Wow.

That sounded like a helluva proposal.

"Wicked," Sniff breathed, his eyes on the blushing Roxie.

Indy bit her lip, but her body was shaking with laughter.

Jet giggled.

My gaze moved over the Hot Bunch and they were all avoiding eyes, shifting on their feet and trying to control grins.

"Um, excuse me, but didn't one of ya'll get shot at this morning?" Smithie barked at the Hot Bunch, jerking us out of our happy moment. "Now, I'm not one to tell anyone how to go about their business..." he went on and Jet made a noise that sounded like a snort and LaTeesha's eyes got huge. "But it's one thing to shoot at your girls while they got *your* badasses covering *their* tight asses, and I'll admit, that's some crazy shit, but it's a whole other thing to break into a house and shoot at a woman with kids under her roof. Now, I'm thinkin' you boys have things to do."

"Smithie, sweetie—" LaTeesha said softly.

"It's covered, Smithie," Shirleen put in.

"Yeah, it'll *be* covered," Smithie snapped at Shirleen. "You're movin' your ass in with me tonight and you're bringin' the boys. LaTeesha, that okay with you?"

"Just fine. I'll make chicken and dumplin's," LaTeesha replied on a wide grin at Roam and Sniff.

"Can we have pizza?" Sniff asked.

Shirleen cuffed him gently up the side of his head. "What's the matter with you, boy? You heard the woman. LaTeesha's makin' chicken and dumplin's. You're eatin' chicken and dumplin's."

"I like chicken and dumplin's," Roam put in.

"See? We'll be fine," LaTeesha finished.

"Yeah, we'll be fine 'cause I got myself a shotgun and I bought you that .38 last year for Christmas," Smithie told LaTeesha. "That'll make us *just* fine."

"I'm not hearing this," Eddie muttered and walked out the door.

"Smithie, I want your address. You just got put on the drive-by route," Lee said to Smithie and he walked out, Smithie following him, muttering what I thought was, "Damn straight".

After that, the Hot Bunch filed out, Luke and Vance after giving Ava and Jules some PDA, Hector after asking me if I knew about the meeting on Thursday with Dixon Jones. LaTeesha followed Matt, who was going to take her to Lee and Smithie. Roam and Sniff followed Bobby, who was going to take them to the TV in the safe room.

This left the room filled with Rock Chicks, Tex and Duke.

And for some reason, everyone had eyes on me.

I didn't think this was a good thing.

Therefore, to deflect attention off me, I turned to Roxie and said, "Congratulations, Roxie. That's cool."

She smiled and replied, "Yeah."

"Ava, sugar, go get Stella a cup of coffee," Daisy said softly, and a chill ran up my spine as Ava nodded and took off on her errand.

"What's up?" I asked as I realized I'd failed at deflecting attention off of me.

"You hear from Mace, darlin'?" Tex asked and I stared at him.

Shitsofuckit.

I had to lie.

"Erm..." I mumbled instead of flat out lying.

"I'm not sure I agree with this," Ally put in, her voice far softer than normal and that chill that went up my spine chased its way back down.

"I don't wanna talk about Mace." I tried to waylay whatever they had planned, but Daisy got up, walked to my chair and pulled me out of it.

"I think you need to be on the couch for this one," she said to me as she walked me to the couch.

Not good.

"Listen, guys, seriously, Mace and I are over and—" I started again, but Daisy ignored me and pushed me down onto the couch.

While Daisy was doing this, Jet pulled Daisy's chair close to me and sat on it. It wasn't her actions that made me stop talking. It was the look on her face.

"Sometimes a Rock Chick needs a little help from her friends," Jet said quietly.

"And sometimes her friends need to know when to back off," I replied just as quietly.

Not being a bitch or anything, but whatever this was, it was unnecessary.

Of course, they didn't know that, but still.

"Yeah, and now isn't one of those times," Duke put in, sitting down beside me, his arm coming to rest on the back of the couch behind me, his big body turned to mine.

"Duke—" I started.

"Would've preferred Mace share this with you in his own time but that time's a-wastin' and bullets are flyin'. It took the girls a while to talk me into this shit last night but they did."

"Really, Duke—" I protested.

"Quiet, girl, and listen," Duke halted my protest then he asked, "How much you know about Mace, his daddy and his sister?"

Oh.

That was it.

"Everything," I semi-lied. I *would* know everything, eventually.

Duke's brows went up. "Everything?"

I nodded.

"You know Mace's sister was kidnapped?" Jet asked softly.

I nodded, this time to Jet.

"You know her Dad hired some commandos to try to rescue her and it went bad?" Jet went on.

Uh-oh.

I didn't know that.

That didn't sound too good.

My heart started beating a mile a minute and I tried to cover.

Nodding again, I lied, "I know everything." Then as proof I offered, "I know she was murdered and Mace holds himself responsible."

"So why're you and Mace estranged, sugar? I can't believe you know what happened and you'd let that man go on alone," Daisy asked.

I didn't have a response to that, so I said, "It's complicated."

"Just knowing about her hand would make it so I never left his side," Ally muttered, my mile-a-minute beating heart skipped to a halt and I stared at her.

She looked a little bit angry and that anger was directed at me.

I didn't have time for Ally's anger.

"Her hand?" I breathed, finding I was fighting for air.

They all looked at each other.

"You don't know everything," Tex's boom was low and he was looking pale.

"What about Caitlin's hand?" I went on.

"Stella—" Duke started.

I twisted to Duke and grabbed his forearm, my voice sounding strained and desperate (exactly how I felt) when I said, "Tell me about her effing hand."

Duke's eyes lifted to Tex. My fingers squeezed his arm, he looked back to me and sighed.

Then he said quietly, "After the commandos botched the rescue job, in retaliation, her kidnappers cut off her hand and sent it to her father in a—"

He didn't finish.

I jumped from the couch, eyes on Indy, and whispered, "Bathroom."

I didn't wait for her to answer, I ran from the room. I got into the hall and Indy was there, hands on me, guiding me. I was making gagging noises, hand over my mouth. I barely made it into and through Lee's office to his bathroom when I hit my knees, tagged the bowl with my arms and hurled eggs benedict into the toilet.

Indy held back my hair as my body lurched through vomiting and then the dry heaves.

When I'd finished, I sat on my ass, back to the wall. Indy gave me a wet washcloth to wipe my mouth as she flushed the toilet.

Then she sat down, close by my side.

I put my hands over my face, the washcloth clenched in one of them. My stomach hurt. I tasted the sour vomit in my mouth, but all I could think about was how Mace was that morning.

"Honey," Indy whispered.

"He loved her hands," I whispered back. "He told me they were exquisite."

All of a sudden, I was in Indy's arms and her voice broke when she muttered, "Oh, honey."

My chest was moving. I felt it, like it was working for air and not getting any. I was breathing through my nose, the breath coming hard. I could feel the exhalations against my lips, but all that work and nothing was getting to my lungs. My eyeballs felt like they'd grown ten times their normal size and wanted to force their way out of my head.

Mace's words sounded in my brain.

Jesus, I'll never forget the way she moved her hands.

"Oh my God," I whispered.

"Shh, honey, quiet," Indy mumbled.

I reared back, looked in her face, which was blurry with my tears, but I could see she was shedding her own. I'd never known Indy to cry. She wasn't a crying type of girl. Even if this surprised and touched me, I needed to move on, and fast.

"Get Duke," I demanded.

"I'm here, darlin'." Duke was standing in the door, all the Rock Chicks and Tex behind him, Ava was holding my cup of coffee.

"Let's go, everyone out," Tex herded the Rock Chicks away as Indy left me and Duke came in.

He sat down next to me, one leg bent, one straight out, his wrist resting on his bent knee.

Tex shut the door and we were alone.

I turned to Duke, and since he wasn't a Rock Chick, I figured Mace wouldn't get mad at me when I blurted, "We're back together. Mace and me. He came home to me last night and we worked it out." I watched the blurry surprise hit Duke's face and continued, "We have to pretend we're not back together because his Dad is playing some kind of game. So we have to keep it a secret."

"All right, love," he replied, his gravelly voice deeper, and I knew it was with emotion, which I had to ignore because I was holding on by a thread.

"He started to tell me about his sister, but it's hard on him. I have to let him tell me his own way," I said.

Duke reached out and slid his fingers through my hair at my forehead, pulling it back away from my face. "You're bein' smart."

"The Rock Chicks can't know about us being back together. And they can't tell me anymore about what happened to Caitlin."

"I'll talk to the girls."

"But you have to tell me."

Silence then a gentle, "Stella, I'm not sure—"

I leaned into him. "Duke, I just hurled because I couldn't take it. If it gets worse, I can't let him see that. I have to be strong for him. He's being strong for me. You have to tell me. I have to be prepared."

"You're allowed to have an honest reaction—" Duke began, but I shook my head.

"No, you don't understand. He loved her. They were close. This is eating at him. I have to be strong. I have to let him give this to me. I've got to be able to take it from him."

Duke's eyes searched mine for a few beats. I watched him come to a conclusion and he nodded. He got closer and his arm moved around me, his big hand coming to the side of my head, pressing against it so my cheek rested on his shoulder.

"Okay, darlin'. Hate to say it, but it gets worse," he said softly, and I sucked breath in through my nose, not at all certain what could be worse than a girl being kidnapped and having her hand cut off. But since it ended in murder, I figured it definitely got worse.

Duke went on, "You need me to stop so you can get yourself together, you just say so."

I nodded my head against his shoulder.

After I did that, he told me.

I didn't make him stop. I listened to the whole thing without making a noise except for my breathing going heavy.

When he was done, we both just sat on the floor, my head against his shoulder, his arm around my waist.

We sat there silent a long time, both of us lost in our own thoughts.

Finally, I said, "I've seen the scars."

"Sorry?"

"From the bullets, Mace getting shot. On his thigh and his shoulder. I didn't think anything of them. He was an athlete, athletes have injuries. I just thought..." I stopped because there was nothing else to say.

Duke didn't reply.

"He thinks he did the wrong thing, calling in the police," I told Duke.

"Far's I can tell, she was dead the minute they took her. Only wrong thing done was her Dad makin' it worse by not doin' everything he could to make it easier for her while they had her. Her Dad knew what he was dealin' with, Mace didn't. He just wanted his sister back. Nothin' wrong about that."

I nodded my head in agreement and pulled in more breath.

Then I whispered. "I'm not going to be able to take them away."

"Take what away?"

"His demons," I explained, feeling hopeless, lost, maybe a little scared, and definitely like I was wrong about my luck changing. "They're never going to go away."

Duke's hand gave me a squeeze at my waist then he got up and left me on the floor. He closed the bathroom door behind him and I stared at it, wondering what to do.

I wanted to go to Mace and put my arms around him, absorb his pain like I was an emotional sponge. I wanted magical powers so I could erase his memories. I wanted to be able to time travel so I could warn him, protect Caitlin. I wanted to give her the life she was supposed to have. Allow her to move to New

York and become a ballerina. I wanted Mace to be able to go to the theater, sit in the audience and watch his sister dance.

Most of all, I wanted to kick his Dad's ass.

On that thought, the bathroom door opened and Duke came back, a toothbrush in its packaging in one hand, a cup of coffee in the other. He put the coffee cup on the back of the toilet and held out a hand to me. He pulled me up and rooted through the medicine cabinet, closed the mirrored door and handed me some toothpaste and the brush. I brushed my teeth, scoured my tongue and rinsed my mouth.

When I was done, Duke put down the toilet seat, guided me to it and I sat down. He handed me my coffee and I took a sip as he crouched in front of me and looked into my eyes.

Then he spoke, "Don't know Caitlin Mason. But I 'spect, she's anything like her brother, you go back in time eight years, sit her down, tell her this was gonna happen, I know what she'd say to you."

"What would she say?" I whispered.

"She'd say 'be happy'."

I knew what he was trying to do.

I also knew it wasn't going to work.

It wasn't that simple.

Nothing about this was simple.

I shook my head and the second wave of tears that hadn't yet come stung my eyes.

Duke continued, "You're right, Stella. This is eatin' him. You say they were close, and that's proved true by the way he's torn apart by this. But any sixteen year old ballerina who loves her brother wouldn't want her spirit to haunt him. She'd want him to let go of those demons and be happy. Your job is to make him understand that's what she'd want."

"How do I do that?" I asked, feeling the wetness start to roll silently down my cheeks.

"By making him happy. You do that, it'll come. He'll let it go."

I shook my head again.

This was not something you let go.

I could make Mace breakfasts of eggs benedict and Belgian waffles topped with strawberries and whipped cream and homemade blueberry pancakes smothered in warm maple syrup and apple coffeecake with a thick crust of brown sugar crumble (or whatever) every morning for the rest of his effing life and it would never make him happy enough to let this shit go.

Duke grabbed my hand and squeezed. "Trust me, girl. I know what I'm talkin' about. I been watchin' the way he is with you. Don't know it all. Don't know what happened to him after it went down. What I do know is he hasn't let anyone in. Not until you. You work at makin' him happy, he'll let it go."

For some reason, that was when I remembered what Mace said to me onstage after I sang "Black".

I can't be the star in your sky when you're the only star left shining in mine.

I wondered what he meant by that.

The only star?

How could I be the only star?

Mace was a good guy. Understandably intense and maybe he had a short fuse, but all the Hot Bunch respected him. More than respected him, they liked him. They weren't colleagues, they were friends.

He had to have a life back then, before that happened to Caitlin.

He had to have people he cared about who cared about him.

He had to have other family.

Friends.

His Mom.

He never talked about his friends, his past, his Mom.

Ever.

And it hit me then.

I knew.

I knew because he was like me.

He was black.

He left his career as an athlete and became a private investigator.

He left his life behind, shut it out, moved on. Everything before Caitlin was gone. He'd pushed it away.

I knew this because I'd done the same thing.

That was when the idea came to me and my back went straight.

I pulled my hand from Duke's, wiped my eyes and asked, "Duke, can you do me a big favor?"

"Anything, love."

"I need Mace's Mom's name and her phone number. But I don't want Mace to know you gave it to me."

Duke stared at me a second.

Then he smiled and said, "You got it."

Chapter 19

Crazy Honkies

Stella

"I saw it first!" Leo shouted.

"I don't care, this tee is *mine!*" Pong shouted back.

I was standing with Indy and Ally, and at the shouts, the three of us looked across Head West to see Pong and Leo standing by a round clothing rack filled with t-shirts. They looked like they were playing tug of war with a rainbow, tie-dyed tee stretched tight between them.

Beautiful.

My effing band.

From the look of it, Annette's store opening was a smash hit. There were people shoulder to shoulder, all of them consuming cashews, olives and Ritz crackers spread with squirtable cheese and drinking Fat Tire beer like these were the finest of delicacies. A lot of those people carried brown paper bags with "Head West" stamped on the side of them in old Wild West style lettering. Bags that held t-shirts, bongs and posters, amongst other things.

It had been fun, thus far, and it was taking our mind off things, which we all needed. That day, Shirleen had been shot at (and lost her couch) and my world had been rocked by all that had happened to Mace. A party, even if it had the weird mixture of olives, squirtable cheese and bongs (though the bongs weren't in use), was exactly what we needed.

Annette was happy as a clam and sifting through the crowd, looking kick-fucking-ass in a cream boat-necked hemp top and khaki loose-fitting hemp trousers. Her feet were bare, all her toes painted in different colors of the rainbow. A thin cream, khaki and green hemp scarf was wrapped around her blonde hair, but lots of that hair was poking out here and there; some of it twisted, some of it braided, some of it curled, some of it just hanging.

The store was one day old but looked like it had been there since the 60's. The walls were covered in Jimi Hendrix, Grateful Dead and Jim Morrison posters and big blankets decorated with Celtic symbols or pot leaves.

There were five big, round clothing racks filled with t-shirts, sarongs and hemp clothing. There were three flipping poster displays showing posters of rock bands, she-devils riding tigers and psychedelic everything with rolled up, plastic-covered posters in numbered slots beside them. There were shelves filled with books like *Zen and the Art of Motorcycle Maintenance* and Jerry Garcia biographies. There were glass-topped and -sided display cases along the front and down one full side of the store, chockfull of bongs of every shape, size and color, one-hitters also of every shape, size and color, Zippo lighters, bumper and other stickers, incense of every scent known to man, as well as a variety of incense burners, candles and an assortment of other head shop paraphernalia.

The Rock Chicks and Hot Bunch were all in attendance, except Mace, who, Luke told me, was working, and for the benefit of the Rock Chicks (something Luke didn't tell me, I just knew), keeping a distance.

The boys were there for security purposes and made this plain by having holstered guns at their belts alongside walkie-talkies. Not to mention wearing identical "Don't fuck with me" expressions on their faces, and for your information, these expressions were Hot Bunch Universal. And with the wide berth they were all getting from the customers-slash-partiers, effective.

The girls didn't go the way of hemp, but at Annette's demand, we were all displaying Annette's wares, wearing jeans and most of us wearing cowboy boots, except Ava, who had on flip-flops. Indy had on a Grateful Dead tee. Ally was wearing a peach and yellow tie-dyed tee with a yellow peace sign on the front. Jules had on a violet tee that said, "Give peace a chance" across the front in psychedelic scrawl. Ava was sporting a vintage Jefferson Airplane tee. Upon arrival, Annette had given me a pink tee with "Flower Power" written across the boobs in cartoon daisies, and like all the other girls, I'd changed in one of the dressing rooms. Roxie had on a killer Indian-style tunic that was also sold in the shop.

Daisy appeared to have missed the dress-code communiqué. She was wearing a white denim miniskirt, a backless halter top made of what looked like tiny silver beads and had a drape at the cleavage that was so low on her enormous bosoms it was vaguely threatening. She'd completed her ensemble with a pair of silver, platform go-go boots and her hair was teased out to *there*.

When I'd looked her from head-to-toe, Daisy told me. "I don't do hippie, comprende?"

I just nodded. There was nothing else to do.

I watched as a scruffy-looking guy, who I knew was a friend of the Rock Chicks because I'd met him at a gig some time ago (he went by the moniker "The Kevster", FYI), shuffled up to Leo and Pong and said one word.

"Dudes."

Then he lifted up both his hands in peace signs like this was going to work.

I closed my eyes in despair, mainly because I knew this wasn't going to work.

"Fuck off, hippie." I heard Pong snap, and I knew it was time to act. With an apologetic glance at Indy and Ally, I pushed forward to take care of my band.

As I made my way through the crowd, I watched The Kevster rear back in offense. "I'm not a hippie. I'm a pothead. World of difference, man."

Leo ignored The Kevster and yanked on the tee. "Let go, Pong."

Pong turned back to Leo. "You let go!"

Leo yanked again and shouted, "No! *You* let go!"

"Dudes, you gotta respect the vibe of a head shop," The Kevster cut in informatively. "It's like walkin' into a Kabbalah Center and starting a bitch-slapping fight. You don't do that shit. You're killin' the vibe."

"Fuck the vibe," Pong yelled just as I made it up to them.

I had bad timing. Pong lost hold on the shirt. He went flying backwards, and since I was behind him, he slammed into me and we both went down. Our arms reeled out to find purchase and we took down two clothing racks with us. They fell to their sides and crashed around us with loud bangs and then started rolling, t-shirts and hemp clothes flying everywhere.

"Chaos!" The Kevster shouted, arms waving over his head. "Chaos at the head shop!"

Ally arrived and pulled The Kevster back, ordering, "Calm down, Kevin."

Kevin didn't feel like calming down. He pointed at Pong then at Leo.

"Eject. Eject, eject, eject!"

"If there's no chaos at the head shop, there ain't no eject either," Pong said from the floor, but The Kevster was having none of it.

"It's about respect, man," The Kevster decreed. "No one brings chaos to a head shop. Everyone knows that!"

Kristen Ashley

Indy was behind me and she pulled me up by my armpits as Hugo made it to our clutch.

He looked down his nose at Pong.

"Crazy honkies," Hugo muttered, making it clear he wasn't there to help.

Shirleen was all of a sudden close and looking at Pong, too.

"Brother, you got *that* right," she said to Hugo.

I'd let this all wash over me without much thought.

This was not unusual. Chaos, in my life (even before the bullets were flying) was not unusual. My band caused chaos everywhere they went.

But at that moment, I was over it.

Effing *over it.*

I'd spent an hour after my time in the bathroom with Duke that morning, sitting in Lee's office while the Rock Chicks guarded the door. I read through the papers that the Rock Chicks, Duke and Tex finally shared with me.

The story about Caitlin was all there, with pictures. Pictures of a beautiful, blonde-haired, blue-eyed, smiling, *tiny* teenage girl. There was even a picture of her with Mace during his surfing days, maybe after a competition. He was standing on a beach in a wetsuit, his hair and suit slick with water, his board planted in the sand behind him. Caitlin, tiny and young, maybe ten years old, was pressed into his side, hugging him around his waist, smiling brightly, her head tilted back to look up at him as his was tilted down to look at her. His arm was around her shoulders, his long, strong fingers curled in, holding her tight. You could see she didn't care, not even a little bit, that she was dry and Mace was soaking wet.

Mace was smiling at Caitlin, too. He was a lot younger in the picture. I had no idea how old, maybe in his early twenties. He smiled at her in a way I'd never seen him before. His face relaxed, open, unguarded, and it hurt my heart to look at it.

I didn't know how much of himself he'd lost after that situation, not until I saw that photo.

When I saw it, I knew he lost everything.

And it was my job to get it back.

I was just damned if I knew how.

I'd learned about Preston Mason, too. A lot about him. Mostly I learned that I wasn't wrong. He was the Supreme Asshole of All Time.

298

I'd read about it all. About her hand. The commandos. And how Mace had watched his sister get her head blown off right before his beautiful body had nearly been riddled with bullets.

This meant Mace had a dickhead father, a dead sister, and now a girlfriend under fire.

That was worth being pissed-off about.

That was earth-shattering.

That could fuck you up for the rest of your life.

I found I no longer had patience with Leo and Pong fighting over a tie-dyed t-shirt of all effing things.

And seriously, could you blame me?

When Pong got to his feet, I moved forward, my cowboy-booted feet treading on t-shirts. I put my hands in his chest and shoved. This surprised him. I'd never done this before and he went back on a foot.

"What's the matter with you?" I snapped.

Pong's eyes got wide as they stared at me and my uncharacteristic loss of control, and he muttered, "Stella Bella."

"No, really. What's the matter with you?" I repeated. "I wanna know."

Pong blinked then he explained, "That t-shirt is the shit."

I leaned to the side, my fingers curled into the t-shirt Leo was still holding and I viciously tugged it free.

I shook it out in front of Pong and shouted, "This? This is worth causing a scene over? This is worth getting in the face of your friend over? You'd never wear this shirt!" I shouted, and I was right. Pong would never wear a tie-dyed t-shirt. Ever.

Then I turned to Leo.

"And you!" Leo took a step back when he saw my face, but I just kept going. "You've got, what? Fifteen shirts just like this!"

And I was right about that, too. He had to have fifteen. Hell, he could even have twenty. Hell, he was wearing one at that very moment!

Leo shrugged and I threw the t-shirt at him. It hit him in the face and he lifted up his hands to catch it as it fell down.

"I'm up to *here* with you two!" I yelled, raising my hand, fingers straight, palm down, up to my chin. "Linnie's dead! *Dead!* Floyd and Buzz are on their way to Oklahoma for her funeral right now and you two are fighting over a t-shirt." Both looked uncomfortable, but I kept shouting. "Damn it, bullets are flying! We're in the papers, like, every day. We're close to something big with a record label which could change all our lives and Mace..." I trailed off when I saw all the Rock Chicks and the Hot Bunch, and incidentally, most of the party-goers were standing around, staring at me.

I clamped my mouth shut, shook my head and forged on, hoping to cover.

"Forget Mace. You two, work this out like the men you are, not six year olds. I'm done with your shit. Done. No more." I swung my eyes to Hugo. "You either."

Hugo's eyebrows went up as did his hands, palms out.

"Shit, mama, what'd I do?" Hugo asked.

"Nothing," I returned. "Nothing to help. You're smarter than that. I know it. You know it. But it's always me that's gotta keep the peace in the band." I threw my hand out. "You're all smarter than this. If we don't keep our shit together, we're gonna fall apart and I'm gonna let it happen because I'm done. Done! Got me?"

They didn't answer, they just stared.

I decided to take that as a "yes" and I pointed to the floor. "Now clean this up, and if you've caused any damage you're paying Annette, even if you have to work it off. Do you hear me?"

They again didn't answer so I leaned forward threateningly and repeated, "I said, *do you hear me?*"

"Shit, Stella Bella, chill," Pong mumbled.

"I'll chill when this is all cleaned up," I snapped back.

"We got it, Stella. No problem," Leo said softly, bending over to pick up t-shirts.

Hugo was still staring at me and he was doing it closely.

"Nothing's going to happen to the band," Hugo told me.

"You're right," I agreed. "Nothing's going to happen to the band. Nothing bad and nothing good, either, if you all don't get your shit together. Do you want to be playing clubs in Denver and Boulder and effing Colorado effing Springs for the rest of your lives?"

Pong, Hugo and Leo looked at each other and then back at me. They'd never considered going further, mainly because I never wanted to take us further.

"We gonna be more?" Pong asked, his voice edged in surprise.

"We could be, if you'd start taking care of your damn selves. We could be a lot more," I answered. "Do you want that?"

More silence, more staring, more obvious surprise.

Finally, Leo whispered, "Shit, yeah."

"Good. Then you have to help me, and you can do that by growing... the fuck... up." On that, I turned to Indy and announced, "I need a beer."

"You're holding one, honey," Indy replied softly.

I looked down at my hand to see I miraculously still had hold of my beer, but it had mostly leaked onto the floor.

"I need a new one," I informed her.

Shirleen's hands came to my shoulders and she started pushing us forward, demanding, "Outta the way. Emergency beer needed!"

"I'm thinking beer isn't gonna be strong enough," Ava muttered to Jules as they shoved in behind us, and all the Rock Chicks followed.

Shirleen pushed me to the back where there was a pocket of space and serenity. Ally came forward and pressed a new, cold, open beer bottle in my hand. Ava took away the old one and put it on a display case.

I took a healthy swig.

"That was righteous," Ally told me.

"Shoulda done that a long time ago, sugar," Daisy said then she gave me a wink.

Before I could reply to Daisy, Annette shoved in.

"Jumpin' Jehosephats, that was fuckin' phat!" she shouted. "I was getting worried that nothing was gonna happen. I'd be, like, totally bummed if I had a party and the Rock Chicks didn't deliver." She shoved my shoulder. "Bitch, you are sofa-king awesome!"

Then she whirled around and shoved away. All the Rock Chicks' eyes followed her.

"I take it she's not mad," I said to Roxie, and Roxie grinned at me.

"Nettie's a little weird," Roxie shared.

"You got that right, sister," Jet muttered.

I took another swig and watched Hector enter the store. His eyes did a scan, found me, and he started pushing through the crowd in our direction.

"I hate to bring this up right now, but we need to talk about Mace," Jet said quietly.

My eyes, and my thoughts, moved from Hector to Jet.

The Rock Chicks hadn't discussed what happened that morning. Instead, Tex loaded me up in his bronze El Camino and took me home after that morning's heartbreaking activities. In his Camino, I'd shared with him, too, about Mace and I being together as he, too, was not a Rock Chick. His response to this was walking me to my apartment and spending the afternoon with me and Juno, eating popcorn and watching action movies.

"Nothin' clears the head like popcorn and Bruce Willis," he'd informed me, shoving a huge fistful of popcorn in his mouth.

This was true-*ish*. Watching Bruce Willis essentially blow up a skyscraper did take my mind off Mace and all our troubles.

For a while.

"I can't talk about Mace right now," I said to the girls.

"She's got a lot to process," Jules told Jet.

"Process, my ass. She's gotta call that boy home, give him the business and get on with it," Shirleen put in.

"They need to talk, not do the nasty," Roxie replied.

"Doin' the nasty *does* the talkin', girl," Shirleen shot back. "You know that more than anyone. Shee-it, just last night, your man gave you a ring *while* givin' you the business. That says it all."

Ally put her hands over her ears and chanted, "La la la, I'm not listening, la la la."

"Sex isn't the answer to everything, Shirleen," Ava talked over Ally.

Shirleen's gaze snapped to Ava. "When's the last time you and Luke had sex?"

"I don't understand——" Ava started but Shirleen cut her off.

"When?" she clipped.

Ava glanced around then shared, "Before coming tonight."

Daisy giggled and the rest of us exchanged grins.

"You two share heart to hearts? Does Luke fuckin' Stark *process* his feelings with you? Or when he's got somethin' to say, somethin' to communicate, somethin' to *process*, does he throw you up against the wall and give you the business?" Shirleen asked, making what I thought was a valid point.

I myself had given Mace the business last night as my way of showing him I was glad he was back. He heard my message loud and clear. Sure, we talked, but only after my message had been delivered.

"We didn't have wall sex. We had dining room table sex," Ava corrected, stubbornly not giving Shirleen her point.

"Oowee, dining room table sex. I like dining room table sex," Daisy burst out. "You two need to get a desk. Marcus and I had desk sex last night. Desk sex is *fine*."

"We have a desk. It kind of... fell over when we tried desk sex," Ava said.

"Luke's a big guy. Your desk is small. You need a bigger desk," Roxie advised.

"Kitchen counter sex is the best," Indy put in her thoughts. "Lee's creative, but when we do it in the kitchen..." she trailed off and started looking dreamy.

"La la la, not listening about Lee being creative, la la la." Ally was back to chanting.

"I'm not sure it's the where, it's more the position," Jules entered the conversation.

"I don't think it's the position, it's all about the intensity," Jet joined as well. "Eddie and I like it hard, rough. That's the best. You know what I mean?"

"Fuck." We heard muttered, and everyone turned to see Hector standing behind Jet and looking at her like he wished he could rip off his own ears after hearing that his brother liked sex hard and rough.

"Whoops," Jules whispered, and everyone started giggling, except Jet, who started blushing.

"Sorry Hector," Jet mumbled.

"Welcome to my world. Now you know my pain," Ally informed Hector.

Hector wasn't about to be dragged into this conversation. His eyes sliced to me and he held up his hand, his index and middle fingers holding a folded piece of paper.

"You wanted a number?" he said to me.

Oh my *God*.

Mace's Mom's phone number.

My breath caught. I felt my eyes grow wide and I nodded.

"Let's go. You got a call to make," Hector finished, and without delay, I put my beer on the display case and moved forward.

"What call?" Ally asked.

"What's going on?" Daisy said at the same time.

"Whose number is that?" Indy put in.

"Leave her be," Jules said softly.

It was at that moment Tod and Stevie pushed into our clutch.

"Oh my *God*. I've been browsing and there is *nothing* here I want to buy. I've never been to a store where there was nothing I wanted to buy," Tod announced, sounding horrified. "Someone check my forehead. See if I have a fever."

"It's a head shop, Tod. You don't smoke pot and you aren't a hippie. Of course there's nothing you'll want to buy," Stevie explained.

"I've seen *Hair*, like, five million times," Tod snapped back, putting his hands to his hips. "Burgundy Rose could kick the shit out of 'The Age of Aquarius'. I've looked everywhere and there's no macramé halter tops *anywhere*."

At Tod's announcement, Hector had had enough. He grabbed onto my bicep and pulled me to him.

Unfortunately, Daisy noticed.

"Hang on. You haven't answered our questions," Daisy called after us as Hector started leading me away.

"I'll explain later," I said over my shoulder.

"You better!" Daisy shouted, and Hector kept going.

Without a word, Hector led me out to an old model, brown Bronco. We were both buckled up and heading to my place when he spoke.

"Do you women always talk like that?" he asked, referring, I knew, to the sex chat.

"Um…" I hedged, because, well, we did.

"I don't wanna know," he cut in.

"Good choice," I whispered.

"Fuck," he muttered.

⚡

The apartment was dark. It was late and Juno and I were in bed when we heard the key in the lock.

Juno was sleeping. I was not.

I was planning.

I rolled when I heard the door open and the alarm start beeping. Juno lifted up and jumped off the bed. I heard the code being entered and Juno's tags jingled as she walked across the room.

I got up on an elbow, pulled my hair out of my face and called, "Mace?"

"Yeah, babe," Mace called back quietly.

I felt my heart flutter then settle. Not that I thought anyone was breaking in, just that I was glad he was home. I was glad to hear his voice say "yeah, babe," like he came home and said that to me every night. I was glad because I thought there was a possibility that he could be coming home and saying that to me every night.

"Just checking," I told him. "Everything okay?"

"As okay as it can be."

That wasn't a great answer, but at least no one had been shot at.

"Are you coming to bed?" I asked.

"In a minute," he replied.

I listened to Juno's tags jingle louder than normal, knowing Mace was giving her a rubdown. Then I listened to Mace move around in the dark, taking off his clothes and the soft rustle as they hit furniture. He walked into the bathroom and the light went on a second before he shut the door.

I lay back in bed. Juno jumped up and started to settle at the foot.

I took a deep breath, quit planning my upcoming War with Mace's Demons Strategy and thought about my night.

Hector had walked me up to my apartment and he'd given me a cell phone to use, saying my cell and landline might be being monitored by Mace's Dad.

I found this creepy as all get out, but then again, Mace's dad was a creep so that wasn't a surprise.

Then, to my shock, Hector stayed. I thought this was a nice thing to do. I wasn't a person who couldn't be alone, but at that moment I didn't want to be alone. Normally, I would choose a Rock Chick to be with me during this, my first important maneuver in my War with the Demons, but since I didn't have that luxury, Hector would work.

I looked at the piece of paper Hector had given me and saw that Mace's Mom's name was Lana. I thought that was a beautiful name. She'd kept the last name Mason so I was guessing she never remarried. I supposed if you were screwed over by the Supreme Asshole of All Time, you wouldn't be keen to jump back into the game.

I dialed her number, got cold feet and hoped she wasn't home.

I had absolutely no idea what to say.

305

Then I got worried she *wouldn't* be home and I had absolutely no idea how to leave a message.

"Hello?" I heard in my ear.

Oh shit.

Too late.

My eyes flew to Hector. He was standing beside me as I sat in my armchair.

He gave me a nod.

"Um, Ms. Mason?" I said back, dipping my chin to look at my knees, and I heard Hector's boots on the floorboards as he walked away.

"Yes?" she answered.

"This is Stella. Stella Gunn. You don't know me. I'm a friend of your son's. I'm a friend of, um... Kai's."

Sheesh but it was weird calling Mace "Kai".

Silence.

Or, I should say, loaded silence.

"Hello?" I called.

"Kai?" she asked and the way she said his name made it sound beautiful. She had a gorgeous voice; soft, feminine, melodic. I liked her just by the sound of her voice. But I really liked her by the way she said her son's name, like it was magic.

"Yes, Kai," I told her.

"Is he all right?" I heard a tremor of fear sift through her voice.

"Yes," I said quickly, then I went back on that word. "No. I mean, he's fine but he's not fine."

Effing hell, this was hard.

Get on with it! My brain shouted at me.

I don't know how! I shouted back.

Well, think of something! My brain wasn't having any of it.

"I don't understand," Lana said in my ear. "You're the girl in the papers, right?"

Oh hell, she'd seen the papers.

I wondered what she knew.

"Yes," I told her. "We're kind of... erm, *special* friends."

Special friends?

I was such an idiot!

"I was getting that from the papers," she said softly. Then she informed me, "You're very pretty."

That was a nice thing to say so I smiled at the phone. "Thank you."

"You're welcome."

What now?

Bloody, effing hell.

"He doesn't know I'm calling you," I told her.

Silence again.

I took a deep breath and forged ahead. "I know about Caitlin. I just found out."

More silence. Again it was loaded.

"Ms. Mason?"

"Call me Lana."

That was nice, too.

"Lana, do you talk to Mace?" I asked.

"Mace?" she sounded confused.

"Erm, it's what his friends call Kai here. Mace."

There was a pause before I heard her say quietly, "That doesn't sound like my son. He's not a Mace."

This made me sad. In the picture I saw that day when Mace was holding his sister, he didn't look like a Mace. He looked like a Kai.

He was definitely a Mace now.

"Do you speak with him?" I asked.

"I haven't heard from him in nearly seven years."

Gut kick, sure and true. In fact, it was *the* gut kick to end *all* gut kicks.

It made me hurt, for Mace and for Lana.

"Oh, Lana," I breathed when I found my voice.

"Why are you calling?" she asked, her voice getting stronger.

"I…" I didn't know what to say. Then I did. "I need your help."

I told her about what was happening. Everything. Sidney Carter. Linnie. Preston Mason. Even my parents. And also Mace's and my history.

I figured she had a right to know. Mace was her son. I took a chance and didn't sugarcoat it, either. I figured since Mace was her son she had to make him who he was at least partly, and I was guessing she gave him the good parts since Preston Mason didn't have anything good to give. Mace had a lot of good parts, so I was thinking her genes had to be stronger so she could hack it.

When I was done talking, Lana immediately asked, "What do you want me to do?"

I looked at Hector. He'd moved away and was sitting on the platform, watching me and scratching Juno's head.

"I need you to come to Denver," I told Lana, taking my eyes from Hector.

"Then what do you want me to do?" Lana went on.

"Nothing. Just come to Denver. I'll do the rest."

"What's the rest?"

I had no effing idea.

I decided not to sugarcoat that either. "I don't know. I'm making this up as I go along."

She laughed quietly and it sounded like a pretty song. "That doesn't sound like a very good plan."

I smiled at the phone again.

"It isn't." I leaned back in the chair, put my heels up on its edge and shared, "But I have to do something. He takes good care of me. It's time someone took care of him. And this, all of this... with his Dad, Caitlin, well, it has to stop."

Silence again, but I felt her warmth coming at me from the phone line.

Finally, she said, "Stella, you should know, he loved Caitlin more than anything else in this world. She didn't have a Dad. Neither of them did, not really. Kai did everything he could so she wouldn't feel that loss, not the way he felt it. When she was taken—"

"Lana—" I cut in.

"No, sweetie, let me finish."

I shut up, mainly because her calling me "sweetie" felt nice. My mother or father never called me anything like that. It was one of the reasons why I liked Mace calling me "Kitten" so much.

I wondered if she called Mace "sweetie".

Lana went on, "When she was taken, I watched my son die."

I sucked in breath. My body got tight, I felt my throat close and my eyes flew to Hector as she continued.

"Kai disappeared. This Mace person has taken his place. You need to understand that he might not want me there. Kai, Caitlin and her Mom, Chloe, and I used to do holidays together. We even did vacations together. We made a family out of what Preston left behind. We all got along great, even if at first,

Chloe and I..." She stopped then started again, "Kai did that. Kai built our family. Kai wanted that for Caitlin and for Chloe and for me."

"And for himself," I cut in.

"And for himself," she agreed softly. "But that's gone now. He wants it gone. And he might not want it back. Not without Caitlin."

"You're his mother," I told her.

"I am, but—"

"And Chloe is all that's left of Caitlin."

"Stella, sweetie—"

"I need to call her, too," I said, a half-baked plan forming in my head.

"I'm not sure that's a good idea," Lana replied quickly.

"He can't go on like this."

"My son's a pretty strong guy. He always was. He can do whatever he wants. He's always done that, too," Lana told me, and she sounded resigned to that.

I wasn't resigned.

"That's true. But now he has to do whatever Caitlin wants. And I don't know Caitlin, but I can't imagine that she would want this. Not for Mace, not for you and not for Chloe. You need to be a family again."

Lana was silent.

"Can you give me Chloe's number?" I asked into the silence.

There was a pause. I heard a deep breath and then, hesitantly, "I'll phone her."

My eyes came up and I smiled at Hector.

"That'd be good," I said into the phone.

"I hope you know what you're doing," I heard Lana say.

"I don't," I admitted. Then, since I was admitting things, I went for the gusto. "But I love him and I have to try."

Another pause then with warmth, "I'm looking forward to meeting you, Stella Gunn."

I smiled again. "Me too."

I asked Hector for the cell number and gave it to Lana. We said our goodbyes and then we disconnected.

My eyes found Hector's were still on me.

"Am I doing the right thing?" I asked him.

"Absolutely," he replied immediately, sounding certain.

"You're sure?" I wasn't so certain.

He got up and walked to me. I sat in silent surprise as he bent down, wrapped his hand around the back of my head and kissed the top of it. When I tilted my face to look at him, his gaze locked on mine.

"I'm sure," he whispered.

"I hope you're right," I whispered back.

He let me go and straightened. "Mace is a lucky guy."

I felt a weird, happy warmth flow through me at his approval.

I smiled up at Hector. "Thanks."

Hector smiled back and my breath took a hike through the trails of the Rocky Mountain National Forest.

Hector Chavez had a fucking great smile.

Shortly after, Hector took off, leaving me the cell. I used it to phone Floyd and make sure he and Buzz were okay. Linnie's funeral was the next morning, and I was cheesed off I couldn't go, but for obvious reasons I couldn't. They were coming right back so they could make the gig on Thursday.

I shared a few things with Floyd while we talked. He strangely sounded both worried and relieved.

Then he passed the phone to Buzz and I shared a few things with him.

"Linnie would be so happy," Buzz told me.

I knew she would and that made me happy, but it also made me sad. I wished that she could be around to see it all unfold, believe in it and maybe believe in herself again.

But my luck hadn't changed that much.

Once I hung up, I made the set list for Thursday's gig and it was going to be a humdinger, designed both for Dixon Jones and Kai Mason, and then I played guitar. After that, Juno and I went to bed and I planned.

The bathroom door opened and I heard Mace moving through the room. I saw his shadow at the side of the bed, the covers went back and then he was in, stretching out beside me and pulling the covers up to his waist.

For some reason I stayed where I was, waiting for him to reach out to me.

He didn't. He was on his back. He put his hands behind his head and I saw his profile facing the ceiling. I was on my side, facing him.

"Lee told me about the fight in the head shop," he said.

Oh dear.

"Pong and Leo got a little out-of-control," I replied.

Mace didn't respond. There was nothing to say. Pong and Leo had a habit of getting out-of-control on a routine basis.

"Daisy and Hector have set a meeting on Thursday with the A&R guy from Black Fat Records," I told him.

"You gonna take the meet?"

I took in a breath then said, "Yeah."

He took his hands from behind his head, turned to his side to face me and murmured, "Good."

"I'm scared," I shared.

"I know," he returned.

Well, there you go. Nothing else to say on that subject.

"I swung by to see Monk today," Mace told me. "Got your money. It's on the kitchen counter. I'll give Floyd, Hugo, Pong and Leo their take tomorrow."

"You didn't have to do that."

"I know that, too."

Well, there you go again. Nothing else to say on that either.

"I didn't call my Mom today," I told him.

"Good," he surprised me by replying. "I want to be there when you do it."

My heart skipped a beat.

God, I loved him.

"Thank you," I whispered.

Again, he didn't respond.

"How was your day?" I asked, feeling weird.

We'd never done this, lying in bed, talking, sharing, even, one could say, *processing*.

It was kind of freaking me out. But in a good way.

"There's been progress. George, the guy from the offices today, is an assistant DA. He's giving us trouble with Sid's case. Hank went over George's head. Presented the evidence to his boss. The boss disagreed with George. He told Hank and Eddie to bring Sid in. The warrant for his arrest went out tonight."

"That's good news, isn't it?"

"Yeah, on the face of it. Sid's gonna be hard to find. He's also gonna retaliate, mobilize his army."

"I thought his army was already mobilized."

"Defensive tactics. He'll go offensive now."

That didn't sound good. In fact, that sounded *way* not good.

"George is pissed," Mace went on. "Hank made him look like a fool."

"Is that gonna be bad?"

"We don't know yet. George doesn't like looking like a fool. He'd go after Hank, but there's nothing to get on Hank. Instead, he'll likely go after Lee and Shirleen as retribution."

"How?"

"Lee'll be okay. He doesn't play by the rules, but he covers his tracks. But Shirleen used to deal drugs." I gasped at this news, but Mace talked through it. "Now she's fostering two runaways, and Jules and another social worker at the Shelter pulled some strings to place Roam and Sniff with her. Roam and Sniff might be moved out. Jules might lose her job."

"Fuck," I whispered.

"It'll be okay," Mace told me.

"It doesn't sound okay."

"Don't worry about it, Kitten." And he didn't sound worried. Not at all.

I trusted him to be right so I let it go.

"Shirleen used to deal drugs?" I asked.

"Yeah. She was never busted and she's been clean awhile."

"I can't believe that of Shirleen." And I couldn't.

"Even good people do bad things, Stella. Shirleen's good people. She just did bad things. Now, she doesn't. She's a good foster carer, she loves those kids. Would lay down her life for them, proved it this morning. She's also a good friend. That's all you need to know. End of story."

It was my turn to fall silent because I trusted him to be right about that, too. And with what I experienced of Shirleen, I knew he *was* right.

Then I shared, "This is weird."

"What?"

"You. Me. Talking."

I heard the smile in his voice when he said, "I like it."

You could hear my smile in my voice when I said, "Me too."

I decided it was time to start beating back those demons. I had to start right away because I didn't like him living with them, and I wasn't going to let him do it one second longer than he had to.

"I like you coming home to me," I told him softly.

The minute I stopped talking the air in the room changed. It felt like it became heavy, close but warmer.

Mace didn't respond, but he did move. Finally touching me, his fingers, whisper-soft, at my waist.

I went on, "I like making breakfast for you. I like you in my kitchen. I like that henley you wore today. It looks great on you."

"Kitten," he murmured, and his fingers shifted down the small of my back. He leaned his body into me and pulled me closer.

My hands hit his hard chest. One slid up and my fingers curled around his neck.

"I like to hear Juno's tags jingle when you give her a rubdown. I like hearing your clothes hitting the furniture."

After I said that, his lips hit my neck and slid up to behind my ear.

I turned my head so my lips were at his ear and I wrapped my arms tight around his middle.

"I'm sorry I fought you, Mace," I whispered. "But now that you're mine again, I'm never going to let you go."

He turned his head and I could swear he was looking at me in the dark. I felt my face grow warm under his gaze, my soft body already warming from his hard one pressing into mine.

Then he kissed me.

Then we used our mouths, tongues, fingers and other parts of our body to process everything else that needed processing.

When we were done processing, when I'd finished purring and we were breathing steady again, when Mace had rolled me and pressed my back into his front, when Juno had come back to bed and settled at our feet, I whispered, "Thank you."

"What're you thankin' me for, Kitten?" Mace asked into the back of my neck, and he sounded amused.

"I'm the Queen of Super Shitty Bad Luck. All my life, my luck has been bad. Not just bad, super shitty bad," I shared. "But not anymore. Now it's good. It's always good when you're around. So I'm thanking you for being my good luck charm."

For a beat, I felt his body go solid as a rock.

Then his arm around my waist got super tight. So tight, it squeezed the breath out of me, and again to the back of my neck, he muttered, "Jesus."

Kristen Ashley

The way he said it, the way he held me close, made me hope that in my first battle, I'd kicked some demon ass.

I considered telling him I loved him, but I didn't want to push too hard, too fast.

My war against his demons was going to take a while. I needed to be patient and strong and not fuck it up.

I could wait.

Chapter 20

Demon Scum

Stella

The next morning, I made Mace apple streusel coffee cake, which, unfortunately, as I was under house arrest (in a way), this necessitated Mace making an early morning trip to the grocery store to buy ingredients, but he didn't seem to mind, as he never did. And anyway, my apple streusel coffee cake was one of his favorites.

While it was baking in the oven, I tried not to make a big deal out of putting Mace's clothes in the closet and the stuff in his boxes around the house.

I wanted him to notice me doing it, but I wanted to make it seem like it was perfectly natural. Like a daily chore, rinsing dishes or feeding Juno.

It was another battle in my War with the Demons, making him feel welcome, settled and at home at my place.

Okay, so maybe it was more like a minor skirmish, but it was still something.

At first, it didn't seem he noticed anything since he was sitting on the couch talking on his cell, leaned forward and writing notes on a tablet on the coffee table.

Considering, even for a normal couple, this would be a huge deal, me moving his stuff into my space, the fact that he treated it like it was perfectly natural, like a daily chore, began to piss me off. So instead of doing it like I didn't want him to notice it, I started banging around while I did it, like he could bloody well get up and help me.

I got down to the bottom of the last box, which was filled with about thirty CDs. When Mace flipped his phone closed, I picked up the box, lugged it to the coffee table and dumped it on his writing tablet.

His head came up immediately. He looked at me and said, "Babe."

I put my hands to my hips and told him, "You need to mark your CDs."

His eyes went to my hips as his brows snapped together.

Then he looked back at me and asked, "Why?"

"Because if you don't mark your CDs, they'll get all mixed up with mine."

I reached in and pulled one out. It was Journey's, "Evolution", which, by the way, featured one of my favorite Journey songs, "Lovin', Touchin', Squeez-in'". I wondered, briefly, if I could fit that song in the next night's set list and decided quickly to do so.

For your information, I had that same CD.

Everyone knew what that meant.

"Who cares?" Mace asked, interrupting my mental set list restructuring. He lifted up the box and set it aside so he could see the tablet.

Obviously, he didn't know what doubled CDs meant.

"I care," I told him. "I have this same CD. How will we know which one's yours and which one's mine?"

Mace sat back and put the sole of his foot against the edge of my coffee table.

"Who cares which one's yours and which one's mine?"

My eyes bugged out right before I said, "*I* care."

"Why?"

"Because I do. Because it's a CD. Because CDs are sacred."

"It's the same CD," he pointed out.

"Yes, but I bought mine at Twist and Shout during my Journey phase, and Twist and Shout is gone now. I was with my old band when I bought it. At my demand, we played 'Wheel in the Sky', like, every night. I loved everything Journey. Even their power ballads. I hate power ballads. But Journey's power ballads kick... fucking... ass. 'Faithfully', 'Open Arms'. Those ballads *rock*."

"So, if we find we're doubled up on CDs, we'll sell mine on eBay."

I made a choking noise, then spluttered, "What?"

Mace was watching me closely, perhaps wondering if I needed an intervention.

Then he repeated, saying the words slowly this time, "We've got any of the same CDs, we'll sell mine on eBay."

I threw my hands up in the air. "You can't just *sell* your CDs on *eBay*, especially if we've doubled up. If we're doubled up then they serve a dual purpose. First, they're backup CDs in case something goes wrong with one, and second, they're material evidence that we should be together because we like the same music. Everyone knows that!"

He shook his head, the expression on his face looking like he didn't know whether to smile or to scowl.

Then he suggested, "If you want to mark the CDs, mark your CDs."

I gasped then said, "I'm not marking *my* CDs. I don't want marks on my CDs. The covers, either." I put in the last as an important afterthought.

He took in a deep breath and I could tell this was an effort at patience before he tried, "Then mark mine."

"You mark yours."

"Kitten, I don't have time to mark my CDs, and I don't have any fuckin' desire to fight with you about this."

Uh-oh.

Were we fighting?

Fighting didn't factor in with my War against Mace's Demons. In fact, fighting would be highly detrimental to my overall Strategy.

"We're not fighting. We're discussing," I told him.

"Discussions between a man and a woman don't include the woman putting her hands on her hips. The minute that happens, it's a fight. And you started this with your hands on your hips," Mace told me.

"I did not," I snapped, but I was worried that I did.

"You did," he returned.

I glared at him. "Well, I was putting your shit away. You *could* help."

"Brody was briefing me on what he's finding on my father. He's coasting on the fumes of seventeen six packs of Red Bull and no sleep for forty-two hours. He's doin' deep hacks, all of them highly illegal, and some of what he's finding pretty fuckin' useful. Sorry I couldn't interrupt the brief to help you hang clothes."

Oh dear.

This wasn't going very well.

I decided it was time I gave in before I left the Demon Skirmish any more bloodied and beaten.

Therefore, I muttered, "Okay, whatever. I'll mark your CDs."

I threw the Journey CD in and put my hands to the box, but Mace was there, too. He pulled the box out of my hands, twisted to the side and dropped it on the floor.

I started to straighten on the word "Hey!" when he lifted in a squat, gripped me at the waist and yanked me to him. I grabbed on to his shoulders and hiked up my heels so the fronts of my calves wouldn't slam into the coffee table. He had me on my back on the couch, him on top of me, before I could say a word.

His face in my face, he said, "Kitten, you gotta know, that coffee cake didn't smell so fuckin' good and I didn't enjoy watchin' you wander the apartment, puttin' away my shit while you're wearin' those cutoffs I like so goddamned much, you'd be a pain in the fuckin' ass."

Okay, so his telling me he watched me walking around the apartment meant that maybe I was wrong about losing the skirmish. Maybe I won and didn't even realize it.

I didn't know what to say that wouldn't give anything away, so I said, "I'm *so* sure."

"Leave the CDs in the box," he ordered. "Once this shit is done, I've decided you're movin' to my place."

My eyes grew round. I forgot about skirmishes and wars and demons and I breathed, "Am not."

"Yep, you are. I like your space, but it's too fuckin' girlie and there isn't enough room. I got a yard for Juno. I got a dining room table so we don't have to eat standing up in the kitchen. We'll move your bed, get rid of your other shit and you can mark the CDs all in one go."

Get rid of "my other shit"?

I did not *think* so!

I crossed my arms on my chest. This took some effort since I had to shove them between our bodies but I did it.

"You seem to have everything figured out."

He grinned, completely ignoring the arm crossing move, which said "fight" far, *far* more than hands at your hips, and said, "Damn straight."

"Your house is modern," I told him.

"Yeah. And?"

"I don't mean to sound funny, but modern's not my gig."

And it wasn't.

His house was, like, three years old, situated in a modern development. No personality. All the houses one of three styles, all of them one of three colors.

Boring.

This hadn't bothered me before since we spent most of our time at my place, but it bothered me now. It bothered me because I knew that his house wasn't his home. It was just a house. After this was over, I didn't want Mace *ever* to live in a house. I wanted to make Mace's house a home.

"Then we'll find another place," he said, like it was all the same to him, and it probably was.

The fight went out of me.

"Really?" I asked.

He watched me a beat and then went back to grinning.

"Really." His head bent and he touched his mouth to mine. "But it'll have rooms."

"I could do rooms," I whispered.

His face got soft and so did his eyes. "You set your music up in the bedroom though."

My body melted under his, I pulled my arms out from between us and wrapped them around his back.

"I could do that, too." I was still whispering.

His hand went to the side of my face, the tips of his fingers slid into my hair at the temple and went back. This made me do a happy shiver. He watched his hand move and his eyes came back to mine. I held my breath at the intensity behind them then something flashed in them. The demons came out, my breath hitched and the guard slammed down.

Even though I thought I lost the moment, he proved me wrong by saying, "When I'm with you, sometimes I forget."

I knew exactly what he was talking about.

I wanted to get up, punch the air and shout with joy, *take THAT demon scum!*

Instead, I put my hands on either side of his face, lifted up my head and kissed him.

He kissed me back.

It got heated.

Some time later, the timer on the oven went off, and against my will, I had to roll him to the side and push away. I got to my feet and he got up to a sitting position. Before I went to the kitchen, standing between his legs in front of the couch, I leaned down and put my hands to his thighs. I brushed my lips against his, kept my mouth there and whispered, "Every time I'm with you, I forget."

I saw another flash in his eyes before I quickly straightened and walked away.

I just stopped myself from licking my finger, pointing it high and slashing my score in the air.

⚜

Mid-morning, after Mace had been gone for an hour, the cell phone Hector gave me rang.

I went to it, flipped it open and said, "Hello."

"Kitten."

I felt another happy shiver.

"Hey," I said softly.

"Hector told me he gave you a clean phone."

"Yeah."

"When'd that happen?"

Oh dear.

"Erm, last night. When he took me home from Head West." It wasn't a lie unless it was lying by omission as to *why* he gave me the phone, and that he stayed while I used the phone for the secret reason he gave it to me.

"Not all fired up about this newfound closeness you got with Chavez," Mace said in a low, unhappy voice.

"Hector's my manager."

Silence.

"So are Daisy and Shirleen. I think the Rock Chicks on the whole are mini-managers, too."

"Jesus," Mace muttered.

"It's all good," I said breezily, even though that was definitely a lie.

Mace decided to move on.

"You wanna come to the offices? Have lunch with me?"

Fuck yes! My brain shouted.

"Sure," I said out loud.

"We'll call your Mom after lunch."

Shitsofuckit.

"Erm…" I muttered.

"Kitten, you gotta call her." This was said softly.

"I know," I whispered, squeezed my eyes shut hard before I said, "Fuck."

"I'll be there. You'll be fine."

At least that made me feel better. "Okay."

"One of the guys'll pick you up."

"Okay."

"Around one."

"Sure."

"You got a list for the grocery store, bring it. I'll swing by King Soopers on the way home."

Another happy shiver.

"You want Belgian waffles tomorrow or leftover coffee cake?" I asked him.

"Coffee cake."

"You gonna be home for dinner?"

"I want to say yes, but we'll see."

"Okay, I'll plan flexible."

"Later, Kitten." I heard the smile in his voice.

"Later." I hoped he heard the smile in mine.

Disconnect.

God, I loved him.

⋙⋘

The cell phone Hector gave me rang at a quarter to noon.

I went to it, thinking it would be Mace again and hoping he didn't have to back out on lunch or dinner, when I flipped it open and said, "Hello?"

"Stella?"

It was Lana.

"Hey Lana. How're you?"

"I'm packing and freaking out. That's how I am. Chloe and I'll be in Denver tomorrow."

Oh my God!

"That's great!" I said to Lana.

"I hope you're right, sweetie. Chloe's freaking out even more than me. Kai and her… Kai was bad after… he thought Chloe blamed him. He convinced himself of it. No matter what she said…" She trailed off then breathed, "Oh *God*."

"It's all gonna be okay," I said like I knew it was true, but I knew no such thing.

"She looks like Caitlin," Lana told me.

Oh man.

Oh shit.

Oh man.

That was it.

No matter what Mace said, I needed the Rock Chicks.

No way *in hell* I was going to be able to pull this off without the Rock Chicks.

"You're gonna be good," I promised. "Mace, I mean Kai, has a lot of friends. Good friends. Good people. We'll take care of you and we'll take care of him."

"If you say so."

Last night, during my planning, I realized that I had to keep Lana, and now Chloe, protected. Not only did we have Sidney Carter to worry about, we had Preston Mason, and maybe that jerky George guy too.

"Don't book a hotel. You have to stay with friends," I told Lana.

"Oh, we couldn't impose."

"You have to," I said quickly. "Kai would never forgive me if I didn't take steps to keep you safe."

Silence, then, "Oh."

"That's okay, too. Safe is these people's middle name." I was thinking about the Hot Bunch. They had other middle names like "Bossy" and "Scary" and "Badass" and "Hot", but I decided not to share those middle names with Lana. She was already freaking out.

"Okay," Lana said.

"Let me know your flight numbers. I'll send someone out to get you at DIA. Okay?"

She gave me the flight numbers and I wrote them down on Mace's tablet. Then I ripped the top sheet off, folded it up and put it in the back pocket of my cutoffs.

While I was doing this, Lana called, "Stella?"

"Yeah?"

"Thank you."

I did another happy shiver, a different kind that didn't involve Mace, his voice, eyes, hands or mouth. But it was happy all the same.

"No, Lana, thank you," I said back.

I programmed Lana's number into the phone under "Bogey One" just in case Mace saw it. I wanted a warning if she phoned again.

I sat on the couch and thought about my options.

Then, because I couldn't decide, I called Fortnum's. I'd talk to whoever answered the phone.

"Hello, Fortnum's Used Books," a woman said, and I knew it was Jane, the super-thin, kind of weird, pathologically shy woman of indeterminate age that had worked there since before Indy inherited the store from her grandmother.

"Jane?" I asked anyway, just to be sure.

"Who's this?" she sounded guarded.

"It's Stella."

Effing hell, now I had to pick someone.

It hit me.

Duke.

Perfect.

"Is Duke there?" I asked.

"No," Jane answered.

Beautiful.

Maybe my luck hadn't changed.

Plan B.

"Okay, then, can I talk to Tex?" I blurted.

"Sure," I heard the muffled noises of a hand covering a mouthpiece, then, "Tex?"

I also heard Tex's muted, impatient boom. "What?"

"Phone," Jane told him.

"I figured that, woman. I got, like, five hundred customers. Take a message."

"It's Stella Gunn," Jane informed him.

"Shit. She's not riddled with bullets, is she?"

I rolled my eyes to the ceiling.

"Are you injured in some way?" Jane asked me in all seriousness.

"No," I answered, but Tex would be if he didn't fall in line with my plan, pronto. "Just tell him it's important."

More phone muffling then, "She says it's important."

I heard incoherent grumbling then Tex came on the phone and instead of saying hello, he said, "I'm gonna fuckin' kill whoever's talkin' to the papers. It's a fuckin' madhouse in here. And most of 'em are new, which means they don't know the drill, like, what I say fuckin' *goes*. They expect me to be nice or somethin'. One told me I needed a customer service trainin' course. What the fuck is *that?*"

"Tex—" I tried to cut in but it didn't work.

"Trainin' courses! Yeah, we need trainin' all right. These fuckers need to learn that I make coffee and they drink it. It doesn't come with a 'hi', 'how you doin'' or 'have a nice fuckin' day'. They order, they move to the end of the counter, they get their coffee and they cease to exist for me. *Fuck!*" he finished on a boom.

"Tex, stop saying 'fuck' so loud!" I heard Indy shout in the background.

"Fuck!" Tex shouted back. "Fuck, fuck, fuck, fuck, *fuck!*"

Oh dear.

"Would it kill you to be a little nice?" I asked when he'd quit saying fuck.

"Yes," he answered immediately.

Okay, I didn't have time for this. We needed to move on.

"Tex, I need a favor," I told him.

"Does it involve me kickin' someone's ass?" he asked.

"No."

"Great. Fuckin' great. I need to kick someone's ass. But do you need me to do that? *No!* You fuckin' do not. Jesus Jones, what is it?"

I told him about my strategy, Mace's Mom and Stepmom's imminent arrival, and I needed the Rock Chicks in on it but sworn to secrecy under threat of certain death if they breathed a word.

"I get to kill 'em if they let the cat out of the bag?" Tex asked.

"Knock yourself out," I replied.

"Leave it to me."

Disconnect without even a good-bye.

I ticked that off my mental list.

Onward.

Mace and I were sitting in Lee's office. I was behind the desk in Lee's chair. Mace was on the desk, sitting close. Next to his thigh were the wrappers from our spicy chicken tortilla wraps.

I sucked on the straw, procrastinating by consuming the watery dregs of a long since dead Diet Coke. I was staring at the phone Mace placed in front of me next to the wrappers.

"Kitten," Mace said softly.

I didn't take my eyes from the phone.

"Fuck," I muttered.

"Do it fast. Get it over with," Mace encouraged.

I looked up at him. I set down my dead Diet Coke. Then I tossed my hair.

"Right. Fast. Over with. Here I go."

I picked up the receiver, dialed the number to my childhood home that even after years I hadn't forgotten, and sat and listened to it ring.

"Hello," my Mom said. She sounded seven hundred years old.

My eyes flew to Mace. He leaned forward, put his hand on my neck right where it met my shoulder and he squeezed.

Strength flowed though me.

That may sound stupid, but it was true.

"Mom?" I called.

Silence.

"Mom? You there?"

"Stella?"

"Yeah, Mom. It's Stella."

"Stella," she breathed.

"Hey. How're you doin'?"

Silence.

Then I heard a hitch, like she was crying.

Stupid.

Stupid, stupid, stupid.

How're you doin'? What kind of question is that? My brain asked.

I ignored my brain.

"Mom, I know what's going on," I told her.

"You do? How do you know?" Mom asked.

"I have a friend who… well, he's more than a friend. He's kind of my boyfriend." I looked up at Mace. He wasn't looking concerned anymore, his mouth was twitching.

Effing hell.

I kept going. "Well, we're actually kind of living together. His name is Kai Mason. I call him Mace. Though, not just me. Everyone does. That is, everyone calls him Mace."

Why was I babbling?

"Anyway, he's nice and he's cute. You'd like him."

Cute?

I was still babbling!

"How do you know what's going on?" Mom got back to the subject.

"Well, he's also a private investigator."

Mom gasped.

"No! No, he didn't investigate you or anything. I mean, well, he did. After we found out from his Dad, who's kind of a jerk…"

My eyes skidded toward Mace's face again, but I couldn't see it as his head was tilted down. His shoulders were shaking however and I knew it was with laughter.

I forged ahead, "Anyway, it's a long story. His Dad told me you were sick so Mace checked up on you and he told me you were in trouble. So—"

"Did you pay the mortgage?"

My hand went to Mace's thigh. I squeezed and his head came up. I was right, he was smiling.

The smile faded when I said, "No, I didn't pay the mortgage. Mace did."

"Your Dad's real mad about the mortgage. Went to the bank and told them to return the money, but they won't do it because we're behind."

"He's going to have to get over it," I told her. "We're sending more money, Mom. Our friends did a collection."

"Don't do that Stella."

"Mom—"

"Don't you do it, girl," she snapped.

All of a sudden her voice had changed and I felt the blood run out of my face.

She could be harsh, but it was unusual. Mostly she was quiet, timid and did everything she could to be invisible.

Mace saw me pale and his eyes narrowed on my face. He dropped his hand from my neck, sat straight and hit the button for the speakerphone.

I still talked into the handset.

"Mom, you have to take the money."

"My life's been a livin' hell since you left, girl." I heard Mom over the speakerphone and her voice was sharp and ugly. "You left me to him. Didn't think for a second about me, what I might go through with you gone. You were always so damned selfish. Then I got the cancer. We don't hear word one from you for years. Now you think you can swoop in, big time rock star, in the papers, datin' a famous athlete, make it *all* better." She dragged out the "all" with acid sarcasm.

I felt my heart lurch and my stomach clench as my mother delivered her gut kick.

She sounded like Dad.

And she'd seen the papers.

Which meant she knew I was the target of a killer.

And she didn't care.

"Mom."

"He's on a tear about this money. You ain't helpin' things. I don't need this. I need to rest."

"Mom, let me help."

"You can help by keepin' your nose outta our business. You wanted to be gone, Stella, you're gone. Let me die in peace."

"Mom."

"Don't call back, and I ain't tellin' him that money was from your hotshot boyfriend, neither. I got enough to deal with."

"Please, Mom, listen to me."

But the phone was dead.

I stared at it, silent.

Mace was not silent.

He muttered, voice low, "You have got to be fuckin' shittin' me."

I didn't look at him. I kept staring at the phone. I was a mixture of mortified and... I didn't know what.

Finally, I put the handset back in the receiver.

"You... have gotta be... fuckin' *shittin'* me," Mace repeated, and finally I looked at him.

Uh-oh.

He was pissed.

"Mace—"

His hands went to the phone. He twisted his torso violently, ripping it out of its socket, the cord flying. He got to his feet and, using the entirety of his upper body for momentum, he threw it across the room.

It exploded against the wall.

Erm.

Wow.

My eyes moved from the phone back to him. "Mace."

His gaze sliced to mine.

"Those ties have been severed," Mace said, his voice trembling with fury.

"Mace."

"You're not phonin' that bitch again. I don't care if she's dyin'."

"Mace."

He exploded, "You're their fucking *daughter!* Do they *not* know how fucking *precious* you are?"

Oh dear.

I wasn't sure this was about me.

Well, maybe it was mostly about me, but it wasn't all about me.

I got close to his tense body and put my hands to his neck.

"Mace, look at me."

His eyes tilted down, but his head didn't. His chest was moving in and out rapidly like he was breathing heavily.

"She called you selfish," he told me.

"Forget it."

"Said you didn't think about her when you left."

"I heard her," I whispered.

"She ever think of you when he was abusin' you?"

"Mace."

"Answer me, Stella."

"No," I said quickly.

"She ever protect you?"

"No."

"She used you to protect herself."

I got closer. "Mace, don't—"

"She did, didn't she?"

"Yes," I said quietly.

"She's worse than your Dad."

"She's not. She's just weak."

"Don't fuckin' defend her. She's worse."

I squeezed his neck.

"Okay. She's worse." My hands slid up to the sides of his head into the hair behind his ears and I pressed with my fingers until his head tilted down. "Don't be angry. They're not worth it."

"I gave them six thousand dollars."

I closed my eyes.

"You know what I'd give to have my fuckin' phone ring and Caitlin's voice comin' at me from the other end?" he asked.

I opened my eyes and saw the demons in his.

Shit.

"What would you give?" I whispered.

"Everything," he whispered back.

"I love you," I said softly, jumping the gun, saying it far faster than I planned.

But I couldn't help it. It just slipped out. I couldn't have stopped it even if I tried.

Mace stared at me.

Even though it scared the effing hell out of me, since I'd thrown it out there, I might as well go with it.

So I did.

"You're the best thing that ever happened to me in my whole life. My hands could be crushed so I couldn't play guitar ever again and I wouldn't care as long as I had you."

Mace continued to stare at me.

I pressed my body to his, got close to his face, looked into his beautiful eyes and made a big mistake.

"It's not my place to say, but I'm guessing, I was Caitlin, I had a brother like you I wouldn't have gone through what I went through. I would have known a good life, a happy life, a lucky life. I bet you protected her from your father. I bet you kept her safe. She was lucky, until the end, to have you."

"Quiet Stella."

"It's true."

"You don't know what the fuck you're talkin' about."

"I bet I do," I whispered.

His hands came to my biceps, his fingers curled around and they did it so tightly, they hurt.

"Quiet," he growled.

I nodded, but I didn't wince and I didn't move away, even as his fingers bit deep into my flesh.

We stared at each other, his face tight. I hoped mine was open.

But he didn't give me anything.

Not even a little thing.

He was closed.

He was gone.

Shit!

The door opened.

I looked around Mace as he twisted toward the door.

We saw Vance swing in. His eyes took in the destroyed phone then skimmed across us both, but locked on Mace.

Then Vance said, "We got trouble."

Chapter 21

Social Call

Stella

I followed Mace and Vance into the reception area. I nearly ran into Mace's back because he stopped dead the minute he hit the room. I stepped around him and stared.

Preston Mason was sitting, legs crossed, calm as you please, on the couch.

As if that wasn't bad enough, Jerky George, the DA, was standing just inside the door next to a somewhat unattractive older woman with a pinched face and bags around the ankles of her hose.

Vance had spirited me into the offices for my lunch with Mace. Shirleen hadn't been around when I arrived, but now she was there. She wasn't seated behind the reception desk. She was standing and she was looking pissed-off.

"You're jokin'," Shirleen snapped in the direction of the older woman.

"What the fuck are you doin' here?" Mace asked, and with a quick glance I saw he was talking to his father.

"Mace," Vance said low.

Preston Mason was staring at me.

"I thought we had an arrangement," Preston asked me.

"Erm..." I mumbled.

Effing hell!

Caught!

"I asked you what you're doin' here," Mace repeated.

Preston's eyes moved from me to his son. His hands came from where they were resting in his lap and he flicked them out to his sides, cool and calm.

"I came to talk to you. But I've been delighted to have the opportunity to watch this drama unfold." Preston motioned between Shirleen, George and pinch-faced lady.

That's when, belatedly, I felt a chill crawl up my spine.

"Shirleen, you okay?" I asked hesitantly.

"No... I... am... not," Shirleen answered.

Oh dear.

"What's going on?" I asked.

"Perhaps, Miz Jackson, we can go somewhere private," the pinch-faced lady suggested.

"Ain't nothin' you can't say in front of my boys." Shirleen gestured to Mace and Vance.

"You have more people in your audience," George told Shirleen, and Shirleen's narrowed gaze swung to him.

"Stella's my girl. And that one's a jackass, so he don't count," Shirleen replied, giving a nod toward Preston Mason.

I nearly laughed but I didn't.

"Shirleen, take it to Lee's office. We'll wait until Jules gets here," Vance put in.

"I'm afraid Mrs. Crowe is likely busy," George told Vance. "You see, King's Shelter is having a surprise inspection today."

Oh hell. That was where Jules worked.

Mace was right about Jerky George, and he wasn't wasting any time in seeking retribution.

"First thing they'll be looking into is your wife's files on the placement of two street kids with a known felon," George continued.

"Interesting," Preston Mason said slowly. "Is she the felon?" he asked curiously, jerking his head toward Shirleen, then his eyes locked on Vance. "Or is he talkin' about you, Crowe? I know *you're* a felon." When the pinch-faced lady gasped, Preston nodded to her and went on informatively, "Grand theft auto."

Oh no.

This was not happening.

Pinch-faced lady stared at Vance for a few seconds before she breathed, "Juliet Crowe is married to a felon?"

"No," I snapped. "She's married to a hot guy."

It was my turn to have pinch-faced lady stare at me then she blinked rapidly and finally turned to Shirleen.

"Miz Jackson, we need to do an immediate intervention," she explained. "Those boys will be placed elsewhere while we look into this matter. You should have expected this as you had your home invaded and fired a .44 caliber weapon during said invasion while both boys were in residence."

"I have a right to protect my home and my boys," Shirleen retorted.

"I'm sorry, but I'm not sure it's policy to allow firearms in the homes of foster carers," pinch-faced lady shot back with saccharine sweetness.

"He shot three times into the livin' room. The night before, Roam had fallen asleep on the couch watchin' movies. He could have been hit!" Shirleen clipped.

"You can explain that while we take your report," pinch-faced lady said. "But those boys are going to need to be moved today."

"Those boys aren't goin' *anywhere*," Shirleen fired back.

I looked across the room and Preston Mason was grinning.

Erm.

No.

Someone had to do something and that someone was going to be me.

"Are you saying Shirleen has to give up her constitutional rights to be a foster carer?" I asked pinch-faced lady.

Pinch-faced lady swung her pinched-face to me. "Who are you?"

"I'm Shirleen Jackson's friend," I answered.

Pinch-faced lady's eyes went to Jerky George and she asked, "Does she deal drugs, too?"

Shirleen growled. Preston Mason laughed. I felt both Mace and Vance go still. My head prepared to explode.

"What did you say?" I hissed, taking a step forward, but Mace moved, his arm came around my waist and he halted my progress by hauling me against his body.

"Everyone knows what she is." Pinch-faced lady pointed at Shirleen.

I leaned toward her, straining at Mace's arm. "I want you to say it. Out loud. So everyone in this room can bear witness to your slander."

"Stella," Mace spoke low behind me.

"No," I twisted to look at Mace. "They wanna dig their hole deeper? We should let them. Hell, we should encourage it!" I ended up yelling.

"Be quiet," Mace ordered.

I was not going to be quiet.

My mother was just mean to me and Mace heard it and it made him destroy a phone.

My father had been mean to me all my life.

In fact, all my life I'd been rolling over and letting people deliver gut kick after gut kick.

I was done rolling over.

I turned around and glared at George. "How stupid are you?" I asked.

His eyes narrowed. "I'm sorry?"

"Have you *not* been reading the paper? Don't you know that everyone who works in this office is famous? We're the darlings of Denver. So if you don't get your," I pointed to both of them, "asses outta here, I'm calling *The Denver Post* and I'm telling them *all* about you. You won't have to wait for Lee to wipe the floor with you. *I'll* do it."

George's eyes moved to Mace and he demanded, "Mason, control your woman."

"Oh no. Not gonna happen," I cut in shaking my head. "Lee said you wanted the Governor's mansion. So when folks go to vote do you want people to remember you as the guy who brought low a good woman, a woman who not only opens her home to runaways, but puts herself in the path of bullets to keep them safe? Oh, I bet the people of Colorado will just *love* that. Coloradans, by the way, don't care about their Second Amendment rights. Don't let that worry you one bit!" I snapped sarcastically and then went on. "And Jules, a social worker who's pregnant for God's sake. She spends her days doing good deeds and you're making her life miserable. And let's not forget the rest of the Rock Chicks, living behind alarms and not able to go anywhere without bodyguards. We were just going about our business and then we all got shot at! I got hit!"

I was now yelling, but I kept right on going.

"Two of those Rock Chicks are fiancées of cops. Cops who keep the streets safe. I'm sure that'll make you *real* popular. And you could stop it, but you didn't. All of this as retribution because you didn't get your way, not because you were fighting for right, for justice, but because you were standing in the way of it while people's asses were on the line. How's that gonna sound? That's gonna make juicy headlines, George. I'm sure I'll find a reporter who'll eat this up. You're gonna be fucked. People will hate you."

I'd run out of steam so I stopped and watched as George's eyes were working. He didn't get a chance to say anything because that was when Preston Mason stood and he did so while clapping.

"Bravo, Stella," he said to me when he stopped his one man ovation. "You're good. I liked the touch with the Second Amendment. I guess you didn't skip that class while you were in school."

"Go to hell," I hissed.

"You have your daughter kidnapped and murdered then you'll know the meaning of hell," he shot back, and I felt the air grow thick as Mace went tight behind me, and I felt waves of hostility coming from Vance *and* Shirleen.

As for me, well, what could I say?

I was on a roll.

"You sure that hell has to do with Caitlin being kidnapped and murdered? Or is it something else, Preston?" I asked. "Maybe that hell is knowing you had a beautiful daughter and an accomplished son and you spent your time making money and screwing people over and not getting to know your own fucking children."

I scored a point. I knew this because his face twisted.

"Shut your mouth." It was his turn to hiss.

"Not a chance," I fired back. "You had your say in the limousine, now I'll have mine. You make me sick. I can barely look at you without vomiting. You think I'm stupid? I'm not stupid enough to throw away something this good." I jerked my thumb toward Mace. "Not like you did, you *fool*. Foreclose on my parents' house while my mother's dying of cancer. Go ahead. That'll just be one more black mark on your soul, but you already have enough to shoot straight to hell when your time's up. Don't you?"

Preston glared at me.

I strained against Mace's arm to lean forward and scream, *"Don't you?"*

I felt Mace lean into me and his mouth was right by my ear right before he said softly, "Enough, Kitten."

At his words, I straightened and sagged into him, spent. He took my weight by wrapping his other arm around me.

Preston Mason's gaze moved between the two of us and stopped on Mace. "I came by to talk deal."

"There'll be no deals," Mace returned in a firm voice.

"Be smart, son," Preston replied softly.

"Maybe I should offer that same advice," Mace suggested.

Preston stared at Mace then he shook his head. "Her parents will be out on the street tomorrow."

"That'll be difficult, considering the mortgage has been made current," Mace retorted.

Surprise flashed across Preston's face before he hid it.

He tried a different tact and nodded at me. "You can do better."

"That's fuckin' hilarious, you givin' me advice on women since you threw away two good ones without battin' a fuckin' eye," Mace shot back.

I looked at Shirleen. Shirleen was grinning at Mace. Then she looked at me and pressed her lips together like she was trying hard not to laugh.

"We going head-to-head?" Preston asked his son.

"Looks that way," Mace answered.

"I always win," Preston told Mace.

"This'll be interestin', since the same holds true for me," Mace returned.

"May the best man win!" Shirleen shouted. "New pool! I got fifty bucks on Mace."

"Don't think anyone's gonna bet against you, Shirleen," Vance put in.

At that, for some reason, Shirleen burst out laughing. I couldn't help it. The situation was just too freaky and scary. I started laughing right along with her.

The door opened and Lee walked in with, of all people, Smithie.

"Well, fuck me," Lee said, looking at George. "Is this a social call?"

I felt the tension ebb out of the room as it moved out of Mace, and the hostile vibes stopped emanating from Vance.

"Nightingale," George replied, but he was looking pale and his eyes were weirdly on Smithie. It was weird because they were on Smithie without ever actually focusing on Smithie, then he said, "Mrs. Armstrong, perhaps we should go."

"But——" pinch-faced lady, or apparently, Mrs. Armstrong, started to protest, but she didn't finish.

"Is that...?" Smithie was looking closely at George. "It is! George Riverside. Well, damn, man. You don't come around much anymore. Where you been, motherfucker?"

I stared between George and Smithie as George's face started getting red.

"Sorry, do I know you?" George asked.

"Sure. It's been a while but you used to come to my club all the time." Smithie leaned toward Mrs. Armstrong. "I own a strip club and Georgie here likes lap dances. Dirty ones. Pays extra to get a little touch here and there from the girls. Usually blondes with big tits. I mean *big*."

Smithie put his hands out in front of him and pinch-face lady reared back.

"Now he goes outta town for his action," Smithie continued.

Pinch-faced lady turned to stare in horror at George as Smithie kept talking.

"Not far to Wyoming, is it George? Still, got a friend up there, he says you're a regular. Damn, ain't cool to take your business out-of-state. What us local guys gonna do?"

Pinch-faced lady stepped away from George and swung her gaze to Shirleen.

"I'll call you Miz Jackson."

"You do that," Shirleen replied, settling in her seat at the same time she was sorting through her pencil holder. She yanked out a nail file and leaned back, crossed her legs and started to file her nails.

On that, pinch-faced lady took off.

"Nightingale—" George started.

"We got pictures, George," Lee cut him off. "And that's scratching the surface. It took me half an hour to find that on you. You want more, you keep this shit up."

George's mouth got tight. Then he looked to his shoes and he left, too.

Preston Mason's cool eyes swung through the room. Everyone stared back. Shirleen even did it while filing her nails.

"Pleasure," Preston murmured and he, too, left.

The minute the door closed, Lee's eyes went immediately to Shirleen.

"You okay?" he asked.

"Will be, once Georgie Porgie gets his ass back to his office and calls the dogs off Jules, Roam and Sniff," she answered.

Clearly, that was good enough for Lee and his eyes cut to Mace. "You?"

"Yeah," Mace replied.

Lee's eyes moved to me. "Stella?"

"You guys know a lot of dicks," I told him.

Lee's eyes crinkled in a smile that didn't quite make it to his mouth, and he said softly. "That's the sorry truth."

"Am I done here?" Smithie asked impatiently.

Lee clapped him on the shoulder. "Thanks Smithie."

Smithie threw up one hand and then he was gone.

Shirleen hit a button on the phone and we heard the speaker click on and the phone ringing.

"Yeah?" Jack's voice could be heard throughout the room.

"You get Stella on tape doin' her 'You won't have to wait for Lee to wipe the floor with you, *I'll* do it' speech?" Shirleen asked Jack.

My body went solid.

"Got it," Jack replied and you could hear him chuckle.

"Get me a copy, I wanna transcribe that fucker," Shirleen demanded. "Luke, Eddie and Hank've gotta hear this shit. Hell, I might get Tom or Malcolm to send out a network-wide email to all the po-lice. Give the boys in blue a good old fuckin' giggle."

I turned and looked up at Mace.

Apparently he was none the worse for wear after our episode in Lee's office and the showdown with his Dad. I knew this because, when he looked down at me, his gaze was warm and he was grinning.

He took one arm away, pointed to the corner of the room and my eyes went in the direction he was indicating. His arms went back around me, he leaned down and said one scary word softly in my ear.

"Cameras."

I stared at the camera.

Effing hell.

I looked back to Mace.

"Is she serious?"

His grin broadened to a smile. "Probably."

"Shit," I whispered.

His arms got tight. "You okay?"

"Your Dad is the Supreme Asshole of All Time."

His smile died and his arms went from around me to my biceps. His fingers curled around, his thumbs stroking the inside skin gently.

"I hurt you?" he asked in a soft voice.

"I'll live," I replied in a softer one.

His eyes flashed, but he let it go.

"Vance'll take you home. We'll talk more later."

I nodded.

From across the room, Shirleen entered our conversation, "Can I just ask what in *the* fuck is goin' on with you two?"

Mace and I twisted to face Shirleen.

"It's a long story," I explained.

"Well, get your ass over here and start tellin' it," Shirleen shot back.

I looked back at Mace. He smiled, bent low and kissed my forehead.

"Got things to do. You got a grocery list?"

I pulled the grocery list out of my back pocket and handed it to him.

Then I stared at the piece of paper in his hand, wondering if it was the grocery list or the flight numbers. I snatched it back and whipped around, flipping it open.

It was the grocery list.

I let out a big sigh, turned back and handed it to Mace again.

His eyes were narrowed. "What the fuck?"

"Nothin', just, erm…"

My mind raced for some reason to explain why I was such an idiot then I came up with something.

"Thought that was the set list for tomorrow. You know I'm weird about those." I wasn't, that was a total lie, which had to be why his narrowed eyes got narrower. "Anyway, it's not the set list. It's the grocery list." I leaned up and brushed his mouth with mine and said, "Now, go forth and conquer bad guys, starting with your Dad."

He stared at me a beat and decided to let it go. He lifted a hand to my neck and gave me a squeeze.

Then he was gone.

For your information, it wasn't lost on me that he didn't say a word about the fact that I told him I loved him.

⌖

"It's covered," Ally said in my ear. "Indy's Dad, Tom, is picking up Mace's Mom and Chloe. They arrive an hour apart. You'll need to call Lana and tell her to tell Chloe that Tom'll meet her at the fountains and keep her company while they wait for Lana."

"Okay, I'll call Lana," I told Ally.

Ally went on, "They're gonna stay with Daisy 'cause they'll probably want to be together and she's got plenty of room. Marcus's boys can't do it, Tom says he'll take them to your gig tomorrow night. Then you can do your thing."

"That sounds good," I replied. "Can you tell Tom that Chloe looks like Caitlin, except older?"

"Sure." Ally hesitated a beat and said, "It doesn't sound like you think this sounds good."

"No, it's all good. It's just..." I stopped, then asked. "Do you think I'm doing the right thing?"

"Shit yeah," Ally answered. "If family's good, family's everything. Mace can't move on unless he sorts this shit out. You're definitely doing the right thing."

I looked down at one of my arms. On the inside, four small, shadowy brown bruises had formed, three fingers and a thumb.

I sucked in a breath and shared, "Mace and I had an episode today."

"What kind of episode?"

"I called my Mom. Mace heard her being mean to me. He freaked out, went ballistic, threw Lee's phone against the wall. It exploded into, like, a million pieces."

"Holy shit," Ally breathed.

"After that, I told him I loved him."

"Holy *shit!*" Ally shouted. "That is *so* cool!"

"He didn't say it back, he just stared at me."

Silence.

I pressed on. "Then, I said I thought he was probably a good brother and he lost it again. He grabbed on to my arms and hurt me."

"Stella—"

"I don't care about that," I cut in quickly. "I get it, all this stuff coming up for him again. It can't be good to see it in the papers. Move around Denver knowing people know. Having pictures of Caitlin in his face."

"No, it can't be good," Ally agreed.

"He's gonna react. I've gotta be able to take it."

"Yeah. Though, chickie, he should be able to control it without hurting you."

"He watched his sister's head explode," I reminded her.

Silence then she repeated, "Yeah."

"I'm not sure I'm getting anywhere with him," I confided.

"Girl, three days ago you were pushing him away. You got to give it time."

She was right, so it was my turn to say, "Yeah."

"You gonna be okay?"

"Sure."

"You call if you're not. We'll talk," she told me. "I'm here, I hope you know that."

That was her way, and since I knew her, always had been. Ally was tough on the outside, but sweet deep down and you couldn't ask for a better friend.

"Thanks, Ally."

"Later," she said.

"Later."

We disconnected and I called Lana immediately. She wasn't home so I left a message about Tom and Chloe and warned her that if she called, I might not be able to talk if Mace came home.

I flipped the phone shut and stared at Juno. I was sitting in my armchair. She was lying on my feet snoozing.

It was late. Mace had come home earlier to drop off the groceries, but he couldn't stay and I didn't know when he'd get back. I'd made myself dinner for one, homemade chicken and rice pilaf, and the round of calls to the Rock Chicks to get them up-to-date and make sure they were keeping their mouths shut. Then I made the round of calls to my band, including Floyd and Buzz who were driving home from Oklahoma. I gave them the head's-up and put them under threat of death if they didn't keep their mouths shut, too.

But now I was sitting there, going over my strategy in my head and I was worried.

Even though both Hector and Ally said I was doing the right thing, I was thinking maybe I was going too fast. Maybe I should wait until all the other stuff was finished. Maybe I should wait until Mace was used to us being back together, until I'd been able to work on him a bit longer. Maybe Mace didn't need to deal with his Mom and Stepmom when bullets were flying and his Dad was being an asshole.

I heard the key in the door and Juno jolted up.

The door opened, the alarm started beeping and Mace walked in, his eyes coming directly to me.

"Hey, babe," he called.

My heart did that settling thing again and I replied, "Hey."

He turned to the alarm, deactivated it, reactivated it then relocked the door as I walked across the room to him. Juno had already made it and he bent low to give her a rubdown while I stopped a few steps away and looked at him.

He looked good; faded jeans, black belt, black boots. Today's short-sleeved henley was dark gray, the sleeves again tight around his biceps, but with the way he was bent and rubbing Juno. The material had also stretched against his back, defining his lats. He was in a partial squat. The jeans, too, had stretched tight against the muscles of his knee and thigh. His dark hair needed a trim. So much so, it had started to have a bit of curl on the ends. But I could still see some skin at the back of his neck. The skin was tan, the shoulders under the tee were broad.

Standing there petting my dog, he was, put simply, beautiful.

I thought for a minute that he had to know it, how beautiful he was, but it didn't matter to him, not even a little bit.

For the first time in my life I found myself wondering how I got so lucky.

He kept bent low, his long fingers sifting through Juno's fur as she wagged her tail and panted, but his head tilted up to me when he noted, "You're up late."

"Yeah," I agreed. "You hungry?"

"No, boys had a meet at Lincoln's. Ate there."

"They pick up Sid?" I asked.

He straightened and shook his head. "Gone to ground. Eddie and Hank had a meet with Turner. They've made a deal with the Feds, workin' together now. They're bringing in Sid's soldiers. The ones they got shit on, they're lockin' up. The rest of 'em, they're shakin' down."

"Progress then."

"Yeah."

"What about George?"

"George has backed down. Lee sent him the photos Smithie got hold of. He *does* like his women chesty, and I won't explain how I know that." I grimaced and Mace kept talking. "George is no longer a problem."

I nodded. We stopped talking and stood there, about three feet apart. Juno had sat down between us and was looking from one to the other, still panting.

Finally, Mace spoke. "You okay?"

I blinked. "Yeah, why do you ask?"

"'Cause your body's wound up tight."

"No it isn't," I lied.

"Babe, it is."

"I just have a lot on my mind."

"You been playin'?" he meant guitar.

I shook my head.

"You should play," he told me.

"I know," I replied.

We stopped talking and started staring at each other again.

Why was this weird?

But it *was* weird, way weird, scary weird.

I worried that it was because I told him I loved him and he didn't know what to do with that.

Things had always been intense between us, when we were together before and getting back to it. He'd told me we were moving in together, really moving in together, even though we were somewhat moved in together now.

With all he was doing, I knew he had to care about me, a lot.

I didn't know if he loved me, but I didn't think he'd think it was a bad thing that I loved him.

So why was he so far away? Why didn't he approach? Why was he staring at me with his face blank like that? Why didn't he even come fully into the house?

"Are you okay?" I asked him.

"Fuck no," he answered immediately.

"What's wrong?"

He took a step forward, just one, but reached out the rest of the way. He grabbed a wrist and gently twisted my arm. You could see the bruises. They weren't angry, but they were there.

"Fucking hell," he muttered, eyes locked on my arm. His other hand came out and grabbed my other wrist, twisted it and his eyes moved to stare at the identical bruising there.

"Mace—"

His gaze came to mine and it wasn't blank anymore. It was tortured, but they were new demons now.

Beautiful.

Just what I needed, *new* demons.

"Never touched a woman like that," he told me.

"Things are intense for you right about now," I said, giving him what I thought was a logical explanation.

"Don't make excuses for me, Kitten."

"I shouldn't have said what I said about Caitlin. I didn't know what I was talking about."

"You were tryin' to be nice."

"Yeah, but I went about it the wrong way."

"Stella—" he started, but I pulled my wrists from his fingers and stepped the last two feet so I was close. Juno backed off and trotted to the couch.

I wrapped my arms around his waist and tilted my head back to look at him. "You said you needed to learn to handle me with care. Well, I need to learn the same thing. You're a pretty intense guy, Kai Mason."

He dipped his head so his forehead was against mine.

"I'll never hurt you again, Kitten," he promised, his voice soft, gentle, beautiful.

"I believe you." And I did.

His arms came around me. "We should talk about some of the other shit you said today."

Oh hell.

"Like what?" I asked, as if I didn't know.

"Like what you said to my father."

"Erm—"

"And you tellin' me you loved me."

Oh effing bloody *hell*.

"Erm, no. Let's just forget about that," I suggested.

His arms went tight. "No fuckin' way."

"It was the heat of the moment," I explained.

His face got soft, his voice went low and it was, as ever, a killer one-two combination. "Best time to say it."

"Mace—" I started, but he was walking me backwards and his head moved, his mouth going to my neck.

His lips against my skin, he kept walking me back while saying, "Let's see if we can create more heat. That way maybe you'll say it again."

My stomach melted.

Oh dear.

I was both glad he wanted me to say it again and scared totally shitless.

"I need my guitar." I tried to delay.

He stopped walking, his mouth slid to mine and he muttered, "Later," right before he kissed me.

My arms went around his neck and I kissed him back.

Okay, so maybe I wasn't pushing too hard, too fast. Maybe I hadn't jumped the gun. Maybe I'd done the right thing.

His mouth moved from mine and he bent low, picked me up in his arms and carried me to the bed.

Once there, he took his time with me, building it so the fire burned deep and he created another heated moment.

He was on top, deep inside me. My legs were wrapped around his hips, my hands sliding up and down his back and our mouths were touching when his hands came to either side of my face and he demanded, "Say it again."

My eyes focused on his and I whispered, "Please, Mace, harder."

He grinned and touched his lips to mine then said, "Not that, babe."

Oh.

Hell.

All right. Whatever.

Both my hands slid into his hair to cup his head before I breathed, "I love you."

I watched as his eyes closed, like they were moving in slow motion then he shoved his face in my neck and started moving again.

This time harder.

⌐⍓

After, I left Mace face down in bed, eyes shut, but I knew he wasn't asleep. I got up, pulled on my underwear, cutoffs and a tank and went to my guitar.

I sat in the armchair, rested the guitar on my knee and started to play.

Then I started to sing to Mace, and what I sang to Mace was another song that said it all between us, a kickass power ballad, Journey's "Open Arms".

After the first verse, I lifted my head and saw Mace was up, still mostly on his belly, but now twisted slightly and up on an elbow.

His eyes were on me.

I kept on singing and this time, I sang the chorus directly to him.

Then, with effort, I tore my eyes from him, looked back down at my guitar and kept singing.

My head lifted again when the song became about the lover coming back, I caught Mace's eyes and I sang that part and the chorus to him as his eyes stayed locked with mine.

I finished singing, dipped my face down to stare at my hands again and mindlessly kept strumming some of the chords to the song.

Mace kept watching me. I knew it. I felt it and I had to admit I loved it.

"What kind of music did Caitlin like?" I asked softly, still watching my hands moving.

"Tchaikovsky," Mace answered immediately.

I lifted my head and smiled at him.

"I don't know any Tchaikovsky," I told him.

He shook his head. His lips turned up in a small grin and I watched him, opening all my sensors to see where his head was at and sensing he was okay (and hoping I was right).

"Do you think she would have liked me?" I asked.

"Definitely," Mace answered, again immediately.

My heart did what was becoming a familiar settle.

"Do you think she'd like me with you?" I went on.

"Yeah," he replied.

"I know it's hard for you to talk about her."

"It's gettin' easier."

I smiled at him. "Good."

Take that demon scum!

"Come to bed, Kitten," Mace muttered.

I quit strumming.

I put the guitar in its stand, took off my clothes, walked to the bed and slid in beside him. I turned to him, wrapping an arm around his waist, cocking a knee, resting it on his hard thigh and putting my cheek to his shoulder. His hand pressed under me, his arm coming up and curling around my waist.

"I love you, Kai Mason," I whispered into his chest, and I found that was getting easier, too.

His fingers dug into my flesh.

"Sleep," he replied.

I snuggled closer. Juno lifted her head and rested it on our ankles.

I fell asleep.

Chapter 22

Even If I Die Doin' It
Stella

"Stop scratching," Mace's sleepy-gruff voice demanded.

"It itches," my sleepy-grouchy voice returned.

His arm went across his body. His fingers wrapped around my wrist, taking my fingers away from where they were scratching around the stitches at my hip. He pulled my hand up and pressed it against his chest.

"It's healin'. You need to keep your fuckin' nails clear," he told me.

"Were you this damn bossy a year ago?" I grumbled.

"A year ago, I was too busy thinkin' about how lucky I was that someone as beautiful and talented as you let me into her bed to be bossy. Now I know you love me, I can be as bossy as I want."

At his words, my head shot up and I stared at him.

It was morning, early morning, the sun just peeping around the now ever-closed blinds.

Mace was on his back, I was tucked into his side. It appeared we'd slept the whole night without moving. His face was still soft with sleep, but his green eyes were alert and on me.

"You thought you were lucky?" I asked.

"Babe, I need to video you onstage. You could be butt-ugly, but the way you move onstage and that fuckin' voice of yours would still make me hard. Singin' or talkin', it doesn't matter. Your voice is the sexiest thing I've ever heard."

Uh... *wow.*

Did he just say that?

"Seriously?" I breathed.

He grinned and rolled into me. "Seriously," he said and went on. "Lucky for me, you also got great hair, great eyes, great legs and an unbelievable heart-shaped ass."

As if to prove his point, his hand slid over my ass and his face went into my neck as he pressed me to my back.

Then he muttered, "Still, I'm inside you and I hear that throaty voice of yours beggin' me to fuck you harder, I swear it takes everything I got to keep control and not come."

I wasn't sure, but I thought I had a small orgasm just listening to him.

I decided to switch topics before I lost what little control *I* had. "Just because I love you doesn't mean you can boss me around."

His head came up and he looked at me just as his hand slid from my ass, up my side, to cup my breast.

"Yeah it does," he said.

"No, it doesn't," I shot back.

He grinned. "It does."

I frowned. "It doesn't."

His thumb slid across my nipple.

It felt so good, my teeth sunk into my lower lip to stop myself from moaning.

His eyes dropped to my mouth.

"Oh yeah it does," he muttered, and he sounded pretty effing pleased.

"I take it back. I don't love you. I think *you're* a pain in *my* ass."

His body started shaking like he was laughing. "You can't take it back."

"I can."

His mouth touched mine before he said, "Jesus, you're cute, Kitten."

"I'm not cute. I'm sultry and sexy," I returned.

His mouth came back to my mouth, his eyes open and staring into mine, his were both soft and amused and I figured, somewhere in his head, that look was kicking demon ass.

"You're that too," he said and did another nipple swipe.

My back arched and my arms wrapped around him. "Okay, maybe you're not a pain in my ass."

His head slanted and his lips hit mine. No touch now, he was serious and I knew it when his tongue slid inside.

My body melted under his.

The phone rang.

"Effing hell," I muttered against his mouth.

He kissed me quickly, did a push up and he was away. I watched as he walked naked across the room and I was so lost in my fascination of watching his body move that it didn't penetrate that it was Hector's "clean" phone that was ringing.

Then it penetrated.

I shot to sitting on the bed and cried, "Mace!"

He had the phone in his hand and was looking at the display when I wrapped the sheet around me and whipped my legs over the side, taking the sheet with me.

Juno woofed in surprise at my swift movements, but I didn't spare her a glance. I was heading toward Mace.

His head came up, his eyes narrow.

I stopped in front of him and he turned the phone to face me.

"Missed call from Bogey One. Who's Bogey One?" he asked.

Think fast Stella, my brain screeched.

I came up with an answer. "How should I know? It's not my phone."

That was when the phone beeped in his hand indicating a voicemail had been left.

I stared at the phone. Mace stared at the phone.

Then he flipped it open and started hitting buttons.

Shitsofuckit!

"Mace, give me the phone." I reached out to snatch it from him, but he yanked it away and his eyes came back to me, still narrow, brows drawn.

"What's the matter with you?" he asked.

"Nothing," I lied.

He watched me a beat then repeated, "Who the fuck is Bogey One?"

"Erm…"

"Start talkin', Stella," he demanded and his voice had gone scary. "Is it Turner?"

I blinked at him, taken aback that he thought I'd hide a call from Eric.

Then I cried, "No! Of course not."

"Then you do know who it is."

Damn it!

Why was I such an idiot?

"Mace—"

"Is it Chavez?" Mace went on.

"No! Mace, I can't tell you. You have to trust me. Just give me the phone." I held out my hand to him, palm up, hoping that would work.

It didn't.

"Last night you sat there singing to me 'nothing to hide, believe what I say' and not ten hours later you're standin' in front of me lyin'."

I closed my eyes then opened them again. "Please Mace, you just have to trust me."

"Trust you with what?" he asked, voice impatient.

"Mace—"

"Trust you with what?" Now his voice was short and pissed-off.

"Your heart!" I shouted.

His body went tight and he blinked.

I ignored all that and went on, "You have to trust me with your heart, dammit. A couple of days ago, you asked me if I wanted into your heart. Well, I'm guessing by now you know that I do. So I'm trying to work my way in there, but you have to trust me. Now give me the *effing* phone!"

He just stood there, frozen, staring at me. This was weird and highly uncharacteristic of Mace, but I wasn't going to look a gift horse in the mouth. I took my opportunity, reached in and snatched the phone out of his hand.

I walked (okay, more like *stomped*) away while flipping it open and finding my way to voicemail. By the time I made it to the kitchen and turned to face him, Mace was tugging on his jeans and Lana's voice was telling me she was on a plane and just about to take off. Red-eye to LA. She'd have to turn off her phone soon, but she wanted me to know she'd called Chloe.

She finished, "See you soon, sweetie."

Even though I wanted to keep a message that had Lana's soft, musical voice calling me sweetie, I deleted it immediately.

Mace had his jeans buttoned and was pulling on the henley he discarded last night by the time I was done.

I opened my mouth to speak, but he got there before me, his voice coming at me like a whiplash. "They cut off her hand."

My breath packed up, and on a direct trajectory, shot straight toward the sun, disintegrating in the heat.

I tried to suck in air but it wasn't coming, mainly because the guard was down. The demons were out, nothing to hide them. Even across the room, I could see they were cavorting malevolently in Mace's eyes and having the times of their lives. Looking at that kind of pain in the eyes of the man I loved, I couldn't breathe.

"Caitlin was kidnapped. My father didn't involve the cops. Instead he hired some fuckin' guys..." He paused then continued, "You wouldn't believe these guys. Knowin' what I know now, fuck, they were the KMart of commandos."

I started toward him, but he put his hand up and clipped, "Don't get near me."

Effing.

Bloody.

Hell.

I stopped.

Juno, feeling the vibe, whined.

Mace kept talking.

"They fucked it up, botched the job. They left a man behind. The kidnappers sent him back in pieces. No fuckin' joke. In pieces."

No gut kick this time. This time my stomach turned and I was worried I might get sick right there.

Duke hadn't told me that part.

"As retribution for that stunt, they cut off Caitlin's hand, sent it to my father. After she died and they examined her, I found out they did it surgical, precise. These guys knew what they were fuckin' doin'. They had training. They had resources. They weren't guys you messed with. My father knew that. He knew it the whole fuckin' time."

I chanced a question. "What did they want?"

"They wanted my father. Even exchange. Caitlin for him."

Duke hadn't told me that, either.

"I take it he wasn't willing to make that deal?" I asked.

Mace laughed, but there was no humor in the sound. "No fuckin' way. Preston Mason sacrifice himself for his daughter? Not a chance."

Mace stopped talking.

It cost me, but I stood still and waited.

After a while, he went on, "I lost patience with my father fuckin' around. I got the police involved, the FBI. Offered myself instead."

I felt my heart squeeze and closed my eyes, but opened them when he continued talking.

"I had no idea who they were, what they wanted. I was relatively famous. I had money. I thought I could bargain with them. I didn't know they wanted my father dead or they wanted him to pay. Not with money; they wanted revenge. It was about revenge. They had no clue our father didn't give a shit about us, and I had no idea what I was doin', but I was desperate so I did it anyway."

He paused and stared at me.

I waited then asked carefully, "What happened then?"

He kept staring at me a beat then he continued, "I got cocky, and gettin' cocky means bein' stupid, but I was desperate *and* cocky so that's a whole other scale of stupid. I fed the media stories. I thought to put pressure on them. A sixteen year old girl losin' a hand, didn't read well in the papers. They didn't give a shit about their reputations. They didn't even care if they came out alive. They were kamikazes, workin' for a larger organization, doin' a job for the greater whole. Makin' a statement in a world that didn't see the light of day. It wouldn't matter how much the papers tried to dig up, they wouldn't find anything. These guys were underground. And when I say that I mean *underground*."

He paused, his intense eyes burning into me and I nodded, thinking he wanted to know that I understood.

Once I nodded, Mace kept speaking.

"The FBI knew what they were up against, but they didn't share this with me. I put pressure on them, too. Fed what I thought was their bullshit to the media to get them to move. It worked. They moved. They had to. It was a PR nightmare for them, Caitlin's pictures in the paper and on the news every day. The way she looked. They had to make it go away. They knew Caitlin wouldn't survive. What I didn't know was they were tryin' to keep me alive."

He stopped. I nodded again and he kept going.

"I made it hard on them. I struck a deal with the kidnappers. Me for her. They sent me in, vest, helmet. I got in there and saw her. They'd had her three weeks by then, but she'd lost so much fuckin' weight, weight she couldn't afford to lose. Her hair was… "

He stopped, closed his eyes. My heart slid up into my throat and he opened his eyes again and kept right on going.

"I didn't take much in. I was only there seconds. They had a gun to her head, blew it off right in front of me, then turned the guns on me. I took a number of hits and went down. They turned the guns on themselves. They were all dead by the time SWAT and the Feds got there."

He stopped talking and I stayed where I was. My heart was still in my throat. I could feel it beating there.

Finally, when he didn't start again, I asked, "Mace, can I come to you now?"

He answered immediately, "No. I'm not done."

What else can there be? My brain asked.

Quiet! I snapped back.

"After that, I gave up everything, went to ground, disappeared. I joined an organization, I can't tell you who and I never will. They trained me. It was specialized training and I needed that training. I did what I had to do to get the job I had to get done done. Then, for years, I did what I did for them at the same time I did what I had to do for Caitlin. I found out my father was involved and how. I can't tell you about any of this shit. If you know, far worse people than Sidney Carter would want you dead and they'd be able to do it. All you gotta know is that by the time I left, I did what I had to do for Caitlin. The person who gave the order to take her isn't breathing anymore, Stella, and I'm the reason he's not. He died like she did, exactly like she did. I made sure of that."

I swallowed. It was hard, considering I had a huge organ in my throat, but I pushed the saliva down.

He kept right on talking and I thought that it was strange and alarming that his voice didn't change. It was strong and sharp and completely devoid of emotion.

"I did shit I'm not proud of and lived in a world you wouldn't be able to imagine and I don't give a fuck. I did what I had to do for Caitlin and I got no problem with that. I can live with it." He paused, his arms crossed on his chest then he asked, "The question is, can you?"

Oh hell.

I didn't know what to say. I needed some processing time and not the kind that involved sex.

When I hesitated, Mace kept at me and he was relentless.

"You told my father he had enough black marks on his soul to send him straight to hell. You gotta know the heart you want into has its own strikes against it. No way to wash off the shit I did. It's marked deep. That the kind of man you want sleepin' in your bed?"

"Well, you haven't given me much choice up to now," I replied.

"Now you got that choice."

"You've never asked me these kinds of questions before," I told him.

"I never expected you to learn this shit before."

I blinked. "You were going to keep it from me?"

"Until the day I fuckin' died."

I couldn't believe that, didn't even want to, and my mouth dropped open before I snapped it shut and asked, "Why?"

"Because I never wanted you to look at me the way you're lookin' at me right now."

Shitsofuckit.

I didn't know how I was looking at him and tried to rearrange my face and shift us into safer waters. "How did you get involved with Lee?"

"Luke knew me, we worked together. He found out I was out. He told Lee to recruit me and now I'm here."

"Luke? He—?"

"Yeah."

"Does Ava know?" I asked.

"As much as she can know," he answered. "Which I figure is about as much as you know."

We stared at each other a few beats then I dropped my head and shifted the sheet tighter around me, thoughts tumbling around in my brain.

I wasn't really sure, but all my thoughts seemed to be about the same thing.

Mainly that I knew, without a doubt, that my luck had changed.

After having a life of no love for so long, finding a guy who could love so deep that he'd sacrifice everything to avenge someone he cared about felt effing *great*.

That might make me a freak, but I didn't care.

I wasn't going to say it out loud, (not again) but for as long as she had him, Caitlin Mason was one lucky girl.

And now, so was I.

"I'll take that as your answer." I heard Mace say and my head snapped up to see he was moving to his boots.

"What're you doing?" I asked.

He didn't look at me when he answered, "Leavin'."

"Why?" His head shot up and I kept talking. "Okay, so, I can't pretend this doesn't freak me out, because, erm… it's freaky and intense, but, well… that

354

was then and this is now. At least I know why you're so effing moody all the time and why you have such a short fuse. I mean, the whole throwing the phone against the wall gig was freaky, too, but now I get it and—"

I stopped talking because he switched directions and was walking toward me.

"What're you doing now?" I asked.

He didn't answer, and right before he made it to me, he dipped his shoulder like the football players do when they're going to make a tackle. It went into my belly and then I was going up.

"Mace!" I shouted. "What are you doing?"

He stalked (yes, stalked!) toward the bed, did a bump with his shoulder and I was flying through the air. I landed on my back on the bed with a soft bounce and Mace was on me.

I pushed against him. "Mace, we aren't done talking."

His face was in my throat and his hands were tugging at the sheet.

"We fuckin' well are," he growled.

"There's more to say."

His head came up and he looked at me just as I heard the sheet tear.

"You still love me?" he asked.

My eyes narrowed. "What kind of question is that?" I snapped.

"Answer it."

"I will not, it's—"

"*Answer it!*" he barked, and I went still at the ferocity in his voice.

Then I whispered, "Of course I do."

"Then we're done talkin'. I'm gonna fuck you until I've erased everything I've said. Until the only thing you can think of is my cock inside you and my hands and mouth on you. Until I hear that fuckin' voice of yours telling me you love me. I'm gonna fuck you until I know it's me you want, despite all this shit, and I don't care if it takes a fuckin' week."

"That'll take, like, two seconds," I told him and watched something cross his face, something that looked a lot like surprise. Then I announced, "Well! There it is! Done! And you didn't even have to fuck me."

He stared at me.

"But you can still fuck me if you want to," I went on.

He kept staring at me.

"Like now. Fucking me now would be good," I prompted.

He kept staring at me.

"Hello? Kai Mason? Are you in the room?" I called, and when he kept staring at me, I kept talking. "Calling Kai Mason, girlfriend needs a good fucking, right... about... now."

That was when he spoke.

And this is what he said.

"God, I love you."

Then he fucked me.

⌖

Even though he didn't have to, Mace fucked me until he erased everything from my head but what he wanted there.

Then he did it again.

Then he did it again.

Then he left me face down in bed. He pulled the torn sheet up to my waist, took Juno out, came back, took a shower, ate a piece of coffee cake and came back to the bed.

I hadn't moved a muscle. I snoozed a bit, but mostly I listened to his noises in my house.

When he sat on the bed and shifted the hair out of my face and off my shoulder so he could lean in and kiss my neck, I asked, my voice messed up because my face was scrunched in the pillow, "How can you move around?"

"Kitten, you need to get in better shape."

"I'm going to have to cancel tonight's gig."

"You'll recover by then."

"You tore my sheet."

"I'll buy you a new one."

"I don't want a new one. I think I'm going to have this one bronzed."

Then he said weirdly, "I understand it now."

My eyes had been closed, but I opened them and shifted them to look at him.

"Understand what?" I asked.

"Why the men put up with the Rock Chicks."

Uh-oh.

I had a feeling we were going to get heavy again.

I came up on my elbows and said softly, "And why's that?"

He didn't answer. Instead he said, "Couldn't believe it, but since I couldn't come up with an explanation, I always thought they were whipped."

I grinned. "And they're not?"

He grinned back. "Men like us don't get whipped, babe."

"Bullshit," I said under my breath, still grinning.

"That isn't it."

"Admit it. It's a part of it," I teased.

"It's easy to find a piece."

As shocking as this statement was, and as much as I should be offended for all womankind, I was guessing he wasn't wrong about that. Not for the Hot Bunch.

"So? What is it?"

He leaned in again and kissed my mouth. "Can't tell you. You know, you'll get cocky."

"It's because we're sultry and sexy, isn't it?"

His eyes went soft and his voice went low. "Not even close." Then he kissed me again and said, "Gotta go."

He got up and moved toward the door.

He'd deactivated the alarm and unlocked the locks when I called, "You keeping me alive tonight?"

He'd opened and was out the door, but he turned, his eyes locking on mine.

"Even if I die doin' it."

Then he was gone.

I laid in bed, up on my elbows, eyes on the door, my heart permanently settled because I knew, without doubt, that he meant every word he just said.

Chapter 23

Family

Stella

"I can't do this," I said into the Explorer.

Jules was sitting up front. Jet was in back, sitting next to me. Vance was driving.

I was freaking out.

Jules twisted around in her seat. Jet reached out and grabbed my hand. Vance's eyes shifted to the rearview mirror to look at me.

"It's going to be fine," Jet said on a reassuring hand squeeze.

"No. No, it isn't going to be fine," I replied and looked at Jules. "What are you even doing here? Bad guys are out there and you're pregnant."

"I'll be all right," Jules told me.

I stared at her then announced, "I need a drink."

"We'll get you a beer when we get there," Jet said.

I looked at Jet.

"I don't need beer, I need tequila," I explained.

"Then we'll get you tequila," Jet promised.

We were on our way to the gig.

Chloe and Lana had both arrived safely and had been whisked to Daisy's house. Reporting in (regularly, as in every half an hour), Daisy told me she'd got them settled in rooms filled with flowers and "big old" boxes of Godiva chocolates.

"Sugar, I said those were from you. Hope you don't mind," Daisy told me, and I didn't. How could I?

She gave them food and drink and let them rest.

Lee dropped Indy and Ally at The Castle and the five of them played Guitar Hero.

I didn't know how I felt about Lana and Chloe playing Guitar Hero with Daisy, Indy and Ally, but I had bigger things to worry about.

Like what I'd say to Dixon Jones.

Like what Lana and Chloe would think about me when they met me. Preston Mason didn't think I was good enough for Mace. Maybe they wouldn't either.

Like if Mace would still love me after I meddled in his life.

Like what I was going to wear to the gig, considering Mace's Mom and Stepmom were going to be there. I felt I should wear something nice, like a pair of slacks or a skirt, but I was a rock 'n' roll singer.

Slacks didn't exactly say rock 'n' roll.

I settled on jeans, a black belt and black cowboy boots. Usually, I wore a t-shirt or a tank, but to dress it up a bit, I wore a black button-up vest with a shiny, satin black panel at the back. I added dozens of thin silver bangles to my left wrist, a wide, hammered-silver band that sat tight on my right wrist, vintage, three-tier chandelier Navajo earrings made of silver and turquoise with dangling, bent spikes of silver at the bottom tier and a black leather thong in choker position around my neck from which hung several small silver discs. I left my hair long and wild, did full on, smoky-eyed makeup and I hoped I didn't look like a rock 'n' roll freak.

I lifted the hand Jet wasn't holding and glanced at it.

It was trembling.

"Look at my hand!" I demanded. "I won't even be able to hold my guitar!"

"Stella, still your mind," Vance said softly.

"*You* still your mind. I'm freaking out!" I screeched.

All of a sudden, Vance pulled over and stopped.

The air in the cab of the Explorer went funny and Jet and Jules exchanged glances.

Vance turned to me.

"You called these women two days ago. They dropped everything to be here. That says they want this to work and they'll do everything in their power to make it work. You did your job. You opened the door. Now you gotta leave it to them to get through it," he said.

"What if he gets angry at me?" I asked, and my voice was low and croaky with fear.

"He probably will," Vance replied and I audibly sucked in breath.

"Crowe!" Jules protested loudly.

"Quiet, Princess," Vance muttered, and to me he said, "It was me, I'd be pissed as hell. Then I'd realize why you did what you did and I'd get over it. Mace'll do the same. You just gotta have the courage to ride it out."

"You're sure?" I asked.

"Yeah," he answered.

"This is serious shit he's dealing with," I shared like he didn't know that.

"Yeah," Vance repeated, because he knew it.

"I'm scared," I went on sharing, with Vance of all people. But, again, I will remind you, I was *freaking out*.

"Means you care. Says a lot. Mace'll know that too," Vance said.

"You think so?" I asked.

"Don't think it, know it," he replied with certainty. "Now, concentrate on something else. Still your mind. You got a big night ahead of you."

He was not wrong about *that*.

Vance turned back around and moved the Explorer onto the road.

Jet gave me another reassuring hand squeeze.

I smiled at her, and as my eyes moved forward, I caught sight of Jules's hand going in the direction of Vance's thigh. I watched her fingers curl around his thigh and I saw his hand come to hers. Then I watched as he twisted his wrist and his fingers linked with hers. He rested the back of her hand on his thigh and kept driving.

I found I had something to concentrate on.

It was the dawning revelation that I knew what Mace was talking about when he said he figured out why the Hot Bunch put up with the Rock Chicks.

Preston Mason had said Vance was a felon. Grand theft auto. Now he was a private investigator married to a movie-star-beautiful social worker. They were having a baby and riding in an SUV to a rock gig, holding hands.

My mind went still, my hands quit trembling and my heart settled.

It was the heart settle Mace was talking about.

He felt it, too.

That was what the Rock Chicks did for the Hot Bunch. That was why they put up with us.

I felt like crying, knowing I'd done that to Mace's heart.

Then I wondered if they knew we felt it, too.

"Oh shit, I think I'm gonna cry," I announced.

Vance's eyes went back to the rearview mirror and Jet did another hand squeeze.

"Why on earth are you gonna cry?" Jet asked.

I looked at her. "Because I think Vance is right. It's gonna be fine."

"Of course it's going to be fine," Jules told me.

I sucked in breath to control the tears. Luckily, since I didn't have a make-up repair kit with me, this worked.

We fell silent. I saw Vance's eyes come back to the mirror and I noticed he looked like he was smiling.

I smiled back.

Vance's gaze went back to the road and he drove us to the club.

⌘

We were playing The Rose, a new club in Lowry that could hold two hundred and fifty people.

The Gypsies liked it because it had a great dressing room backstage and the staff usually left us a tin tub filled with ice and Fat Tire beer.

Tex met us at the backdoor and told me, "Fuck, I'm nervous as a fuckin' jackrabbit."

I looked up at him with surprise. Tex wasn't the kind of guy who got nervous.

"Why?" I asked.

"Family reunions. They freak me out," he answered.

I stopped dead. "You think I'm doing the wrong thing?"

His hand settled on top of my head. "No fuckin' way."

I let out the breath I was holding.

"Still," he went on, "Mace is a big guy and fuckin' moody as all hell. He loses it, be a bitch to lock him down."

Beautiful.

"Shut up, Tex," Jet snapped.

"Be cool, Loopy Loo," Tex shot back.

"Tequila," I blurted.

Tex's gaze came to me.

"Tequila. Right. I'm on it," he said and peeled off, going toward the bar.

That afternoon, when Roam and Sniff got out of school, Pong, Leo and Hugo picked them up and came to get the equipment. The stage was set, and I had one thing to thank Sidney Carter for: I didn't have to lug amplifiers around town.

I knew because Daisy called and told me that Lee and Tom had picked up Daisy, Ally, Indy, Lana and Chloe and they were already backstage.

We made it to the dressing room door. I stopped dead again and stared at the closed door.

"It's gonna be okay," Jet said.

I turned to her. "I don't look like a rock 'n' roll freak, do I?"

She smiled and shook her head, then whispered, "No, Stella, you look rock 'n' roll *amazing*."

I nodded because she sounded like she meant it. I took in a breath and opened the door.

Daisy, Ally and Indy had been joined by Floyd, Duke, Roxie and Ava.

Two women were with them.

One was petite, blonde and blue-eyed with a pretty face and sun-kissed skin. She was wearing a pair of designer boot-cut jeans, black strappy sandals on dainty French-pedicured feet, a complicated woven black leather belt and a white tuxedo blouse. Her hair was pulled back in a soft ponytail.

The other was older. Tall, slim, had long, shining black hair left loose, fantastic skin, warm brown eyes and she was stunning. She was obviously one of those older women who never lost their cool, was sexy as hell and always would be until the day she died. She was wearing faded jeans, black flip-flops and a black Stella and The Blue Moon Gypsies tee, the "o's" were little blue moons.

I didn't know who gave her the tee, but if I had to put money down on it, I would guess it was Ally.

When they saw me, both of their mouths dropped open.

I did a stupid little wave and said, "Hi, you must be Lana and Chloe. I'm Stella."

When I spoke, the blonde, who I was guessing was Chloe, burst into tears.

This alarmed me.

I took a step forward. She lifted her hand as if to ward me off.

Erm, not good.

I stopped and my heart started slamming in my chest.

363

"Chloe, sweetie," Lana's soft, melodic voice called.

Chloe's eyes were locked on me.

Then she whispered, "She's perfect."

Lana's eyes came to me.

She smiled and said, "Yeah, she is."

Wow.

This was good.

Way good.

Happy shiver good.

I smiled back at Lana.

"Oh crap. I'm gonna cry," Indy blurted, her hands coming up and she started fanning her face.

Duke slid his arm along Indy's shoulders and I moved toward Lana. As I did, she stepped toward me, her hands coming up in front of her. I took them and she held on tight.

"I'm scared to death," she told me.

I squeezed her hands and admitted, "Me too."

She started laughing. It was just as melodic as her voice, and it washed over me like soothing water.

Chloe approached and I smelled her perfume. It was a sophisticated floral scent that was like smelling heaven.

One of Lana's and my hands unlocked, both of us reached out to Chloe and she grabbed on tight.

Holding their hands and taking them in, I thought that maybe Preston Mason wasn't the Supreme Asshole of All Time. Instead, he had to be the Stupidest Man on the Face of This Earth.

"Thank you for asking me to come," Chloe said, her face still wet with tears.

"Thank you for coming," I said back.

"I'd do anything for Kai," she told me softly.

I swallowed the tears that climbed up my throat and squeezed her hand, too.

The door flew open. Our hands detached and we all jerked toward the door. Pong was pushing in, behind him was Leo, and I could see Buzz and Hugo pulling up the rear.

"Oh shit. Double, double, toil and trouble. Mace is fucked," Pong announced, eyes on Lana, Chloe and I.

Hugo pushed in and slapped Pong up the back of his head. "Shut up, Pong."

"Dude, you totally agree with me," Pong replied.

"We're here to give you moral support," Leo said, eyes on me.

Moral support from The Gypsies.

That I did not need.

"Why don't you give me moral support in the form of finding out what's taking Tex so long with that tequila?" I suggested.

"Don't need tequila. I got a doobie in my guitar case," Leo replied.

"Leo!" Buzz snapped. "Maybe these fine ladies don't smoke dope."

"Ever a time to start, this is it," Hugo muttered.

I looked at the ceiling then I looked at Lana and Chloe.

"This is my band, The Blue Moon Gypsies, Buzz, Leo, Pong and Hugo. I think you've already met Floyd." I indicated each as I said their names. "Except for Floyd, they're lunatics. Take no notice of them."

"Bitch, your tee is the shit," Pong informed Lana, proving me right.

"Thank you. I like it," Lana replied, her lips forming her son's beautiful smile, which she directed at Pong.

"Don't call Mace's Mom a bitch," Buzz snapped and came forward, hand up, smiling the smile that made a thousand groupies cream their pants. "Ladies, nice to meet you."

Pong, Hugo and Leo learned to mind their manners for just long enough to greet Mace's Moms.

While they did so, Floyd got close to me.

"You okay Stella Bella?" he asked softly in my ear.

"No," I replied.

His arm slid around my waist and he said, "Proud of you."

I closed my eyes.

When they opened them again, I was a lot more okay than I'd been for days.

I leaned into him, put my arm around his waist and my head on his shoulder.

My eyes moved to Buzz and I whispered, "How's Buzz?"

"We had a talk on the drive home. This may sound funny, but I think the funeral was good. Closure. Her folks are good people and they knew Buzz tried to take care of her. You could tell they were grateful." I nodded and sighed and Floyd went on, "Still, he's a little lost without Linnie, but I think he's gonna be okay."

I gave his waist a squeeze right before the door opened again and everyone in the room jumped and turned toward it.

Hector and Shirleen were walking in with Dixon Jones.

Shitsofuckit.

This is just your life, your career, your world, my brain said to me. *No reason for you to be nervous.*

Why are you such a pain in the ass? I asked.

It's the job of every neurotic artist to have a brain that tortures them, my brain answered.

Well, fuck off, I demanded

Then to Dixon I said, "Hey."

I moved forward, my eyes going from Dixon to Hector, who gave me a nod, then to Shirleen, who was watching me closely, and back to Dixon. "Glad you could make it," I finished.

We shook hands.

"Would you like to meet the band?" I asked.

Shirleen shouldered close. "No time for that. Who knows what's gonna happen? Could be snipers. Could be time bombs. We gotta get down to business." She turned to Dixon. "Let's go, times wastin'. What you got to say to my girl?"

Dixon looked at Shirleen, then me. From what he said it appeared he, too, didn't want to waste any time. "Feel like headin' to the studio?"

I got that freaky thrill that was half terror, half elation, bit my lip and looked at Floyd. Then I looked at Hugo then Pong then Leo and finally Buzz.

My eyes went back to Dixon and I said, "Yeah."

Dixon looked at Leo and Buzz. "You boys got enough new material to fill a CD?"

"Sure," Buzz said. "But we're The Gypsies. We gotta do a couple covers."

"No covers. We do new shit," Hugo put in.

"Dude, we so have to lay down 'Ghostriders', at least. I'm thinkin' 'Sister Golden Hair', too," Pong decided.

"Not 'Sister Golden Hair', 'La Grange', we kick 'La Grange' in the ass," Leo demanded.

"'La Grange'! We do covers, we ain't recordin' 'La Grange' before we record 'Ain't No Easy Way'," Hugo snapped.

Maybe I should have intervened, but I didn't. Dixon Jones had to know what he was getting himself into.

He did.

Pong, Buzz and Leo had all opened their mouths to speak, but Dixon got there before them.

"'Ghostriders'," he said decisively and his eyes cut to me. "And we'll talk to Joel's people, get permission for Stella to do 'And So It Goes'."

"Righteous," Ally breathed.

"You bring papers?" Hector asked Dixon, and he nodded.

"In the car. I'll give them to you, but you get someone who knows what they're doin' to look at them."

For a second, I felt relief. It wasn't unusual for hungry new artists to get fucked in the signing process, but it didn't seem that was Dixon's gig.

My relief disintegrated when I got a look at the scorching hot glare Hector was directing at Dixon. His glare said he wasn't used to anyone taking him for a fool and he didn't like it much.

Dixon caught it, too, took a small step back. He decided (wisely) to change the subject.

"How soon can you get them into the studio?" he asked Hector.

"What studio we talkin' 'bout?" Shirleen asked Dixon.

"Our set up in LA," Dixon answered. "Black Fat'll pick up all expenses. They'll have rooms at the Chateau Marmont while they're workin'."

Effing hell but he wasn't messing around.

All-expense paid trip to LA staying at the Chateau Effing Marmont?

Jim Morrison stayed at the Chateau Marmont, dangled from a drain-pipe there, hurt his back.

And Led Zeppelin rode their motorcycles through the effing lobby.

My heart skipped a beat at the thought of Pong, Hugo and Leo at the Chateau Marmont. The only thing that made me feel better was that I heard somewhere the hotel was supposed to be earthquake proof which meant The Gypsies couldn't destroy it.

And if Zeppelin could ride their motorcycles through the lobby, the staff probably wouldn't blink at the shenanigans of The Gypsies.

"Kick fuckin' ass!" Pong shouted, hands up in the air in a devil's horns "rock on" gesture.

Hector delivered the buzz kill. "Stella doesn't step foot out of Denver until she's safe."

"Dude, you guys could provide security for Springsteen and the entire fuckin' E Street Band," Leo whined. "You could get us to LA."

"You're not goin' anywhere until Stella's safe," Hector said in a tone that made Leo snap his mouth shut.

"Agreed," Dixon put in readily.

Hector nodded to Dixon, turned and pointed to me. "Backstage fuckin' passes." He looked back to Dixon and said, "Let's go to your car."

Then they were gone.

Everyone stared at the door.

"What just happened?" Chloe asked Lana quietly.

"I'm not sure," Lana replied.

"Nothin' much," Daisy declared nonchalantly. She then turned to Chloe and Lana and screeched. "Just that our girl and her band are about to get signed by a red-hot record label!" She threw her hands in the air and shouted, "*Yee ha!*"

"Holy crap, now I really think I'm gonna cry. God dammit!" Indy yelled, back to fanning her face.

"I'm already crying!" Roxie wailed, and it was true.

Lana smiled at me. "Oh sweetie, that's great!"

"It's not great, it's *righteous!*" Ally screamed.

"Rock 'n' roll!" Ava shouted, hands up, doing her own devil's horns.

Everybody started jumping up and down, screaming, shouting and hugging.

"Champagne, we need champagne!" Daisy squealed right before the door opened.

Mace and Lee stood there.

The room went still.

Effing *hell*.

Unfortunately (or fortunately, depending on how you looked at it), I was standing next to Lana, my arm around her shoulders, hers was around my waist.

The minute she saw Mace, her body went solid and her fingers dug in.

Everyone was silent.

Mace's eyes were locked on his Mom.

I held my breath.

His gaze unlocked and sliced to Chloe.

I heard Chloe suck in breath.

His eyes cut to me.

Oh dear.

I gave Lana a squeeze.

"Babe?" I called to Mace. "We got some special guests tonight, otherwise known as Bogey One."

I saw his jaw grow tight and I watched as his tongue traced his teeth behind closed lips.

For your information, I did not take this as a good sign.

I saw Vance and Luke behind Lee. Luke entered the room. Vance leaned in, grabbed the doorknob and shut the door, him behind it. Lee and Luke positioned themselves in front of it.

My eyes moved back to Mace and he'd twisted his torso to watch this. Lee put his hands to his hips. Luke crossed his arms on his chest. Both men's eyes were leveled on Mace.

Well, one thing was certain, the Rock Chicks took their assignments seriously. They'd done everything I asked to the letter.

Mace turned back toward me.

"Kai? Sweetie?" Lana called in her soft voice.

Mace closed his eyes, but even so, you could see the pain slash through his face at hearing his mother's voice.

"Maybe we should give them privacy," Jules whispered.

Mace's eyes opened and cut to her, pain gone, fury in its place.

Shit!

"Don't you fuckin' move," he growled.

Jules went still and so did everyone else.

"Mace," Lee spoke low behind him.

Mace looked over his shoulder at Lee.

His voice was dangerous when he said, "You wanted a show? You'll get a show."

Lana tried to take a step back, but my arm went tight around her.

"Mace, look at me," I demanded.

He didn't delay. His eyes cut to me and I thought I might melt under the heat of his glare.

"You arrange this?" he clipped.

"Yes," I answered.

"Why the fuck would you do that?"

I looked toward Duke. He pressed his lips together and nodded his head.

My gaze returned to Mace. "Because Caitlin would have wanted it."

The air in the room went so thick it was like we were breathing soup. Chunky soup, with bits of carrot and celery in it, enough to make you choke.

It took everything I had, but I ignored the chunky air.

"You did what you had to do for her," I said quickly. "Now I'm doing what she'd do if she was here. She wouldn't want you tortured by those demons in your head. She'd want to chase them away. She's not around to do that, so I figure, since you said she'd like me with you, then she'd give that job to me. I took it. I'm going to chase them away."

I let go of Lana and moved toward Mace. He stood frozen, scary frozen. Not like he was in shock, like he was holding his body still so he wouldn't hurt someone.

I didn't let that faze me as I moved toward him until we were toe-to-toe.

I tilted my head back to look at him and rested my hands lightly on his chest. I felt his heart beating hard and fast under my hand.

This frightened me, but I pushed on.

"And don't tell me I don't know what I'm talking about. I know you didn't want me to but, I've seen the papers, Mace. I saw the photos of her. I saw the photo of her with you. She loved her brother. She'd want you to be happy. You need your family. Everyone in this room is your family. Everyone's here because they care about you." I hesitated, smiled and then said, "Well, except maybe Pong and Hugo. They're here because there's usually free beer in The Rose's dressing room."

I was trying to be funny, cut the tension.

It didn't work.

Mace stared at me. I stared back.

Mace's stare got scarier. So much scarier it scared me, but I took it and stared back.

There was movement at our side. Mace and my heads turned and Chloe was there.

She lifted her hand as if she was going to touch Mace. His eyes moved to her hand and they narrowed so she dropped it.

She took in a breath and held it.

On the exhale she said, "She's right, honey. Tiny would want that."

Mace's body jerked when he heard his sister's nickname, but he didn't say a word. He just stared at her.

This isn't going very well, my brain informed me.

Shut up! I returned.

Chloe lifted her hand and touched my arm. She put pressure there so I moved to the side. Now Lana was there, standing next to Mace, across from me. But my eyes were on Chloe. She had her hand in her jeans pocket, and when she pulled it out, a chain was dangling from her fingers.

I watched in stunned, frightened silence as Chloe pulled in a breath so deep her chest visibly expanded with it. She let the breath go and leaned into Mace. She got up on tiptoe, put her arms around his neck, the chain between her hands, a tiny ring dangling from it. She clasped the chain around Mace's still frozen neck.

Chloe settled back on her feet, but lifted a hand to touch one finger to the ring that was now resting at his throat.

"She loved that ring. Never took it off. I've been wanting to give it to you since..." She stopped and shook her head slowly then went on, "You gave her that, remember? On her fourteenth—"

She didn't finish. Mace's arms shot out and he yanked her to his body so hard her head jerked back and she let out a small cry. His back arched as he buried his face in her neck.

My throat closed and I felt the tears immediately fill my eyes and spill over.

She hesitated, likely still recovering from all of a sudden being in his arms. Then Chloe wrapped her arms around his neck and held him tight.

"Out, now." I heard Lee say, and there was movement all around us.

Lana threw her arms around the two of them and I took a step back. The others were leaving and I was going, too. This family needed space.

I didn't get a second step. Mace's hand darted out and closed around my wrist. His head came up, his eyes locked on mine and pinned me to the spot.

He didn't have to say a word.

I settled in.

He let me go and turned to his mother.

She slid into his arms as if she'd been there only yesterday.

As Mace hugged his Mom, I looked to the door.

Floyd was there.

So was Lee.

Floyd winked at me.

So did Lee.

Floyd went out first.

Lee closed the door behind him.

"And it's your turn, girl, to cry," I sang into the mic.

I started the "na-na's" of Journey's "Lovin', Touchin', Squeezin'", the band kicked in the second time through, and the entire crowd shouted them back at us, hands up in the air, jacking out the beat. The crowd included Lana and Chloe, who were front and center with the Rock Chicks.

Lana, I noticed right off, was super comfortable up front at a rock gig. I'd watched as she sung out loud, knowing every song we played, except the three new songs of Buzz and Leo's, of course. She danced and swayed, and let's just say that Mace's Mom could *move*. She was sexy as all get out and I could tell she loved rock and roll.

For Lana, an afternoon of Guitar Hero was definitely the way to go.

On the other hand, it took Chloe awhile to get into it (her favorite music was probably Tchaikovsky, too). Still, The Gypsies were on a tear and it didn't take very long for her to feel the vibe and let it take her where she needed to go.

The security detail was the same as the other gigs, except Hank and Eddie weren't there because they were dismantling Sidney Carter's operation. In their place was Indy's Dad, Tom, and Hank, Lee and Ally's Dad, Malcolm. Tom and Duke both were close to the stage guarding me and the Rock Chicks.

I'd had just enough time after the reunion to tell Mace about Dixon Jones and the Chateau Marmont and to let his smile of approval and his lip touch give me a happy shiver. Then Chloe and I let him alone with Lana.

In order to give them privacy, instead of hanging backstage with the band as normal, I sat at the bar, drinking beer with the Rock Chicks and Chloe, who didn't drink beer. She drank martinis. Chloe was one classy lady. At the bar, I talked to some of my fans with Duke plastered to my side until it was time to take the stage.

I was smiling as I sang the "na-na's", my arm up in the air, moving back and forth. The crowd caught my rhythm and, as one, their arms moved with mine and they chanted the "na-na's" with the band.

My eyes slid through the crowd and I saw Luke at the doors, back to the stage, arms crossed on his chest, talking to one of the club's bouncers.

I kept singing, my eyes kept moving and I saw Mace standing head and shoulders above the crowd. His eyes were scanning.

I waited, and just as I knew it would, his gaze came to me. I didn't know it, but the minute his eyes hit me, my smile grew brighter. I also didn't know that Lana and Chloe caught my smile and turned around to see what I was smiling at. Further, I didn't know, when they saw it was Mace, Chloe burst into tears again and Lana hugged her.

Mace's eyes left me to scan the crowd again and my eyes kept moving, still singing the "na-na's", still living in my happy place, my *lucky* place. The place where my band was heading to LA to record an album. The place where I'd chased Mace's demons away and gave him back his family. The place where I lived now. The place where Mace loved me.

My eyes traveled the length of the bar and something shifted in that happy place. I couldn't put my finger on it but something was wrong.

Still chanting with the crowd, my hand in the air, my eyes went back up the bar.

Then down it.

Then back up.

Then it dawned on me that Tex wasn't sitting at the bar.

And Tex never brought the tequila.

Automatically, the band and I finished the "na-na's" as my eyes flew through the crowd, searching for but not finding Tex.

The band stopped playing and I said into the mic, "We're gonna take a break, be back!"

The crowd roared and I gave them a wave and a smile, keeping up appearances, but as fast as I could, I moved offstage.

Duke was there with a beer and he shoved it in my hand.

"Girl, normally you kick ass but tonight, I gotta tell you darlin', you are the *shit!*" Duke said to me, and normally I would be stunned, maybe even moved by his compliment. Duke didn't hand out compliments very often.

Instead I looked up at him and asked, "Where's Tex?"

Duke's body went still then his head jerked around to scan the bar.

My band had come down behind me and the Rock Chicks were rounding the stage, but I didn't look at them.

I moved.

I shoved though the crowd. People were trying to get my attention, to stop me, to talk to me. I heard their words as I moved, shoving through until I saw Mace coming my way.

I stopped in front of him, put my hands on his chest and tilted my head back.

He was looking down at me smiling, face soft, voice low, "Babe—" he started.

I cut him off, "Where's Tex?"

His head jerked then shot up. He, too, scanned the bar.

My fingers curled into his t-shirt. "When I arrived he met me at the back-door. He went to get me tequila. I haven't seen him since. With everything that happened, I didn't think—"

I didn't finish. Mace's hand wrapped around mine and he started pushing through the crowd. By the time we got to the side of the stage, the Rock Chicks were looking pale and the Hot Bunch was in a huddle. Lee sliced an unhappy look at Mace and got on his phone.

"Has anyone seen him?" Roxie asked.

"When we arrived, but I haven't seen him since," Jet answered.

"Fuck," Duke muttered.

"What's happening?" Lana asked, getting close to Mace and me.

"One of our people is missing," I told her and looked up at Mace. "We need to make an announcement. Stop the show," I said.

Lee flipped the phone shut and addressed the group, "The girls are going home. Then I want everyone in the field. Bobby, Matt, Duke, Tom and Dad will stay on Stella and the band. Matt, you're responsible for getting Stella home. Dad, arrange police escorts for every band member when the gig's over. Yeah?"

Malcolm nodded.

"Fuck!" Duke exploded. "How did we miss this?"

"It's my fault," I whispered.

Lee's eyes sliced to me.

"Get that out of your head. Finish the gig," he ordered, then his gaze moved through his men as Hector and Darius arrived at the huddle from wherever they'd been. "Luke, you got Ava and Ally. Darius, you got Shirleen, Daisy, Lana and Chloe. Hector, you got Jet and Roxie. Vance, you got Jules and Indy. Mace, you're with me. Let's go."

They went, except Mace, who looked at Matt. "I gotta know you got this."

Matt nodded. "I got it."

Mace's eyes went to Tom and he skewered Tom with what could only be described as *a look*.

Tom said, "We got it. Go."

Mace looked at me and I started babbling, "It's my fault. We didn't think. We didn't catch it. Everyone was caught up in my shit, your shit, Dixon, your Mom, Chloe. I knew I should have waited until all this was over. If something happens to Tex—"

His finger went to my lips, effectively quieting me, then down and his hand curled around my neck. He stared at me as he gave me a neck squeeze.

Then he was gone.

Fear streaming through my system, my eyes were locked on the backstage door Mace went through following Lee.

"It's all my fault," I whispered.

Chapter 24

No More Fucking Hugging

Jules

My cat Boo and I didn't sleep well, tossing and turning all night, waiting for Vance to come home or phone to say everything was okay.

He didn't.

The alarm went off and I got out of bed, fed Boo and did my morning business. I was standing, hips against the counter, eating slightly toasted toast.

I was trying, with limited success, to learn how to cook. I'd tried but never got the hang of making toast, and since the morning sickness was sticking with me, slightly toasted was a lot better than fully burnt.

I was slightly toasting toast when Vance walked in the backdoor.

His eyes cut to me and he said, "Hey, Princess," before he turned to deactivate and reactivate the alarm.

I waited and he came to me, put an arm around my waist, brought me to him and touched his lips to mine.

I knew this wasn't good. If the news was good, he wouldn't have had to put his arm around me before giving it to me.

After he'd lifted his head, he said softly, "We got nothin'."

I closed my eyes and opened them when Vance's arm went tighter around my waist.

"I gotta shower and get to the office. We're havin' a briefing and we're all goin' back out."

I nodded and asked, "Do you know what this means?"

He shook his head. "Sid's usually communicative, lets people know what he wants or what he's done and why. No word."

"Do you think Tex is all right?"

His face went tight and I had my answer before he said, "Sid doesn't mess around. It's not lookin' good, Jules."

I bit my lip and tried not to cry.

"Hank says Roxie's a mess," Vance told me. "Can you take some time today, get to her?"

I swallowed back my tears and nodded.

Tex was Roxie's uncle. He'd been estranged from his family for decades, but through letters, since she was a kid, they'd been close. Eight months ago, she'd done for Tex what Stella had done for Mace last night. She'd brought him back into the family fold.

Vance kept talking. "I'm gonna be busy, Princess, so you need to call the real estate agent. Put in an offer on that house."

"It can wait," I replied.

His arm got tight again and his hand came to the side of my face. "It's the only place we've seen we both like. It's right. You'll still be close to Nick and I'll be close to the office. I don't want to lose it. Make the offer."

"I can't think of anything but Tex right now. There'll be another house—"

"Let us worry about Tex. You take care of our family."

"Crowe—"

His body shifted back a few inches and his hand went to my belly. He liked to put his hand there. These days he slept with his hand there.

It should probably be said I liked it when he put his hand there. Maybe even more than he liked to have it there.

"I want to be settled before he comes, Princess," Vance said quietly. "Make the offer."

My eyes narrowed at what he'd slipped in, thinking he could get away with it.

We'd been having an ongoing argument about the baby's sex since I hit my second trimester. Neither of us wanted to know so we hadn't asked the doctor.

For some reason, probably hormones, this argument honestly annoyed me. Vance (and now Nick was in on the act) thought it was hilarious. In fact, they both brought it up regularly and it had advanced. Now we were fighting about names.

"It's not a he. It's a she. And her name is going to be Rebecca Ann, for Auntie Reba."

His lips formed a small smile. His hand left my belly, he got close again and both his arms went tight around me.

"As much as I'd like you to have a girl to name after your aunt, it's gonna be a boy. And we're namin' him Max," Vance returned.

See what I mean?

"It's a girl, but *if* it should be a boy, we're naming him Harry," I shot back.

"I'm not namin' a kid Harry."

"Yes you are. Harry's a good name."

"Harry's a name for someone else's kid, not *my* kid."

"Crowe—"

His face came close. "You know I enjoy fightin' about this with you, Jules, but I got shit to do."

My body got still and I nodded. His mouth came to mine and he gave me a brief kiss. Then he walked away, hands at his belt.

"You want toast?" I yelled to his departing back.

"I'll make it," he yelled back, disappeared into the bathroom and shut the door.

"I'm thinking that's a good choice," I told Boo who was sitting on the kitchen floor, his big, black, bushy tail sweeping widely, giving me a kitty pouty face, not at all pleased that Vance had come in and given me all the attention.

"Meow," Boo agreed.

⋈

I hit King's Shelter, getting there by police escort, something which, hormones or not, I found annoying, since in my day (as in, a few months ago), I could kick some serious ass. I no sooner got through the door when May was bearing down.

May was a volunteer at the Shelter and even though she was thirty years older than me, she was my closest friend. She had a tough hide, a soft center (literally and figuratively) and a heart of gold.

"We got a problem," she announced.

I opened my mouth to ask, but I saw what the problem was immediately. Roam was in the room.

"I'll take care of this," I told May and stalked to Roam.

The minute I made it to him, I demanded, "What are you doing here? You should be in school."

Roam was with Clarice, who was a runaway, too, but now she spent a lot time with the tutors, a lot of time with Daisy, and even though she was just seventeen, was more like a volunteer than one of the kids. She kept the kids in line, helped to get them off the streets, quietly fed info to the social workers and sometimes talked the kids into sessions with the tutors.

Roam and Clarice were talking with a couple of other kids, both of whom were new around the Shelter so I didn't know them very well.

Roam's eyes came to me and he got up from where he was sitting on the back of the couch.

"Law," he said and that was it.

He walked several steps away and I assumed he expected me to follow.

When he stopped and gave me a look, I realized I was not wrong.

Roam had been one of my kids. In a way, even though he was sixteen now, living with Shirleen and growing up fast, he still was one.

A special one.

Seven months ago, he took a bullet to save my life. In turn, I took two to save his and killed a man. We didn't talk about this, but obviously, we were close. With May and Sniff, he'd stood up with me at my wedding.

Vance had taken both Roam and Sniff under his wing, and when they weren't at school, out on dates with girls, doing homework or being given tough love by Shirleen, they worked the surveillance room at Nightingale Investigations. It was unusual, but sometimes they went on ride-alongs with Vance, and lately, Luke had been taking them out, too.

However, Roam calling me by my street name and then arrogantly expecting me to follow him smacked way too much of the Crowe Effect. In fact, it was so Hot Bunch-like that I was thinking maybe he should have his time at Nightingale Investigations curtailed.

Even though I wanted to say something, I followed him. The kids at the Shelter respected him. He'd been out on the street a long time and made it through. He'd lost his best friend to bad drugs and he'd taken a bullet for me. Now he was in a good home, getting an education, and there was no other way to say it, he was a Nightingale Investigations Apprentice. The Nightingale Men had badass reputations. Roam hanging with them was huge.

When I made it to him, in a low voice, I snapped, "Why aren't you at school?"

"May have a line on Tex," he replied.

I blinked, but the rest of my body froze. I came unstuck, grabbed his arm and pulled him further away.

May came up to us and got close. "What's goin' on?"

I ignored May, my eyes glued on Roam. "Talk."

"Some kids saw somethin'. They know who Tex is, gave me a call. Sniff and I snuck out last night, took Shirleen's Navigator and started checkin' things out. Sniff's watchin' the building the kids said they took him into. I been makin' the rounds, askin' questions. I think it might be true," Roam answered.

"Have you told Vance this?" I asked.

"Didn't want to look the fool if it wasn't gonna—" Roam started but I interrupted.

"Call him. Right now. Tell him everything you know."

"I still haven't made certain—" Roam began again.

I leaned in. "You know better than that. It doesn't matter. Any lead needs to be followed."

He looked at me a beat, nodded and yanked out his phone, took two steps away and hit a button. I watched him put the phone to his ear and he started mumbling into it.

"That boy," May said, and she sounded both proud and exasperated.

"Yeah," I agreed, and both May and I kept our eyes on Roam.

I felt my ass vibrate just as I felt my stomach churn.

I was looking forward to having Vance's baby, *really* looking forward to it. Because once I had our baby then I wouldn't be sick all the fucking time (amongst other reasons).

I pulled the phone out of my back pocket and swallowed my nausea.

The display said, "Sniff calling".

My eyes flew to May. I flipped open the phone and put it to my ear.

"Talk to me," I demanded and I heard panting but no words. "Sniff?" I called sharply I saw May's eyes go narrow and felt Roam's slice to me.

"Law?" Sniff said through the panting.

I started moving to the door. "Keys," I snapped at May, and her body jerked then she started running toward the kitchen where she kept her purse.

Into the phone, I asked, "Where are you?"

"Runnin' from the building. Tex is with me. It... fuck, Law, he blew it up," Sniff told me.

I stopped moving. "What?"

More panting, but he talked. Sniff talked a lot. It would take more than running from an exploded building to get him to shut up.

"Tex blew up the fucking building. It was *insane*."

Kristen Ashley

"Give me that fuckin' thing," I heard Tex boom through his own panting and then I heard him in my ear. "Jules?"

At the sound of his voice, my hand went to my throat, tears hit the backs of my eyes and I shifted my body until it was close to a chair. I was sinking into the chair when I asked, "Are you okay?"

"Fuckers conked me a good one. I got a splittin' fuckin' headache," he answered. "We need a ride," he said this last like he'd been at a party, the designated driver ditched him and he was partially annoyed but still enjoying the party.

In other words, Tex was all right.

May was running up to me.

I turned to her and shook my head.

"Where are you?" I asked Tex.

I heard scraping on the mouthpiece then, "Where are we, kid?"

"Commerce City," Sniff replied, and I heard him giving some streets and cross streets. My eyes moved to Roam who'd come close and I snapped my fingers for his phone.

"Hang on, Tex," I said, snatched Roam's phone out of his hand and put it to my other ear. "Vance?"

"You got me, Princess," he replied.

"I've got Tex on my phone. He's fine. He's with Sniff." I gave him all the info I had.

Vance repeated the streets in my ear. Likely he did this for the benefit of whoever he was with. Then he clipped, "Roger that, Jules. You still got him on the line?"

"Yeah. He's on Sniff's phone."

"Get off. Darius is closest. He'll call Sniff."

"Okay."

"You said he blew up a building?"

"That's what Sniff said."

Silence for several beats then, "Christ, we got it on police band now."

Then he started laughing.

"Crowe! There isn't anything fucking funny about this!" I yelled and everyone turned to listen.

"You're right." He was still laughing, then he said, "Out."

Disconnect.

382

I flipped Roam's phone shut and went back to mine. "Tex, you there?"

"Where the fuck else would I be?" Tex boomed, and even though this was rude, it was Tex and he was alive and well enough to be rude so I could have shouted with joy.

"Vance knows where you are. Darius is in the area. You'll have a pick up soon. Keep the line open for Darius's call."

"Gotcha."

Disconnect.

I looked at May, but it was Roam who said, "Law, you shouldn't say fuck."

I growled.

Then I felt it coming. I ran to the bathroom and puked.

⇥⇤

About an hour later, Bobby came to get me and Roam. Stella and Ava were already in his Explorer.

We all went to Fortnum's.

Tex was behind the espresso counter when we got there. Roxie was close by his side. Jet, Indy and Ally were all behind the counter with them. Lee, Eddie, Hank, Sniff and Darius were all standing in front of the counter. Duke and Jane were standing at the end. There were no customers. Fortnum's was officially closed.

Tex swung a portafilter at us the minute we entered the store. It was still full of used coffee grounds. The grounds flew across the room and splattered next to a table.

"If you girls get near me, I swear to God, I'm gonna rip someone's head off!" he boomed. "I'm all right. No more *fucking hugging!*"

We all reared back, and Ava even put her hands up.

"All right, all right. No hugging," Ava said and we cautiously moved into the store.

Roam went to Sniff. They didn't hug, either, just did some complicated handshake and moved away from the adults.

"Tex, I'm happy you're alive and all, but I kid you not, you toss a portafilter filled with grounds around one more time, *I'm* gonna rip *your* head off," Indy snapped.

This made Tex lose his scowl and grin at Indy.

"What happened?" I asked when I got close to the counter.

"He hasn't said," Ally informed me.

"I'm gonna tell the story once. Daisy and Shirleen ain't here. If I told it to Indy and Jet when I got here, I would have had to tell Ally when she got here, and then Roxie when she got here. Now you. Then Daisy and then Shirleen. You're gonna have to fuckin' wait," Tex boomed.

"He blew up a building!" Sniff shouted, deciding he liked the adult conversation better than the teenage one.

Ava and Stella both gasped. Obviously, they hadn't had the full brief yet.

"You blew up a building?" Stella stared wide-eyed at Tex.

"Morons took me to a building with chemicals," Tex explained.

"He built a bomb!" Sniff shouted, coming to the group at the front of the counter.

Everyone's eyes moved to Tex and he shrugged then said, "They'd locked me in. I had to get out somehow."

"So you blew up the building?" Stella asked.

"I just meant to blow open the door. But, like I said, the place was filled with chemicals," Tex replied.

"So, once you blew open the door, the entire building blew up," Stella said, clearly not able to take it in.

Tex shrugged again. "Shit happens."

The bell over the door went and Ally shouted, "We're closed!"

Everyone turned to the door as the unwitting male customer muttered, "But, it's Friday. Everyone's open on Friday." He pointed at Tex. "And it says in the papers his coffee is the best in Denver. Maybe even America."

"He just blew up a building," Ally told the customer. "He might still be contaminated with chemicals. Like the sign on the door says, we're closed."

At Ally's words, the customer's eyes grew round and moved through all of us.

Finally, he breathed, "It's true. Everything they say about all of you is true." His eyes focused on Stella. "Oh my *God*. You're Stella Gunn."

"Dude. Do you *not* know what 'closed' means?" Ally snapped.

Lee walked toward the customer and his eyes skittered to Lee.

"Wow, I know you. Saw your picture in the paper. You scored the redhead and you own Nightingale Investigations," the customer said, wide eyes on Lee, and I couldn't help it. I had to laugh a little because he was looking at Lee like he was an honest to goodness movie star. "Are you gonna, like, throw me out?" he asked Lee as if he wanted him to do it.

"No, you're gonna walk out, like, right now." Lee answered.

The customer's mouth dropped open at Lee's deep voice and threatening tone then he whispered, "Have you ever killed anyone?"

Lee leaned in threateningly. "Do you mean today?"

At that, the customer took the hint, did another store swipe with his eyes and he took off.

Lee locked the door behind him.

"It's like that all the fuckin' time," Tex boomed. "I'm gonna kill whoever's talkin' to the papers. Either they act star struck, like I'm Paul Fuckin' Newman, or they expect me to be nice to them, like I fuckin' care they're breathin'. Only good thing about it is the tip jar needs to be emptied three times a day. I'm thinkin' about getting one of those kitty water bowls that refill with fresh water all the time, like a kitty fountain."

Stella was still staring at Tex who had, not five minutes ago, talked about blowing up a building, and now he was talking about kitty water fountains.

Nobody else thought this was unusual.

Mainly because it wasn't.

There came knocking at the door and Daisy, Lana and Chloe were there with Mace. Lee opened the door and they rushed in.

"Any of you hug me, I'm gonna snap your neck," Tex boomed.

Lana skidded to a halt. Chloe went pale. Daisy ignored Tex totally. She powered through the store, shouldered through the people behind the counter and threw her short arms as far as she could get them around his wide bulk.

"Woman!" Tex shouted, aggrieved.

"Shut up," Daisy whispered, but her voice broke in the middle and we heard a muted sob.

The room went still. Everyone looked at everyone else and I saw Roxie's eyes fill with tears.

Tex relaxed and his arms moved around Daisy.

"I'm okay, darlin'," he muttered.

That was when Daisy reared back and started hitting him with her little fists.

"Don't you scare me like that again, Tex MacMillan, or I'll kick your ass!" she yelled.

For a second, Tex looked surprised.

Then he let out a bark of laughter.

"Shit woman, like you could kick my ass," Tex hooted.

Roxie pulled Daisy away and suggested, "Why don't you let Uncle Tex make you a latte?"

"Damn straight," Daisy snapped. "Mocha, double chocolate," and she swiped at her running mascara.

"Maybe you should go to the bathroom and do that," Jet suggested.

Daisy whirled on Tex and pointed in his face. "Now you've ruined my mascara!"

On that, she stomped off to the back of the store where there was a staff-slash-Rock Chicks and Hot Bunch-Only bathroom.

"It's okay. We're not normally this crazy," Jet told Lana and Chloe.

"Yes we are," Ally muttered.

"What am I standin' here for, my health?" Tex boomed, already banging out Daisy's mocha. "Anyone need a fuckin' coffee?"

Duke moved forward to take Lana and Chloe to the counter.

I turned and saw Mace had claimed Stella. She was tucked to his front, her head under his chin, her arms around his waist, his arms around hers. One of his hands lifted and he curled his fingers around her neck. Her head tilted back and he smiled down at her.

I'd only seen Mace smile a few times in our acquaintance, but I'd *never* seen him smile like that. You could actually see her body melt into his as she returned his smile.

I turned my eyes away because I found something about this too intimate to watch.

I'd known Mace for months, but he was the only Nightingale Man I didn't know well. Now, knowing his story, I knew why.

Everyone thought Vance's and my story was heartbreaking, but Mace's made ours look like we'd grown up with Ozzie and Harriet.

Stella was a flat out miracle worker.

"Never thought I'd see *that*," Ava whispered to me, a jerk of her head indicating Mace and Stella, but her eyes weren't on them either.

"Nope," I agreed.

"It's good to see," she went on, and I grinned at her.

"Yep," I agreed.

Vance came home late that night, climbing up to the platform where our bed was and waking me. I usually slept hard and deep, but I always woke when Vance got home, even if it was for a few moments.

"Hey," I whispered.

"Go back to sleep," he muttered, fitting himself to my back from shoulders to heels and putting his hand to my belly.

I rolled, and Boo, who was tucked into the crook of my lap, got up on a disgruntled, "Meow!" and stalked off the end of the bed.

Vance shifted so I could press us together front to front.

I put my hands on his chest and asked softly, "You angry at Roam?"

"I was workin' my way to that. But seein' as it worked out in the end, I didn't see any reason to get in his face about it. We had a talk though. If there's a next time, he knows to call me," Vance answered. "Anyway, he told me what he did. They'd checked out the building. No cars, no noises, no people they could see. Tex was in a windowless room, and for obvious reasons, not makin' a lot of noise. They thought the place was empty. Sniff's orders were to phone if anyone approached the building. Roam was gonna call if they had company. There were some errors in judgment, but it was good work. He's learnin'."

I relaxed into him.

Vance was a patient teacher.

He was going to make an excellent father.

"You get anything you could use out of Tex?" I asked.

"A little. He was unconscious most of the time. The rest of the time he was alone and makin' a homemade bomb," Vance answered.

"I thought you said Carter didn't mess around."

"Usually, he doesn't. It's likely they wanted to play with him and wanted him conscious when they did it. They left Tex tied to a chair. He scooted to some metal shelves, used the sharp edge of the shelves to cut through the plastic. They probably didn't expect him to get loose. They definitely weren't expecting him to know how to build a bomb. We're guessin' they were goin' back, but they got lots of other shit keepin' them occupied these days."

That was a lucky break. A scary one in *many* ways, but lucky all the same.

"Do you think he'll give up?" I asked.

"Carter?" he asked back.

"Yeah," I answered. "First Shirleen guns down one of his assassins in her living room then Tex blows up one of his buildings," I explained. "Any sane person would give up."

"Sidney Carter is a lot of things. I'm not sure sane is one of them."

This was not good news.

"Eddie and Hank getting anywhere?" I continued my mini-interrogation.

"Yeah, Carter's operation is in disarray. Some of his men are talkin', makin' deals. More warrants are goin' out. It's takin' time, but it's lookin' good."

"So, it'll be over soon?"

"Maybe. They don't find him, Carter's gonna start gettin' desperate. That's what I'm worried about."

I snuggled closer. "It'll all be okay."

Vance sighed then shared, "I don't know if you noticed this, Princess, but we started with Indy getting kidnapped repeatedly. Jet nearly got raped. Roxie got the shit beat out of her. You were shot, twice. Ava was violated and nearly exploded in car. Now everyone's a target and there's a man out there who's desperate. I don't like it. It does not give me a good feeling."

"We'll survive," I whispered.

"Yeah, let's just hope Hector and Ally get somethin' on. That way, we can kill two birds with one fuckin' stone and be done with this shit."

At his words, I burst out laughing.

"I wasn't bein' funny," he told me.

I wrapped my arms tight around him. "I hate to disappoint you, honey, but Jet told me that Ally told her that Hector's like a cousin or something."

"Fuckin' great," he muttered, and I let out a small giggle.

It was his turn for his arms to grow tight.

"Love to hear you laugh," he muttered, and my belly did a swoop.

We fell into a comfortable silence for several long minutes.

Then I told him, "They accepted the offer on the house."

His arms went even tighter. So did mine.

It was a great house, just a few blocks away, only a couple doors down from where Lee and Indy lived. It had a nice, tidy yard with excellent landscaping, beautiful plants and mature trees. It had character, warmth and even a white picket fence.

It made me want to laugh.

I used to be a vigilante, head-crackin' mamma jamma who carried a gun, patrolled the streets, and one time took down a bail-jumping pimp and two of his working girls, one after the other.

Vance still was a badass mother.

And we were moving into a house with a white picket fence.

I couldn't wait.

"I'll call the agent tomorrow, get him to fast-track it," he told me.

"What are we gonna do with three bedrooms and two and a half baths?" I asked.

"Fill them with babies," he answered, and the belly swoop dipped deeper.

Still, just to be annoying, I said, "This is the only child I'm having. Morning sickness sucks."

I heard him give a low, soft laugh before he informed me, "We're havin' four kids."

"Four!" I cried, my head tilting back to look at him in the moonlight.

I loved looking at Vance any time, but the best time was in the moonlight, when the planes and angles of his face were shadowed, both hard and soft but all beautiful, like he was to me.

His chin tipped down and he looked at me. "Yeah, four."

"No way am I gonna have four kids."

"Four's a good number."

"*You* carry four children in your body, puking every five minutes from morning until noon."

He grinned then his mouth touched mine. "Okay, then three."

I thought about it, pressing my lips together, then I said, "All right. Three."

I saw, even in the moonlight, the looks of satisfaction and amusement that passed on his face, and I realized he'd only ever wanted three kids.

He'd just played me.

"You're annoying," I told him.

"You've mentioned that before," he said back.

His hand went up my back and into my hair, tipping my head down and pressing my face into his throat. It moved away from my head but stayed tangled in my hair, and I felt his fingers start to play with a tendril.

We kept our silence and lay still and comfortable in each other's arms.

Finally, I asked, "You tired?"

"Wiped," he answered.

I pressed deeper and kissed his throat.

"Any chance of nighttime sex?" I asked there.

He waited a beat then dropped to his back, taking me with him. In a flash, his hands were on my nightie, going up, and the nightie was gone.

"You want it, you gotta do all the work," he answered.

I smiled.

I wanted it, so I was willing to do all the work.

In fact, I didn't often get a chance to do all the work, so I was looking forward to it.

⤗⤎

It was some time later. I was on top, Vance inside me. I was moving at my pace and enjoying every stroke. One of his hands was at my hip, the other one between my legs, creating magic.

"Closer, Princess," he muttered and I leaned toward him. The fingers on his Magic Hand moved and I had to stop my descent to throw back my head and moan.

"Closer," he repeated when I'd stopped moaning, but I had started panting, and I got closer.

My face was in his face. The hand not between my legs went from my hip into my hair.

It fisted right before he said, his voice husky, his breath short, "I love to watch you ride me. Do you know how fuckin' beautiful you are?"

"Do you know how beautiful you are?" I returned on a pant, because he was seriously causing some sensations between my legs and I was about ready to explode.

He didn't answer my question. Instead, against my mouth, he noted, "You're close."

I nodded.

"I wanna hear it," he told me. His voice had moved from husky to hoarse and I knew what he meant.

"Vance," I whispered, like I always whispered, *always*, right before he made me come.

⤗⤎

"Jules," Vance said sharply in my ear, his arm, tight around my midriff, was shaking me.

I jolted awake, sweating and breathing heavily. When I opened my eyes, the shocking, bloody images from my subconscious were still vivid.

"I'm awake," I whispered, but I was trembling and I felt Vance's lips against my neck and his arm stayed tight. "I'm okay," I told him.

"I want you to see someone about these fuckin' nightmares," he growled against my skin.

I had nightmares about what happened. Mainly, that I shot someone in the head and killed them. Sometimes I'd dream about me getting shot, but mostly it was about me taking another person's life.

"After this current drama is over," I told him.

"Promise me, Jules," he demanded.

I scooted backwards and nestled my bottom into his groin. "I promise."

We fell silent and I waited for him to fall asleep, like he normally did after he woke me from a nightmare.

He didn't fall asleep.

Instead, he said, "You did what you did because you are who you are. I wouldn't change one piece of you. You did it for Roam. You did it for survival."

"I know," I replied quietly.

Vance pressed closer. If you'd asked me if he could get closer, I would have said no, but he did.

"He was scum, Princess," he murmured to the back of my head. "If we'd had two minutes to get to him, if Luke and I made it to him before shots were fired, either one of us would have taken him down. And doin' it wouldn't give either of us nightmares."

"I know," I repeated.

"He'd already killed Cordova. He'd beat the shit out of Roam and would have killed him, too. You did what you had to do."

I closed my eyes tight and said, "I was the reason he was on a rampage."

"You blow his sister's head off while he watched?" Vance asked.

My body went still as his point penetrated deep.

"Of course not," I whispered.

He put a hand to my midriff and pushed me to my back then he went up on an elbow and looked down at me.

"You poured vegetable oil on dealers' cars. You threw smoke bombs. Retaliation for that isn't murder."

He was right.

"You're right," I told him. "Except it was canola oil," I corrected to lighten the mood.

Vance didn't feel like lightening the mood.

"What are the alternatives for that night?" he asked me and I blinked.

"What?"

"You're a good shot. You could have kept him alive even though he was aimin' to kill. You kept aimin' to maim, what would have happened?"

"He probably would have shot me in the head," I told him, and this was true.

"Roam too," Vance pushed and I shivered.

"Roam too," I whispered.

"Which means Sniff would be alone. No you, no Roam."

That didn't bear thinking about so I shoved it aside immediately.

Vance went on, "And I wouldn't have you and you wouldn't be pregnant with our son."

"Daughter," I corrected quietly.

"I don't give a fuck what it is. It exists. It's yours and mine, and it's gonna be here because of the split second decision you made to put a bullet in his brain."

"Crowe—"

"Part of the reason I love you is because, despite the kind of person he was, you're the kind of person who'd let this haunt you." His mouth came to mine. "But, Jules, now you gotta let it go."

He was right about that, too.

I hated it when he was right.

But I loved it when he told me he loved me.

"I love you," I said against his lips.

I felt his mouth grin. "That's good, since you're married to me and havin' my baby."

He gave me a swift kiss, pushed me back to my side and fitted himself against my body from shoulders to heels.

His hand came to my belly.

I was almost asleep again when I heard him say softly, "Anything happened to you, I'd be Nick."

I knew what he meant. My Uncle Nick had never recovered from Auntie Reba's death. He existed, and on some level, he enjoyed life. He loved me and he respected and cared for Vance. We had a nice little family. But the light had gone when Auntie Reba died and it was never coming back.

I knew this about Vance. I knew this was how much he loved me. I'd known it for ages.

"I know," I said.

"I experienced that feeling for six hours while you were in surgery. I never want it back."

"Vance—"

"I never want it back, Jules."

"Okay."

"You made the right decision when you aimed to kill."

I linked my fingers with his and held on tight. "Okay."

"Go to sleep."

I sighed, then snapped, even though my heart wasn't in it, "Stop telling me what to do."

His fingers tightened on mine, but he didn't answer.

We fell asleep.

And, for some reason, I never had another nightmare about that night.

Never.

Chapter 25

Gonna Pick a Fight with You Every Day
Stella

I woke when Mace and Juno's weight hit the bed. I was so deeply asleep, I hadn't even felt Juno leave the bed when Mace arrived at the door, nor did I hear his key in the lock or him moving around the apartment.

I was dead asleep because the night before, with Tex gone, and seeing as it was all my fault, I hadn't had a wink of sleep. It didn't help that I didn't hear one word from Mace all night until he phoned mid-morning to say Tex was all right and that Bobby would be picking me up and taking me to Fortnum's.

"Mace?" My voice was husky with sleep.

"Yeah, babe." He was on his back and he rolled me into his side.

His arm curled around my waist as I rested my head on his shoulder.

"What time is it?"

"Quarter after midnight."

"Everything okay?" I asked.

"As far as I know," he answered.

"You would know?"

His fingers gave my waist a squeeze as he said, "Yeah, I would know."

I rested my arm on his abs and my body relaxed into his.

"Do you wanna talk?" I mumbled into his shoulder, already halfway to dreamland.

"If I had any energy, Kitten, I'd use it to fuck, not talk."

Well, one thing you could say for that, it proved Shirleen right.

I was almost in dreamland when I muttered, not even knowing myself what I was saying, "Love you, Kai."

And, being so close to dreamland, I didn't feel his body get tight when I called him for the first time by his given name.

"Kitten," Mace said in my ear, and I felt his arm, tight around my waist, give me a gentle shake.

I opened my eyes. It was morning.

We'd shifted in the night. I was turned away from him. Mace was pressed to my back.

"Stella," Mace said, giving me a less-gentle-but-still-gentle shake and I blinked.

"I'm awake," I told him.

"It's a big day, shit to do. But before we get to it, we gotta talk."

It *was* a big day.

It was Lee and Indy's wedding day.

Luckily, since I'd been invited to the wedding and the bachelorette party that was supposed to be last night, I hadn't scheduled any gigs for the weekend.

Unfortunately, since we were all in danger of being kidnapped and/or murdered, Lee had cancelled his bachelor party and at the same time cancelled Indy's bachelorette party.

Incidentally, just as an FYI, Lee's party was meant to be at Lincoln's Road House and, in a bizarre Rock Chick/Hot Bunch twist, Indy's was scheduled to be at Smithie's Strip Club.

The cancellation of the bachelorette party had not gone down well. Ally went berserk when Lee had cancelled the party that she'd spent months planning. He'd made his announcement after everyone had checked in to see with their own eyes that Tex was still breathing, so everyone was around to get the news firsthand *and* witness the knockdown-drag out fight that ensued.

I didn't have any siblings but always wanted one; until seeing Lee and Ally fight.

After it went on awhile, Hank got involved, trying to be the diplomat (and failing), and then it escalated.

Then Eddie and Indy got involved and it exploded.

We all watched as the five of them shouted at each other about stuff that was so historical no one knew what they were on about.

They were yelling about some kegger Indy and Ally had masterminded in high school, which for some reason ended with Hank, Lee, Darius and Eddie being picked up by the cops, and we learned that Hank, who had been at the University of Colorado, was nearly suspended and he wasn't happy about this, even years later.

"You haven't changed one fuckin' bit, either of you!" Eddie shouted, pointing at them both.

"Good!" Ally shouted back.

She planted her hands on her hips and I immediately saw where Mace was coming from with the hands-to-hips business.

"Gotta tell you, beautiful, never liked the idea of you havin' a bachelorette party. You and Ally plus the Rock Chicks equals disaster at the best of times, and these are far from the best of times. I'm fuckin' thrilled I got a reason to cancel it," Lee said to Indy.

Indy let out a gust of air between pursed lips and turned to me. "Tell me he did *not* just say that."

Instantly, Mace was at my ear. "For fuck's sake, don't speak."

Tex boomed, "Jesus Jones, but I'm glad I wasn't whacked last night. If I was dead, I'd've missed *this!*"

"We'll have a party after ya'll get back from your honeymoon," Daisy tried to play peacemaker.

"If you do, Jet's not goin'," Eddie announced.

Uh-oh.

"What?" Jet, who had been keeping herself removed, asked.

"Roxie either," Hank threw down.

Uh-oh again!

"Sorry?" Roxie's eyes narrowed.

"Oh my," Lana, standing beside me, breathed.

"You're not goin'," Eddie repeated to Jet.

"You heard me," Hank said to Roxie.

"They scare me," Chloe, who was on the other side of Lana, whispered. "But still, I think those boys might want to quit while they're ahead."

They didn't hear Chloe and were on such a tear, without remorse, Eddie and Hank dragged Jet and Roxie into the fight and it degenerated to the point where I feared the roof would blow off Fortnum's.

"*Quiet!*" Darius all of a sudden shouted. Everyone went quiet and looked at him. "Jesus, you never learn do you?" he asked the warriors.

Then he turned and pointed at Mace. "He knows." He turned to Vance and pointed. "He knows." Then he turned to Jules and said, "She knows, too. And you all know *I* fuckin' know. You gotta learn life's too damn short for this shit."

He got up close to Indy and Lee and clipped, "You two've been in love since you were kids. Tomorrow, you're gettin' married, and today you're fightin' about what? What're you fightin' about?"

Lee's face got tight and Indy looked at her feet while Darius went on.

"Eddie's right and he's wrong, it ain't just Indy and Ally who've never changed. It's all you all." His finger circled the lot of them as he continued, "How fuckin' lucky are you, even with all the shit that's gone down, that you haven't learned what we've learned?" he asked, throwing his arm around the room and ending with his fist thumping his chest. "Rejoice, for fuck's sake," After that, Darius turned to Tex and said, "Good to see you're alive, big man."

Then he turned on his boot and he was gone.

"He scares me, too," Chloe mumbled.

I stifled a giggle.

Indy bit her lip and turned to Lee. "Can we chat, um… privately?"

Lee's face went soft, his arm went around her shoulders and they disappeared into the books.

So did Hank and Roxie, Eddie and Jet.

Ally looked at everyone else.

"So I'm an idiot. This isn't news," she announced.

"Well! Thus ends another white people fight," Shirleen declared.

"You!" Tex boomed and he was pointing at Lana. "And you!" His finger moved to Chloe. "Learn quick, it ain't ever borin' around here."

"I'm getting that," Lana replied, and luckily, her mouth was twitching.

Things calmed down after that. The men went off to do whatever it was they did and the women, along with Tod and Stevie, Duke and Tex, hung around Fortnum's chatting, gossiping and doing the minor changes they had to do so that Lana and Chloe could come to the wedding.

"Oh, we couldn't," Chloe protested. "We barely know you."

To which Indy replied with a smile, "Family's family, and like it or not, the minute you got on that plane, you became family."

This was sweet as all get out and Lana and Chloe thought so, too.

Instead of a bachelorette party, we had pizza delivered and Tod and Stevie ran out and got beer. We ate pizza and drank beer at Fortnum's. The chatting and gossip degenerated to sex talk, but since Mace's Moms were there, I kept silent on that particular subject. They were not used to drinking beer at altitude and did not. Chloe, I learned, had been married to a guy named Ben for five years. It was clear he was a good guy (in *a lot* of different ways). Lana was single, and apparently enjoyed her status.

After a while, the sex talk downshifted to game after game of Yahtzee.

We sipped beer, shared and played Yahtzee until, at around ten, our escorts arrived to take us home.

I snuggled back into Mace's body and mumbled, "I have to get to The Castle. I'm not a bridesmaid, but I'm invited to the pre-wedding festivities."

"You'll get there after we talk and after we fuck. First, the talk," Mace replied, and I noticed two things right off the bat.

One was that he was being bossy.

The other was that he sounded serious.

Very serious.

Instead of getting angry at him for being bossy, this made me get tense and I turned to face at him.

I tilted my head back to look at him and saw he was definitely serious.

My breath, feeling adventurous, headed up the Inca Trail.

"Is something wrong?" I asked.

"You said you'd seen the papers."

"What?"

"You said, the other night, backstage, that you'd seen the papers."

I blinked. "Yeah? And?"

"If you saw the papers, when I told you about Tiny, you already knew everything."

I was confused. "Are you angry about that?"

"Yes and no."

"What's the 'yes' part?" I asked hesitantly.

"You stood there as I told the story, actin' like you didn't know."

"Well, I didn't know all of it."

"I know the part you didn't know. No one knows but the men. But you acted like you didn't know any of it."

"There were other parts I didn't know," I tried.

"You acted like you didn't know any of it," he repeated.

"Mace—"

His arm went around me, he pulled me close and tipped his chin down further so his face was in mine. "Kitten, this is gonna work, you don't lie to me. Ever. Got me?"

I blinked again.

Now hang on a second.

"These are pretty extreme circumstances," I defended myself.

"Yeah, that's the 'no' part and why I'm lettin' you get away with bringin' Mom and Chloe here without talkin' to me about it."

I blinked.

Yes, again!

Letting me get away with...

"Mace—"

He interrupted me. "We're done talkin' about this. I said what I had to say. I think you get me."

Oh, I got him all right.

He made to move into me, but I scooted away and got out of bed. I stood at the side in my panties and tank, put my hands to my hips and glared at him.

I was pissed way the hell off.

I'd gone through emotional hell to do what I did.

And he...

He...

"I never thought I'd say this in my whole effing life but *how dare you!*" I screeched.

Juno got to her belly and woofed.

Mace got up on an elbow and his eyes narrowed.

"Get back in bed," Mace growled.

"Fuck off!" I snapped.

"Get back in the fuckin' bed," Mace clipped back.

"Don't tell me what to do, Kai Mason."

"That's another thing," his voice rumbled with anger, "you don't call me Kai."

"In about three seconds, you don't back down, I'm never gonna call you *anything*," I retorted, then I moved to flounce away, and I must admit, as embarrassing as it was, I was definitely going to flounce.

Before I got even a step his fingers wrapped around my wrist. He gave a sharp tug and I was back in bed, Mace on top of me. Juno woofed again and quickly exited the bed.

"Don't you walk away from me," he rumbled.

"I'll do what I want."

"We got a disagreement, we talk and work it out. You don't fuckin' walk away."

"For your information, *Kai*, we're not disagreeing, we're *fighting*."

"Okay, Stella, we get in a fight, we talk and work it out. I repeat, you do not fuckin' walk away."

"And I repeat, I'll do what I effing well want!"

He looked furious, furious enough to explode, but instead, his head slanted and he kissed me.

It was a hot kiss. Fueled by the fight and such an intense kiss, we were all over each other. Hands and mouths everywhere, the anger turned to something else entirely and I liked it a lot.

He tore down my underwear as I pulled off my tank. Luckily, he was already naked.

Then his lips were on my belly, his hands spreading my legs and his mouth was right where I needed it.

He was good at this. If I had to rank his talents, oral sex was arguably top of the list. Therefore, he had me squirming and panting under him in no time.

Then he came up over me. I thought he'd enter me but he didn't. His hand moved to cup me between my legs but that was it. No finger action, no movement, just holding me there. His mouth was at my throat.

"What do you want?" he asked there.

I didn't hesitate, couldn't. I was in a state.

"I want you to fuck me," I breathed.

"Beg," he ordered. and my eyes, which had been closed, flew open.

"No."

His head came up. His eyes captured mine and his fingers, finally, did a swirl.

One slid inside, out then back in.

While he was doing this, he repeated, "Beg me, Kitten."

"No," I repeated, but it was still breathy.

His hand kept moving.

His lips came to mine and he whispered, "Beg me, babe."

I was no match for his hand, which I was thinking was as talented as his mouth.

Therefore, I whispered back, "Please, Mace, fuck me."

His hand stilled and my mind went blank.

Kristen Ashley

"Say it again."

I said it again.

I no sooner finished the words than his body disappeared.

Before I could figure out where he went, he whipped me to my belly. I looked at him over my shoulder and he was on his knees between my legs. The minute his eyes caught mine, he lifted up my hips and slammed into me.

Effing hell.

It was heaven.

My head jerked back and I moaned, "*Yes.*"

His hands at my hips, he drove in again and again. Just as I was about to explode he pulled out and I groaned in protest.

He fell to his back and moved me over him.

"Mace…" I breathed against his mouth, but he was jerking my legs at the knees so I was straddling him. He pushed me up, entering me at the same time.

I looked down at him.

Lordy, but he was beautiful.

"Now, Kitten, you fuck me," he demanded, his voice thick.

Without hesitation, I did.

As hard as I could, as rough as I could, and as fast as I could.

I threw my head back with my climax and he whipped me on my back and finished by driving in deep, making my second orgasm ride the wave of the first.

When he was done, I took his weight and he kept moving inside me, gently pressing his hips between my legs while I purred.

Finally, he stopped and he did something with his body, his weight still on me, but I wasn't taking all of it. One of his hands was stroking my side from hip nearly to armpit.

His face was in my neck.

"I like fightin' with you, babe," he told my neck.

Oh dear.

He was gonna piss me off.

"Don't piss me off," I told the ceiling.

His head came up. My eyes shifted to him and he was grinning at me. "We should have fought a lot more a year ago. Would've never left you."

Now, I was getting pissed-off so I decided to share.

"Erm… you're pissing me off," I warned him.

"Gonna pick a fight with you every day," he informed me.

"Mace—"

His face came closer and my head pushed back into the bed, but it didn't get very far and his mouth touched mine.

"Forgot how much I like you on your knees," he muttered against my mouth. "Your heart-shaped ass right there for me."

"Mace—" I tried again.

"I'm beginning to change my mind," he told me conversationally, his mouth moving from mine to my jaw. "Pretty soon, you'll be famous. Everyone'll want what I got right here." His hips moved again, as he was still inside me and I was tender, I let out an involuntary short, rough purr. His hand moved up my side from my hip and in, cupping my breast. "But it's mine," he whispered against my cheek and then his mouth moved to my ear. "All... fuckin'... mine."

Even though I liked what he was saying, like, a lot, I still felt it important to stay on target.

Therefore, I informed him, "I'm not done being mad at you."

His head came up and he was still grinning. "I'm all right with that."

It was safe to say I wasn't getting pissed anymore. I was there.

I gave him a hearty shove. We disengaged and he rolled to his back, but I got the distinct feeling (and that pissed me off too) that he let me get away with this. I was rolling the other way when he caught me at the hips and whipped me around so I was on top of him.

I pushed up, but he kept me pinned with both arms tight around my waist, his long legs tangling with mine.

"Talk to me," he demanded, but he said this with his face soft and his voice low and I'd never been a match for that combo, so I did.

"The Rock Chicks intervened. That morning when Shirleen shot that guy. They were worried that we were over and they decided to tell me what happened to Caitlin. I tried to stop them, but before I could do that, they told me about her hand."

Mace's arms got tighter, but I kept talking.

"When I heard that, I got sick, as in, literally. Straight to the toilet and then no more eggs benedict."

I watched him flinch and when he was done, I saw his eyes had grown warm.

"Kitten," he mumbled, but I shook my head to let him know I wasn't done.

403

"I knew you'd tell me, but I had to be strong for you. When you told me, I couldn't lose it, make something that needed to be about you about me. So I talked Duke into telling me the whole story. He didn't want to, but he did. After he told me, they gave me the papers."

He rolled me to my back and was half on me, half off, up on one elbow, his other arm across my midriff.

"All you had to do was tell me this," he said softly.

I shook my head. "I never wanted you to know. Not about me losing it. I just wanted to be there for you."

The tips of his fingers went to my temple, and whisper-soft, they sifted into the hair there.

"I appreciate that," he muttered. His head bent to kiss me, but I jerked my mine back and to the side. His brows drew together and he asked, "You still pissed?"

"Um... yeah." I answered in a tone that stated, *isn't it obvious?*

"Why?" he asked.

"I don't make you explain your every movement. I don't boss you around. I trust you."

His head jerked. "Didn't I just spend a week workin' at winnin' you back because you *didn't* trust me?"

Effing hell.

I forgot about that.

Cover! My brain screamed.

"That was then, this is now," I returned.

He stared at me then he sighed. "All right, Kitten. You wanna stay pissed, stay pissed. I'll be here when you're over it."

That, for Mace, apparently was that.

He did a push up and exited the bed, got dressed, grabbed the lead and whistled for Juno. As he was doing this, I pulled up the sheets, laid in bed and watched. When he was gone, I got up and stomped to the bathroom. I was out of the shower and standing at the sink wearing my robe, my wet hair combed back, brushing my teeth when Mace walked into the bathroom. He came up behind me, put an arm around my waist and kissed my neck where it met my shoulder.

His eyes came to mine in the mirror. "Done bein' pissed at me?"

I wasn't.

But as I stared into his beautiful green eyes, I noticed they were a strange mixture of wary and amused, as if he was preparing for a negative response, but any response he was going to get would make him laugh.

I kept brushing and looking at him in the mirror noticing something was missing.

For a second, it escaped me.

Then I realized it was the guard. The guard was not down over his eyes.

And there were no demons.

It was just Mace and me in the bathroom.

My eyes moved to his throat and I saw his sister's tiny ring resting there.

I wanted to take a moment and mentally do a triumphant war dance of glee at my trouncing of the demons.

Instead I took the toothbrush out of my mouth and answered through a mouthful of foaming toothpaste, "Yeah. I'm done."

Just like I thought, what I said made him laugh.

I watched that, too. Then I leaned forward and, while I spit and rinsed, I allowed myself a mini-mental war dance of glee.

Ha!

Die demons die!

He was still behind me when I straightened and his other arm joined the first around me.

"That didn't take very long," he told me.

"You're infuriating and bossy, but you're hot. You're lucky you're hot. If you weren't, I wouldn't put up with you," I said it but I didn't mean it, (at least not all of it) and it didn't sound like I meant it, either.

His mouth went back to my neck.

"Bullshit," he muttered there.

I ignored that and asked, "Is your suit for the wedding here?"

"Nope, tux is at the office. We'll drive by there on the way to Daisy's to pick it up."

"You're wearing a tux?" I asked, surprised. It was an evening wedding, but still.

"I'm in the wedding," he informed me and my eyes grew round.

"You are?"

"Yeah, standin' up with Lee."

I blinked.

"You are?" I repeated.

"You didn't know that?" he asked.

"No. I didn't know that. You didn't tell me."

"Indy didn't tell you?"

"I'm not *sleeping* with Indy," I reminded him.

"I thought you women talked wedding shit all the time." He sounded surprised.

"We talk about sex and we talk about rock music and sometimes we talk clothes. Tod talks about the wedding."

He grinned. "You talk about sex?"

"Yeah, Eddie likes it rough and hard and Luke and Ava fell off when they tried desk sex."

He winced and muttered, "Too much information."

I was intrigued at his reaction and turned in his arms to face him. "Don't you guys talk about sex?"

"Fuck no," he said immediately.

"No locker room talk?"

"No."

"While you're sitting surveillance?"

"Again, Kitten, no. We don't talk, probably because we don't wanna know."

"But the Rock Chicks are sultry and sexy. I thought you all would want to brag."

"Don't need to brag."

"Why not?"

Mace gave me a look that said it all, his arms got tight and he replied, "Babe."

I grinned and decided to tease. "Indy says Lee's great at kitchen counter sex."

He frowned. "Stop talking."

I didn't stop talking. "And I think Vance is creative with positions. I find that interesting. Maybe you two can chat, get some ideas."

"Stella—"

"Hank proposed to Roxie while he was giving her the business," I informed him.

"Be quiet," he growled.

"And Daisy and Marcus——" I didn't finish. I squealed because he bent, put a shoulder to my belly and carried me out of the bathroom. He threw me on the bed and stalked back to the bathroom, slammed the door and I heard it lock.

I giggled to myself.

Juno loped over to me and nudged my calf with her nose.

"That was fun," I told Juno.

Juno woofed.

I gave her a head scratch and looked at her bowl.

Then I shouted, "Mace, you didn't feed Juno!"

He shouted back, "I walked her, you feed her!"

I heard the shower go on.

Still smiling, I fed my dog, made coffee, then I made Belgian waffles for Mace.

Chapter 26

Something Borrowed

Stella

We were sitting around Daisy's dining room table, which was littered with every beauty implement known to womankind, from moisturizers to makeup to false eyelashes to bronzing powder to shimmer powder to hair dryers to curling irons plus brushes, combs, teasing combs, bobby pins, hair spray, gel, mousse, pomade, finishing wax and shine elixir.

Indy was sitting, drinking a latte Tex brought her from Fortnum's, which was closed for the day. Then he hightailed it out of there, saying he was meeting "the boys" for lunch.

She was calm and chatting with Lee's mom Kitty Sue, Roxie's mom, who was in from Indiana for the wedding, Trish, Eddie's mom, Blanca, Jet's mom, Nancy, Duke's wife, Dolores, Lana and Chloe.

She was wearing a beautiful, pale pink, kimono-style silk robe with a huge, intricate flower embroidered on the back, a bridal gift from Roxie, Jet, Ava and Jules, her hair up in a towel, her legs crossed, leaned back and at-ease.

In fact, everyone was calm and chatting.

Daisy had put on a huge, gourmet, catered buffet for our lunch which was sitting on the sideboard. She'd had a half dozen bouquets delivered that were the same as Indy's wedding flowers, pale pink and white gerbera daisies, white roses and pale pink and white peonies, and these were decorating the room. She'd not gone rock 'n' roll, but instead a Chopin CD was playing softly in the background. Daisy was floating around in her own robe, her hair back in a wide band, her face devoid of makeup, offering refills to those who wished to imbibe early from a champagne bottle she was holding.

Out of nowhere, Tod rushed in wearing a beautifully tailored navy suit, a pink shirt, monochromatic tie and a harried expression. His shiny, Italian leather shoes clattered on Daisy's floorboards with his frenzied approach.

His dramatic entrance shattered the peaceful, feminine serenity.

Stevie, also wearing a beautifully tailored suit, followed more sedately.

Tod took in two breaths, his hands up, one clamped around a clipboard and he pressed the air down.

"Okay, okay. Update. Just got back from the club. They're about to start setting up. They have the right colored linens and the florist has already been there. I called her to give her a piece of my mind since she wasn't supposed to deliver the flowers to the club for another hour and they might get droopy. She *promised* me she wouldn't be early with your bouquets. I told her she must go back to the club and *personally* check that not one *single* petal droops before we arrive at seven."

When he paused to take in a breath, Ally suggested, "Tod, calm down, have a glass of champagne."

Tod's head swiveled toward Ally.

"Can't you see I'm in the middle of a briefing!" he screeched and then he looked back to Indy, face composed and voice back to normal. "Where was I?"

Indy was looking a little concerned with the possibility that Tod's head might start revolving three hundred and sixty degrees, so she said softly, "Petals drooping."

"Right. Okay."

He looked down at his clipboard, and as he talked he made checkmarks on whatever was on the board.

"The cake has been delivered and they're putting it together now. It looks beautiful. Perfect. The Lana-slash-Chloe update has been noted by the caterers and staff." He looked at them, pointed to them with the end of his pen and bounced it back and forth between them as he spoke. "You're sitting with the out-of-towner Rock Chick people. Trish and Herb'll take care of you, but I moved Stella to your table just in case."

Back to his clipboard, he checked something off and kept talking.

He gave updates on absolutely everything, including the state of the asphalt of the drive up to Cherry Hills Country Club, a location that Daisy and Marcus, as members of the club, arranged for the reception, saying, "They sealed that crack I noticed last week, thank *God*."

"Tod, darlin', did you just say they sealed a crack in the asphalt?" Trish called out.

"Yes, thank *God*," Tod repeated.

Trish shook her head. "Son, as Roxie used to say to her Dad when she was growing up, you need to take a chill pill."

Tod's eyes narrowed on Trish and everyone sucked in breath.

"I want this to be *perfect*," Tod retorted.

"And it will be. You been working hard on it for months. Now enjoy the fruits of your labors." She pointed at the buffet. "Have some of that cold, sliced chicken. Kid you not. Melt in your mouth."

"Trish, there's a million things to do!" Tod shot back.

"Nothing you haven't already checked and double-checked, I'm sure," Trish returned.

"Yes, but—" Tod started, but Trish leaned forward.

"Tod, won't say it again. Sit yourself down, take a load off and do what your friend here really wants you to do." She indicated Indy with a jerk of her head. "Which is enjoy her day *with* her, not running around like a chicken with its head chopped off." She looked at Nancy and said, "Yeesh, young people these days."

Everyone stared at Tod and Trish, wondering what might happen next.

Stevie sat at the table and called, "Daisy, I'll take some of that champagne."

"Sure thing, sugar," Daisy scooted around toward Stevie.

"Get Tod some, too," Indy put in.

"You betcha," Daisy said.

Indy put down her latte, got up and moved to Tod. When she arrived at him, she put her arms around him and whispered in his ear. His face got flushed and his eyes started to fill with tears.

Indy's back was to me but I could see Tod's face, though he wasn't close enough to hear.

But it didn't take a lip reader to see he said, "Love you, too."

⌇⌇

The Hot Bunch

"'Nother round for you boys?" the waitress asked on a flyby.

Lee's head came up and he did a chin lift indicating a positive response.

The waitress stopped, hitched a hip, smiled and said, "Lee, honey, I hear today you are oh-fficially off the market."

"Been off for a while, Betty," Lee replied.

"My heart's breakin'," she told him and looked around. "You boys're droppin' like flies." Her eyes moved from Hector to Darius to Willie to Mace. "Least there's four of you left."

"Three," Mace said.

"Oh, honey, now you just went and ruined my day." She grinned. "Saw the papers. 'Bout time you got your head out of your ass about Stella."

The Nightingale Men, Hank, Eddie, Malcolm, Tom, Roxie's Dad, Herb, Jules's Uncle Nick, Willie and Duke were at Lincoln's Road House waiting for their lunch to be served. Tex had not yet arrived.

At Betty's comment, some heads dropped to look at the table, a few eyes slid to the side and there were a couple of chuckles.

Mace made no reply. Betty had been serving Mace food and beer for years and didn't expect one. She winked at Mace and went to get their beer.

"You comfortable with the arrangements?" Malcolm asked Lee.

Lee's eyes moved to his father. "Yeah, Dad. I'm pretty comfortable with personal security in the form of half the Denver fuckin' Police Department off-duty, eatin' Indy's catering and carryin' concealed."

"Indy isn't payin' for that catering, I am," Tom cut in. "And what it costs, you boys better eat it and enjoy every scrap."

"Please tell me it's steak and potatoes," Bobby muttered.

"Not even close," Tom told him. "Don't remember much, but something's wrapped in filo pastry."

"What in the Sam Hill is that?" Herb exploded.

Tom shrugged.

Herb looked at Lee. "You have a hand in the menu?"

Lee shook his head.

"You have a hand in *anything?*" Herb asked.

"I have to be in a tux and at Red Rocks at five and get Indy to Cherry Hills Country Club by seven. Indy put her foot down that we have to stay until eleven before we can get the fuck out of there and we got a suite at the Brown Palace," Lee responded. "That's all I know about today. That's all I want to know about today."

Herb's eyes moved to Hank. "Listen to me now, son, you better get involved. You asked Roxie to marry you, you gotta remember, she's draggin' us all along with her. I ain't payin' for no fuckin' pastry. Good old roast beef carved right on the spot, potatoes, maybe some of them fancy green beans and fuckin' weddin' cake. Got me?"

"Roxie told me Tod's already started her wedding book," Hank replied.

"What's a wedding book?" Eddie asked.

Hank shrugged. "Hell if I know, but Roxie says Tod's got one for Jet, too," Eddie closed his eyes and Hank's gaze moved to Herb. "If Tod's involved, I'm out. Roxie knows that and she's good with it."

"Sounds like you did the right thing," Luke said to Vance.

"What'd you do?" Herb asked Vance.

"Justice of the Peace." Vance replied.

Herb nodded. "Problem is, you knocked up your girl. That's the only way women'll allow you to get away with a Justice of the Peace." Herb looked back to Hank as many of the men coughed to hide their laughter. "That's the ticket, son, only way to save us all. Start workin' on makin' a baby."

Hank was taking a drag off his beer. He choked on it and his eyes slid to Herb.

Herb kept talking. "Don't worry. You have my permission."

Hank looked at Lee and muttered, "Fucking hell."

Lee was too busy laughing to reply.

So was everyone else.

Tex arrived at the table and boomed, "What'd I miss?"

⇥⇤

Stella

The Rock Chicks, Tod, Stevie and Kitty Sue were all in Daisy's massive master suite.

The stylists and makeup artists had come and gone. Indy's bridesmaids, Ally, Roxie, Ava, Jet, Daisy, Jules and two of her other friends, Marianne and Andrea, were all done up in subtle rosy-cheeked makeup, shimmer powder and beautiful, pale pink, wispy, chiffon dresses with short trains and graceful drapes of material at their arms that looked like they'd slid down from their shoulders, but actually were meant to be like that. Their hair was all in soft updos with tendrils hanging down. They all had brand new pearl studs with a single diamond at the bottom in their ears, bridesmaids gifts from Indy.

Their dresses and hair made them look like they were drifting around caught in a romantic modern day fairytale.

Who would have thought India Savage, Rock Chick, would be into romantic weddings?

Then again, Indy hooking up with Lee after loving him since he held her hand during her mother's memorial service when she was five years old *was* a modern day fairytale.

So there you go.

I'd done my hair and makeup at the dining room table while the stylists were seeing to the wedding party and changed into my dress in the room Mace and I shared what seemed like years ago.

I'd bought my dress well before all the drama started and the day after a really good take at the Palladium. I'd curled my hair and left it long at the back, but pulled it away from my face in some soft twists secured by hidden pins at the top and sides. My dress was deep burgundy satin, strapless, skintight with a slit up the front. I was wearing a pair of pointed-toed, pencil-heeled satin slingback pumps that had been dyed to match the dress. I had a long necklace of garnets, but I'd wrapped it around my wrist and I had some teardrop, chandelier garnet earrings at my ears.

I was sitting on the bed between Jules and Jet when Indy's head emerged through the top of the dress Kitty Sue and Ally were putting on her. The dress slid down her body and settled.

Unlike the romantic visions her bridesmaids were, Indy's dress wasn't wispy chiffon and romantic.

It was angelic.

Ivory satin, v-necked, another, deeper V in the back, the front of the dress and the back of the dress held together by loops of thin ivory cords at her shoulders, which were stitched through gathered material. The dress fit her like a glove and had a wide skirt, a huge slit up the front and a long train. There was no diamante, stitched pearls, lace or sequins in sight. The only jewelry she wore was her engagement ring, a triple-tiered pearl bracelet that was Ally and Kitty Sue's present to her, and her mother's pearls at her ears.

The dress looked exactly like what an angel would wear.

If that angel were a sexy, sultry redhead.

Her hair was down in curls and waves (the way she said Lee liked it) and her makeup was subtle but exquisite.

She wasn't going to wear a veil.

It was beautiful, but that beauty all came from Indy.

Kitty Sue was standing back and staring at her.

Then she said softly, "I just need to go check something," and she ran from the room.

Indy and Ally watched this. Everyone else in the room was silent.

Then Indy turned to Ally, put her hands out to her sides and asked, "What do you think?"

Ally gave her a once over, and when her eyes moved back to Indy's, you could see the tears.

"Righteous," Ally whispered. She gathered Indy in her arms and gave her a hug.

"Old, new, borrowed, blue. Old, new... blue." Tod was surreptitiously studying his clipboard and muttering to himself. He leaned toward Stevie and whispered, "Shit, I think we forgot the borrowed."

"Man in the room," Shirleen announced, walking in followed by Mace, who'd changed and was now wearing a tux.

I took one look at him and the sight of my gorgeous boyfriend in a tux sent my breath on a cruise of the Caribbean.

It was clear Indy wasn't going the romantic route with Lee's groomsmen because it wasn't your average, everyday tux. It was a *hot* tux. It was black on black: black suit, black shirt, black silk tie, and not a bowtie either. I could tell immediately it wasn't rented. It was tailored to fit perfectly.

Shirleen kept talking. "He's here for Stella, Lana and Chloe."

She wasn't wrong. He was our ride.

Though it was kind of weird she brought him up to the bedroom.

I watched and wasn't insulted when his eyes caught on Indy and didn't move.

"Shirleen! You don't just bring a man into a bedroom filled with ladies dressin'!" Daisy snapped, even though everyone was already dressed. "Especially if one of those ladies is a soon-to-be bride!"

"What? It's Mace. He's taken. It ain't like he's out on the cruise," Shirleen snapped back.

Indy looked at Mace through the mirror, smiled and greeted, "Hey Mace."

He gave her a chin lift.

"Indy, honey, I don't mean to alarm you but we forgot the borrowed," Tod called.

"What?" Daisy asked.

"We got old, her Mom's earrings, new, Ally and Kitty Sue's bracelet, blue, her garter, but nothing borrowed," Tod explained.

"Oh shit," Ally mumbled.

Shirleen looked at Tod. "Borrowed is easy. Anyone can give her something borrowed. Shit, she could use a borrowed bobby pin."

"Her hair isn't up, Shirleen," Ava told her.

Shirleen looked at Indy then muttered, "Oh yeah, right."

"I'll get my jewelry box, see what I have," Daisy announced and ran to her dressing room.

"A hankie's good. Anyone got a hankie?" Roxie called out.

Since I was watching everyone search for something borrowed, I almost didn't catch Mace walking toward Indy. His arms were around his neck and then the chain with his sister's ring on it was off and dangling between his fingers. He upended it on one side, the ring falling out into his palm. He shoved the chain in his trouser pocket, stopped in front of Indy, took her right hand and slid the ring on her pinkie finger.

Only Jet and I caught this, and watching it we both were breathing so heavily trying to rescue our makeup, we sounded like we were hyperventilating.

Indy looked at the ring then up at Mace. She curled her fingers around his bicep, leaned into him until their faces were close and smiled.

The sun from the windows highlighted the tears glistening in her eyes.

Jet and I looked at each other. She reached out, grabbed my hand and squeezed.

We looked back to Indy as she took her hand away from Mace's arm, swiped under her eye, turned to the room and announced, "I'm good. Borrowed needs a checkmark, Tod."

"What? Where?" Tod asked, jerking his head around, looking at the floor as if he'd been told to capture an invisible rabbit in the room.

Mace came to me sitting on the bed. He leaned in, grabbed my hand, pulled me up and said, "Let's go."

We got into the hall when he asked, "Where's Mom and Chloe?"

"In the dining room, drinking champagne with Trish, Dolores, Nancy and Blanca."

"Oh fuck," he muttered.

I looked up at him. "What?"

"They're with Trish. Roxie's parents are nuts. They make Tex look adjusted," Mace told me.

I laughed. "I've been noticing that."

We were down the stairs and nearly to the dining room when I pulled at his hand to stop him.

He halted and tilted his head down to look at me, body still facing forward.

"Babe, I'm a groomsman, I gotta—" he started but I interrupted.

"Kai, what you just did for Indy—"

His face went hard and his body turned toward me.

Then he leaned in and clipped, "I told you, don't call me Kai."

I blinked because I hadn't even realized I'd done it, but even so, I was stunned at his reaction to it.

Then I felt my eyes narrow and my blood pressure skyrocket. "Sorry, Mace, it just slipped out and the only reason I can think of as to why is because what you just did for Indy was something a good man named Kai would do, not a badass called Mace."

I yanked my hand out of his, muttering under my breath about how moody he was and started to stomp away, but he caught me and whirled me into his arms.

"Effing hell, are we gonna fight again?" I cried as I tilted my head back to look at him.

I no sooner got my eyes on him than his mouth was on mine.

He kissed me, deep, slow and sweet.

When he was done, he didn't move his mouth from mine when he said, "You're gonna have to be patient with me, Kitten. This isn't fuckin' easy."

At his admission, my blood pressure settled.

I put my hand to his face and whispered, "Okay."

His eyes traveled my face and down, his arms gave me a squeeze and he whispered, "Babe, you look great."

I eyed his tux. "Not as good as you." I pulled out of his arms, grabbed his hand and went on, "Now, let's go get your Moms."

His brows went up and he didn't move, even though I was tugging at his hand. "My Moms?"

I went back to him, lifted up on tiptoe, put a hand to his chest and touched my lips to his. "Don't ask, just go with it."

He shook his head, but he followed me to the dining room anyway.

Chapter 27

Confession

Stella

I was standing in a corner with Ava and Luke, listening with half an ear to Ava doing everything she could (and *seriously* failing) to get Luke to dance, but watching the dance floor with frightened eyes.

Tom and Lana were cutting a rug. Tom was flinging Lana around while Nick, who was Indy's DJ, played The Brian Setzer Orchestra's "Jump, Jive an' Wail".

I already knew Lana could move, but Tom was something else. He couldn't just boogie, he could boogie *woogie*. He might be a bit older, but the man was *strong*. He flipped Lana around like she weighed as much as a wet towel.

They'd been nearly inseparable since the dancing started, after Lee and Indy's first dance and the father-daughter/mother-son dance and the wedding party dance, of course, and I wondered how Mace would feel about his mother hooking up with Indy's dad.

"Stella." Luke's deep voice came at me.

"Uh…" I muttered, eyes still glued to Lana and Tom, mind still engaged with images of Mace going berserk.

"Earth to Stella, come in Stella," Ava called.

My body jerked and I turned to Luke and Ava. Luke was looking at me. Ava was looking at the dance floor.

"Do you think Mace will go ballistic if something happens between Tom and Lana?" I blurted.

Luke's eyes moved to the dance floor. Ava's came to me.

"Crap, I hadn't thought of that," Ava breathed.

Luke's gaze came back and he asked, "They're all adults, including Mace. Why would it be a problem?"

"Mace can be unpredictable," I told Luke.

At my words, Luke threw his head back and let out of bark of laughter like I was being funny.

I was, by the way, *not*.

Ava and I stared at him.

When he was done laughing, his dark blue eyes were dancing and he informed me, "Mace is the one of the steadiest men I know."

I stared at him a beat, wondering if he knew a different Mace than I knew, then I mumbled, "Obviously you've never pissed him off."

Luke started chuckling and said, "Nope. Try to avoid that."

"Shit, what do you think *Indy* will think of Tom and Lana?" Ava put in, and we all looked back to the dance floor.

Indy was dancing with Malcolm, and as our eyes hit them, Malcolm swung Indy out and she collided with Lana. Both women's bodies tumbled, Tom's arms went around Lana and Malcolm jerked Indy into his before she could fall. Indy and Lana's gazes locked, Indy burst out laughing and gestured to Lana. They pulled away from the men and started swinging each other around.

"Don't think she'll mind," Luke muttered.

I smiled at Ava.

The wedding had gone off without a hitch. This was mostly due to Tod's impeccable planning. It was also partially due to a number of off-duty but still-uniformed Denver Police checking everyone's names against lists Tod made for them and patrolling the Red Rocks Amphitheater and facilities so no one was kidnapped or shot at, which would have ruined the vibe for sure.

Indy and Lee had been married on the Upper Terrace at Red Rocks with nothing but the panoramic views as decoration. There were no flowers, no ribbons, no urns, just some chairs set up and only the romantically-clad Rock Chicks, the angelic Indy, the Denver skyline and the red rocks formations setting the scene.

It was perfect.

They could have had the reception there, but Indy and Tod decided not to because they didn't want folks getting snockered so far away from a taxi call.

Indy had said that Lee wasn't into "this wedding business", but I found myself thinking he changed his mind when Tom guided Indy onto the terrace. You could hear all the air being sucked out of the night sky when his eyes settled on her.

She was smiling at him and looked as calm and serene as she had all day.

Lee wasn't smiling. He stood frozen and was, no other way to put it, staring with slightly parted lips as if he'd never seen her before in his life, but he still was going to carry her to a deserted island and ravish her the instant their toes touched the sand.

Hank was best man and standing next to Lee, then it was Eddie, Darius, Luke, Monty, Mace, Vance and Willie. Ally was maid of honor, then Andrea, Marianne, Ava, Jet, Roxie, Daisy then Jules.

Lee's eyes never left Indy, not when Tom was giving her away, and not when Tom gave her the father's kiss.

But when Tom placed Indy's hand in Lee's, his fingers closed around hers and you could see the sharp tug right before her body slammed into his. One of his arms went around her waist, the other hand bunched in her hair, and he kissed her right then and there.

And it wasn't a chaste peck on the lips either.

He went whole hog. So whole hog it took Ally doing a catcall and the preacher touching his shoulder to stop the make out session.

Everyone in the congregation and wedding party chuckled except Lee and Indy. Lee took his time finishing the kiss. When he'd lifted his head an inch, he whispered something to her that made her press her lips together, probably in order not to cry.

Then he turned to the preacher and said in a deep, authoritative voice, "Carry on," like he was officiating the ceremony.

Lana, who was sitting next to me, leaned in and whispered, "I think I like Kai's boss."

I grinned at her because I *knew* I did.

Other than that, the ceremony was simple and short. Neither bride nor groom were traditional. They didn't bother with the reception line, they stood smiling at folks, embracing, talking and shaking hands while they let their guests and their photographer take pictures. Indy wanted no posed photos, only candids, and that's what she got. After that, they took off in Lee's Crossfire.

Indy had built in a goodly amount of time for them to get to Cherry Hills Country Club, but Daisy confided in me, mostly it was so they had time to get home "to consummate the marriage, compende?" and get to the Club.

They arrived half an hour late.

No one cared.

The Brian Setzer Orchestra finished, Lana and Indy stopped swinging each other around and Nick's voice came over the sound system.

"Got a request," he told the crowd. "From a man named Kai."

There was some general muttering, but my eyes flew to Nick. My breath caught and before I could unhinge it, a hand was at the small of my back. I looked over my shoulder and Mace was standing behind me. He started pushing me toward the dance floor as Billy Joel's "And So It Goes" started playing.

We were on the dance floor, one of his arms sliding around me, the fingers of his other hand drifting down my forearm when I found my voice.

"Mace…"

His arm went tight around my waist bringing my body full frontal to his. The fingers of his other hand laced with mine. He brought our hands up, twisted his wrist and rested the back of mine against his heart.

"Dance with me, Kitten," he whispered.

That was all he had to say.

I melted into him.

Mace and I had never danced before, and he was good at it. Not like he was a ballroom dancer, just that his body fit perfectly into mine, swayed with a natural grace and he was so strong, mine went along for the ride.

"Got a confession to make." He'd tipped his head forward so his smooth cheek was against mine, his mouth at my ear.

"What?" I whispered into his.

"Went to The Bear to watch you play. I don't like missin' your shows and I wanted to talk to you after the gig, work out our shit." His hand gave mine a squeeze. "I saw you singin' this to me."

My head jerked back, my face coming to the side to look at him. His head lifted an inch and his eyes locked on mine.

Before I could say a word, not that I had any words to say, he kept talking. "Watchin' you sing that, hearin' the words, knownin' what it meant, it was then I knew I loved you, Stella."

I wanted to find words but I couldn't. So instead, I slid the hand he wasn't holding from his shoulder to around his neck and I got on my toes and kissed him.

He kissed me back. When he was done, he put his cheek back to mine and we finished the song, bodies pressed together, cheek to cheek.

For your information, it was the single most beautiful moment of my life.

Outside of the first time he told me he loved me, of course.

When it was over, he touched his mouth to mine again. We disengaged and he started to guide me off the dance floor, but our eyes hit Chloe and Lana, who were standing together at the edge of floor and watching us. Chloe, definitely a crier, had tears in her eyes.

Lana smiled at me.

I smiled back.

Mace caught the smile exchange. His hand slid from the small of my back to around my waist and he gave me a squeeze.

We arrived at Lana and Chloe and I was going to say something, but I saw movement at the entryway. Roam and Sniff were standing there. Sniff was bouncing on the balls of his feet and grinning ear to ear. Roam gave me a chin lift.

"Erm, excuse me," I mumbled to Mace, Lana and Chloe.

I turned and raised my hand to motion to Nick. I'd primed him earlier so he gave me a nod, a grin and he grabbed the microphone.

"If everyone could go out onto the patio," he announced.

A murmur went through the crowd and the guests all looked at each other in confusion. Then slowly, with more guidance from Nick, they did as they were told.

Mace's fingers tightened at my waist. "What's goin' on?"

I smiled at him. "Nothing, just..." I paused, "I'll see you back there."

I pulled free and went out the front door. Floyd, Pong, Hugo, Buzz and Leo were all waiting for me. Buzz and Leo were holding their guitars. Pong was holding his drumsticks. Floyd had my guitar.

I took my guitar from Floyd and nodded to my band.

Then I said, "Let's go, guys."

We walked through the club, and by the time we got back to the patio where Roam, Sniff and the Gypsies had set up our amps, Pong's drums, Hugo's keyboards, a set of bongos and wheeled out the Club's piano, all the guests were gathered around. The band took their places and plugged in while I went to the mic.

I put the strap of my guitar around my shoulder as my eyes found Indy and Lee.

Once I did, into the mic I said, "Don't have a lot of money so we thought we'd give you a memory."

Indy pulled in her lips, Lee's eyes crinkled and I nodded to Pong.

He started the beat.

Then I started to speak the first words of Shania Twain's "You're Still the One".

It was hokey, but for Lee and Indy it was just perfect.

Hugo started at the keyboards, and as I finished speaking, Floyd's piano came in. Then I hummed a sweet, "Mm, yeah," and I began to sing a sweet, hokey, perfect love song that said it all as my band played.

When I started singing about them taking the long way, I saw tears filling Indy's eyes. And when I was singing about them holding on, still together and strong, Indy was flat out crying.

My band stepped up to their mics and sang the title of the song as I kept singing.

As we played the crowd swayed, but I kept my eyes on Indy and Lee.

When I started singing about them beating the odds together, Indy turned to Lee. He had an arm wrapped around her, his other hand went to her jaw, her arms were around his waist, her head tilted back and she sang the rest of the song with me, but to her husband.

Hugo's keyboards played as the band sang their "oo's" when I watched Lee's head dip low so his forehead was resting against Indy's and they both closed their eyes and held on to each other.

I started singing again. Indy's eyes opened and so did Lee's. his hand slid down to her neck, his thumb stroking her jaw as she kept singing right along with me.

The band went silent and I finished with just my guitar as Indy kept singing to Lee, but my eyes moved to Mace. They locked with his and I sang the last two lines of the song direct to him.

I stopped singing and the guests cheered. Ally and Daisy let out catcalls and Tex gave a war whoop.

Mace just shook his head.

Then he smiled.

I smiled back.

Indy and Lee weren't cheering. They were making out, *again*.

It was the best present I'd ever given in my life.

The band didn't hesitate. Hugo moved to the bongos and started the rhythm, Floyd started to play piano and I took the microphone in my hand.

"Enough of that," I said to the guests. I looked back at the band and shouted, "Let's roll."

That's when we played Joe Cocker's "Feelin' Alright".

Everyone started dancing, and even Indy and Lee began to sway with the music. When it was time for the chorus, the entire crowd put their hands into the air and sang it with us.

Floyd was laying it down when my eyes found Mace's. He was standing with Luke and Vance, but he was smiling at me in a way that was heart wrenchingly familiar.

It was the same, sweet, unguarded smile he wore in the photo of him and Caitlin I saw in the paper.

I was "onstage", so unfortunately, all I could do was smile back.

But in my head, I gave one of the dying demons a last, vicious, sucker kick to the gut.

Then I focused on rock 'n' roll.

We went from Cocker to Three Dog Night and played "Shambala", then on to The Doobie's "Jesus Is Just Alright". After that, I let Buzz take one and he sang America's "Sister Golden Hair". We turned it up a couple notches, going straight into Boston's "Peace of Mind". Finally, I strapped on my mouth organ and we finished with one of our signature songs, the Black Rebel Motorcycle Club's, stomping, twanging, kickass "Ain't No Easy Way".

With our "thank you's" said into the mics. We left the instruments but the guests shouted and hooted until we were forced to go back and do an encore of "Ghostriders in the Sky".

For your information, the vibe of the set list was the happiest we'd ever played.

Chapter 28

Swen and Ulrika Are Gonna Be Pissed

Stella

Mace and I were in an Explorer on the way to my apartment after the reception and I was riding a killer happy buzz.

I was with my man. I loved him. He loved me. He was holding my hand against his thigh. My band was going to head to the studio for recording time on an impending recording contract. Two people I cared about just had a kickass wedding. And no one had been shot at or kidnapped all day.

"Happy buzz," I muttered to the window, grinning at it like a lunatic.

"What?" Mace asked as he turned onto my street.

I looked to him. "Happy buzz."

He glanced at me briefly, his beautiful jade eyes smiling, then back at the road.

I tested the boundaries of my seatbelt to lean in to him, pulling my fingers from his hold only to curl them around his thigh. I kissed his strong, square jaw as I heard him engage the turn signal before pulling into my drive.

"Never been happier, babe," I whispered, my lips moving against his jaw.

Mace didn't reply, but I felt his jaw get hard under my lips.

This surprised me so I pulled back a bit. I looked at his hard profile then followed the direction of angry gaze and saw a limousine at the end of the drive.

Shitsofuckit.

As we pulled up, the backdoor opened and Preston Mason folded out of the backseat.

Just as I suspected.

Shitsofuckit!

"Great," I muttered. "If anyone could kill this happy buzz, The Supreme Asshole of All Time could do it."

Kristen Ashley

Mace ignored my comment and ordered, "Stay in the truck," as he came to a halt, then put the SUV in neutral and set the brake without turning off the ignition.

"Mace—" I started, thinking good advice would be to suggest he ignore his father, I ignore his father, we walk in, forget he existed, resume the happy buzz and get on with our night, which would consist of making our happy buzz way happier.

He turned to me and gave me a look.

I shut up.

He threw open his door and angled out of the SUV.

I sat and watched him approach his father. Then I sat and watched him have words with his father. Then I sat and glared at his father as his condescending gaze came to me. Then I sat and watched as Mace's eyes did a sweep of the area while his father jabbered, probably being a serious dick, before Mace's hand came up abruptly, palm out. Preston clamped his mouth shut and Mace turned and strode angrily to the truck.

He yanked open the door and reached into the ignition, but his eyes were on me.

"Inside, babe," he ordered. I nodded then he went on, "Wait for me to get to your door."

I undid my seatbelt and Mace switched off the ignition, pulled out the keys and rounded the hood, his head turned to his father, his deep voice sounding, though I couldn't make out what he said. Mace made it around, pulled open my door and put his hand to my arm to help me out. He marched me to the side door where Preston was waiting.

Fabulous. Now we were going to have unwelcome company *in* my pad.

I tried to shoot daggers out of my eyes at Preston Mason as Mace and I approached, but unfortunately, this didn't work (though that didn't mean I quit).

Eventually I had to give up when Mace got the side door open and propelled me inside with his hand now at the small of my back, and I had to start concentrating on walking up two flights of steps in high heels without falling on my face.

We made it to my apartment successfully without me turning and giving Preston what-for for ruining my happy buzz, but worse, pissing Mace off when I knew he, too, was experiencing a happy buzz, Mace-style. And a Mace-style happy buzz when I was in close proximity usually included me getting laid, thoroughly, and very, very well, which made it even harder for me not to let loose on his dick of a Dad.

Mace dealt with the alarm and I saw Juno was lying on the bed, clearly tuckered out from a day of sleeping. She woofed at us in greeting but made no move. She did, however, train her doggie eyes on Preston in a confused but alert way, and it was good to know my dog could read a different kind of vibe, one she'd never had to read before, and that was when her people didn't much like someone.

I moved around to turn on lights and as I did this, Preston murmured, "Charming."

I stopped turning on lights and looked to him to see he was studying my space and obviously didn't think much of it.

Seriously, Mace's Dad was a dick. My apartment was small, sure, but it still rocked.

"Kitten, do me a favor." I heard Mace say, and my annoyed gaze went to him to see he was talking to me but his eyes were locked on his Dad. "Get changed in the bathroom and hang there. Do your thing, give us some time."

Um.

Hell no.

I had not just been through two weeks of the emotional ringer to end all emotional ringers, letting Mace back in my heart, trusting him, finding out what happened to Caitlin and taking our future in my hands to reunite him with his family, only to have his dick of a Dad give him shit without me taking his back.

Unh-unh.

No way.

"No," I replied and Mace's eyes sliced to me. I knew he was ticked. Hell, even if I just met him, the look on his face would tell me he was ticked, so I quickly explained, "No one fucks with my man."

Mace drew in a breath but some of the anger slid from his face.

Then he started, "Stella—"

"No, Mace. Your Dad is a dick and he's not gonna be a dick to you without me at your back." Before Mace could reply, I turned to Preston and stated, "We've had a really, *really* good day and those have been few and far between lately, so say what you have to say and then get out so we can forget you exist and get on with making it a really, *really* good night."

Juno woofed her agreement to my invitation and Preston's lip curled at my insinuation.

"Well?" I prompted when Preston didn't speak.

I walked to Mace and didn't give him a choice as I burrowed a shoulder under his armpit so he had to wrap his arm around me. When he did this, I wrapped one arm around his back and rested my other hand on his abs.

Preston studied us and his lip stayed curled.

Then he replied, "I assume you're not going to offer me a drink."

Totally a dick.

"Sure, I'll offer you a drink," I told him. "If you're here to apologize to Mace for being The Supreme Asshole of All Time, beg his forgiveness and promise to dedicate all your energies to philanthropic work from today until the day you die. No, if you're here to continue to be a dick."

Preston looked at his son.

"Seriously, Kai, is this your choice?" he asked, throwing a hand out to me.

Mace's body went rock-solid.

Oh shit.

"Moving on!" I declared quickly. Then to Preston, "Say your piece and go."

Preston looked back at me. "Fine, Stella, but I advise you not to be here when I say my piece, as you so eloquently put it."

I opened my mouth to speak but didn't get a word out.

"Your cracks at Stella end right fuckin' now," Mace growled.

Preston's eyes went to his son, and so did mine. I knew Mace pretty well. I loved him and I hoped to spend the rest of my life with him, but that didn't mean his look wasn't really freaking scary.

That said, it was also hot and he was pissed on my behalf so it also felt really freaking good.

I turned my eyes back to Preston, trying hard not to smirk, only to see he had entered a staring contest with Mace.

This went on awhile.

Considering father and son clearly had a life edict that included "never say die" I lost patience and snapped, "Seriously! Let's get on with this."

Preston's eyes slid to me. His jaw got hard and he looked back at Mace.

"I think you know you're treading on thin ice," he announced.

"I do?" Mace asked.

"Don't be stupid, Kai," Preston whispered. "You never were before, except once and it ended in tragedy. Don't do it again."

If Mace's body was rock-solid before, it was marble now, but I didn't really notice since my vision exploded in sparks of red and I instantly decided I was done. I didn't know why he was there. I didn't know why Mace allowed him to come up.

And at that moment, I also didn't effing care.

"Get out of my house," I hissed and Preston looked to me.

"You don't—" he began.

"Get... *the fuck*... out... *of my house!*" I bit out.

"The receptionist at his place of business dealt drugs," Preston informed me.

"Get out of my house," I kind of repeated.

"Her nephew, Kai's colleague, was in business with her," Preston went on.

Really?

Darius?

Yikes.

Oh well. Past tense. If it didn't bother Mace, which obviously it didn't, it didn't bother me.

And anyway, Darius was cool.

"Get out of my house," I repeated again.

Preston continued, "His organization was involved in a clandestine operation which culminated in an officer employed by the Denver Police Department discharging a weapon and wounding a man, something that has never been reported to the police."

Oh dear. That probably wasn't good, and it was probably worse Preston knew about it.

I powered through my worry and again demanded, "Get out of my house."

"His employer is on retainer with Marcus Sloan. Shady dealings with a man who is not shady but entirely criminal, running guns and peddling flesh."

Yikes again!

Marcus ran guns and peddled flesh?

Whoa.

Preston wasn't done. "And the wife of one of his co-workers filed fraudulent reports with Child Protective Services in order to place two runaways with a known felon."

Well, at least I knew about that one.

I quit repeating myself and just glared at him.

Preston held my glare and stated, "Routinely, a man in Liam Nightingale's employ performs illegal hacks, not only on private accounts but also on local, state and federal government sites."

I wasn't a computer person so I thought that was actually kind of cool.

Obviously I didn't share that.

Then, softly, he said, "The man you cling to so desperately has taken lives."

My glare intensified.

I was hardly clinging to Mace *desperately*. Lovingly, definitely. Supportively, sure. Desperately, *no*.

"Many of them," Preston whispered.

He fell silent so I asked, "Are you done?"

"No," he replied and looked at Mace. "Your play, son, is to speak to Nightingale, tell him to agree to my investment. I obtain controlling interest in Nightingale Investigations. I clean up the cesspool that is your business, take out the trash, including Darius Tucker, Vance Crowe, Lucas Stark and that hideous receptionist, all of whom, due to their past activities and associations, leave much to be desired. You'll keep your job because, clearly," he threw out a hand again, "your woman cannot provide for you if you should need to get back on your feet, which you will, considering the fact you just gave six thousand dollars to her family, which significantly depleted your reserve. Nightingale steps aside and I call the shots."

Uh-oh.

I felt my body get tight.

Mace spoke.

"You're saying you'll leak this information if I don't do as you say."

Preston nodded. "Chavez will lose his job and he'll not find one on my payroll when I take over Nightingale Investigations. He might even face charges. Shirleen Jackson will lose custodial care and those boys will either go back to the streets or into the system. Juliet Crowe will also find herself unemployed.

Brody Dunne and Lee Nightingale will likely be questioned and possibly arrested for their activities—"

Mace cut him off, "That all you got?"

I felt my body jerk, seeing as I thought all this sounded pretty bad. I looked up at Mace to see his face was bland, almost uninterested, as if this information wasn't damning and more than a little scary. But instead, Preston was telling him that he knew Lee and his boys had trampled a few flowers in a public garden for shits and giggles.

"Kai—" Preston started, but Mace didn't let him get any further.

"First, you should know that Stella's place is wired, cameras with microphones. Your blackmail attempt was caught on tape."

Preston's body gave a small start, almost imperceptible, but I caught it and I also held my breath.

"I—" Preston began again, but Mace's head turned away from him, the movement so sudden, Preston stopped speaking.

Mace looked at something across the room. What, I didn't know, then he looked back at his father.

"Cameras are off now, Dad," he said quietly and I again tensed. "Now, it's just you and me and this is what I got."

Oh man.

I figured what Mace had was probably a lot so I settled in, but I did it while I braced.

"Brody's good, you know that so you shoulda been a lot smarter." Mace was still talking quietly. I was thinking his quiet was not an indication he felt he had the situation under control, but instead an indication that he was close to losing his mind at having to deal with this bullshit, or his father at all, and I bit my lip. "You know I know you fucked up. You know I know what you did that got Caitlin killed. You *fuckin'* know."

"I didn't do a thing to—"

Mace interrupted, "Oh yeah you did."

"Not one thing, Kai," Preston clipped.

"Arms, Dad," Mace returned.

Oh man.

Arms?

As in weapons?

What the ef?

"There's not a shred of evidence to support that," Preston retorted swiftly, now also talking quietly, but his face had shifted, gone more vigilant, surprisingly giving it all away.

"There isn't?" Mace asked, and I watched Preston's body straighten.

Mace kept going.

"What you don't know is that we know that you haven't stopped what you were doin' to get Caitlin killed."

"Kai—"

"Government contracts you got for your munitions plants, Dad. Probably the Feds won't be real thrilled to know your guns that are supposed to be in the hands of our boys in uniform are also finding themselves in the hands of not only enemy factions, but seven terrorist sects."

Oh my God!

"APM Holdings have absolutely no dealings in munitions," Preston replied.

"You're right," Mace agreed then disagreed, "But *you* do."

Oh. My. *God!*

"Nonsense," Preston returned.

Mace studied his father. He did this for several long beats. I waited while consciously breathing because I knew something had changed, something was not right, my man was struggling.

Then I knew why when he whispered, "They blew her head off."

I pressed closer to Mace and held on harder.

Preston paled, but his eyes narrowed before he replied, "And whose fault was that?"

At that, Mace leaned forward and exploded, "*They blew her fuckin' head off!*"

The hand I had at Mace's abs slid around so I was holding him close with both arms.

Preston leaned forward too and hit back, "You never should have—"

"Given a shit about Tiny?" Mace returned. "Is that what I shouldn't have done? Because, Dad, I was willin' to go down for her, and I almost did. You didn't do shit and you were the reason she endured that fuckin' nightmare before they blew her head off and you didn't do *shit*. Except, of course, after they ended her life, you gave in and started trading arms with them again, so the next time it wouldn't be you direct they played with."

Things had degenerated to a place I did not want Mace to go, therefore I decided to intervene and I did this by declaring, "I think we're at a stalemate, boys. Why don't you retreat to your corners—?"

"Mouth shut," Preston ground out, eyes cutting to me. "This is none of your concern."

That was when, no matter how hard I was holding onto him, I lost hold on Mace as he moved, swiftly and purposefully, tearing out of my arms and closing the distance between him and his father. He was three inches taller and several decades younger, but he got toe-to-toe and bent his head to get nose-to-nose with him before he commenced in delivering the death blow.

"I warned you, now I'm tellin' you. Do not *ever* fuckin' speak to my woman again. I don't give a shit what comes out of your mouth, never again. I don't even like you lookin' at her. You never speak to her or my retribution will be physical. Hear me and believe me, I am *not* joking."

Preston drew in a swift breath, because even an arrogant, thinks-his-shit-doesn't-stink dick like Preston could see that Mace was definitely not joking, but Mace was far from done.

"You are dead to me. You treated me like shit, Mom like shit, Chloe like shit and *Caitlin* like shit, and you got her dead. You know it. I've been itchin' to let loose the shit I got on you, itchin' to do it for... fuckin'... *years*. I got a new family now and you think you can fuck with them, piss in your goddamned corner, prove you're the man with the biggest dick by playin' with them, think fuckin' again. I will bring you down and I'll smile doin' it. I know you found out where your guns were goin', you found out your partner was fuckin' you, you put a stop to it and the men who were gettin' those guns didn't like it. They pushed, you pushed back, but you didn't do it smart. Thought your fuckin' money made you untouchable, but you... were... *wrong*. You had no clue what you were dealin' with and weren't smart enough to learn. They pushed harder, took Caitlin and you let her swing in the wind for *your* fuck up. There are so many reasons you're a piece of shit, it'd take me a decade to count them down. But from this point on, your shit does not encroach in my life. Not again. You took my sister, and every fuckin' day I think of her and my mind bleeds for your fuck up. That's *all* the shit you get to shove at me, but that's fuckin' more than enough."

435

Preston had straightened his spine to face down his son and when Mace was done talking, he shot back, "You have no evidence to support those accusations, Kai."

"You wanna try me?" Mace returned.

"That evidence doesn't exist," Preston replied.

"The only proof I'll give you that it does is to feed it to the media, Dad. There is no show and tell with this shit. You do not back down and slink away, I'll bring you down. You try to fuck with Eddie, Shirleen, Lee, any of them, I fuckin' promise you, you'll have an indeterminate stay at some government facility no one even fuckin' knows exists, courtesy of me. And trust me, post-9/11, the people who're gettin' your guns, the Feds don't care how much money you got. That's a good deal, Dad, 'cause just thinkin' about you or thinkin' about Tiny and what you did to her makes me lose hold on the control that keeps me from exposing you for the total, stinking piece of shit you are and always have been. And I think about Tiny all the time. Every day, every hour, every minute she's in my head, beautiful and whole, then thin, broken and terrified and finally very fuckin' *dead*."

"You have no evidence," Preston persisted, his face beginning to get red.

"You believe that, call my bluff," Mace invited.

"Your friends are on the line, Kai," Preston reminded him.

"You think you got us by the balls, call... my... *bluff*," Mace bit off.

Preston glared at him.

Mace glared back.

Personally, if you asked me, I thought Mace's glare was a lot better.

This went on a long time, too, but I didn't try to intervene and even Juno sensed she had to let this play out, so, along with me, she remained silent.

Finally and suddenly, with some surprise, I watched Preston Mason's face twist and he whispered so low it was nearly inaudible, "I had no idea Caitlin—"

But Mace didn't let him finish.

"I know you didn't, which makes your monumental fuck up a colossal fuck up because even after you fucked up, you fucked up again with those god-damned commandos, then again when you didn't come clean to the FBI and work with them to find a way to get her out of that fuckin' mess. Then *again* when you let me walk in there and watch my sister die."

"Kai, I had no—" Preston started again.

"You think I give a fuck?" Mace whispered and the tortured way those words came out made my stomach clench and even Preston flinched. "Honest to God, you think I give a fuck about anything that has anything to do with you? They tortured her, Dad. They cut off her fuckin' hand then they took her fuckin' life and all that is on *you*. This is not a fuck up like you grounded her for too long because she missed curfew and she's pissed like any teenager would be pissed because their Dad is an asshole, *for fuck's sake*."

Mace spit the last three words out and kept going.

"You fucked up and her life ended. Even after it was done, I cleaned up your goddamned mess and kept my mouth shut. Way I see it, you owe me. You owe me huge. You owe me a fuckin' sister and there's no way to repay that so I'm tellin' you now, you repay by getting the fuck *out* of my life and *staying* out."

Preston held his son's eyes.

Then, because he was a dick, he kept trying.

"Every day, I think of her and—"

Mace took a step back, most likely to retain a shred of control even as he lost it and roared, "*Fuck! I do not give a fuck!*"

That was when Juno woofed, but her woof was not a woof of solidarity with Mace. It was a different kind of woof. It was the kind of woof that made Mace's head whip toward her, so my head whipped toward her and I saw she was on all four paws on the bed, staring at the wall.

She woofed again as she jumped off the bed. Then she didn't woof but barked, straight out, sharp, agitated. A warning. She immediately started dancing along the wall, sniffing, restless then more barking.

"Goddamn it," Mace clipped, reaching into the jacket of his tux to pull out his phone, but it started ringing before he got to it as did the phone in my house. "*Goddamn it!*" Mace barked then shouted. "Get down!" When both Preston and I hesitated a millisecond, he roared, "*Down!*"

On his word, the windows exploded. I hit the deck and I hit the deck with Mace's body on top of me.

"*Juno! Come!*" Mace shouted.

I tried to look, but he had an arm over my head, his body covering me as gunfire sounded from what seemed like all around, piercing my eardrums.

"Talk," I heard Mace growl, probably into his phone then, "No shit? You hear that. We're under heavy fire. Units. Every available man. Now."

I heard the flip of a phone closing just as the gunfire stopped, and I felt the fur of Juno pressing to my arm.

Thank God, she was close.

I thought that then thought no more. Mace was up and he was hauling me up with him.

"Move," he ordered when he had me on my feet, but he didn't need to, he had my hand and he was dragging me to the door. "Come!" he commanded Juno, but he didn't need to do that, either, because she was right at our sides, crowding us.

That was when I heard several very scary noises, noises the like I only ever heard in movies. I stupidly stopped, turned my head and saw them.

I saw them.

Mace didn't stop. He didn't even hesitate. I knew he heard it, too, and I knew he knew what they were without looking at them. I knew this because he went faster, as in *a lot* faster, as in *running* faster and my feet had to move again or he would literally be dragging me.

But I saw them.

I saw them

Grenades.

Not one.

Three.

Three!

I realized then that they blew out my windows at an impossible angle if they were firing from the ground, or they did it from higher ground but at a distance, only so they could launch the grenades in and blow us to bits.

Shit.

Shit!

We were out the door on a run and sprinting down the stairs, Juno at our sides, Preston following close. When we hit the first landing, multiple explosions rocked my apartment and tossed us as they blew out the wall above our heads. We flew to the side. Mace slammed into the wall and I slammed into him while plaster, wood splinters and probably bits and pieces of my possessions shot over our heads and rained down on us.

It took Mace a nanosecond to recover before he was dragging me down the next flight of stairs, this time tucked close to him, his arms crossed and covering my head.

We hit the second floor landing when he stopped us and shoved his phone in my hand just as he reached into his jacket at his waist and around his back where I knew he had a holster. I heard the click of him releasing the strap and he came out with a gun.

"Call back last call in my call history. That's the control room. They gotta have a status update. Give it," he ordered, then his eyes slid to his father and he went on talking as I flipped open his phone and shakily found his recents screen. "Stay here with Stella. Do not move unless I tell you to."

I looked up to see Preston getting close to me. I looked to Mace to see him moving cautiously toward the mouth of the flight of stairs that led to the first floor.

He didn't move cautiously back. He jerked back as gunshots went up the stairs, bullets embedding in the ceiling. I swallowed a scream, and to stop my instinct to throw myself at my man, I pressed into the wall. Preston pressed into me. Juno pressed into me. Mace ran to a door, tried the handle. He found it locked, took a step back and slammed forward using his shoulder and the door blew open.

His eyes sliced to me. "Follow me, Kitten, at my back. Close. Now."

I moved, got close to his back feeling Juno's fur brush my bare legs as I did, as well as feeling Preston keeping close.

Mace moved and we all moved into the second floor hall. Mace shifted and we all shifted. Mace pushed the broken door to, pulled a narrow table from the side wall until it was blocking the door and he shifted again, moving down the hall, quickly but stealthily, head up and sweeping side to side.

We all moved with him.

I kept close to his back, my fingers shoving up under his jacket to curl into the waistband of his trousers and I looked back at the phone. I hit go on the last call and put it to my ear.

It didn't even ring before it was answered.

There was no greeting, just a barked, "Status."

"Um... hi," I said. "This is Stella."

"Right, Stella, status," the man's voice replied, not a bark this time but still sharp, urgent.

I thought it was Monty, but I wasn't sure and didn't give it headspace at the time because Mace moved us toward a wall, stopped and was doing hand motions to his father. I felt Preston's fingers curl around my arm as I felt Mace's fingers curl around my wrist to detach my hand on his slacks. He stared into my eyes a beat before he turned and moved back where we came.

Oh man.

I got down to business and said into the phone, "Okay, multiple grenades just blew up my apartment. We're cut off at the backstairs. We're in the hall on the second floor and Mace is going back toward the backstairs."

"Stop him."

Shitsofuckit!

"Mace, stop," I called, quiet and quick. "Monty says stop."

Mace stopped, twisted and looked at me.

"More," I said into the phone.

Monty didn't hesitate. "You're surrounded. All exits cut off. They've disabled the outside cameras. We tried to turn on the inside cameras, but they're off-line. Before they got to the cameras, we saw at least six of them approach and breach the house. They're inside. First unit to the scene, ETA, five minutes. Mace needs to hole you in until backup arrives. Out."

Without delay I relayed this information to Mace. "Surrounded. No exit. Outside cameras disabled. Inside off-line. At least six men inside. Backup five minutes. Monty says we need to hole up."

Mace started moving back just as more bullets tore through the door we just went through.

When this happened, I didn't think. I'd been shot at a lot recently and been caught unaware and therefore didn't respond appropriately.

Not this time.

This time I dashed to the next door off the hall, opened it and raced in. Juno came with me. So did Preston. Mace followed and slammed the door, locked it and then turned to his father.

"Move this shit," he ordered, circling his hand around in the air. Preston nodded and immediately father and son started moving jumbles of furniture in front of the door.

I slunk to the back of the room with Juno, crouched low, knees to chest and went back to Monty.

"We're in, I think, the third room down to the left coming down the hall from the back. They're on our floor."

"Hang tight," Monty advised.

Right. Hang tight. Great. Good advice.

Effing hell.

"Roger that, hanging tight," I whispered, deciding against doing this with sarcasm as Mace shoved a huge, old rickety wardrobe in front of a dresser his father had shoved in front of the door.

I stared at the furniture noting that unfortunately none of it was made of steel.

Effing, effing, hell, hell, *hell*.

"Stella, a squad is three minutes out. Another unit two minutes behind them. Luke one minute behind them. You're good," Monty assured.

Gunfire exploded, loud and terrifying, bullets thudding in and *through* the furniture in front of the door. I went down to a hip and thigh, my arm with the hand not holding the phone shot out, curled around my dog and I pulled us both down so far my forehead was resting on the dusty floor.

The gunfire kept sounding, hideous, excruciatingly loud. I felt my lungs seize, my breath evaporating. Not on a joyride, beaming to a different galaxy in order to get the eff out of Dodge even as I felt Mace crouch low beside me.

We were good.

Right.

Not even close.

More gunfire, but this was Mace returning fire, probably warning shots to let them know he was armed. He only shot twice, but the gunfire outside ceased.

I sucked in breath.

"Two and a half minutes, Stella," Monty said in my ear.

"I'm movin'," Mace whispered to me. My heart froze, my neck twisted, my eyes shifted to his hard, determined face and my breath disintegrated again.

It came back in a fiery rush and I whispered frantically, "No. They're two and a half minutes out."

"Babe, these guys are not stupid, but they are desperate. They'll aim low or kick in. They got no time, they know it, and they got six men. We got one with one gun. We don't have two and a half minutes."

My hand went from Juno, shot out and I grasped the material of the arm of his tux. "No," I pleaded.

"Stay low," he returned.

"No," I whispered, not to his order but to his going.

He didn't listen. He jerked his arm free and his eyes shifted to his father.

"She's in your care," he whispered. The words held weight; they had meaning no one could miss, then he moved. Crouched low, he went to the side wall then around the furniture and I lost sight of him.

"Oh my God, Monty," I whispered into the phone. "Mace is on the move."

"Fuckin' fuck, fuck, *fuck*. Maverick. *Fuck!*" Monty clipped in my ear.

I didn't feel particularly soothed by this reaction and because of that I felt tears well in my eyes. I felt Preston close and heard Juno whine. I looked to my dog to see her low on her belly but her eyes were aimed at where Mace disappeared.

My dog loved my man.

I loved my man.

And he was going to keep me safe.

Or die doing it.

Oh God.

"Monty," I breathed, my breath now coming fast, in pants, more adrenalin tearing through me. So much, I was tingling from head-to-toe. So much, I could feel it saturating my system. I was drowning in it.

"He's good, Stella, he knows what he's doin' and he's been in worse spots than this," Monty told me.

This was not exactly welcome information. It was actually scary information, but nowhere near scarier than my current scary situation so I let it slide.

Then I thought no more when the sound of more gunfire filled the air, but through this I heard furniture move (no joke!) and a door open (oh God!) then a grunt, a shout, more gunfire, more gunfire, still more gunfire, another grunt, a thud, a man's scream, more gunfire, another thud, another man's shout, the sickening sound of bone breaking, a man's strangled cry, more gunfire...

Then silence.

I held my breath, eyes on my dog, Juno's eyes not having moved from the spot where she last saw Mace.

"Stella?" Monty called in the phone.

My head turned and my gaze shifted, catching Preston's. He was on his knees, bent forward, torso twisted my way, his body mostly shielding mine from the door. His eyes were on me and I saw it, clear as day; fear was written all over his face, and not the kind of fear a man feels when his life was in imminent danger. The kind of fear a man feels when his mind is consumed with the possibility that another one of his children had been struck low.

Even considering the terror I felt, which took most of my attention, it was still difficult to witness.

"Stella?" Monty's voice was sharp in my ear.

"Monty," I whispered back, having nothing else to say. Holding Preston's gaze, reading his look, knowing I was wearing the same terror with only a nuance of difference on my face.

"Please, God, not again," Preston breathed. My heart twisted. It hurt like a mother, then we heard footfalls.

We both jerked our heads toward them. My neck went way back and my eyes filled with wet that instantly spilled over when I saw Mace casually striding toward us.

His jacket was torn at the shoulder.

That was it.

Just his jacket was torn at his shoulder.

Lordy be.

I surged to my feet and rushed him. He took my full body impact without even going back on a foot as Juno woofed excitedly over and over again, and I felt her body brushing ours as she circled us. Mace's arm wound around my waist, going tight, and his other hand slid the phone out of mine.

I shoved my face in his chest, pressing close, deep, hard, holding him tight and bawling like a baby as I heard him say into the phone, "Current threat neutralized."

For some bizarre, insane reason which likely had a lot to do with the fact that I was temporarily unhinged due to the extreme relief washing through my system, his words made me laugh through my tears, still burrowing, his arm getting tighter as I did so.

That was when I heard the sirens.

Okay, now I believed we were good.

But only because my man made us that way.

On that thought, I stopped laughing, gulped back a sob and more tears flowed.

━━━

I stood outside at the edge of the activity, still wearing my heels. My feet were killing me, as was the gunshot graze at my hip which I'd landed on when

I went down on it in that room. It hadn't really hurt for days, just itched. Now it hurt.

I had a blanket wrapped around me, a blanket Mace had wrapped around me, and this was because even though it was summer and still warm, it was late at night and I was trembling, and not because it was late at night.

Juno was sitting at my side, her big body leaning into my legs, her eyes riveted to Mace, who was standing fifteen feet away where he had walked not thirty seconds ago to talk to Eddie and Hank.

My eyes were riveted anywhere but at the body that was on the ground, under a sheet, next to Preston's limousine.

His driver had been taken out. One minute, innocently chauffeuring a rich guy (or whatever), the next minute, dead.

I couldn't deal with that so I was ignoring it.

The place was crawling with cops, squad cars, forensic personnel, paramedics, ambulances. Big lights had been set up and trained around the space so they could see what they were doing. And, lastly, there were Nightingale men.

In fact, the only Nightingale man not there was *the* Nightingale, Lee, who I was told briefly by Mace was not let in on this fiasco seeing as it was his wedding night.

After Mace imparted this information on me, Luke had noted that Lee would likely be displeased about being kept in the dark.

I had noted, but silently, that Lee *and* Indy would likely be more displeased at having their big, happy day and its culminating, arguably happier festivities interrupted by mayhem.

If the guys took shit from Lee, they did. Luckily, they were badasses, so even though Lee was also a badass, I doubted they'd have difficulty dealing.

There were bystanders and media at the edge of the property, cops and police tape holding them back.

I was counting as the stretchers came out of the building.

Two men fully covered.

Dead.

Four men still alive, but even from a distance seriously not in good shape.

Mace didn't fuck around.

This would probably fascinate anyone else; how he did it, how he pulled that off. Holed in a room one second, one against six armed men the next and besting the lot.

Not me. I didn't want to know and I was never, *ever* going to ask.

Mace was breathing. I was breathing. My dog was breathing.

That was good enough for me.

The good news was this was the last hurrah. I knew this because Luke told Mace while he was holding me close, his hands running soothingly up and down my back as Luke gave his briefing.

The six men Mace neutralized were the final six men in Sidney Carter's army. Sidney was still unaccounted for, but his operation was fully dismantled. He had no more soldiers. They were still looking, but they suspected once he heard that this last mission was not successful, he would cut and run. They were covering trains, airports, bus depots and the Highway Patrol was on alert. They'd even contacted Border Control.

I was not really processing this information. I was concentrating on my teeth not chattering.

This was what I was concentrating on when I caught movement out of the side of my eye. My head turned and my mind was not switched on enough to react to seeing Preston Mason suddenly, for some reason, sprinting my way.

The only thing I thought was, he wasn't exactly young but the guy could still move.

Then I heard him shout, "*Sniper!*"

At his shout, the air went thick and electric. My body twitched first then instantly jerked to the side in preparation to run (again), and the second it did I heard the whiz and thud as a bullet slammed into the dirt just beyond me.

I was tackled from behind as I heard a second hiss split the air. I hit the soft, thick grass in Swen and Ulrika's side yard with a painful thud that was made more painful by the weight that landed on me, and Juno barked.

I lay there, face down, and whoever was on me didn't move.

There was rushing all around me. I twisted my neck and saw men running and one of those men was Mace.

But he was running somewhere else.

I had no chance to react to this as I felt Juno's nose snuffling around my neck and hair and felt my body being crushed by the one on me. I tried but failed to heave the weight off and saw the hems of uniform pants and shiny policemen shoes, and the weight on me was rolled off. I rolled with it, to the other side, and instantly saw Preston lying on his back beside me, a cop on his knees by him, carefully rolling him back to his belly and shouting, "*Medic!*"

Medic.

Oh God.

Medic.

He'd been hit!

Someone tried to pull me up, but I yanked my arm away and got back on my belly, flat, pressed to the ground. Even my cheek was in the grass, my face super close to Preston's, my eyes locked to his pained ones.

"You with me?" I whispered.

Hands were at my back but I ignored them. Preston stared at me as I heard more running feet and bodies landing on their knees around Preston.

My hand darted out and caught his, my fingers curling around.

"Preston, stick with me," I urged, my fingers squeezing.

"*Gurney!*" I heard shouted.

Preston blinked.

I scooted closer and held his hand tighter.

"Hang on," I whispered.

I watched his eyelids lower a millimeter and his mouth went slack.

And I knew.

I knew.

I knew. I knew. *I knew.*

"*Hang on!*" I shrieked, then I was up, arms tight around me, one at my chest, one at my belly and I struggled against the hold as they lifted Preston lifeless body onto a gurney. "*Hang on!*" I screeched.

They strapped him in.

"*Hang on!*" I screamed.

They pulled the gurney up to its full height and wasted not a second in rushing it in a roll across the lawn, the drive and into the ambulance.

"Please hang on," I whispered.

The fight left me, oozing out, and my body went slack in the arms surrounding me.

When it did, those arms turned me. I looked up at Willie Moses just as his hand curled around the back of my head and he shoved my face in his throat.

I again burst into tears, my legs collapsing from under me as the weight of knowing a man might have lost his life to save mine settled on me, the weight heavy, crushing, and Willie's arms got tighter.

"Find Mace." I felt as well as heard Willie order. "Now." Then, into the top of my hair, he whispered, "Hang on, honey."

I felt Juno's body press against the side of my legs and somehow found the strength to lift up my hands, curl them in Willie's shirt and hang on.

⌖

Mace

Mace slid the dark, heavy hair off Stella's neck, eyes locked to her sleeping profile.

He pulled in breath.

Then his hand moved from his woman to her dog. He slid his fingers through the fur on Juno's head and he whispered, "Stay with her."

Juno blinked up at him then shuffled on her belly closer to Stella.

Mace straightened from sitting on the side of the bed in one of Daisy's guest rooms. He switched out the light and walked out the door.

He was nearly to the stairs when Daisy made it up them.

She stopped, as did he.

Her blue eyes captured his, her head tipped to the side then her hand came up. She rested it gently on his jaw and pressed lightly as her eyes held his. She let them and her hand communicate for her.

Her hand and her eyes had a lot to say; they didn't waste time, and all of it was beautiful.

She dropped her hand and whispered, "Your Momma and Chloe are in the great room."

Without waiting for a response, she skirted him and walked down the hall without looking back.

Mace watched her while he thought, not for the first time, that Daisy Sloan was a good woman.

He walked down to Daisy and Marcus's great room where Chloe was sitting on a sofa staring vacantly into the dark, unlit fireplace, and his Mom was standing at a window staring vacantly into the dark night. They were in their own thoughts; not pleasant ones, as they wouldn't be. An attraction, a bad decision, giving their heart to the wrong man, and then no end to heartache.

Now, closure. But not the right kind.

The instant he entered, Chloe's neck twisted, her eyes shot to him and she asked, "How is she?"

His Mom turned from the window as Mace answered, "Out."

"She take the pills?" Lana asked.

Mace nodded, stopped and sat on the armrest of the couch.

He was wiped, fucking shattered. He felt like he could sleep for a god-damned week. He not only felt like it, he wanted to do it.

But he wanted to do it somewhere where there was a beach right outside his room, Stella in his bed and no one around for miles.

Lana moved toward him saying, "She'll be okay, sweetie."

Mace knew that. He knew it.

He knew it because if Stella didn't wake up that way, he'd make her that way even if it took a lifetime.

Lana stopped two feet in front of him and looked down at him.

Softly, she asked, "Okay, now, are *you* okay?"

"He died for her," Mace replied bluntly, and Lana drew in breath through her nose as he felt Chloe tense down the couch from him.

"Why the fuck would he throw himself in front of a bullet to save Stella and he wouldn't—?" Mace started and Lana moved.

Closing the distance between him, her palm came to his cheek, fingers curled around his jaw forcing his face to look up at hers.

Jesus, he missed her touch.

Jesus.

He should have fucking remembered his Mom could soothe a hurt just with her touch.

He didn't remember.

Jesus.

"You'll never find answers to your questions, Kai," she said softly, and it hit him, not for the first time in the last few days, how fucking much he also missed her voice. She could soothe with that, too. Effortlessly. "So please, sweetie, *please,* right now, with me and Chloe, let them go. He did what he did and it's done. Your beautiful girl is upstairs sleeping. You caught that Carter man, and even if he wasn't going down before, you caught him with his rifle so he'll go down for what he did to your father. It's done. Your father is gone, but his death is avenged. Life goes on. Live it. Enjoy every minute of it and let this go."

The minute his father shouted "sniper", Mace knew just how desperate Carter was, not for freedom, for vengeance.

Sidney Carter was a trained sniper. The first Iraq war. It wasn't something they didn't know. He'd just stopped doing his own dirty work a decade before.

Instead of going down like a man, he decided to do his own dirty work, the stupid, sick, demented fucking *fuck*.

But what his mother said was true. Carter was already going down, but now there was no way Carter wouldn't stay down.

Mace thought his thoughts, drew in breath. He stared into his mother's eyes, and not for the first time in the last few days or in the last seven years, he realized how much he missed them. As he did this, he felt his hand taken in Chloe's.

Lana's hand dropped to his shoulder as he looked to Chloe.

"We love her," Chloe whispered, changing the subject to Stella. "She's perfect for you."

She was not wrong.

"Totally," Lana muttered, and Mace looked back up at his Mom.

"She's beautiful. She's talented," Chloe went on, and Mace turned his gaze to her to see her face soft. "And she looks at you like you turn on the sun in the morning and switch it off at night."

"Totally," Lana repeated on another mutter, and Mace felt his lips twitch.

"Tiny would absolutely *adore* her," Chloe went on. Mace's lips stopped twitching and Mace saw her turn to Lana. "Wouldn't she, honey?"

"Oh yeah, heck yeah," Lana answered, and Mace's eyes went back to his Mom just in time to watch her say, "Tiny thought you turned on the sun in the morning and switched it off at night, too. She'd definitely adore Stella. Two peas in a pod, the way they love you. Two peas in a pod."

Mace sucked in breath. He did this to fight the burn that threatened to consume his chest.

He could control it, had been for years. It was only recently when he started to believe he could beat it, move past it and maybe find a life where his memories focused more on his sister's grace, her smile, her giggles, her easy affection and less on watching her life end way too fucking soon.

That was because only recently he'd finally come to understand that he wouldn't be able to accomplish that alone.

Luckily, he'd also recently come to understand he was far from alone.

Mace stood and both women disengaged from him, Lana taking a step back.

Then he muttered, "Wiped," and moved to his mother. He wrapped his hand around the back of her head and pulled her to him as he bent to touch his lips to her forehead. There he whispered, "Missed your voice, your eyes, your touch, even your smell."

Mace heard her draw in a sharp breath. Her hands went to his waist, fingers digging in, but she didn't say a word and he said no more. He also didn't move. Not for a while. He breathed her in, felt her touch and let it heal.

He should have remembered.

He didn't.

Now he did.

Thank Christ.

He kissed her forehead and pulled away. She let him go. Feeling his mother's gaze soft on him, he turned to Chloe. Ignoring the tears shimmering in her eyes, he bent and did the same, but saying nothing, just touching his lips to her forehead and pulling back.

She sniffled.

He looked between them and muttered, "See you in the morning. We'll all go out and have breakfast," he paused then finished, "If Daisy lets us."

"Right," Lana agreed, her voice husky.

"Oh… okay," Chloe stammered, her voice trembling.

Mace started to move from the room, but stopped at the door and looked back. Then he smiled at his "Moms".

They smiled back.

He walked out of the room and back up the stairs.

In the darkened room he was sharing with Stella, he silently accepted Juno's soft, welcome back woof. He took off his clothes, stood by the side of the bed and repeated the actions he'd done once that day. He lifted his arms, undid the chain at his neck, brought it down, upended it and Tiny's ring Indy had returned to him with a kiss to his cheek before getting into Lee's Crossfire at the end of her wedding night dropped into his hand. He set the chain on the nightstand, pulled back the covers and slid in behind Stella.

His arms moved around her heavy, sleeping body. His fingers found her right hand, and he lifted it and slid Tiny's ring on her pinkie.

When he did, she moved, nuzzling back into him and muttering groggily, "Grenades. Jeez, babe. Swen and Ulrika are gonna be pissed."

Then her body settled and Mace knew she was again asleep.

He lay in the dark listening to her breathe.

It was the most beautiful sound he ever heard.

Then her words hit him.

And he couldn't help it. His arms closed tight around her. He buried his face in her hair, smelled mint, decided he seriously fucking loved that smell and he burst out laughing.

⌁

Stella

I woke and blinked at the tight hold of the arms around me and the sound of Mace laughing into the back of my hair.

That's weird, has he cracked up? My brain asked me.

I listened to his laugh, felt his warm strength curled all around me and considered this for a millisecond.

Then I decided if my man had gone insane and Mace's brand of insanity meant he was holding me close and laughing, I didn't give an eff.

And on that thought, I went back to sleep.

Chapter Twenty-Nine

Rock Chick

Jane

One week later...

Jane slid through the shelves of Fortnum's unnoticed by customers. Then she slid behind the front counter unnoticed by Rock Chicks, unnoticed by Hot Bunch, unnoticed by Tex and by Duke.

"It has to be *somebody*," Ally stated, and Jane looked to the couch faced by two armchairs, all of which sat in front of the huge front window.

Mace was sitting on the arm of the couch, Stella held close in front of him between his legs. Daisy and Shirleen were in the sofa. Hector was seated on the other arm of the sofa, unlike Mace, who had one foot in the sofa seat, one on the floor. Hector had both feet on the floor, his back slightly to the couch, slightly removed.

His mind was somewhere else.

Jane briefly wondered where it was.

Then her eyes moved to Ally, who was in one of the armchairs across from the couch. Stevie was in the other one, his dog Chowleena on her belly beside his chair taking a snooze.

Tod was on a flight. Seeing as he was a flight attendant, that frequently happened, which meant he often missed the action. This annoyed him, and he let this be known as only Tod could do. Then again, he had drag queen outfits to buy and someone had to pay for them so off he went, grumbling and/or throwing attitude all the way.

Jane found this amusing.

Then again, Jane found a lot that happened in Fortnum's amusing.

Her eyes moved again and she saw Roam and Sniff sitting at a table, coffee cups in front of them. Roam was lounged back, one long leg bent, foot to floor, one long leg stretched out. He had his phone to his ear. Sniff was sitting across from him, shoving the contents of the bag of fast food he'd brought with him into his mouth.

Three girls around Roam's age were at an arrangement of chairs two tables away from him. All of the girls had been in before. All of them frequently. All of them were now staring at Roam, which was what they did if they were lucky enough to time their visit when he was hanging. And all of them were doing it in a way that it was clear they wished it was the other way around.

Jane knew why. When she first saw Roam some months ago, she thought you had to be blind not to see the promise of good looks. They were stamped on him. In just months, this had grown with his confidence. The bulking out of his body along with his understanding of what it could do, his quick and acute awareness of his surroundings, his alert eyes that held a wealth of experience far beyond his age, and just simply the fact that he was maturing into his features.

It was plain to see he was going to be beautiful mostly because he was nearly there now.

It was also plain to see he was following close in the footsteps of his Hot Bunch mentors. Jane knew this because he was oblivious to the looks he was getting. Completely.

The girl who caught Roam's eye and held it would not look. She would do the opposite and he would thrill to the chase.

It was just the way of the Hot Bunch.

They didn't do easy.

Well, that wasn't true. They did a lot of easy. They just didn't install it in their bed for a lifetime.

Jane's eyes continued to move and she saw Tex and Duke behind the espresso counter, bickering. About what, Jane couldn't hear at that moment, but with practice, eyeing them for a moment, she knew everyone would hear it in approximately two point seven five minutes.

Jane continued to scan and she saw Eddie standing at the end of the espresso counter, Jet in his arms. Jane couldn't see Jet's face and only could see Eddie's profile. His head was bent and he was whispering in her ear. As he did, Jane watched observantly and noted Jet pressed closer, then closer.

And Jane knew, for Eddie and Jet, the world had ceased to exist. There was Eddie and all there was for him was Jet. Then there was Jet and all there was for her was Eddie.

Jane decided in that second that Eddie and Jet were going to be her favorites for the day. She changed them every day depending on what she witnessed. Sometimes it was Lee and Indy. Other times, Hank and Roxie. Others, Jules and Vance or Luke and Ava, and now Mace and Stella.

Today it was Jet and Eddie.

Jane's eyes moved from them back to the couch. They fell on Stella and Mace and she instantly changed her mind.

Stella was leaned into Mace, her arms wrapped around the one he had at her stomach. Her head had fallen back on his shoulder, turned slightly so her temple was pressed to the side of his throat.

Jane studied them.

Mace looked content.

Stella looked well beyond that.

This would be surprising for normal folk, considering a week ago Stella's apartment and most of her belongings had been blown to smithereens and Mace's Dad lost his life to save Stella's.

Then again, the two things most important in her life, both of which breathed, weren't blown to bits, so with the Rock Chicks at her back (*sans* Indy, who was still in Barbados on her honeymoon and would be for another week), Stella did what she could with what was left and was now living with Mace at his house.

That was to say, she was doing this in the short-term, considering they were already searching for a new place and had arrived at Fortnum's thirty minutes ago after spending the morning viewing three properties.

No matter what, life for the Rock Chicks and Hot Bunch always just went on.

As for Preston Mason dying, Jane had listened (as she always listened, avidly) and she knew, although it wasn't nice to think, his life ending was not a big loss to the world. And she knew from experience that whatever Stella was enduring due to a man dying so she could live and Mace was enduring because he lost his father, they'd make it through, and they'd do it because they had each other.

Preston Mason bequeathed his vast holdings to his son.

His son had turned them over to his mother and stepmother. They were in turn making enormous donations to a variety of charities.

Most of them having to do with the arts.

And most of those having to do with giving underprivileged children opportunities to learn to dance.

Jane, still unnoticed, always unnoticed and liking it that way, continued to study them.

She had watched Kai Mason now for months and months. Jane had spent most of her life being quiet and watching. Therefore, she saw things others didn't. On the rare occasion, she had noted Mace showing humor. But that was rare.

For months and months she saw only pain in Kai "Mace" Mason.

Today she saw no pain.

This made her smile a little, unnoticed smile.

Her eyes dropped to Stella's hand, and at her distance, she could just barely make out the gold ring on Stella's pinkie finger.

Just the other day, she overheard Jet telling Jules that Stella never took that ring off.

Never.

Jane sighed.

So there it was. Stella and Mace were now her favorites for the day.

She wasn't fickle. No doubt Eddie or Jet would do something, and soon, to regain the title.

"Mystery for the ages," Stevie replied with unconcern to Ally, and Jane's eyes moved to him.

"I think not," Ally shot back. "It has to be part of the inner circle. No one knows all that shit. Someone spilled. And that is *way* uncool."

Jane didn't think so, but she wouldn't, considering she was the one who talked to the reporters, and Jane knew Ally was talking about whoever talked to the reporters. She knew this because Ally had been talking about it a lot.

She felt no guilt. Jet and Tex's tips had quadrupled. Tex had a nest egg, but Nancy was moving in with him the next week and she wasn't able to work but part-time, and not at a job that paid very much.

Further, Jet wanted a KitchenAid and she'd wanted one awhile.

So Jane got it for her, kind of.

Not to mention coffee sales had seen that increase, too, and even book sales.

Lee wasn't hurting for money.

Now Indy wasn't either.

No, Jane felt no guilt. None at all.

Anyway, it was a week ago and it had all already blown over.

All of it but the increase in customers.

So there.

"No one is copping to it, and in this crowd, someone did it, they'd cop to it or they'll *never* cop to it," Shirleen decreed, and Jane looked to her, thinking she was right.

Jane would *never* cop to it.

"We'll never know," Shirleen finished.

Hmm.

Jane didn't know if she was right about *that*.

"It's still uncool," Ally mumbled.

Whatever, Jane thought.

Without a word, but with a chin lift at Mace, Hector got up.

Jane tensed.

Then she watched as he moved toward the door, carrying his takeaway coffee cup.

Jane's hand darted to the drawer where they kept their purses. She opened it and nabbed hers, shut the drawer and scurried after him.

No one noticed her go.

Hector's Bronco pulled into a spot across from the art gallery in LoDo, or Lower Downtown Denver, and Jane pulled into a spot two car lengths down on the opposite side of the street.

Hector sat in his beat-up brown Bronco, head turned, eyes aimed into the art gallery.

He did this awhile.

Jane watched awhile.

Finally, Hector put his Bronco in gear, pulled out of the spot and drove away.

Jane switched off the ignition to her car, exited it, locked it, fed the meter and walked into the gallery.

When she did, she smiled.

A petite, curvy, very well-dressed, strikingly beautiful woman with a mass of golden-cream-strawberry blonde hair that was a riot of soft ringlets mixed with full waves that floated down her back and all around her exquisite face and shoulders was standing behind the counter.

She looked like a fairy princess.

Jane especially liked her hair. It was fabulous.

Jane suspected Hector Chavez liked her hair, too.

But he probably liked her curves better.

"Hello." Her soft voice sounded as her pretty eyes smiled.

Mm-hmm.

This was good.

Jane approved.

"Just looking," Jane muttered. The woman tilted her head welcomingly toward the gallery and Jane spent the next fifteen minutes pretending to look as she surreptitiously watched the blonde doing whatever she was doing behind her counter.

Then Jane bought three postcards that had prints on the front of art displayed in the gallery. Postcards she would never use.

After she did that, she left.

⚶

Jane waited for her computer to boot up as she turned on dim lighting around the room and lit a scented candle.

Cotton flower.

Pretty and soothing.

She sat at her desk, moved her mouse and opened her word processing program.

Then she centered the cursor, turned on bold, set the font size at eighteen and typed.

Rock Chick.

She hit control at the same time she hit return, starting a new page, changed the font size to fourteen and typed.

Chapter One.

She hit return, turned off bold, turned on italics and changed the font size to twelve and typed.

The Great Liam Chase.

Then her eyes went fuzzy and her memory was swamped with the image of Liam Nightingale embracing his very soon-to-be wife in her angelic wedding dress prior to being declared man and wife.

Jane smiled.

She was a romantic and she felt the world needed to learn about this love affair.

She felt this because it was beautiful.

They all were.

So Jane refocused on her monitor and started typing.

Epilogue
Get Out Here, Babe, I Wanna Kiss You
Ava

Five years later...

I was sitting, cross-legged, smack in the middle of Luke's and my big bed.

I could hear Shirleen downstairs, talking to Gracie while Shirleen (and Gracie) banged around the kitchen.

I told Shirleen that she should come with us tonight, but she wouldn't. She'd fashioned herself into the Rock Chick version of Auntie Mame and it was clear her favorite of the Rock Chick/Hot Bunch progeny was, by far and away, Gracie. If Luke and I came home to find Gracie and Shirleen spirited away in the night with a note explaining that Shirleen had kidnapped her and would never return, I wouldn't have been surprised. She loved that child nearly as much as Gracie's father and I did.

It was lucky for Gracie, Shirleen had a lot of love to give, and I was happy she wanted to give it to my daughter.

The shower turned off and my attention went to the door of the bathroom.

Within minutes, the door opened and Luke was there.

He was clean shaven, and his hair, worn much longer now than the way he used to wear it when we first got together (that was to say it was thick, wavy and *lush*), was wet. He'd long since shaved off the killer mustache he used to have, much to my despair. But with the time he spent with me and Gracie and at Nightingale Investigations (not to mention spending time at our cabin in Crested Butte, where, if we were there very long, which we were a lot these days, he'd usually grow a beard) he said he didn't have time for 'tache maintenance.

He'd done his usual half-assed job at toweling off. There were droplets of water clinging to his beautiful shoulders and perfectly formed just-hairy-enough-to-be-sexy-as-all-hell chest and he had the towel wrapped around his waist.

"Towel off much?" I teased and his dark blue eyes sliced to me.

He stopped moving toward the dresser and one side of his mouth went up in a half-grin.

"Babe, get dressed. We're gonna be late," he ordered.

"We won't be late. I'm totally ready."

I watched as one of his dark eyebrows went up.

"You're in a robe," Luke pointed out.

"I just have to put on clothes," I replied.

"And half a ton of silver."

He was right about my silver. I still wore a lot of silver jewelry, even though Gracie was usually tugging at my necklaces. I was constantly in danger of her choking me to death. She was like he-baby, she was so damned strong. That she got from her father. Not to mention she kept shoving my rings, while they were on my fingers, in her mouth and biting hard, and that child had the jaws of death, kid you not. I should know. I nursed her. She was teething and the silver must feel cool on her gums so I didn't mind, much. I was pretty sure one day I'd find the baby Gracie gum mark grooves in my rings cute.

I decided to change the subject to one I wanted to talk about.

Luke had made it to the dresser and was rooting through a drawer.

I winced as he rooted. Our drawers were painstakingly tidy. I liked them like that and put a lot of effort into it. Everything folded neatly and organized by color or color combination or long-sleeved (then by color) and short-sleeved (then by color), etc. I had a system. A *tidy* system.

Luke didn't do tidy and he wasn't all that hot on any of my systems either, no matter how often I explained them to him, which was a lot.

I got over Luke's ruthless rooting and asked his naked, muscular, sexily dotted with droplets of water back, "What do you think of the name Maisie?"

Luke's body went completely still. Then, very slowly, he turned to me and his eyes locked with mine.

"Repeat the question," he demanded.

"You heard me," I said softly.

Quick as a flash, Luke was across the room, I was flat on my back, he was on me and wrapping my legs around his hips.

"Luke!"

"Quiet," he muttered as he yanked the towel away and then kept muttering, as if to himself, "Please God, don't be wearing any underwear."

I slapped his shoulder, "Luke, Shirleen is…"

He kissed me to shut me up (he did this a lot).

When his mouth moved to my neck, I was breathing faster, but I still said, "We're going to be late."

"We'll be quick."

"Luke, seriously…"

His head came up. His eyes caught mine and I went quiet at their intensity.

"You sayin' you're havin' my baby?"

I nodded.

His face went soft and, just as soft, he said, "Then we're celebrating."

I smiled at him. There was no denying Luke when he was in the mood to celebrate. Not that I'd want to.

"Okay," I whispered.

He kissed me again.

I kissed him back.

⚜

Sometime later, we were both yanking on our clothes, way late, and Shirleen was shouting up the stairs for us to get a move on.

"You never said what you thought about the name Maisie," I said to Luke.

"I don't give a fuck what the name is, long as you come out of it alive."

I felt my breath catch.

All the Nightingale Men got off facing all kinds of uncertain situations and hair-raising danger, but they became a wee bit edgy when their women got pregnant.

This was because Indy had nearly died while having her and Lee's first, Callum.

I'd known Lee a long time and I'd never seen him the way he was in the hospital that day when the doctor ejected him from the birthing room. He was always cool and in control. Ultra-cool and in control.

That day, he was not cool and in control.

He was so not cool and in control, I thought they'd have to tranquilize him.

In the end, it was surprisingly me who calmed him down.

It was funny how life came around and then went around. Lee had been the one to find me at my worst, my most humiliated, beaten up and taped to a pole after my ex violated me. He had taken care of me, doing so gentle and sweet.

Years later it would be my touch that stopped him from losing it.

I'd put my hand on his arm. He'd frozen at my touch right before he turned into me, slid an arm around my shoulders and yanked me to him, shoving his face in my neck.

I remembered it like it happened two minutes before. Then again, it was something you never forgot.

"Fuck, Ava," he had said into my neck as his other arm wrapped tight around my waist.

I slid my arms around his waist, turned my head and whispered in his ear, "I know, Lee."

"She was screaming."

I shut my eyes tight and held on tighter.

"I won't be able to..." he started and his voice was hoarse.

"You won't have to," I cut him off.

He pulled me deeper into him and I thought he'd crush me, but I didn't make a peep.

"Fuck," he murmured and said no more, just held on. So I did the same thing.

Indy and Callum had made it, though the drama wasn't over. A year later she announced she was pregnant again and Lee went berserk. I'd never seen anything like it, and I'd seen Luke go berserk once, and let me tell you, when one of these boys lost it, it wasn't pretty.

It was Vance who cooled him off that time.

Vance and Jules had been riding the wave of baby number three. At that time, Jules was due any day. She'd had a difficult first pregnancy, sick through-out it and nearly two days of labor, a lot of it *hard* labor, when she had Max.

Jules had glowed through her second pregnancy with Sam, though, and breezed through the delivery. The pregnancy with what would become Harry was like it was with Sam.

Vance explained that to Lee. Lee sorted himself out and settled in for the long haul. Even though for him, and thus everyone around him, it was a *tense* long haul. Indy ignored this and carried on as always, which was to say, she was her usual crazy self, which made Lee all the more tense.

Indy had been the same as Jules when she bore and delivered Alison (named after Ally, but to keep it all straight, everyone, for some reason, called Indy and Lee's Alison "Suki"). No problems during the pregnancy or delivery. But Lee took matters into his own hands after that and had what Ally described as "The Operation" in capital letters *with* the air quotation marks she always used when referring to it, as she would lift her hands and jerk her index and middle fingers up and down.

It was Indy's turn to go berserk. Lee had had "The Operation" without consulting her, and Indy wanted three kids.

I had kept it between Lee and me, but when Indy looked like she was going to hold a grudge for perhaps ever, I shared with Indy the episode in the waiting room while Indy was delivering Callum. Indy got over her tizzy pretty damn quick after hearing that.

I smoothed my tee down over my belly and left my hands there.

Soon, I wouldn't be able to wear my jeans, which would suck.

Other than that, my pregnancy with Gracie had been pretty good, outside of the crippling migraines I had in the first three months, which I had no idea (until Daisy confided in me after Tex confided it in her after Gracie was born) drove Luke straight to Lincoln's Road House. There he and Lee would drink themselves to oblivion, talking drunkenly about how they should never have let the Rock Chicks "fuck with their heads" and getting into in-depth conversations about the pros (there were many) and cons (there were none) of adoption and Tex or Hank or Eddie would be called to drive them home.

As I stared at my belly, I smiled. I didn't mind being pregnant. I hadn't lost all my pregnancy weight after Gracie. Not because I didn't want to, but about ten pounds to goal, Luke put a stop to all dieting by showing me in his unique way how much he liked my curves.

I looked at Luke, who was sitting on the side of our bed and pulling on a pair of boots.

"I'm going to get fat again," I told him.

His head came up and he looked at me.

"You're pregnant. Pregnant is not fat."

"Pregnant is fat," I retorted.

Luke lost patience. "For fuck's sake, are we seriously having this conversation?"

"You know how I feel about being fat!" I snapped. I'd once been huge and I'd worked hard to lose the weight. I never wanted to go back there.

Luke looked back at his boots. "I don't care if you're big as a house, just as long as you never cut your hair or lose your sense of humor."

I stared at his bent head like it had split open and a dancing mini-Luke popped out wearing a top hat and tails singing "Thank Heaven for Little Girls".

I mean, seriously, was he for real?

"Luke?"

His head came up then his eyes narrowed when he saw I was still not ready.

"What?" he asked impatiently.

Crapity, crap, crap. He *was* for real.

"Nothing," I muttered. I turned away and started to pile on my silver.

I really love him, Good Ava, my sweet little angel, said in my ear.

You think we have enough time to jump him again before going to the concert? Bad Ava, my not-so-sweet little devil, asked in my other ear.

Jeez, Bad Ava was such a slut.

⟩⟨

Daisy was staring around Sports Authority Field at Mile High which was packed to the gills.

"Do you believe this shit?" she breathed.

I looked around the stadium. I believed it.

The Gypsies had started out in Denver. This was a hometown gig. There was no way the people of Denver were gonna let Stella and her boys down.

What I did find hard to believe was watching Stella on television. Now *that* was weird.

Though she looked good on the red carpet, dressed rock 'n' roll cool but couture chic and hanging on to Mace's arm while walking up to some awards ceremony.

The Blue Moon Gypsies were huge. They were the new definition of cool. They were, as the magazines said, "Bringing rock back to its roots," and it was true.

They didn't do slick, produced, music videos. Most of their videos were clips from concerts or them playing a song, live, on a sidewalk in Vegas, for which they didn't get a permit so they got arrested. This was also touted as bringing rock back to its roots, but it wasn't original. U2 had done much the same for their kickass "Where the Streets Have No Name" video. Or they'd shoot the video while playing in a small, cool-as-shit but seriously dive club somewhere, thus making the club famous and jacking up their revenue.

It didn't hurt that Stella was gorgeous and the boys in the band not only weren't hard on the eyes, but they also drank a lot, screwed around a lot, got in trouble a lot and were generally just pure, old fashioned rock 'n' roll.

We had a roped off section, front and center. We also had backstage passes hanging around our necks.

Stella took care of the Rock Chicks.

The entire gang was there. Indy and Lee, Roxie and Hank and Ren and Ally (the Nightingale offspring's parents, Kitty Sue and Malcolm, were watching Callum and Suki, Hank and Roxie's kids Leah and Tex, as well as Ren and Ally's daughter, Katie); Jet and Eddie and Hector and Sadie (Hector and Eddie's Mom, Blanca, was watching Jet and Eddie's brood, Alex, Dante and Cesar and Hector, and Sadie's daughter, Lola, and newborn son, Gus); Jules and Vance (Jules's friend May was watching Max, Sam and Harry); Daisy and Marcus; Sissy and Dom; Tod and Stevie; Nick; The Kevster; Ralphie and Buddy; Tex and Nancy; Duke and Dolores; Annette and Jason; Smithie and LaTeesha; Tom and Lana; Chloe and her husband, Ben; Roam and one of his (many) girls (this one was new; I didn't know her name); Sniff (who was alone, for once) and Floyd, his wife, Emily, and his two daughters.

Floyd was now The Blue Moon Gypsies' Manager, though on occasion (or more often than "on occasion") Stella coaxed him onstage. Floyd wasn't

Kristen Ashley

backstage during this gig. He was going to hang with the crew since it was a hometown show.

We all hadn't seen Mace and Stella in a while, though they kept in close touch, or at least Stella did.

At first, Mace stayed working for Lee while Stella and the band traveled, toured and promoted albums, but they kept their home base in Denver. A few years ago, when her popularity moved outside The States and she'd have dates in Europe and Asia, Mace quit Nightingale Investigations and went with them.

This worried me. Mace was action man. I didn't see him as a member of an entourage.

He wasn't one for long.

Some crazed fan had broken into Stella's dressing room before a gig and did things that were so freaky and gross, Luke wouldn't tell me what they were. Mace now oversaw the entire band's security detail.

There was never a repeat of The Dressing Room Incident (as it came to be known), though none of the Rock Chicks, not even Indy knew what happened (and Stella never spilled, no matter how hard Ally pushed it). But also he was so good at it and such a tough guy, badass, macho man that other rock stars and movie actors heard of him and now he was in high demand. He moved Stella and his home base to Los Angeles, started his own security business based in LA, and had even more tough guy, badass, macho men in his employ than Lee did.

The crowd was getting restless, beginning to chant and stomp. The Gypsies were half an hour late taking the stage.

They were probably fighting, as usual.

All of a sudden, Luke slid his arm around my shoulders and kissed the side of my head. I looked at him and my heart jumped when I saw his face.

One could say my husband was pretty damned happy I was having his baby.

"Don't get all squishy on me. I married a tough guy, macho man. You get squishy, I'm gonna have to find someone else," I told him.

This was a lie. I'd seen Luke (almost) squishy a lot with Gracie and I didn't mind it in any way, shape or form. He didn't do baby talk or any of that crap, but his soft, sweet looks for me were nothing on the way he looked at his daughter. I thought he'd be pissed he didn't have a boy, but he didn't care at all.

Luke wasn't fazed by my lie.

Instead, he said, "If you get those fuckin' headaches again, I'm movin' out of the house for three months and livin' in the cabin in CB. I don't even want to hear about them from Daisy or Shirleen."

I just stopped myself from smiling. "Vance refuses to take assignments out of state when Jules is pregnant. He won't even miss a single day of her pregnancy," I informed Luke, pretending to sound hurt.

"I'm not Vance," Luke informed me, not pretending anything.

This time, I couldn't stop myself from smiling. "No, you aren't."

He bent his head and kissed my neck. I felt the thrill of it from neck to nipples.

When he lifted his head and looked at me again, I asked, "Do you want a boy this time?"

He answered immediately, "I want a healthy family. Mom, Dad, kids, whatever way they come."

I also answered immediately, "God, I love you."

He tilted his head and rested his forehead against mine. "Don't get soft on me. I married a bitchy woman. You get soft, I'm gonna have to find me another bitchy woman."

I smiled at him and lied again, "Okay, I'll try to be a bitchy woman."

He grinned at me, not halfway, but full on this time. I felt that in my nipples, too.

That was when the lights went low and the crowd went wild.

I jumped out of my seat, and ran forward, and, per usual, joined the Rock Chicks at the edge of the stage.

Stella walked out and I held my breath at the sight of her.

She looked great. She didn't even look like she'd had baby Tallulah only six months ago. She was wearing jeans, cowboy boots, a killer belt and a light blue, teeny little t-shirt that said "The Gypsies" in cool, electric-blue glitter script across the boobs.

"I want one of those shirts!" Roxie yelled to no one.

"Right on, sister," Ally yelled back.

Stella strapped on her guitar, walked up to her mic, and she was so close, we could touch her boots.

I'd seen Stella play a lot before she got famous, and all the girls had caught every concert she did close to home after. Every time since she made it big, just like tonight, she pointed down to us, wrapped her hand around the mic and, first thing, told the crowd, "My girls are here tonight."

The crowd went wild. Indy, Ally, Jet, Roxie, Jules, Sadie, Daisy, Annette, Sissy and I jumped up and down and screamed like we were fifteen year old groupies.

"Rock Chicks, wouldn't live without 'em," Stella muttered into her mic with a smile down to us, and the crowd roared again. Stella looked away from us to the arena. "Seeing as we're home…"

She didn't finish. The crowd didn't let her. They belted out a whoop that was deafening.

When they calmed, she went on, "As I was saying, seeing as we're home…" Another deafening whoop, but Stella kept talking this time, "we're gonna do it like we did it before. None of this new shit we've been doing, we're going vintage."

The crowd went absolutely nuts.

"Holy fuck, they're gonna tear the place down," Vance shouted from behind us, but the Rock Chicks ignored him, mainly because we'd likely be right in on any "tearing the place down".

"Though, not that vintage," Stella went on. "Just a little something I like that says it all."

Stella looked behind her to Pong at the drums then to her left at Leo and Hugo then to her right at Buzz and she nodded. Then Stella, Buzz, Leo and Hugo all stepped up to their mics in a line at the front of the stage.

"This is for Kai," she told the crowd, and since everyone knew Mace, being hot as he was, and being famous in his past, and being famous for what went down with Stella in Denver, and being famous because those books came out, and, well, again being hot, the crowd descended into bedlam.

The minute she finished saying Mace's name, the guitars and drums started. They started *hard* and they started *loud* and I felt the thrill of them in my toes, straight up my body to the very ends of my hair.

Stella lifted her mouth to the microphone and started to sing Blink-182's totally kickass, rockin' love song, "All the Small Things".

The Rock Chicks banged our heads and jacked our hands in tandem with the beat, arms lifted high in the air and when the boys in the band took to their microphones and sang, *Na na, na na, na na, na na na-na, na na, na na, na na, na na, na-na,* we sang it with them.

Stella had stepped back from her mic to jam, her own head banging with the "na na's". Then she riffed, dancing gracefully and swaying her body, so cool it was unreal.

She stepped back to her mic to sing as everyone in the entire stadium sang with her.

Leo, Buzz, Hugo and Pong went into the "na-na's" again, and we all danced and sang with them as Stella went off, working the stage, working the crowd, nodding and smiling to her fans.

"Jesus," Luke muttered behind me. I turned to him and his eyes were locked on Stella.

He'd never been to one of her gigs except the ones where he was protecting her and all the Rock Chicks, and he'd been kind of busy during those.

"She's the shit," I shouted at him and his eyes moved to me.

Luke was about to speak when something caught his eye and he looked up again.

I turned back around and saw Stella at the mic. The music had slowed in order to own the crescendo and her eyes were looking to her right, not to Buzz, but offstage.

"Get out here, babe, I wanna kiss you," she said into the mic, but she most definitely wasn't talking to the crowd.

She stepped back from the mic, once, twice, her body facing forward, her head twisted to the side, all the while she played her guitar and then, all of a sudden, the smile on her mouth went radiant.

I looked to my left and saw Mace was walking out onstage. His eyes were on Stella, a small smile on his face, and he was shaking his head, walking slow, looking good (as usual).

All the Rock Chicks and Hot Bunch stopped dead and stared as Stella swung her guitar behind her back, ran the rest of the distance between her and Mace and launched herself at him.

He caught her, hands at her ass. Her arms wrapped themselves around his neck, her legs wrapped around his hips. He tilted his head back, she tilted hers down and she kissed him.

The crowd shouted, screamed, whistled. They were nearly louder than the music as Buzz, Pong and Hugo kept singing "na-na's" and Leo took over the lyrics.

One of Mace's hands left Stella's ass, went up her back and into her hair to cup her head.

He broke the kiss, and with a huge smile on his face, he leaned over at the waist like he was going to drop her. Stella held on tight, threw her head back and let out a piercing, laughing scream that we could hear, even over the crowd. Her hair swept the stage and her guitar hung off her back.

They stood there like that, both laughing into each other's faces, oblivious to the tens of thousands of people watching them, totally into each other.

My heart went into my throat. I leaned back against Luke, his arm moved to wrap around my chest and we watched two people we both cared a lot about.

They were in love, they were healed, and most of all, they were outrageously happy.

I thought, for the rest of my life, I'd never forget seeing them horsing around and laughing onstage in front of a hometown crowd.

I never *wanted* to forget.

I didn't have to worry.

Someone caught them with a camera. Mace bent over holding Stella and laughing. Stella wrapped around him, her magnificent hair fanned on the stage, her guitar hanging off her back, her head thrown back, her neck arched...

Her smile lighting up an arena.

The picture was on page fifty of the next edition of *Rolling Stone*.

The Rock Chick ride continues
with **Rock Chick Regret**
the story of Hector and Sadie